The Myth and the Monster Copy

The Raven Society Book 2

R.L. Geer-Robbins

Dark Rose Publishing Company

Book Cover by GetCovers.com

Editor- Latisha Felty

2nd edition 2003

ISBN- 979-8-9875639-9-1

Contents

"The art of living well and the art of dying well are one."
– Epicurus

Dedicated to everyone who thought their story wasn't good enough to be told.

Introduction

'Warnings Are Nothing but Predictions and Possibilities.' -Book of the Veiled Instructions

No AI was used in the creation of this book.

If I had used it, then I wouldn't have spent hours trying to figure out how to explain how to 'whisper yell' at someone. An ability I have a natural talent for when shopping with my husband, but I can't seem to figure out how to write what it looks like.

If you do find any editing issues, please let me know. I have learned that one set, two sets, or three sets of eyes are still not enough to catch all the errors. And even though I'm in my 40's – the words 'Wednesday' and 'supposably' still elude me and spell check. I would rather have the chance to fix the errors than live with the dark cloud of a failed spell check.

No characters in this book were harmed. However, I do allude to some distressing events and subjects, such as SA, prejudice, religion, and injustice. These moments are not to trigger anyone but to stay true to mythology. If you find yourself uncomfortable, please skip ahead, put the book away, or call someone. I understand. There is pain in healing, but as in the case of the stories you are about to read, I hope everyone finds peace.

Just like in The Writer and the Librarian, if you find tear stains on the pages, ignore them. I promise they are tears of joy mixed with tears of frustration and maybe a few drops of blood from papercuts.

And finally, my friends, I hope you enjoy the story you are about to read. It was written with a lot of love and more coffee than my doctor is comfortable with.

Keep Reading and Stay Caffeinated!

Prologue

'Even One Story Left Untold Is A Tragedy.' -Book of the Veiled Instruction

*T*he chronicles of history will judge my every move. I've been weighed on the scales of eternity from the moment I stepped onto this path. The verdict of history will stand for all time, and I will not be able to defend myself.

That is nothing new. Monsters rarely have the chance to tell their side of the story.

I am the mother of all supernatural. I am the creator of nightmares and dreams. Your fantasies of dark witches wielding power, vampires shimmering with unholy energy, shapeshifters morphing into dangerous beasts, and warriors ready for battle all come alive through me. Unleash your imagination and feast your eyes on a world of pure magick.

It is time for the world to remember.

It is what is owed to me.

One man has rewritten my history. And I will not stand for it anymore.

Let me tell you my truth.

I am an elemental spirit of fire, water, earth, and air. Born of the lingering magick of this world and created by the gods, I do not remember my creation. One day, I did not exist, and the next, I did. I was the first of my kind to walk on this earth.

I was blessed with grace, handsome looks, a cunning mind, and knowledge, and then sent to the mortal realm with a gift from the gods. My life had been an unending stream of pleasure, passion, and sensuality. With my looks and my wits, I had won the hearts of kings and queens and built a kingdom out of my desires.

Now, I look back on my life with a sense of loss.

The world was different back then. Lush, green, and unspoiled. Animals I haven't seen in thousands of years wandered in herds across the massive territory. Fields of crops and fruits grew everywhere, unaided and plentiful. The land stretched out mile after mile, as far as the eye could see, constrained only by the horizon. There were no walls, only endless fields spotted with flowers, grasses, and trees. It was a beautiful world, and I remember being in awe.

Then it all changed—humanity's desire to expand and build increasingly encroached on the land. Families became progressively larger, then homes, towns, cities, and finally, countries were established. Instead of seeking peace and abundance, wealth and authority became the rallying call of the mortals. They viewed the supernatural with hatred. For them, only our deaths satisfied their desire for dominance.

But I was given the key to ending the chaos. The item the gods had given me was sealed in a container, untouched and overlooked until it called to me. A sweet melody echoed through the air, promising retribution for my children's untimely end.

And I answered the call. Holding it in my hands, it shined like the sun, blinding me to its contents. Lights danced and flashed around me in a myriad of colors as if a prism was set aflame. It was a box made of cypress wood, light honey brown, with a golden sun engraved on one side. The other side was smooth and unscratched, with a word engraved that promised revenge.

Inside the box lay a jar, a key, and a note. The key was warm to the touch, searing my hand with its heat and brimming with magick. The message from my creators reminded me of my purpose for being sent.

The gods had sent me as punishment. My sole purpose was to bring despair and destruction to the unworthy. The box smelled of blood, death, regret, and loss. It was bitter and vile, like acid on the tongue, like honeysuckle wine left out in the sun for far too long, the taste of a broken heart.

One word.

It takes only one word to know the meaning of true evil.

Pandora.

Chapter 1- Medusa

13th Century BCE, Sarpedon Island

The silence engulfs me, a deafening orchestra of emptiness. It is a haunting symphony that plays in an endless loop. A constant reminder that I will never hear another mortal's voice again.

Unless it is screaming.

The haunting memories of my hunter's final moments will forever remain mine. Unless, by chance, you visit my garden. There, among the overgrown vines and wilting flowers, you can witness for yourself the stark reality of death in all its unfiltered rawness.

Eternity.

Have you ever wondered how long that is? Even if you multiplied a billion by a billion, it would not compare to a single fraction in the vastness of infinity.

That was my sentence. An eternity of silence. A cruel punishment for a crime I did not commit.

My story will forever remain untold, buried in darkness and forsaken by those in control. When even the gods fear you, they will stop at nothing to eradicate your existence.

But I'm ready to share my story with you. Even the memories that haunt my dreams.

And once I've shared my truth, it will be up to you whether or not to remember it.

My name is Medusa. I was formerly the high priestess, a sister, and the most beloved woman in the country.

Now, I am a monster.

Chapter 2- Medusa

13th Century BCE, Athens, Greece

Medusa was just a child when she and her sisters were shepherded to Athena's temple in Athens to start their training as future priestesses. Old enough to understand the magnitude of the honor bestowed upon them. Young enough to be naive about how it would change their lives.

Especially Medusa's.

Their parents were caught off guard when Athena suddenly announced that their daughters were now under her guardianship.

Their mother tried to prepare them. Warn them about the potential dangers of being a follower of Athena.

But the allure of the bustling streets and the grandeur of the temple were too captivating for the young girls to ignore.

It wasn't until years later that Medusa would look back on their first day with a heavy heart. Regretting deeply her decision not to heed her mother's advice and escape.

Over the next decade, the sisters were fully immersed in their studies, attending a diverse array of classes. They delved into the intricacies of music and art, explored the depths of history, pondered the complexities of philosophy, honed their social etiquette, and committed to the memory of the pantheon of gods and their unique abilities.

None more important than Athena, of course.

All their hard work and preparations had led up to this moment.

The city was abuzz with anticipation as it readied for the Panathenaea, a festival dedicated to honoring Athena. Amidst the excitement, all eyes were on Medusa, who was on the brink of her first official appearance as the newly anointed high priestess.

With an unwavering devotion to her goddess, Medusa meticulously managed every aspect of the event - from organizing meals to overseeing the construction of a new stadium for the competitions. Her dedication was palpable, and it was this commitment that earned her the respect and admiration of the city.

As the first day of celebration dawned, Medusa was not filled with excitement but annoyance.

A servant had rudely awakened her to deal with a heated dispute between the butcher and chef over the quality of a recent meat delivery. Their argument echoed through the halls as Medusa groggily stumbled out of bed, threw on her robe, and hastily pulled back her hair. She reluctantly made her way towards the kitchen, rubbing the sleep from her eyes, anticipating the chaos that awaited her.

The butcher and the chef were constantly arguing. Medusa had hoped that today, of all days, they would put aside their differences, but it seemed that the gods had ignored her prayers.

Thankfully, she managed to diffuse the situation, taking responsibility for inspecting the delivery herself. For two long hours, she carefully scrutinized each cut of meat and slab of fish, enduring the pungent smells of raw oysters and uncooked liver that filled the kitchen chamber.

By the time she was done, she made a solemn vow to never subject herself to such torture again. But she left with the butchers' sincere gratitude and a guarantee from the chef that the meal would be the star of the event.

Medusa's problems didn't end there.

As she made her way down the dimly lit corridor towards her room, she collided with a young accolade who had been searching for her. Wide-eyed with fear, the girl ushered Medusa toward the temple.

Urgency filled the air as they hurried past the towering pillars, intricate tapestries depicting the creation of Athens, and elaborate murals of Athena's conquests.

As the heavy doors flew open, Medusa covered her mouth with the sleeve of her gauzy gown, shielding herself from the thick smoke and spicy scent of incense that permeated the air. Her eyes welled with tears as she stepped into the room, gasping in shock at the sight before her.

The flickering light from countless candles cast an eerie glow on the walls, giving the illusion that the entire room was engulfed in flames. A thick haze of smoke hid the altar as Medusa stumbled through the room, searching for the artist she'd hired, ready to throttle him.

According to the accolade, he'd fled in a panic after setting one of the priceless tapestries on fire. With a frustrated sigh, Medusa spent the next hour scurrying through the temple, gathering and hiding half of the candles and incense, stashing them in a back closet, locking the door, and swearing never to hire the bumbling artist again.

Athena would not tolerate anyone burning down her temple.

Covered from head to toe in a thin layer of soot and ash, Medusa trudged wearily towards her quarters, the weight of the day already weighing heavy on her shoulders. Before she got to her door, a servant ushered her outside to yet another problem that demanded her immediate attention.

Powerful winds had ravaged the once neat rows of tents set up along the sandy shorelines of the Argean Sea, their flimsy structures no match for the storm. An unusually high tide had swept away the carefully laid-out racetrack, leaving nothing behind but scattered debris and destruction. Where there had been spectator seating, large boulders were haphazardly strewn about in a chaotic mess.

Gods help us all, Medusa thought as she rubbed her temples.

She had no doubt it was the work of Poseidon. Despite the city's official declaration of Athena as its patron, the rivalry between the two gods never ceased. The devastation before her was just another demonstration of their ongoing war.

As men scurried about, clearing away the wreckage and resetting the area, Medusa stood at the edge of the churning sea. She held out a small offering, a humble plea to Poseidon, whose moods could destroy all of her hard work. Her voice rose above the waves, begging him to leave Athens alone for the week and promising he had not been forgotten.

She knew the gods were fickle creatures, swayed by flattery and appeased by stroking their egos. If she played along with his childish demands, he would stop acting like a child throwing a tantrum.

An hour later, the winds died, and the sky cleared, revealing a stunning, cloudless afternoon.

Medusa was staring into the distance, deep in thought, when her sisters found her. Looking over her shoulder, she smiled as they walked up. Stheno's fierce emerald green eyes gave away her annoyance as she approached, looking like she was preparing for war. On the other hand, Euryale had a playful grin on her lips as she pushed back a stray strand of her luscious copper hair.

The sisters' resemblance was striking, but that's where the similarities between them ended.

Stheno, the eldest, was a formidable force to be reckoned with. Her eyes, sharp as daggers and fiercely protective of her younger sibling, could strike fear into even the bravest warriors. She stood tall and unyielding, bearing the weight of their family's reputation on her shoulders.

When the sisters were reprimanded for even the slightest infraction during their training, Stheno always stepped forward to take the blame. She was their unwavering guardian—their rock in times of turmoil and their champion in times of need.

Euryale, the middle child, had a natural charisma that instantly put others at ease. Her kind smile and gentle presence were contagious. When they first arrived in Athens, it was Euryale who stayed up late at night, telling Medusa stories and easing her homesickness.

Her talents went beyond emotional support. She oversaw tending to the sick who sought refuge at the temple, caring for them with tireless patience and always crediting the gods for their miraculous recovery.

Medusa was destined to become the high priestess, but her sisters had carried her to the altar.

"Medusa, it's time," Euryale called out softly.

Medusa glanced over her shoulder to take in the sea one last time, sighing heavily, wishing she could escape into its depths. She squared her shoulders, eyes shining with determination, and announced, "Let the games begin."

Chapter 3- Danaë

8th Century BCE, Argos, Greece

It had been ages since I last thought of her.

Whenever memories come flooding back, I distract myself. Reading, painting, sewing, or pacing around my room—anything to push away the thoughts of the person I had sentenced to death.

A life for a death. Not a fair exchange, but one I made willingly.

I feel Charon's presence nearby, waiting for my impending death and ready to ferry me to the Otherworld. I just don't know what is taking him so long.

Unless it's because he has been told not to.

I wouldn't put it past the gods.

All I have left is the deafening silence: silence and constant reminders of my sins. My only regret is that my story will never be shared. It will remain hidden in the shadows of history, slowly fading into oblivion.

I have been nothing but a pawn in a twisted game of power, moved across the board by the hands of those who were supposed to protect me.

Until the day I was given the power over life and death.

Now, I face the consequences of my choice. But before I go, I want to reveal my life's raw and unfiltered truth to you. Then, you can decide if my name deserves to be etched into history's memory.

My name is Danaë. I was once a princess, a beloved wife, and the woman who sent a child to find a weapon that could kill the gods.

Now, I am a murderer.

Chapter 4- Danaë

8th Century BCE, Argos, Greece

Danaë steps echoed across the marble floors of her father's palace as she anxiously paced back and forth, waiting for his return. For days, she couldn't shake the sinking feeling that he had gone to seek advice from the Oracle of Delphi on her behalf.

She wasn't sure for what, but it couldn't be good. Kings only consulted the Fates when they were in desperate need. The kingdom wasn't at war. The citizens had had years of exceptional harvests and prosperity. Her father's crown sat securely on his head.

That left only Danaë. Something had to be wrong with her. Knawing on her fingers, Danaë resumed her pacing, pausing occasionally to peek out the windows, hoping to see her father's figure approaching in the distance.

"Danaë, sit down. You're giving me a headache." Rhea glanced up from her sewing, giving her young charge a pointed look. "Staring out the window won't hurry him along."

"Yes, Rhea," Danaë mumbled, her words thick with frustration. Rhea couldn't understand the overwhelming sense of dread weighing down on her shoulders. She didn't realize that her entire life was hanging on by a thread, and the Oracle held the scissors.

She was the daughter of King Acrisius and Queen Eurydice, rulers of Argos. From birth, she was destined to carry on her family's legacy and secure their future by producing an heir. It was her sole purpose in life, ingrained in her since she could understand the concept of duty.

But despite all her best efforts, Danaë had yet to fulfill her destiny. Every passing day brought more pressure and disappointment as she remained unmarried and childless.

It wasn't from a lack of trying.

Countless suitors had arrived, but no one asked for her hand in marriage. Many of them wouldn't even meet her gaze. The most recent suitor used Danaë's beauty as an excuse. Another complained that she talked too much, while another said she didn't speak enough. One bold suitor went so far as to criticize her hips, claiming they weren't wide enough to bear healthy sons.

Each rejection was painful and humiliating—a slap to her dwindling pride.

A harsh cough escaped Rhea's lips, and Danaë turned to look at her nursemaid. Rhea pointed to the chair next to her. After a tense pause, Danaë scoffed and continued pacing.

Ever since she was a baby, Rhea had taken on the responsibility for her upbringing. Constantly finding fault with Danaë's lack of sensibility and pose, she labeled her charge as 'a work in progress,' pointing out her clumsiness, commenting that her voice was as irritating as nails on stone, and reiterating her parents' opinion that Danaë should have been a boy.

As a child, Danaë imagined Rhea would say something so horrendous that the gods would strike her with fury. But no matter how much she prayed or how many sacrifices she made, Rhea remained unscathed by their divine wrath.

Instead, she used her sharp tongue to remind Danaë of her many failings.

Then again, Danaë thought, *maybe she was right.* King Acrisius clearly thought so. The mere fact that he was willing to embark on the perilous journey spoke volumes about his desperation. He wouldn't have taken such drastic measures unless he thought his daughter was incapable of finding a suitable husband.

"The Oracle only opens the temple doors once a month. One month to travel there, another to prepare for her vision, and another to return home, assuming everything goes smoothly," Rhea reminded her for the fifth time that day.

Danaë rolled her eyes, glancing at the courtyard below. Rhea wasn't sharing anything she didn't already know.

"Instead of all your pacing, you could help me finish this tapestry before your father arrives," Rhea remarked with a pointed gaze at the loom in front of her. The two had been working on it since her father's departure, hoping to present it to him as a birthday gift.

The depiction of Argolis' rise to power was stunning. When finished, it would be able to cover a wall, showcasing the grandeur and majesty of Argos and her family's legacy.

At the center stood a larger-than-life image of Zeus, masterfully crafted by Danaë herself. Every detail, from the strength in his muscular form to the wisdom in his eyes, spoke volumes about what she desired in a husband- someone who would be devoted to her and their kingdom and kind and wise in their rule.

Danaë grumbled as she walked towards Rhea, "If I must."

With a snort, Rhea passed a bundle of vibrant blue wool to Danaë, motioning for her to wind it into a ball. Danaë settled onto her stool and began the task, her fingers deftly twisting and turning the soft wool.

The sun moved across the sky as they worked, casting long shadows on their bent-over bodies. As noon approached, a servant appeared with a platter overflowing with freshly baked bread, creamy cheese, fresh figs, and a jug of deep red wine for their midday meal.

They made their way to the windows, gazing at the courtyard below as they settled in to eat. Danaë slipped off her sandals and wiggled her toes, relishing the heat bathing her legs.

"If you had one wish, what would it be?" Rhea asked as she poured their wine.

Danaë shrugged. "The same thing every woman wishes for. A husband, family, a warm bed, and an honorable death."

What more was there to be said? She was the daughter of a king. As a woman, she had no rights, and as an only child, she carried the burden of her kingdom's future on her shoulders. There was no destiny for her except the one already paved.

"What if the Oracle saw a different future? What would you do then?" Rhea pressed, popping a fig into her mouth.

The question took Danaë aback. She hadn't considered the possibility of another route. "I suppose the Oracle would know best," she said slowly. "Why?"

Rhea refused to meet Danaë's gaze, instead focusing on the garden below them. After a tense silence, she reached out and tenderly patted Danaë's cheek. "Whatever path the Fates may lay before you, remember that you hold your destiny in your hands."

Danaë nodded, surprised at Rhea's rare display of emotion and kindness. Through the window, she caught sight of her father's favorite horse, flanked by his loyal guards, heading towards the courtyard. Relief washed over her like a wave, and she sighed. Surely, she would get the answers she needed now.

Danaë waited for her father.

But the king never came to see her.

King Acrisius secluded himself in his chambers for weeks, emerging only to attend to matters he could not delegate. A whirlwind of activity enveloped the palace, with advisors bustling about, architects fervently sketching plans, and priests murmuring prayers as they moved through the halls.

It was as if some divine directive had been issued, and the entire kingdom was on a mission to fulfill it.

Despite her persistent inquiries, Danaë remained clueless about what the Oracle had revealed to her father. Her mother evaded the topic or redirected the conversation whenever she tried to bring it up. Deep down, Danaë knew her mother was keeping something from her.

But she didn't know what.

Until her parents summoned her to the throne room to announce their decision.

Danaë was being sent away.

Chapter 5- Lilith

Modern Day- City of the Unspoken

"**B**edtime," Lilith's voice echoed through the dimly lit room, breaking through the hushed conversations and muffled laughter of The Untold Stories Book Club.

For years, she had been gathering with the children once a week to delve into the pages of books found in the Library of the Unread. These were the stories of forgotten myths and legends, some banished from memory, others twisted beyond recognition.

As the hour grew later, the members showed no signs of concluding their meeting, instead sinking deeper into their plush armchairs that had seen better days. Lilith savored the moment, relishing the sound of disappointment that filled the air in a chorus of boos from her charges.

"You can't stop the story there, Aunt Lilith!" a voice shouted. "We want to know what happens next."

Lilith's gaze roamed the back of the room, finally resting on Jacob. She couldn't help but smile. It had been a while since he had attended one of their meetings. The last time she remembered seeing him was right before his father left.

Lilith's breath caught in her throat as Jacob's eyes met hers. He was the spitting image of his father, Cain, with sun-kissed brown hair and an olive complexion. His bright eyes sparkled like a warm summer day.

A smudge of dirt adorned his cheek, and Lilith had to resist the urge to wipe it away.

It didn't surprise her. Jacob spent all his time in the gardens, caring for the vibrant flowers and trees in the City of the Unspoken. He had inherited his father's green thumb and was responsible for managing the city's harvest since his father left.

To Jacob, it was a way of coming to terms with the fact that the Fates had dealt him and his family a cruel hand. With his parents gone from the city, he and his sister were left to pick up the pieces and rebuild their shattered lives. It was difficult, but they knew why their parents had decided to leave.

Cain didn't tell anyone where he was going, but Lilith knew. He'd gone searching for the Fates, seeking absolution for his sins and retribution for crimes committed against his wife.

Even though Lilith missed Cain, she supported his decision just like he had always supported hers.

Never forget who you are. Those were Cain's last words to Lilith. A reminder that she still had work to do. Not only for herself but for her family.

"It's getting late, Jacob." Lilith flashed him a warm smile as his face fell with disappointment.

"I know, Aunt Lilith, but you're getting close to the best part," he complained.

"Yeah, the part where Danaë is locked into the tower," a cheery voice encouraged. Lilith glanced over to see Aurora, the daughter of Medea and Helios, sitting next to Jacob. She was a lively and unpredictable girl who had a new love interest every month, leaving behind a trail of heartbreak in her wake.

Lilith looked around the room and sighed in mock frustration. She could never say no to the kids. She enjoyed spending time with them, and it was her way of ensuring they never forgot who they were and where they came from.

She refused to let anyone else experience the same agony she had endured. Her story had been twisted and altered so often that she struggled to separate fact from fiction. Lilith felt like a piece of her true self was lost each time it was retold.

But Lilith had a plan.

It'd taken considerable effort and strategizing, but she had managed to maneuver everyone onto their designated positions on the metaphorical chessboard. As the endgame drew near, everything appeared to be aligning perfectly.

The key players were en route to the City of the Unspoken.

Granted, there had been a few hiccups along the way. Like Moll showing up at the gates to the Otherworld with some unexpected guests.

Lilith had wanted to leave Aelle and Max behind, but Vivian insisted on bringing them along. It was the first time Vivian had seen her daughter since she was an infant, and while Vivian was ecstatic about the reunion, Aelle had been less than thrilled.

Lilith understood why Aelle was weary. The revelation about her mother's identity had been a bombshell, and she needed time to digest the information. She just hoped that Aelle could accept the truth of who she was. And soon.

If not, it could pose challenges for her plans.

"Aunt Lilith?" The sweet, innocent voice of a curious child rang out like a bell in the quiet room. Lilith's gaze snapped up, startled by the unexpected interruption. She blinked, momentarily disoriented, before focusing on the small figure sitting before her with wide, curious eyes. "Why is Medusa a monster?"

"What?"

"Medusa?" the child repeated. "Why is she a monster?"

Lilith's brow furrowed as she considered explaining such a complex and dark concept to a young mind. "It all depends on how you define a monster, Penelopa. In Medusa's tale, maybe she wasn't the true monster; maybe it was the person who created her."

"Like Frankenstein," a teenager from the back cried out. "He wasn't a monster. The mortal who created him was."

"No dummy, the monster was a monster," another boy scoffed as he hit his friend over the head.

A girl with a tangle of long, dark hair interjected with a sneer, flipping her hair over her shoulder. "Actually," she declared triumphantly, "Dr. Frankenstein was the true monster. He created a creature, but in doing so, he became one himself."

Penelopa's sharp gaze swept over the group, taking in every detail of their banter with cool calculation. Her intense, icy eyes settled on Lilith, a smirk playing at the corner of her perfectly sculpted lips. "Who created Medusa?" The question hung in the air, heavy with unspoken judgment.

Lilith was just about to recount the story when she caught sight of a familiar figure entering through the back door. The sound of a cane thumping against the floor was unmistakable, and Lilith smiled as her friend entered the room.

Moll took in the curious and surprised faces of the children, who turned to look at her unexpected arrival. She smiled warmly, trying to put them at ease. "Who are we discussing tonight?" Moll inquired with interest as she shuffled towards the group.

"Medusa," Jacob answered as he rose to help Moll.

Lilith watched closely, her sharp gaze taking in the pained expression on Moll's face as she lowered herself onto the seat. She could see how much weaker Moll had become since her arrival; the shawl wrapped tightly around her shoulders was a testament to her declining health.

It was a cause for concern. If Lilith's plan failed, Moll would soon become the next forgotten tale lost to the City of the Unspoken.

"Ah, that's a fascinating story," Moll exclaimed as she tucked a thick woolen blanket around her lap to ward off the night chill. "What part did you get to?"

Penelopa's voice erupted excitedly, carrying over the crackling fire as she announced, "Medusa just became the high priestess!" A smile spread across her face as she rose from her seat with regal confidence. She sauntered towards Lilith, mimicking Medusa with a playful sway in her step, and exclaimed, "I bet she looked stunning!"

Jacob leaned close to Moll and whispered, "We were discussing who the real monster was. The creator or the created?" Molls' eyes widened in surprise as she turned to face him, taking in his intense gaze fixed on the endless rows of books that disappeared into the darkness like an ominous mist.

His parents' story was somewhere on the cluttered shelves, but no one could find them.

"Who do you think creates monsters?" Moll shivered, pulling her shawl tighter around her shoulders as she gazed at the teenager. His features twisted into a sneer in the dim light, and his eyes glinted with unmistakable disdain and hatred.

"Writers," Jacob's voice dripped with venom. Moll cringed under his intense stare.

Lilith started to interject, but Moll gave her a subtle head shake. She wanted the children to express themselves freely, and she needed to hear it as much as they needed to say it.

Penelopa narrowed her eyes, looking suspiciously at Moll as Jacob slid closer to stand beside her. "Aren't you a Writer?" she asked, her tone laced with accusation.

"Yes," Moll admitted. "Now, I'm trying to fix what I helped break."

"How do you plan on doing that?" Penelopa asked. "Aunt Lilith says that once something is broken, no matter how much you try, it'll never be the same."

Moll nodded. "I couldn't agree more," she said softly. "Like a vase that has been shattered - even if it's glued back together, there will always be imperfections. But those cracks can also add character and strength to the piece." She glanced back at the shelves of books behind her. "Sometimes the most beautiful things are the ones that have been broken and put back together."

"How?" Jacob asked curiously.

"I'm going to write the truth, in all its brutal honesty. Then the reader can determine who is a monster and who is not."

But deep down, Moll knew the truth.

She was the true monster in the room.

Chapter 6- Chloe

Modern Day- Otherworld

I tossed and turned in my sleeping bag, the haunting visions that invaded my mind refusing to release their grip.

Two women.

One standing in a towering window, her delicate porcelain skin marked with teardrops that glistened in the dim light. She gazed down at me with a bittersweet smile that held a multitude of emotions within its curves: sorrow, loneliness, and guilt.

The other one stared at me from a shoreline with a frown. She held a smooth, green sea stone in her clenched fist, its colors swirling like the ocean's depths. She stepped towards me, her long hair whipped around her face like snakes striking out, and she shook her head at me to not come any closer.

The air between us was thick with tension, pulsing with raw emotion. I instinctively stepped back, feeling her cruel smile piercing the barrier of reality and vision. A chill ran down my spine as the disturbing image faded. Drenched in a cold sweat, I sat up, glancing over at Eidolon to see if I had woken him up. To my surprise, he was still asleep, his body cocooned in his sleeping bag, his arm tucked under his head, and a soft snore escaping his lips.

Holding back a chuckle, I studied him, noting the toll the past three months had taken on his body. A scruffy layer of stubble covered his chin, and worry lines were etched into his forehead like permanent scars. Despite his attempts to hide his exhaustion, the dark circles under his eyes gave away the countless sleepless nights he'd endured.

And it was all my fault. The guilt weighed heavily on me as I sighed. Everything would be different between us if I had just told Eidolon the truth from the beginning.

Maybe we wouldn't have spent last night arguing.

To be fair, I wasn't the one who started the argument; Sydney did. He wanted to devise a strategy for rescuing Moll, Aelle, and Max from the City of the Unspoken. As we all shared our thoughts and suggestions, each one more outlandish than the last, it quickly became evident that we were not on the same page.

Not surprisingly, Eidolon and I were on opposite ends of the spectrum—my preference for a diplomatic approach clashing with Eidolon's desire to storm through the city gates. The debate raged for hours without actual resolution before Victor suggested we call it a night to clear our heads. We all agreed.

Eidolon didn't say a word to me as he laid out his sleeping bag next to mine. He just rolled over with a muffled, 'See you in the morning.'

I spent the next two hours staring at the stars, watching as a golden shower fell from the heavens. It would have been beautiful if it didn't feel like a warning.

Realizing that sleep was not in the cards for me, I reluctantly crawled from my sleeping bag and slipped on a sweatshirt. If I had time to kill, at least I could do something productive.

Trying not to wake anyone, I grabbed my copy of the Book of the Veiled and walked down the narrow path to the riverbank. The sky was starting to awaken, a gentle pink spreading like a soft blanket across the horizon. I scanned the area for a suitable spot and finally settled on a sizable boulder perched precariously at the edge of the rushing water.

Careful not to slip on the moss growing up its sides, I ascended to the top and settled onto the worn surface. It was a perfect spot, a notch that fitted my curves as if it were made for me. I took a moment to appreciate the book, my fingers tracing the leather cover and name etched on the bottom. 'Chloe.' Opening it to a blank page, I took a deep breath and let the musty aroma of parchment and ink envelop me.

Nothing was more invigorating for a Writer than a page waiting to be filled with words and a world waiting to be created. As the sky slowly changed from its dark pinks to vibrant blues, I lost myself in a realm of visions, prophecies, and inevitable death.

I was penning the last line when a chill ran down my back. The feeling intensified as the sound of massive paws crunching on the rocky bank crept closer.

"Hello, Arawn," I called over my shoulder, not bothering to turn around. "For what do I owe this honor?"

"Can't a god come and chit-chat with one of their favorite mortals without being questioned?" Arawn's voice, rich and smooth like melted chocolate, filled the air as he casually leaned against the boulder.

I glanced over and realized that we were at eye level, and I couldn't help but marvel at his impressive size. His dark, wild hair cascaded around his broad shoulder, and his piercing silver eyes danced in amusement as he smiled at me.

"It's your world," I shrugged, pulling my unruly hair back into its usual messy bun.

I watched as Arawn's loyal hellhounds bounded toward the shore, their powerful muscles propelling them through the water. As they played, the waves crashed against their glistening snow-white fur, revealing a carefree side to their typically fierce persona. I laughed as their barks echoed across the beach with unbridled energy.

"Did you sleep well?" Arawn smiled as the smallest pup of the litter and my favorite, Hester, hopped onto the back of the pack leader, playfully nipping at his ears. Hester's barks were full of mischief, and her red eyes glanced at Arawn with a mischievous glint. He nodded his approval as the hellhounds went on with their antics.

"Yes and no," I answered, tracing a jagged crease in the rough rock. I shifted my gaze upward, taking in a breath. "I had a dream about Medusa and Danaë."

"Ah, yes," Arawn sighed, running a hand through his long hair. "Sad story. I was sorry to see how it ended."

"You were there?" I looked at him in surprise.

Arawn flashed me a sly grin and let out a small laugh. "I know it's probably hard for you to grasp, but I've been alive for quite some time."

"Did you know them?" I pressed, my voice laced with curiosity and a hint of urgency.

Arawn's face betrayed a brief moment of regret, his eyes dropping to the ground before meeting mine again. "Yes, I did." His eyes lit up as he continued with a grin. "But they're not the same people anymore."

I tilted my head in confusion. What did he mean they weren't the same people anymore? "Why do you think I had a vision about them?"

"You're the Writer. You tell me why," he scoffed.

I released a deep exhale and tossed a stone into the rippling river. "I don't know, to be honest. I didn't see much in the vision. But I can tell you this: Medusa is one scary woman. I just don't understand what Greek mythology has to do with the Book of the Veiled."

"Seems to me you have some research to do then," he interjected, arching an eyebrow.

My jaw clenched as I bit back a retort. Adjusting my glasses, I fixed Arawn with a piercing stare. "Helpful as always." I tried to keep my voice steady despite the rising irritation in my chest. "Do *you* think it has something to do with the Book of the Veiled?"

Arawn shrugged, his attention focused on his hellhounds. "Maybe. The Fates rarely tell me what they're up to." He gestured into the distance with a chuckle. "I'm afraid you will have to ask them yourselves."

"Marvelous suggestion," I huffed, not amused. "You got a phone number for them? Or an address? Something a bit more helpful?"

He snorted. "If I knew, don't you think I would've told you already?"

Honestly, I wasn't sure if the god would have told me. We were all guilty of keeping secrets from one another, especially Arawn. An uneasy quiet hung between us as I fiddled with a jagged stone shard. At last, I mustered up the bravery to voice the question weighing on my mind.

"Do you think he'll forgive me?"

I could see the gears turning as he contemplated my question, his features shifting into a pensive expression.

"I don't have an answer for that either." Arawn's expression soured as he continued, "It's inexcusable not to know one's identity. You and Moll could have given him some clarity, but you chose not to."

I opened my mouth to protest, but he quickly silenced me with a look.

"Let me finish. No matter how well-intentioned you thought you were, you became a part of the problem." His eyes narrowed. "Isn't that why you came to the Otherworld? To give the lost souls their stories back? But then you turned around and denied Eidolon his."

"I didn't intend to." My voice was barely audible as the words stumbled out of my mouth. Arawn had a knack for making difficult situations even more daunting with his opinions. But he was right; I couldn't undo what I'd done. And if I were in Eidolon's position, I wasn't sure I could forgive myself either.

My thoughts must have been written on my face because Arawn gave my shoulder a reassuring pat. "It won't be easy. But I think you'll find a way to fix it."

"Thanks, Arawn," I grimaced. "I appreciate you coming to check on me."

"No need to thank me," he said with a grin. "I just came over to remind you that you still owe me that Scotch pie you promised. The rest of it was a bonus." He walked off, leaving me staring after him. It took all my willpower not to stick my tongue out at his retreating form.

Asshole. Wide-eyed, I darted a look to make sure he didn't hear my thoughts. His laughter told me he did. Embarrassed, I turned back to the river, lost in thoughts about Medusa, when Eidolon snuck up on m e.

"I thought I might find you down here," Eidolon said, watching the hellhounds play. A soft whistle escaped his lips. The pack immediately responded, their fierce gazes turning towards us as they barked and raced over. They sat before him, their tails wagging in excitement and tongues lolling out from exertion as they panted heavily. Eidolon reached down and scratched Hester behind her ear.

"I wanted to get some writing done," I said as he clambered up beside me. I shifted over to make room for him, uncomfortably aware of how close he was to me.

"Dreams?" Eidolon asked knowingly, glancing at me. A piece of his dark hair fell over one of his eyes, and I fought the urge to brush it away.

"Yup," I nodded, sitting on my hands. "About Medusa and Danaë. Before they became *THE* Medusa and Danaë."

Eidolon's gaze drifted towards the City in the Mountain. When he turned to face me, his expression was pensive. "I met someone named

Danaë while you were away," he said. "She didn't say much, just insisting that we find her. But she never specified who 'her' was."

The words inscribed on his skin started to twist and morph as he spoke, drawing my gaze. I studied them closely, wishing for the same clarity they had provided in the past. However, this time, there were no definitive answers. The words disappeared, leaving behind a faint haze of grey smoke surrounding Eidolon.

Disappointed, I shifted my focus back to the hellhounds. I wasn't sure how my vision fit into the bigger picture of Lilith and the Book of the Veiled. But everything was interconnected. I just needed to find the right thread to unravel the mystery. But before I could do that, I needed to clear the air.

Inhaling deeply, I gazed up at the sky and decided to take the risk of starting another argument. "Eidolon, I *am* sorry. I didn't mean..."

Eidolon cut me off, leaning back and gazing up. "I know, Chloe. I just needed some space to wrap my head around everything." His tone was grim, and I cringed.

Fiddling with the sleeve of my sweatshirt, I refused to look at him, not wanting to see the disappointment on his face. "Don't blame Moll too much. She was trying to protect you."

"Chloe, there's a fine line between protecting and deceiving someone." He turned to look at me, his eyes darkening. "I understand you were trying to keep me safe, but Moll and I made a promise to always be honest with each other. No matter what."

"So, what do we do now?" I whispered.

Eidolon paused before saying, "We go to the City of the Unspoken. Find Moll and the others. Confront Lilith and find the missing books. Hopefully, the Fates decide we are worthy enough not to snip our lifelines along the way," he chuckled. "If we survive by some miracle, I'll have a long talk with Moll to set things right." Eidolon nudged me with his shoulder. "Then you and I can get a proper cup of coffee and split an apple fritter in celebration."

"Sounds like a plan to me," I said, trying to quell the butterflies in my stomach as relief washed over me. Despite everything, Eidolon still had me in mind. "What could go wrong?"

He exaggeratedly sighed before getting down and looking up at me. "Sydney's insatiable appetite and rocky relationship with Bree," he started counting off. "Victor's annoying habit of spouting off useless trivia. Isabelle's unpredictable magickal mood swings, Watson's relentless need to provoke others, and Arawn's pack of hungry hellhounds." He glanced at the creatures, who perked up their ears at the mention of their master. "No offense," he added with a smirk toward them

.

"And make sure we're home before dark," I playfully reminded him, relishing the easy back-and-forth banter. "Eidolon," I started, wanting to apologize again, but he waved me off.

"We are fine," he reassured me. I eyed him. He crossed his heart. "I swear."

I jumped down, slipping on the moss. Eidolon caught me before I could hit my head on the boulder. "How about you try not to get yourself kill," he muttered I bit back a retort.

I wished people would stop saying that to me.

Chapter 7- Medusa

13th Century BCE, Athens, Greece

Medusa's soft leather shoes crunched on the pebbles as she made her way up the steep path. She struggled through the thick forest of seagrass until she was greeted by a breathtaking sight: the moonlit sea glimmering in the distance just beyond the cliffs.

She often came up here when she needed a moment to think. And this evening, she had a lot on her mind.

The games had been an astounding success, with participants from all over the country fiercely competing for the coveted Athena breastplate. Two competitors had caught her eye - a musician and a horseman. Nothing was exceptional about them, but their friendly faces drew her attention.

They had approached her confidently, without fear or awe, looking deeply into her eyes and smiling. That was rare: men were usually intimidated by her position or fixated on her body. But they never made eye contact.

These two men were different. They saw Medusa for who she was, not as a high priestess but as a woman. As she presented their rewards, electricity coursed through her body. It was a sensation she'd never experienced - a mix of excitement and vulnerability.

"It looked like Cleanthes and Arrian took a liking to you," Stheno said with a sly smile as the trio trailed back to their chambers on the final evening of festivities.

"I have no idea what you're talking about," Medusa replied, looking over her shoulder at her eldest sister. Euryale laughed, and Medusa scowled at her. "Don't get started," she said before picking up her pace.

Her siblings were always teasing her, but this time, it stung more than she wanted to admit.

She was jealous. Jealous of every woman who could flirt back, fall in love, get married, and have a family.

Everything that she wasn't allowed to experience.

Perched precariously on a boulder that jutted out over the churning sea, Medusa absentmindedly plucked small pebbles from the ground and cast them into the foamy waves below. She was consumed with dreams of a family she could never have, watching as her fantasies dissolved into the ocean's vastness.

She was alone. A solitary sentinel destined to observe but never partake in the pleasures of life.

Yes, she was the high priestess. Yes, she was honored and respected. And yes, it was everything she thought she wanted. But too many days were filled with silence and prayer. Too often, she had to divert her eyes when a man glanced at her for fear of appearing unchaste.

What she wanted most at this moment was to find someone to love. Unconditionally and freely.

"The stars are beautiful this time of night," a voice called out beside her. Medusa leaped to her feet in surprise. A deep, booming chuckle reverberated in the air, causing the ground to tremble beneath her feet. "Why so nervous, Medusa?" the voice rumbled, its vibrations sending shivers down her spine. "We're old friends," they added with a hint of amusement.

Her initial fear faded as she recognized the god beside her. "Poseidon," Medusa bowed her head in respect. "For what do I owe this honor?"

Poseidon's eyebrow arch in amusement, "Owe? Nothing, high priestess. I was just wandering by and happened to see one of my favorite mortals sitting all alone. How could I resist the urge to come over and try to cheer them up?"

Medusa fixed him with a pointed gaze. "You."

Poseidon feigned shock. "My dear high priestess, I'm not as terrible as you make me out to be."

"Your reputation deems otherwise," Medusa muttered dryly, shifting her gaze to the long blades of grass tufting around the boulder.

"Come now, don't believe everything you hear. Now sit down and tell me what is bothering you after such a triumphant week."

Medusa was torn. Poseidon had invited her to sit and talk, but etiquette demanded that she remain standing with her eyes lowered before a god.

Was this a trick? Medusa considered her options and decided to take a risk. Poseidon's expression appeared sincere. And it would be rude to decline his offer.

"Nothing is wrong," Medusa declared as she returned to her spot, drawing her legs up and wrapping her arms around them. "I just needed time to sort out my thoughts." With her face pressed against her knees, she turned to look at him for the first time and carefully studied the god.

Poseidon was striking, with tanned skin glimmering with sea droplets. He kept his long black hair in a braid down his back, and his eyes mirrored the tempestuous sea - a mix of gray, blue, and silver. Unlike his fellow gods, Medusa had never seen him with any facial hair, highlighting his youthful appearance.

His tunic and cape clung to his frame, emphasizing the chiseled lines of a flawless physique. Medusa wanted to touch the midnight blue fabric, wondering if it would be as smooth as silk or soft like fine cotton. The moonlight danced across the sparkling sapphire eyes of the dolphin brooch pinned to his shoulder, giving the appearance of amusement in its twinkling gems.

"Why don't you just go to the temple?" Poseidon asked, intrigued. "Isn't that where priestesses usually go when they have questions?"

Medusa stared at him in surprise. Poseidon wanted to know about her life. Before she lost her nerve, she answered, "I have." She turned to look back at the ocean. "I just didn't get an answer."

Poseidon chuckled. "Ah, the curious role of a high priestess. Expected to have all the answers, but never given any. I've seen this before."

"You have?" Medusa asked, intrigued. It would be nice to know that she wasn't the only one who felt this way.

"Too many to count," he sighed. "Struggling with the same questions and disappointments. And they all ended up here, on this very spot - the border between Athena's home and mine." He gestured towards the shore, where the waves crashed against the rocky cliffs. "You've finally come to understand that the path of purity, while noble, often leads to a lifetime of alienation. And even beyond that."

A lifetime of alienation. Medusa had not thought of her position in that manner before, but Poseidon had a point.

Even in death, when Charon arrived to ferry her onto eternity, she would be secluded from the other souls because of her role as high priestess.

She would be alone forever. Her position demanded it. Was this to be her fate? The thought crushed her as the air grew heavy like a thick, suffocating stew. Medusa's vision blurred, and a searing pain raced through her head like a stampede of bulls charging.

"Head between your knees before you pass out," Poseidon instructed as his mighty hand gently guided her head down. "Wouldn't want Athena thinking I killed you. Can you imagine the backlash from that?" he joked as Medusa struggled to regain control of herself.

Was he laughing at her?

Rude.

After a few moments, Medusa struggled to sit up straight and meet the gaze of the massive god before her. His eyes held a mesmerizing sway, like trying to resist a tidal wave of intense emotions and memories.

He smiled as she leaned forward to see more.

It wasn't a memory. It was a prophecy. A future in which Medusa strolled alongside a child in one hand and held another on her hip. The scene shifted to her sitting at a table surrounded by a loving family, her face etched with wrinkles and her hands dotted with age spots.

It was everything she wanted. And more.

No! Medusa forcefully turned her head, gasping for air. She refused to entertain these thoughts. This was not her destiny. As the high priestess, she was devoted to Athena and willingly offered herself as a sacrifice for Athens. That was her path. Nothing else.

Damn, Poseidon, for putting these thoughts into my head!

Medusa rose to her feet, smoothing out her dress and getting her emotions under control. She was wise enough not to heed the words of the god who toyed with human emotions as capriciously as the tides changed. "I am grateful for your time," she said, turning to face him and bowing respectfully. "But I must return before my absence is noticed."

He nodded once in the direction of the rising sun, smiling.

How long had she been sitting there? It couldn't have been all night. Her sisters would kill her if they knew, not to mention what Athena would do. With one final bow, Medusa turned and made her way back down the path towards the temple. It would be another day filled with endless prayers, meetings, and preparations for the upcoming festival.

The same as it would be for the rest of her life.

"We shall meet again, Medusa," Poseidon's voice echoed. "When you're ready, I'll be here."

Despite herself, Medusa smiled. She didn't trust the god more than she could throw a boulder into the sea. But it would be nice to have a friend.

Even if it was Poseidon.

Chapter 8- Medusa

13th Century BCE, Athens, Greece

For three weeks, Medusa returned to the same spot on the cliffs overlooking the Argean Sea every evening. She told herself she went there to get away and clear her head, but in reality, she went there to meet Poseidon.

And every night, he came.

Medusa cherished the time, not because he was a god, but because she had someone to talk to.

For the first time, she chatted about her childhood before coming to the temple and the challenges she faced as a high priestess. She told him about the drama between her head chef and butcher. And in a rare moment of honesty, Medusa told him about her sisters, her doubts about her life, and her dreams for the future.

In return, Poseidon told her about his life, including his struggles with Zeus, the war between the Olympians and the Titans, and what living in the ocean was like. He regaled her with stories of formidable warriors and terrifying sea monsters he battled.

The more Poseidon opened up, the more Medusa saw just how much control he possessed. With a mere wave of his trident, he could create islands or destroy them in an instant. Yet, his favorite memories were the ones he shared with other sailors about their adventures on the vast seas.

She longed to be part of that world.

"Have you ever considered leaving the temple and trying something different?" Poseidon asked as he leaned down. His hand shifted through the sand, finding a smooth piece of sea glass.

Medusa paused, mulling over his question. "I've thought about leaving," she confessed, "But where would I go?"

"You could come to my realm," Poseidon offered, handing her the pebble. His fingers brushed against hers, and Medusa's cheeks flushed as she closed her hand around it. "I have plenty of room," he chuckled, gesturing toward the ocean. "And I promise I won't make you clean my temple," he teased, staring at her.

Medusa froze, unable to find the words to reply. Shaking herself out of her stupor, she massaged the bridge of her nose, considering his proposal. Poseidon was offering her the chance at a new life, away from the constraints of Athens and Athena's growing disapproval.

Could she accept?

Could she leave everything she knew behind for the unknown?

And what exactly was Poseidon asking for in exchange? She flushed under the intensity of his stare, a fiery passion that hinted at a desire for more than friendship. He wanted something more intimate and personal.

Was she willing to become his lover?

With the heavy weight of the decision pressing on her, Medusa squared her shoulders and took a deep breath. She couldn't give up everything she had built for herself and her sisters. "I appreciate your offer, but I must decline."

His eyebrows arched in surprise. "No?" he asked incredulously, the word hanging like a thick cloud.

"Why should I?" Medusa challenged, needing to hear his reasoning.

"Why wouldn't you?" Poseidon shot back.

Medusa let out a deep sigh, turning the smooth sea glass over in her hand. She thought for a moment before speaking her truth, "I would only consider leaving if I found true love." Shifting to face him directly, she crossed her legs and smoothed down her dress. With a coy glance from beneath her eyelashes, she posed the question, "Is that something you can offer?"

Poseidon's piercing blue eyes narrowed, and impatience flickered within them. He understood Medusa's insinuation all too well. "Gods are not monotonous."

"But why?"

"Mortals die," he huffed as if that was the only answer she needed. To Poseidon, the conversation was over.

Medusa disagreed. "You have the power to change that," she insisted, "if you found the right woman."

With a deep, guttural growl, Poseidon slammed his hand down on the boulder, ripples of power spreading down to the shore. His anger was palpable, swirling and churning in the depths below as whirlpools formed and threatened to pull everything into them. Above, the sky darkened with heavy clouds, a thunderstorm brewing and crackling with energy. "Absolutely not," he spat out.

Medusa tried not to flinch. "Why?"

Poseidon's hand curled into a tight, white-knuckled fist, his lips pulling back in a grimace. "To cheat death is to lose one's humanity and become a monster. No love is worth such a sacrifice."

"Love?" Medusa whispered.

Poseidon averted his gaze, frustration evident in the hand he ran over his face. "Don't ask me again," he ordered through clenched teeth. "I have watched as my brothers condemn women to a similar fate, and it never ended well."

"And it couldn't be different for us?" Medusa pressed.

The sea god's voice boomed as he stood, his towering form casting a shadow over her. His eyes blazed with anger as he turned to face her. "No," he thundered, "it could not."

Their gazes locked; tension thick between them like a tangible force. As they waited for the other to act, unspoken words hung in the air, palpable and heavy. In the distance, seagulls' cries mixed with the rhythmic crashing of waves against the shore, creating eerie yet beautiful music to their stand-off.

With graceful and deliberate movement, Medusa unfolded her long, slender legs and rose to her full height. Tilting her head back, she squared her shoulders, drew a deep breath, and steadied herself. "Thank you, Poseidon."

He scrutinized her in surprise. "Thank you?"

She nodded once. "Yes, thank you. For telling me the truth. I appreciate the offer, but I cannot accept it."

Medusa's chest constricted with pain when she witnessed the brief expression of hurt on the god's face, but she pushed it away. She refused to be just another one of his conquests, a pawn in his manipulative games. She pushed past him, and with each step, her heart felt like it was breaking into smaller and smaller pieces until it turned to dust.

"The offer stands," Poseidon called after her. "When you are ready, I will be waiting."

Medusa didn't stop walking.

But she couldn't help but wonder if she'd made the wrong choice.

Chapter 9- Danaë

8th Century BCE, Argos, Greece

Time became a cruel master as Danaë sat trapped in her father's desolate prison.

King Acrisius spared no expense in constructing his monumental masterpiece, hiring only the most skilled engineers and craftsmen to bring his grand vision to life. The tower, constructed with unyielding stone, loomed over the desolate landscape like a predatory giant. Each stone was meticulously chosen and fitted to blend seamlessly with its surroundings. The walls were fortified with hearty mortar, guaranteeing the tower's unshakable shape and deterring any rescue attempts.

A fortress constructed to stand the test of time. And Danaë was confined within its walls like a wild animal in a cage.

The days blurred, marked only by the slow crawl of the sun across the small opening that served as a makeshift window. She stared out of it, yearning for the cool touch of grass beneath her bare feet and the comforting warmth of the sun on her face. Memories flooded her mind of the few times she and Rhea would dance in her room, the pranks played by the mischievous servants, and the lively bustle she would experience when she ventured into the city center.

She held onto the memories like precious gems, keeping them close to her heart as a course of hope and strength. But as the days turned to weeks, even those recollections faded, replaced by a bleak resignation settling heavily in her chest.

Danaë spent hours pacing back and forth through the room to maintain her sanity. Her frustration and anger only increased as time passed until she couldn't bear it. Rushing to the window, she screamed, hoping someone would hear her.

But all was silent outside. With nothing else to do, she counted the stones on the tower wall one by one, trying to distract herself from the overwhelming sense of being trapped.

14,025 stones surrounded her. 3,214 stones made up her floor. And a countless number of seconds to go insane.

Fueled by desperation, she snapped off one of the stool's legs and used it to etch crude drawings onto the walls. But even this outlet could not calm her racing mind and growing agitation.

The dried food her father left for her in a trunk was unappealing, so she resorted to tossing it into a mug, piece by piece, cheering each time she made the shot.

Time soon slowed to a crawl, hours turning into days. Sleep provided only temporary relief. But even that became a distant and fleeting memory as her body struggled to endure the harsh conditions.

Her once lush lips dried and cracked, occasionally bleeding from the extreme elements. A constant bitterness lingered in her mouth, a mix of smoke and decay. Her skin grew pale, stretching over her protruding joints, and her once beautiful hair hung limp and greasy, matted with filth. Once a symbol of elegance and grace, her dress was reduced to tattered rags stained with grime and filth.

She dared to peek at her reflection in a bowl of water only once. The image staring back at her was haunting. Her once bright and lively eyes were sunken, resembling two black pearls buried in their sockets. Dark circles encircled them, smudged with dirt and traces of dried tears.

Unable to bear the sight any longer, she flung the bowl across the room, relishing the sound of it shattering into pieces.

Danaë resigned herself to her fate; she would die alone. The reason would forever be a mystery. She spent her days waiting for Charon's arrival, lying on the frigid stone floor, prepared to welcome his icy touch of death.

But he never came.

Danaë couldn't decide which was more painful: being rejected by her parents or the crushing realization that death would not come for her.

What had she done to anger the ferryman?

What had she done to her parents?

Why had the gods doomed her?

What words had the Oracle spoken to her father that condemned her to a fate of agony and suffering?

Negativity constantly spun and weaved, haunting her thoughts. She tried to block out its cruel words, but even closing her eyes couldn't shield her from its taunting presence.

You are nothing.

Your parents should have had a son.

Death is a release you don't deserve.

With her hands buried in her hair, she let out a primal shriek that reverberated through the air. A sound so piercing and raw that it froze the gods in their tracks. The cry of anguish and despair echoed with the weight of all her pain and sorrow. As she released the sound from deep within her, she felt a sense of catharsis wash over her, like a cleansing fire burning away all her pent-up emotions.

Danaë collapsed against the moss-covered tower walls, mentally and physically drained. She closed her eyes and drifted into a fitful sleep. It wasn't long before a faint rustling sound jolted her awake. Rubbing her throbbing head, she opened one eye and scanned the room.

No one was there, but she couldn't shake off the feeling that someone or something was watching her as the hairs on her neck stood in alarm.

There was only one person who could find her.

With effort, she struggled to sit up and face the figure in the room. "Charon?" she croaked, her eyes locked on a shadow standing in the corner. "I'm ready," she whispered, surrendering to whatever fate awaited her beyond the River Styx.

A gentle hand rested on her shoulder, comforting and reassuring.

"I am ready," she rasped again as her eyelids drooped and warmth coursed through her frozen body. The effects of weeks of starvation faded as satiety took over. Another soothing hand rested on her forehead, and her plea for death gave way to an instinctual drive to survive.

"Hush now, little one. Sleep." The soothing sound of the voice lulled her into a peaceful state, quieting her restless mind and troubled sanity. She couldn't resist the urge to close her heavy eyelids as she was gently placed on a soft surface. A comforting weight covered her body, followed by a gentle touch that tucked a stray strand of hair behind her ear.

"I will be back," the voice echoed further away.

Danaë fell into a deep, dreamless slumber.

Chapter 10- Danaë

8th Century BCE, Argos, Greece

As the first light of dawn filtered through the window, Danaë basked in its warm glow, which spread across the entire tower. She stretched her limbs luxuriously with a deep sigh, no longer feeling discomfort or pain. Her fingers glided delicately over her face, feeling soft, velvety skin and eyes no longer swollen from the tears she had shed the night before.

She turned her attention to the luxurious mattress, enjoying the thick quilt that cocooned her in warmth and the silk pillows surrounding her. Her fingers traced the patterns of the coverings as she marveled at her soft skin and strong nails. She couldn't help but smile as she examined every inch of her hand, amazed by the transformation that had taken place.

Slowly, she turned her head to take in her surroundings, her eyes widening in shock and wonder at the change.

The tower radiated a warm and welcoming ambiance. Vibrantly patterned rugs in blues, greens, and grays blanketed the floor. A tall shelf sat tucked in the corner, adorned with a steaming water pitcher and the bowl she shattered the day before, now whole once more. Sitting up, she saw an open wooden chest at the foot of the bed, revealing stacks of dresses, undergarments, and an exquisite cloak in midnight blue.

Danaë's heart dropped when she saw a large oak table covered in various dishes. Tears welled in her eyes as she saw platters of meat, pots of warm soups, and bowls brimming with fresh fruits. She quickly jumped out of bed and grabbed the cloak to wrap herself in, sinking her toes into the soft rug as she hurried to wash off the remnants of sleep.

She piled her plate high with some of everything in minutes. Danaë savored each bite with a satisfied hum until she was full and even had a few extra bites just to be sure. Pushing back from the table, she struggled to move her heavy body back to the bed, feeling satisfied for the first time in months.

Nestled under the generous covers, grateful for the smooth sheets and cool pillows, she smiled for the first time since she arrived at the tower. As Danaë drifted off to sleep, she couldn't help but wonder if the mysterious person from the night before would return so she could express her appreciation.

Danaë's recovery took four days, and she felt entirely rejuvenated. Mysteriously and without fail, the room was restocked daily with food, firewood, and hot water. One evening, she was surprised to discover books and a painting kit sitting at her bedside. As she turned each page or started a new painting, she whispered prayers of appreciation and admiration to Artemis, convinced that the goddess had aided in her recovery.

Even when her parents failed her, the goddess came through.

But Artemis never responded.

Restlessness and boredom consumed Danaë by the end of the week. The stone beneath her feet bore witness to her agitation, slowly wearing away at its surface with each passing step. As she paused near the window, her eyes darted out over the vast valley below, searching for release. The atmosphere hung heavy with her irritation and repetitive intruding thoughts.

Her parents sent her away.

The gods abandoned her.

Death refused to take her.

In a storm of anger, she grabbed the plates and flung them across the room. They swirled and tumbled in the air, ricocheting off the rough stone walls before landing safely back on the table.

Tears of frustration streamed down her face as she turned to the cups, gripping them tightly in her trembling hands. With a primal scream, she hurled them toward the ground, their fragile bodies bouncing off the unforgiving stone floor.

She shifted her attention to the tall and sturdy chairs around the table, mocking her rage. With a furious kick, she sent one toppling over and then another, relishing the sharp pain shooting up her foot. But no matter how hard she tried, they would not stay down, stubbornly righting themselves like obedient soldiers.

Irritation seethed through her.

"Why. Won't. Anything. Break?" Danaë screamed as she tore her pillow to shreds.

As her emotions drained away, she collapsed onto the rug, convulsing with uncontrollable laughter. Her eyes blurred with tears as she came to a terrifying realization - she was being consumed by madness, gripped tightly in the clutches of the goddess Lyssa.

She'd become the madwoman imprisoned in a tower.

The thought made her laugh harder.

"Are you done?" a lazy voice asked from across the room.

Danaë 's heart pounded as she froze. She closed her eyes and took two deep breaths before cautiously peeking over the mound of destroyed pillows and stray feathers. To her surprise, a man sat at the table, sifting through a fruit bowl. He plucked an apple from the bunch, grinning as he took a big bite.

"Quite the spectacle you put on," he remarked, pointing the fruit in her direction. "I was worried the tower wouldn't hold up."

Danaë offered a timid smile to the stranger, her cheeks tingling with embarrassment. It had not been her proudest moment, but to be fair, she had no idea anyone was watching. The realization made her stop in her tracks. How could someone witness her private spastic episode?

She was trapped. Alone. In a tower.

She rubbed her eyes in confusion. Was the man real? Or had she finally slipped the final inches into insanity?

"I'm real." With a graceful hand, he poured himself a generous glass of rich wine, sniffing it in pleasure before taking a sip. He gestured towards the table. "Please, join me," he invited warmly. "I brought your favorites."

Danaë's eyebrows shot up in surprise as she looked at him. What did he mean by saying he brought her favorite food? As she peered into the bowls, she discovered a spread of all her favorite dishes: fresh figs, succulent roasted duck, sweet apples drizzled with syrup, and delicate pastries dusted with powder. "You did all this?" she asked in astonishment.

"Does anyone else know you're here?" he asked, arching a perfectly sculpted eyebrow in amusement.

Danaë couldn't resist the shiver that ran through her body as she met his gaze. His stunning appearance was like a magnet, drawing her in. She took in the waterfall of golden hair cascading down his neck and the warm bronze tone of his skin shimmering with flecks of gold. His full lips were tempting, and his molded jawline rivaled temple statues.

She remained still, watching as he rose from his seat and advanced towards her with a mischievous gleam in his eyes. Like a predator closing in on its prey, his movements were calculated and graceful, sending an electric sense of peril through the air. Her heart raced with every step he took closer to her until he was mere inches away.

With one hand, he gently brushed her hair away from her face. Danaë shivered at the contact but didn't pull away. Instead, she leaned into him, her body trembling with anticipation.

With one touch, she knew who had saved her.

Zeus.

The king of the gods.

Chapter 11- Lilith

Modern Day- City of the Unspoken

After some convincing from Lilith, the book club postponed hearing the end of the Medusa and Danaë story until their next meeting. The children reluctantly returned to their rooms with a mixture of frowns, laughter, and secret plans to meet in the kitchen later for a pantry raid.

Lilith and Moll stood, exhausted and emotionally drained, watching the children skip away. Their bodies were heavy and weary from the long day, but their minds were even more tired from trying to keep up with Lilith's charges' endless stream of curious questions.

In need of a stiff drink to soothe their frayed nerves, they made their way to the bar for a well-deserved drink. The warm aroma of wood smoke and spiced cider welcomed them, wrapping them in a comforting embrace as they settled into plush armchairs by the crackling fireplace.

Moll's tense muscles relaxed as she idly traced the intricate design on her glass before setting it down on the coffee table. "If I'd known what was in store for me today, I never would have left my room," she lamented, rubbing her forehead.

Lilith's eyes flicked to the side, "Children have a way of forcing us to confront our inner demons, do they not?" The subtle curl of her words hinted at a deeper meaning, as if she had been on the receiving end of their interrogation before and knew all too well what Moll was feeling.

Moll nodded, her brow furrowed in deep thought as she scooted closer to the blazing fire. She held her hands before her, palms facing outwards, savoring the warmth radiating from the flames. "Yes, they do," she murmured, the crackling of the fire accompanying her words.

As Lilith eyed her, she took in Moll's appearance. The past three months had drained her, evident by her tired eyes rimmed with exhaustion and translucent skin that revealed the blue veins running underneath. It was concerning how much her body had weakened.

Moll was running out of time.

"They're almost here." Moll turned her head to glance back at her friend, offering a tired smile. The thought of seeing her grandson again filled her with dread. She couldn't bear the guilt of knowing she had been keeping secrets, breaking a promise never to hide anything from him. But she couldn't tell him the truth just yet. Not before she found her daughter.

Moll just hoped Eidolon understood.

Lilith twirled her drink, watching as the ice cubes slowly melted. She was anxious about the upcoming family reunion and how Moll would handle it. "How long do we have?"

"A few days, maybe. Not long."

"Are you sure this is what you want to do, Moll? It's not what we discussed."

Moll laughed humorlessly. "Do we have a choice?"

Lilith gave a meek shrug. "I hoped that when I told you where Diana was, you would give me Arawn's book and let me handle everything. You need to rest," she finished with a pointed look.

Moll's shoulders shook with a raspy, ragged chuckle, her breath rattling in her chest. A fit of coughing overtook her, but she stubbornly pushed through, determination blazing in her eyes.

"I've had enough rest," she declared hoarsely, gasping for air. "It's time to end this once and for all."

In one swift and graceful motion, Lilith rose from her seat and knelt beside Moll. Her hands moved in gentle, circular motions as she massaged the tension from Moll's legs. "Moll..." Lilith's voice was a sweet, soothing, calming melody as she looked at her friend in worry.

"Don't start with me," Moll snapped, her voice laced with venom as she dismissed Lilith with a cold glare. The intensity of her gaze sent a chill down Lilith's spine, and she retreated to the safety of her chair. Moll's recent unpredictable nature made Lilith feel like she was constantly treading on thin ice, never knowing what would trigger her sharp-tongued outbursts.

Moll reclined, allowing her head to rest against the plush headrest. Her eyes closed in exhaustion as she spoke, her words dripping with resignation and a touch of bitterness. "I'm dying," she admitted, her weary voice barely above a whisper. "I knew before you showed up with your outrageous request." She glanced over at her friend with feigned resentment.

Lilith raised an eyebrow in amusement, pursing her lips. "In my defense, I thought you knew I was coming."

Moll shrugged in response, letting out a small sigh and closing her eyes.

"You haven't answered the question. Are you ready?" Lilith questioned again.

Moll turned her head and opened one eye, eyeing Lilith with determination in her bright blue eyes. "It's the only way." She turned back to face the fire.

Lilith's slender fingers twirled her wedding ring as she asked, "Is there no other option?" She had poured endless effort into reaching this pivotal moment, but now that she was standing at the crossroads of their future, doubt seeped into her like a poisonous fog.

"No." Moll was firm in her conviction, leaving no room for further discussion.

That was fine with Lilith, but she had one more question that had nothing to do with the Raven Society or the Book of the Veiled. "Lucifer?" her voice trailed off.

"He's alive," Moll reassured with a knowing smile. "And causing all kinds of hell," she chuckled at her own joke.

Lilith's tense muscles relaxed as she breathed out a sigh of relief. The bond between her and her mate had never disappeared, but it had been a faint whisper for centuries. The only physical reminder of their connection was hidden in the library, and she promised to protect it until his return - whenever that would be.

"I wouldn't fret," Moll soothed, guessing Lilith's worries. "We've been careful."

The silence lingered, and Lilith decided to change tactics. She knew Moll had been keeping things from her, and now that the time had come to implement the next stage of their plan, she hoped her friend would be a little more forthcoming.

"Where did you hide it?" she asked, pretending it didn't matter. Lilith may not have needed to know in the grand scheme of things, but she still *wanted* to. While mankind's survival depended on Lilith, Moll guarded the book that determined the fate of the Otherworld.

"You know better than to ask," Moll said with a scowl. "But for your peace of mind, I'll tell you it's safely hidden at the beginning."

Lilith huffed, crossing her arms over her chest. "Helpful," she grumbled under her breath. The beginning was such a broad concept that it could refer to anything - the beginning of time, the beginning of the world, or the beginning of the end.

But there was no use pressing Moll for answers; she wouldn't budge. Still, she couldn't help but wonder if Moll's recent visit to the Fates had something to do with it all.

Moll shuffled across the dimly lit library to pour herself another drink, hoping it would distract her from the heavy atmosphere. She stole a glance over her shoulder at Lilith, staring at the dancing flames. Lilith was annoyed with her answers, but this was best. No matter how much it would hurt in the end.

As Moll sipped her drink, she couldn't help but feel a twinge of pity for Lilith. The fire's soft glow cast shadows on her delicate features, emphasizing the sadness in her eyes that made her seem much younger than she was.

The ancient entity was older than the very foundations of the Otherworld—older even than the fallen angel Lucifer. Only the original gods, who had long since faded into legend and myth, could claim a longer existence than her.

Lilith lived in a world before heaven and hell were even a concept.

Growing up, Moll heard countless tales about a resentful and vindictive woman banished from Eden for her disdain for mortals. She'd been branded as a prostitute. A villain. The lowest of the low.

But Lilith was none of those things. She was kind and witty, had a weakness for chocolate cake, and bore the burden of humanity.

But Lilith also had her secrets. And Moll was determined to discover the truth before the rest of the Raven Society arrived.

Moll let out a deep sigh as she sank into the soft cushion of her chair. She gently rested her cane on her lap, running her fingers over the detailed carvings. "Why *did* you take the Book of the Veiled? Don't get me wrong, I've enjoyed the adventure. But what was the point?"

Lilith sighed heavily, unfurling her long legs and stretching them out in front of her. Her body was tired from the journey, but her mind was even more exhausted from the weight of her burden. "It was the only way to save the stories," she explained to Moll, who looked at her with wide-eyed surprise.

"Whose stories?" Moll asked, intrigued.

Lilith directed her attention towards Moll, her eyes narrowing as she chose her next words. "Mine," she declared in a definitive tone. Then, she listed the names on her fingers, each carrying significance and weight. "Taliesin, Morrigan." Lilith paused. And Chloe."

Moll froze. Fear icing over her heart. "Chloe? Why would you need to save Chloe's story?"

Lilith paused mid-drink, looking at her friend over the rim. "That's not the right question."

"What's the right question, Lilith?" Moll asked, exasperated.

Lilith took a drink before responding, her gaze returning to the crackling fire. "The issue with Writers is that they can only see one part of the whole picture. Instead of worrying about where the books are, you should question why the Fates allowed two Writers simultaneously."

Chapter 12- Chloe

Modern Day- Otherworld

"Let's go!" Sydney yelled as he gathered his thick mane of chestnut hair and secured it in a low ponytail, revealing glimpses of silver at his temples. Grinning confidently, he adjusted the straps of his rucksack and patted his thigh to ensure all his knives were within reach. "We've got people to save."

He'd been impatient since breakfast, ready to storm the City of the Unspoken, armed only with a small arsenal of weapons and a burning need to face a dragon. Isabelle and Watson argued with him about the absurdity of his plan, but they soon found themselves engrossed in a heated discussion about the best methods for battling trolls.

Usually, I would've joined in on the conversation, but until today, I didn't even know trolls existed, and I sure as hell didn't want to meet one.

The last book I read said they like to eat people. Granted, it was a fairy tale, but I was beginning to realize fairy tales were not just the product of overactive imaginations. They were a warning to mortals. And I, as the only real mortal in the group, was scared shitless.

Did they not care that we were about to face one of the most formidable supernaturals of all time or that I was the only one with no capacity to protect myself?

A witch with no witchy ability, I winced, recalling the conversation I had with Taliesin and Diana. Despite being born into a powerful family of witches; I didn't inherit any of their abilities.

Unfortunately, my greatest claim to fame was knowing how to use the Dewey Decimal System. And last time I checked, that knowledge was about as useless as knowing you can't hunt camels in Arizona.

If Lilith did decide I was the enemy, what was I going to do to protect myself? I nervously gnawed at my fingernails, my imagination conjuring up all sorts of terrifying possibilities.

I *could* run.

On the other hand, the farthest I had ever run was down the block to the local bakery before they closed. That's not really all that impressive.

Victor's inquisitive gaze shifted to where I stood, his sharp eyes taking in my tense posture. "Are you okay, Chloe?"

"Yeah, just thinking." I bent down to retrieve my pack, settling its weight on my shoulders. He nodded once and whirled around to walk away when I called out, "Hey, Victor? I got a question for you."

"Sure. What's on your mind?" Victor asked, reaching into his pocket and pulling out a granola bar.

Holding it out to offer me a bite, I shook my head. I couldn't eat if I wanted to—a sure sign of my fear. I *never* turned down food. "What do you know about Lilith?" I asked.

His eyebrows raised in question as he leaned against a tree. "I can only tell you this much: Lilith is neither human nor deity. A study I read discussed different speculations about her origin - some say she was Adam's first wife, others claim she was Lucifer's companion, and some believe she was the serpent who tempted Eve." Victor leveled a look at me. "But really, no one knows who she is."

"That's sad," I whispered, my eyes following a leaf as it fluttered from the branch above me. "Which one do you think Lilith was?"

"All I can say for sure is every story has a glimmer of validity." His earnest gaze hinted he wanted to say more, but he remained silent

Arawn had said the same thing to me before. I couldn't wrap my head around how Lilith could embody everything the legends claimed. Or had her tale been rewritten so many times that the truth of who she really was had become lost in history?

I was about to ask when Sydney's voice boomed, urging us to hurry.

Victor shook his head and rolled his eyes, muttering, "Does that man have only one volume? Loud?"

I laughed as we walked back to the group.

"Finally," Sydney sighed, exasperated when he saw us. "We're wasting daylight." He turned to Bree with a glimmer of excitement in his eyes. "Do you think we'll get to meet Odin? I've always wanted to see Valhalla. Just imagine what fun we could have." He playfully nudged Bree's shoulder. "Of course, you've already been there. Lucky duck."

As he rambled, Bree froze, her lips pressed in a firm line, her piercing blue eyes blazing with anger.

Oh, she is mad! I worriedly glanced at Eidolon as he positioned himself in front of me, shielding me from the potential battle brewing.

He raised an eyebrow. *You think?*

Bree's sneer transformed her face into a mask of pure fury. "No, I wouldn't," she spat, her jaw clenched tightly. "Odin's curse barred me from entering the sacred land. So no, I have no idea what it looks like." The pain in her eyes burned as bright as Asgard's flames, and her words echoed with the weight of centuries of bitterness and resentment.

Sydney's eyes widened as he realized the gravity of his mistake. His hand raked through his hair as he tried to find the right words to make amends. "Bree, I had no idea."

Bree shook her head and brushed off his apology as she secured her weapon on her back. "It is what it is," she replied before walking to Arawn's side.

Arawn scowled at Sydney as he wrapped an arm around her shoulder and guided her down the path away from us. The gods quiet words intertwined with her fiery insults as she glared back at the shapeshifter with rage.

Sydney's shoulders slumped in defeat. He had clearly developed feelings for the Valkryie despite his attempts to keep it hidden. Unfortunately, Sydney tended to say the wrong things at the wrong moments, especially when Bree was involved.

"I think I hit a nerve," he mouthed, and I nodded in agreement.

I knew Bree wasn't thrilled with seeing Odin again, but there was something else off about her. She was on edge and easily irritated, a noticeable change from her usual demeanor. She grew increasingly somber and withdrawn as we neared the City of the Unspoken.

Breaking the tense silence, Victor cleared his throat and asked, "So, have we come up with a plan for getting to the City of the Unspoken yet?"

"Arawn said it's a week away by foot," Isabelle shuddered, rebraiding her hair. "Maybe a little longer if we run into any issues."

"That sucks," I muttered, missing my coffee pot. Eidolon glanced at me and smiled, nodding.

Victor pivoted in Isabelle's direction with a worried expression. "What issues?" He glanced at Eidolon and me, back to Isabelle. "I thought we brought Arawn along to prevent any 'issues' from arising," he added, using air quotes.

Isabelle shrugged. "Who knows what can happen? We *are* in the Otherworld."

"Don't tease him, Isabelle. It's not kind," Watson scolded with a chuckle as Victor's complexion turned pale and his gaze shifted nervously. "But he brings up a good question. How will we reach the City of the Unspoken?"

"Got it covered," Arawn called out as he walked up. Bree trailed behind him, looking like she would rather be anywhere else.

"Great. What's your plan?" Watson asked, his eyes flickering over to the god as he guided Isabelle's pack onto her shoulders. His lips brushed against her forehead in a tender kiss before he stepped back. Isabelle patted his cheek with a smile.

"The hellhounds, of course." Arawn crouched down to stroke the head of one of the beasts by his side. The hound stared at him with adoring eyes and a slight tail wag. He chuckled, reaching into a pouch on his belt to give it a treat. "So demanding," he teased. "They wouldn't mind a run. It's been a while since they had a good workout."

"Not enough souls to chase?" Victor muttered, eyeing them with uneasiness. His eyes darted up to Arawn, fear dancing across his features. "Don't they eat people for fun?"

A mischievous smirk appeared on Arawn's face as he responded, "Only those who are hiding something." The hellhounds perked their heads up and grinned in agreement. Slowly, they all stood up, stretching their limbs, preparing for the journey.

"There are only three of them!" Victor pointed out, taking a step back. "How do you expect them to carry us all?"

"Trust me, little man. You can only see three, but it doesn't mean there aren't more," came the reply. Five more massive hellhounds materialized out of thin air and perched next to their owner, beaming at us all.

I couldn't help but chuckle as Victor's jaw dropped in surprise. The beasts were enormous, their white fur bustling with power and their fiery red eyes fixed on us eagerly. It was terrifying and awe-inspiring.

"They're beautiful." Sydney approached the closest one, urging them to come closer with a soft voice. The hound cautiously peeked at him, then at Arawn, before advancing for a quick sniff. Arawn nodded in approval, and the hound leaned in for a friendly lick on Sydney's hand. "I shall name him Balto," Sydney declared with a broad smile.

Watching Sydney interact with Balto, I took my chances, approaching the smallest of the eight. The moment our eyes met, an instant connection was forged. As my fingers stroked her fur, it felt like I was running my hand through the finest strands of silk, each one smoother and more lustrous than the previous. She greeted me warmly, nuzzling me with her wet nose, and I chuckled.

"I'll call you Hester Prynne," I said, bending down to see her eye to eye. "She had her share of mistakes, but she loved fiercely and defended her family until her last breath." Hester's stunning ruby eyes locked with mine, and I knew she understood.

Feeling his stare, I glanced over at Eidolon watching me. He gave me a slight nod and a whisper of a smile, his lips curving up in a mysterious way that made my heart skip a beat. With effortless grace, he settled into his seat of one of the larger breasts. Eidolon led him in a slow circle, carefully adjusting the dagger on his thigh to ensure it didn't impede the hellhound's movements.

"Time to go," Isabelle sang as she tied a scarf around her hair. She and Watson were already atop their hounds, seated like seasoned equestrians.

"All righty! Time to save the world!" Sydney exclaimed, raising his arm and clenching his fist, ready for battle.

Bree's thick, unruly curls bounced as she leaped onto her hellhound. She leaned forward, her lips moving as she whispered soft commands into its pointed ear. The creature let out a deep, guttural bark and pranced about, its powerful muscles flexing with each step.

"And try not to die," Victor muttered, shifting his pack and begrudgingly mounting his rebellious hellhound. The creature fought back, determined to throw Victor off its back. I tried to keep a straight face as I witnessed the ridiculous struggle. Victor eventually gained the upper hand but was clearly displeased with the situation.

Watson's deep chuckle echoed through the clearing as he rode his hound over to Victor. With a playful nudge to the shoulder, he exclaimed, "Cheer up, mate! With your gifts, you're the only one guaranteed to walk out alive."

"Just because I can heal myself doesn't mean it doesn't hurt." Victor swatted at him. "You try to mend your bones with no pain meds," he grimaced. "I'd rather spend an hour listening to Aelle explain some obscure historical point and its implications for current political turmoil."

I couldn't hold back a laugh. Not because I disagreed but because I agreed wholeheartedly. Healing my bones without medication was infinitely more appealing than being alone with Aelle for an hour.

"Time to go," Eidolon called out, and we followed Arawn as he led the way down the path surrounded by trees toward the City of the Unspoken. Eidolon rode alongside me, his leg brushing up against mine. I blushed as he winked at me.

My own knight in shining armor, I thought happily.

I told you everything would work out, Watson said as he glanced over his shoulder at us.

Whatever. I rolled my eyes and glanced away. He and Isabelle were always the optimists.

But I hoped I could find a love like theirs, a love in which 700 years plus 700 years was still not enough.

Chapter 13- Chloe

Modern Day- Otherworld

For four grueling days, we pushed through treacherous landscapes and uncharted territories, stopping only for quick meals and short breaks at night.

Through it all, Isabelle and Watson provided a welcome distraction with their tales of past exploits. Watson regaled us with stories of summers spent traveling with a circus, mesmerizing audiences with their daring feats. They laughed about the time Watson decided to try running with the bulls and failed miserably. Isabelle shared that Watson proposed under the twinkling lights of the Eiffel Tower but forgot to bring the ring.

I looked forward to the stories as they provided a much-needed respite from our physically taxing expedition.

Sydney and Bree were constantly at odds, arguing over everything, from the best weapons to use in a battle to the most efficient way to carry gear to the sharpness of their swords. They found something to bicker about even during mundane tasks like cooking dinner or starting a fire.

Despite their constant disagreements, they remained inseparable, always within arms' reach. It was as if their arguments drew them closer rather than further apart.

To pass the time, Arawn, Victor, and Eidolon delved into intense debates on a range of topics. They discussed the limits of mortality and the ever-evolving relationship between science and religion. The air was charged with intellectual energy as they challenged each other's beliefs and ideologies, engrossed in the thrill of debate.

I didn't talk. I had too much on my mind. Eidolon respected my space, allowing me to work things out for myself. However, he always kept an eye on me, never letting me stray too far from his sight.

My mind was consumed in a whirlwind of thoughts when Arawn's voice bellowed through the dense forest, commanding the hellhounds to halt near the river we had been following for hours. Hester joined her friends at the riverbank's edge, her expression both curious and wary as she sniffed the air.

I scanned the surroundings, taking in the rushing water that reminded me of the River Tweed. After my previous encounter with the call of the Siren, I was nervous.

"We're here," Arawn said as he jumped from his hellhound.

With a collective, weary sigh, we all dismounted and stretched our cramped limbs. The soft rustle of leaves and the gentle murmur of running water broke the silence as Bree and Sydney disappeared into the forest, their arguments echoing back as they gathered wood for the night's fire. Isabelle and Watson wasted no time unpacking our meager supplies, laying them out to prepare dinner.

I sat next to Hester, watching as Eidolon and Arawn strolled away, a nightly ritual they began during our journey. Their voices carried in the breeze; their words shrouded in mystery. Even though I couldn't hear what they were saying, I could see the intensity of their discussion. Whatever they were talking about always had Eidolon returning with a distant look in his eyes. And resolve.

Are you okay? I asked when they returned, handing him a plate of mysterious meat and thinly sliced apples that Isabelle prepared.

Feigning nonchalance, Eidolon replied with a casual shrug and dug into his food, avoiding the question. His fork scraped against the plate, the sound grating against our silence. Something was bothering him, but I knew better than to push for answers when he wasn't ready to share.

I shrugged, tuning into the ongoing argument between Bree and Sydney over proper hunting techniques. Across the campfire, Isabelle and Watson's laughter rang out as they shared a private joke, and Victor and Arawn debated the likelihood of hellhounds digesting mortals.

As the night wore on, exhaustion finally caught up to us, and we retreated to our sleeping bags. The campfire gradually dwindled to embers, casting a gentle light over the area, and the sound of snoring from Sydney and the hellhounds filled the air.

No matter how hard I tried, I couldn't fall asleep. Laying on the ground, the blades of grass poked through my sleeping bag, and I stared up at the twinkling stars above. The vastness of the sky reminded me of how small and insignificant I was in the grand scheme of things. I felt utterly alone with my thoughts, with no one to talk to.

Moll was in the City of the Unspoken. Eidolon was dealing with his own thing, and I couldn't call my mom. Things were not looking too good for me, and I fought the urge to go down the rabbit hole of despair.

Moments after finally drifting off to sleep, the sound of my name jolted me awake. I blinked groggily, trying to adjust my eyes to the darkness as I propped myself up. The moon cast a pale light over the landscape, illuminating the tall glass and scattered trees. Beyond that, I saw no one.

Laying back down and rolling over, I found the source—a lone figure sitting under an old oak tree that appeared out of nowhere. With a mixture of curiosity and caution, I got up and hesitantly walked over. A woman lounged against the tree trunk, leisurely munching on an apple while studying me curiously.

She sat confidently, exuding the energy of a seasoned warrior dressed in well-worn leather. Her pants were faded and marked with scars and signs of countless battles fought. I eyed her worn boots, covered in a layer of dust and what looked like splatters of blood, wondering whom it had belonged to, but too afraid to ask.

With a simple gesture, she invited me to sit. I obliged, settling down next to her.

"You seem lost," she commented, taking another bite. I raised an eyebrow in question. She shrugged, tapping her temple with a grin, "I heard your thoughts." When our gazes met, I was immediately drawn to the vibrant emerald hue of her irises, speckled with glimmers of gold, similar to mine.

She seemed familiar. But I didn't know how. I wanted to ask but decided that she would tell me if she wanted me to know. Instead, I threw a small rock.

"It's been a rough couple of weeks," I confessed, surprisingly willing to share my story with the mysterious woman.

The woman raised an eyebrow, silently telling me to continue.

"I was invited to join a secret society, and all hell broke loose." I took a moment to gather my thoughts, unsure how to describe my journey. How did one articulate the magnitude of everything I encountered? It sounded far-fetched even to me. After inhaling deeply, I decided to lay it all out on the table.

"Then I was informed that I was the new 'Writer,' I air-quoted, "even though I don't know what that means. Now we're on this wild goose chase looking for Lilith, who may or may not have taken my friends and may or may not be plotting to destroy the world." I furrowed my eyebrows and scowled. "Or maybe it was the Otherworld she wanted to dismantle? I'm not sure, really."

"Lilith?" the woman questioned, looking at me strangely.

I nodded. "Allegedly, she stole the Book of the Veiled. But I'm not entirely convinced." I raised my gaze to the sky above, marveling at how the stars twinkled and danced above us. With a thoughtful expression, I plucked a smooth pebble from the ground, relishing its comforting weight and texture as I rolled it between my fingers. A deep snore from behind me had me looking over my shoulder. I snickered as Hester snuggled up against Eidolon's hellhound. "Then there are the visions."

"Visions?"

My gaze flickered back to her. "Visions. They come to me at the most inopportune times, and then I write them down in the Book of the Veiled—a sort of dream journal if you will."

"I thought you said Lilith stole them?"

"Not all of them. Just three."

"Three?"

"Yup, three. We are heading to the City of Unspoken to get them back."

"The City of the Unspoken?" the woman questioned slowly.

I pulled my hair out of the bun and shook it out, letting it flow around my shoulders. Frowning, I started picking out twigs and an alarming number of dried leaves stuck in my curls. "That's where Arawn says she is."

"Well, then," the woman chuckled. "If Arawn says she's there, it must be true. It sounds like you've had a busy couple of weeks.

"Understatement of the year. On top of that, Taliesin said I was a descendant of a powerful deity, but I didn't get any of her abilities." I wiggled my fingers. "A witch with no witchy powers."

"You sound disappointed," she pointed out, smiling.

"I am," I grumbled. "I wanted to be part of the cool kid's club. Instead, I'm on the fringes of the playground, hoping somebody will invite me to play on the swings."

The woman laughed, "I don't think it's as bad as you're making it out to be."

"No?" I huffed. "I just set an all-time world record for the shortest relationship with someone who could have been my soulmate. To top it off, I haven't had a decent cup of coffee in weeks, and I'm suffering through withdrawals."

"Now, that sounds dreadful," she admitted, her green eyes locked on me. "But you know Eidolon is the only one who can help himself, right Chloe?" I nodded, my eyes dropping to my lap. She went on. "Relationships are always complex - no guarantees of smooth sailing. But that's your path with him." She paused, searching for the right words. "As for your abilities, not everyone is meant to be a superhero. Some are meant to endure when others believe they'll fail. What they do in the face of extraordinary challenges makes them true heroes."

"How can you be so sure?" I asked doubtfully.

The woman smiled sadly as she looked up at the sun rising on the horizon. "We are alike, you and me. Destined to be forgotten while the world remembers everyone else."

"Way to boost my morale," I frowned.

She smirked. "It's our destiny." Her eyes sparkled with wisdom and guidance as she placed a hand on my shoulder. "Keep your focus, Chloe. Trust that everything will fall into place one day, and you will understand why you are on this journey." With a graceful movement, she rose to her feet, brushing off the dust from her pants. Offering a hand to help me up, she continued with a hint of mystery in her voice. "I have no doubt we will cross paths again soon, lil' Writer."

I nodded, unsure of what to say, as she walked away.

"Oh, and Chloe?" she called out to me before disappearing into the forest.

"Yeah?" I spun to face her.

"Try not to die along the way."

She disappeared into the darkness, and I realized I never got her name.

Chapter 14- Chloe

Modern Day- Otherworld

The mysterious woman's words resonated with me. There were people in the world who were not supposed to be in the limelight, and it seemed like I was one of them.

So, I spent the day watching and listening, marking our route in case a sudden escape was necessary. As we approached the City of the Unspoken, the landscape grew darker and more ominous. The trees loomed above us, spindly branches reaching towards the sky like desperate hands or sharp claws trying to snatch the moon from the heavens.

I jumped in my seat every time angry ravens echoed through the woods, their harsh caws filling the air, interrupted occasionally by the hoots of owls swooping in for their next meal. I couldn't shake the unease that settled on my skin like a damp cloak. This is what I'd imagine the Otherworld to be.

Haunting. Dangerous. The stuff of nightmares.

The trees grew thicker and taller, forming a natural barrier between us and the City of the Unspoken. Their sturdy roots writhed out of the earth in a complex pattern, twisting and turning around clusters of prickly bushes. In the distance, barely audible moans echoed through the darkness, begging someone to remember who they were.

The Otherworld wasn't somewhere where souls went to be tortured. It was a place where they were sent to be forgotten, not forgiven.

The thought was somehow more frightening than an eternity of punishment.

An endless silence. Was there anything worse than that?

Arawn's expression turned bittersweet as he caught my eye and shook his head in understanding. He knew what was running through my mind. I met his gaze, lifting my chin in determination, silently promising to do whatever was necessary to restore the Otherworld to its former glory. He nodded once before he spurred his mount towards our final destination, his laughter passing through the forest.

At last, as we curved around a sharp bend, the majestic City of the Unspoken revealed itself before us. A stunning sight, the city radiated with an ethereal beauty that danced and shimmered under an unseen light. The grandeur of its glass and stone architecture stood proudly on an isolated island, surrounded by inky, foreboding waters and haunting mist. I was instantly mesmerized by its beguiling obscurity.

The Library of the Unread rose like a dark monolith from within the city's heart, its imposing height dwarfing the surrounding buildings. The walls were constructed of solid obsidian, a deep black that absorbed the city lights. No windows or doors were visible, giving the structure an impenetrable and mysterious air. As we drew closer, I saw ancient markings etched into the surface, their edges worn and faded but still holding onto their secrets.

"Legend says that inside those walls is the knowledge Odin sacrificed himself for," Arawn told us as we all stared at the sight, speechless.

"Well, shit," Watson whistled. "That is more of a fortress than a city."

"Who built it?" Eidolon asked, glancing at Arawn.

Arawn's shoulders rose and fell in a resigned shrug; his brow furrowed in deep contemplation. "I don't know. One day, this land was an empty field; the next, it was here." He turned to meet Eidolon's stare. "I asked the First One, but they never answered."

Victor's sharp eyes swept the area, searching for any sign of a bridge or makeshift means to cross the dark, murky waters. Each time he thought he had spotted something, it turned out to be nothing more than a trick of light on the water. His frustration mounted, and he spun around to face Arawn. "How in the world are we supposed to reach the other side?"

"You have to take the ferry across," Arawn chuckled.

Sydney scrunched his eyebrows in confusion. "What ferry?" he asked, his voice muffled in the dense fog creeping toward us. I strained to hear the faint sound of water hitting a dock somewhere, but I couldn't pinpoint its location.

Arawn rocked on his feet, smiling. "Charon should be here soon."

I turned to him in surprise and asked, "Charon? Don't we need to pay him to cross?"

"Mortals and their misinterpretations," Arawn scoffed, rolling his eyes. "There is no cost to crossing in the Otherworld. At least not monetary."

"What does that mean?" I narrowed my eyes to him. "Monetary."

"It means there will be a cost." Arawn looked at me with pity in his eyes. "It's different for everyone."

Watson wrapped his arm around Isabelle, pulling her closer to him. He ran a hand up and down her arm. "That doesn't exactly reassure us, Arawn."

"Too late," Arawn warned.

My eyes followed his pointed finger to an opening in the thick mist, revealing a lone figure standing on a deck, watching us. I eyed him cautiously, my heart pounding.

He was a shadow of a person, barely discernible in the dim light. His long gray robe was splattered with dark river mud and torn at the hem.

His piercing silver eyes glowed, revealing his sharp features and unkempt appearance. Charon was neither young nor old, and his face held no defined attractiveness or repulsiveness. It was simply a real, human face that unsettled me more than any monstrous creature ever could.

The dock beneath him was a testament to its age, weathered and worn with cracks and splinters running through its surface. The boards sagged underfoot, precariously tilted towards the churning river below. With each crash against the beams, the water left behind a frothy trail of foam before swirling away. It was a perilous platform to stand on, yet the ferryman remained confident and unmoved.

"Is there time to rethink this?" Victor asked, running his hand through his hair.

I was with Victor and stepped closer to him in silent support. We exchanged worried glances before the fog cleared, revealing a small boat floating towards the edge of the dock.

Charon motioned for us to approach.

"Here we go." Sydney's voice was barely a whisper as he and Bree proceeded forward, their footsteps crunching on the gravel path. Isabelle and Watson followed closely behind, with Watson holding onto Isabelle's hand to steady her. Victor trailed behind, but Arawn stopped me in my tracks. Eidolon appeared by my side, his tall figure providing a sense of protection, and I smiled at him gratefully.

"What's up?" I asked the god, looking up at his towering figure.

He looked at me worriedly and shook his head. "I've done all I can for you," he said, his expression turning into a frown. "If I proceed any further, it will seem like I'm interfering." He shifted his gaze to Eidolon. "However, I'd like to share two pieces of advice with you." I raised an eyebrow in anticipation, but his attention remained fixed on Eidolon.

"First, stop holding onto the past. Clutching onto 'what-ifs' and 'maybes' will keep you from moving forward.

Eidolon eyed him wearily, but we nodded in understanding.

"And the second?" I asked, knowing what he was about to say.

His piercing eyes fixed on me, and I swallowed. "Try not to die. It would be most inconvenient."

I sighed exasperatedly, rolling my eyes. Arawn chuckled and strolled off, whistling to the hellhounds for them to follow. Hester hesitated, her gaze flashing uncertainly between me and the god, unsure what to do.

"I'll be back soon," I assured her. Hester's eyes flickered with doubt, but she nodded once before bounding off, her long tail trailing behind her like a wild banner in the wind.

I watched until she disappeared from view, feeling a pang in my chest at the thought of not seeing her again. Despite our brief time together, she had already become vital to my story—I just didn't know how yet.

"Eidolon?" I asked, turning to face him, pushing the hair out of my face.

"Yea?"

"Why does everyone keep telling me not to die?"

Eidolon's arm wrapped around me, warm and comforting, as he squeezed my shoulders. "I wish I knew Chloe," he said with a wistful sigh, his gaze drifting towards Charon.

We walked towards our destination together, shrouded in shadows but beckoning us forward.

Chapter 15- Chloe

Modern Day- Otherworld

We scrambled onto the small boat, jostling for a place to sit and praying it wouldn't capsize under the weight of seven fully grown adults and the ferryman. To our surprise and relief, the boat held steady and seemed in decent condition despite its age and constant use.

Without a word, Charon guided the boat through the dark and mysterious waters. The vessel glided smoothly over the murky surface, skillfully avoiding the jutting rocks that threatened to capsize us at every turn. Occasionally, a creature would leap out of the water, its shimmering silver scales catching the faint light. Each time, my heart skipped a beat, unsure of what other dangers lurked beneath the surface.

Arawn's words of warning echoed in my mind, and I couldn't help but wonder what he meant by there being a price to pay. I wanted to ask, but after a glance at Charon, I decided against it. Our guide didn't seem like the chatty type. Instead, I nervously shifted in my seat and focused on the path ahead.

Eight massive towers stood guard over the city—their sharp edges and imposing height were a formidable barrier against any potential threat. The walls protected centuries of history and witnessed empires' rise and fall and time. As I gazed up at them, it dawned on me the significance of the expression: *If these walls could talk.*

Excitement filled me.

I was about to cross the threshold of the library of all libraries. A sacred place that held the answers to all history's mysteries. My heart raced as I imagined the countless volumes and scrolls within, waiting to reveal their secrets.

The weight of my worries about the stolen Book of the Veiled, missing friends, and the impending end of the supernatural world lifted from my shoulders like a soft breeze on a warm spring day. Even the tension between Eidolon and myself dissipated, replaced by intense curiosity and determination.

The world around me faded into the background, my thoughts consumed by a single, intense desire. I was no longer worried about what I needed to do or what others expected of me. All that mattered was my wants and needs, pulsing through every inch of my being like a powerful current. In the moment, nothing else mattered but satisfying my cravings and fulfilling my dreams.

I wanted the knowledge. Nothing else mattered. No one else was worth my time.

And then, like a wave crashing onto the shore, pitch blackness consumed my mind. It enveloped me in its suffocating grip, leaving me struggling to grasp reality. The urge to scream built, but I fought to keep it contained as voices whispered and murmured all around, beckoning me to join them.

They don't want you.

You're a failure.

Eidolon doesn't trust you.

You're a liability.

Everyone dies when you're involved.

My hands flew to my ears, trying to block out the voices. "No, no, no," I whispered.

Of course, you would deny the truth. You are too weak. Nobody wants you around. Take a good look at yourself. You were willing to abandon your duty for books. Your friends will die because of you.

Memories of my many mistakes in my short and tumultuous life raced through my mind like a high-speed train. Each one hit me with full force, leaving its mark. I was weak. Afraid. And I was undeserving. I would be the reason my friends died.

I was selfish.

The mystical, eerie Siren calls echoed through the air, entrancing me with their enchanting song. My worries and uncertainties dissipated in its wake, replaced by calm and tranquility. I turned towards the source of the melody, finding solace in the gentle water lapping against the boat. The Sirens were leading me toward a haven, and I wanted to follow.

Water.

Ever changing and moving.

Predictably inconsistent.

I would be safe in the water.

"Chloe!" Eidolon's voice reverberated in the distance. I whirled around to find him, but he wasn't there.

Why would he be? Eidolon had avoided me for days, a consequence of my own mistakes. I turned back toward the enchanting sound and mentally moved in its direction, curious to see where it would lead.

Peace. The voices promised me peace. The group would be fine without me. I was a witch with no witchy abilities. Anyone can write a book; it's not that complicated, damn it.

Right?

"Chloe!" Eidolon called out again. "Don't listen to them. They're not real."

"They are," I murmured, wading deeper into the water. "You have no idea. It would be easier for everyone if I weren't here." My feet moved closer to the seductive music as the icy river engulfed my legs like chains. The chilling sensation was a stark reminder of my mortality, and I welcomed it with open arms.

"Please don't go," Eidolon pleaded. I stopped to listen. "Don't leave me too."

His voice was filled with raw emotion, and a shiver ran down my spine. I couldn't leave Eidolon. I knew what it was like to be left behind. A fate worse than death. Determined, I turned toward him, confident that staying was my only choice. Before I could take a step, hands dragged me into the murky depths of the River Styx.

"Eidolon." A guttural scream tore from my throat as I struggled against the relentless pull of the water. It flooded my mouth and stung my eyes with its salty bite, blurring my vision and disorienting me. Like a wild animal caught in a trap, I thrashed and fought against my captives, but their grip was too strong to break. The crashing waves swallowed my desperate cries for help.

Fool, he doesn't want you. Why would he?

Come with us, Chloe.

We will keep you safe.

Forever.

I fought harder, desperately trying to keep my head above the water. I attempted to grab anything, but there was nothing to hold onto. Fear consumed me. I knew I wouldn't make it out alive. No one would come to save me, and I was too exhausted to save myself.

With a final gasp for air, I thought of Eidolon and wished I could've said goodbye before I succumbed to the water.

Chapter 16- Medusa

13th Century BCE, Athens, Greece

Medusa spent the next three weeks pouring herself into her work and responsibilities. Anything to keep her thoughts from drifting back to Poseidon. Their last conversation left her more determined than ever to follow through on her role as the high priestess.

Every day, Medusa woke up before sunrise and headed to Athena's temple before anyone was awake. She dedicated hours to studying ancient texts, performing rituals, and leading ceremonies. When she wasn't at the temple, she oversaw the training of the temple's acolytes or met with local leaders to discuss matters of state.

And every night, she retreated to her quiet sanctuary for her personal devotions. She allowed herself to be enveloped in the familiar routine of lighting candles and incense and repeating the same prayers.

Poseidon was wrong. Athena loved her.

Medusa pleaded with the goddess, hoping for some acknowledgment. But Athena remained silent.

It wasn't for a lack of trying.

She followed every ritual and made each offering perfectly. Instead of being treated as a high princess, Medusa played caretaker—a glorified housekeeper.

As she carefully wiped the dust off Athena's marble figure, Medusa felt the familiar pang of resentment. She'd always been a devout follower, but her pleas were unheard.

And she didn't know why.

With a heavy sigh, she moved on to the next statue, running her fingers over the delicate carvings in the stone. As she worked, her mind wandered, and she lost herself in thought.

What would it feel like to possess the power of the gods? The ability to manipulate and shape the world as you please, with no limits or boundaries. To exist forever, free from the constraints of time.

The gods had it easy. If they made a mistake, they could start over from scratch and try again—no harm, no foul.

But for mortals, there was no second chance at life. A single misstep, one incorrect choice, and there would be no turning back.

Even if she chose a different path, opting for the realm of Poseidon instead of the temple of Athena, it would only grant her a few years of pleasure.

Medusa's confusion stemmed from one question: Should she choose a short life filled with happiness or tie herself to an eternity of servitude?

Desperate for an answer, Medusa fell to her knees in prayer.

Steel-eyed Athena, wisest of goddesses, daughter of thundering Zeus and Metis of good counsel, patron of great heroes and adventurers, advisor of princes and kings, your favor falls on the bold and the clever, on those who dare and those who tempt the noble Fates.

Athena, weaver of the finest, fairest tapestries, teacher of art and craft to mortal artisans, worker of metals, your soft hands guide the flow of molten ore.

Leader of battles, warrior maid, of tactics and strategy you know all, of clever trickery and wiles you are the master; with words and wit you may win much, with the strength of arm and sharpened sword, at need, you take all contests.

Athena of wisdom, Athena of skills, goddess of the agile mind, for your works, I praise you.

Medusa's eyes shifted to Athena's statue, pleading for mercy. Time dragged on in excruciating silence, each passing second feeling like an eternity. Exhausted and drenched in sweat, she fought through the headache that was forming and the piercing pain in her knees from kneeling too long.

"Why don't you answer?" Medusa screamed at the marble.

All she wanted was assurance from Athena that her sacrifice was worthwhile. A sign that Poseidon was wrong. She needed it more than ever. The Winter Solstice was right around the corner, and Athens was preparing for its week-long celebration in honor of the sea god.

Medusa had never been involved in previous events, but this year would be different. And more difficult for her.

She missed him.

Medusa sat up straight, focusing on her prayers. However, her thoughts kept drifting back to Poseidon's proposition. Would anyone notice if she left? Would they care?

My sisters, Medusa thought. *My sisters would know.*

They would be so disappointed if she abandoned them.

Of course, she couldn't be a consort. She was a high priestess, a virgin, the one person entirely off-limits to even the gods. She was destined to be alone in life and death.

"Medusa!" Stheno's voice echoed through the halls.

Medusa sighed deeply, taking one last look at the statue before slowly rising to her feet and shuffling toward the entrance. Every step was torture as blood rushed back to her legs. She grimaced as she stopped to rub her calves, leaning against a panel.

"Medusa!" Stheno called again, louder. More desperate.

"I'm here," Medusa shouted, pushing herself off the wall. She approached the large opening to the gardens, shielding her eyes from the sun. Her sister bolted towards her, her flowing auburn mane coming undone from its braid and swaying behind her like flickering flames. Beads of sweat glimmered on her skin, highlighting the contours of her figure beneath her tunic.

Stheno, the most composed of the sisters, sprinted towards the temple with a sense of urgency Medusa had never seen before. And it scared her.

"What's happened?" Medusa called out, rushing to meet her.

Stheno stopped, hunching over and gasping for air. She slowly stood upright, pushed her hair out of her face, and wiped perspiration off her brow. Pointing towards the city, she explained breathlessly, "It may be nothing, but it could become a problem." She grabbed Medusa's arm and turned toward the town center. "I need you to come with me." Without waiting for Medusa's response, Stheno pulled her down the narrow path.

"What in the gods' name is going on?" Medusa's panicked question echoed through the garden as she struggled to keep up with her sister.

"Poseidon is unhappy with the festival plans and is threatening that he won't come," Stheno explained as she walked faster.

Medusa's steps faltered, shock etched on her face. Poseidon never missed a festival, especially one in his honor. Stheno must have heard wrong. "Are you sure?"

"Of course I am," Stheno snapped. "The butcher found me when Poseidon's high priest canceled the order for six cows. A servant told the butcher that he had overheard Poseidon telling the priest that he wouldn't show up if you didn't come to negotiate his demands."

"Why didn't the priest tell me himself?" Medusa wondered.

Stheno glanced at her sister knowingly as she explained, "The high priest was angry because Poseidon chose you instead of him. I think he planned to blame you if anything went wrong."

Medusa struggled to conceal her smile and maintain a facade of worry, even though she was secretly delighted. Out of all his devotees, why did he choose her to fix the problem? Did he miss her as well? She bit her lip in delight.

Stheno narrowed her eyes. "Do you have something to tell me?" she asked. "Like why Poseidon summoned you?"

Medusa shrugged, avoiding her sister's gaze. "I don't know; it's as much of a mystery to me as it is to you."

Medusa's denial didn't convince Stheno, but she respected her sister enough not to press further. She knew Medusa had been meeting the god but assumed their clandestine meetings had ended since she hadn't seen her sister return to the cliffs in a while.

Stheno spent hours on her knees, day after day, pleading with the gods to end the affair. She feared the growing tension between Poseidon and Athena could have disastrous consequences for Athens if they went to war over her sister.

Despite her reputation, Stheno was not without compassion. She sympathized with her sisters, who would never experience love. Stheno was content with her own life, but she knew Medusa and Euryale were struggling with their predicament.

But no matter what they did, they could not deny or change who they were meant to be—servants to the goddess.

Stheno just hoped Medusa recognized it as well.

"Do you want me to come with you?" Medusa looked at her in confusion. Stheno sighed. "To meet Poseidon."

"No, I can manage," Medusa assured her. She'd been hoping to see Poseidon again, and this was the perfect excuse. After all, no one could be upset with her if the god summoned her. "He'll just moan about something trivial like he always does. I'll fix it and be back before dinner." Medusa turned quickly on her heels, heading to the shoreline, her sister's disappointed stare burning into her back.

Stheno turned her attention back to the temple, resolved to send more prayers, and hoped Medusa knew what she was getting herself into.

Chapter 17- Medusa

13th Century BCE, Athens, Greece

With each step, the crunch of gravel under Medusa's feet echoed through the serene surroundings. As she approached their favorite spot overlooking the Aegean Sea, she could see Poseidon already perched on a large boulder, his muscular frame silhouetted against the warm glow of the sun. The breeze carried the faint scent of salt and seaweed, mixing with the sweet aroma of blooming cliff roses.

"I was wondering when you would show up," Poseidon greeted without looking up.

"You didn't give me a choice," Medusa replied, striding forward to stand next to him.

"We all have a choice. It's up to you to decide if the outcome is worth it." Poseidon glanced at her with a sly grin before gesturing for her to take a seat.

"And if I hadn't come?" Medusa's hair swayed in the cool breeze as Poseidon offered her his cloak. She draped it over her shoulders, inhaling his familiar scent of seawater and warm sand.

"We both knew you were coming," he said with a wink. "You missed me."

"I don't know what you're talking about." Medusa turned away from the god's intense gaze, feeling a flush spread across her skin. The heat of his stare made her uncomfortably warm, and she tried not to squirm under his penetrating scrutiny.

"You're lying," he chuckled, the sound bouncing off the wave. "You missed me just as much as I missed you, priestess." Poseidon raised an eyebrow in question. "And, given how quickly you responded to my threats, I assume you still haven't heard from my niece."

Medusa brushed a strand of hair behind her ear, feigning sincerity as she said, "I will. She's just busy."

Poseidon's head shook in disbelief. He couldn't fathom why Medusa couldn't believe that Athena wasn't busy. She was playing a game with her high priestess. A contest of wills that Medusa was destined to lose. "That is where you are wrong. The gods do not ignore their followers, especially the faithful."

The air between them became heavy as Medusa wrapped a piece of seagrass around her finger. She reclined back on her arms, tilting her head back to gaze at the clouds. In a soft, resigned voice, she asked, "Athena doesn't find me worthy, does she?"

Poseidon considered the question before answering truthfully. "Athena is not inherently vindictive. But if a mortal fails to meet her standards, she has been known to disregard them." He shrugged. "It doesn't mean you've done anything wrong or that your devotion is in question; it simply means you don't fit into her expectations."

"Oh." Medusa hugged her knees to her chest. She wasn't sure what hurt more—that Athena thought she was just another devotee or the feeling of being nothing special.

Feeling her inner turmoil, Poseidon gently took hold of Medusa's hands. The warmth of his touch flooded through her body like a powerful surge of molten lava.

"You are not a prisoner. You can leave." His eyes burned with passion as he continued, "I want to show you the world. No more temples, no more tedious prayers, no more drawn-out ceremonies. Just you and me, experiencing everything the world has to offer."

Medusa gazed down at the contrast of their intertwined hands: hers small and delicate, his large and calloused. She traced the intricate swirling tattoos that adorned his forearm with her eyes, mesmerized by their complexity and beauty. "You would do that for me?" she asked, her voice trembling with emotion.

"Medusa, I am offering you the universe on a platter. All you have to do is say yes." Poseidon's sincerity rang true, and for the first time in her life, Medusa felt truly seen and desired. Every inch of her being longed to say yes to the once-in-a-lifetime offer.

But, just because it was an option didn't necessarily make it the best choice. She hesitated, her mind racing with questions. "If I were to go with you, would Stheno and Euryale be able to come?"

Leaving Athens and her position would be a sacrifice, but she would happily go as long as her sisters were by her side.

Poseidon's brow furrowed in thought before he replied, running a hand through his hair. "It's possible. There's plenty of room. I'm sure I could find something to occupy their time."

Medusa's grip on his hand tightened, her emotions swirling in a tumultuous mix of relief and disbelief. Poseidon was offering her a second chance—a chance at the life she'd always dreamed of—a life filled with love, acceptance, and freedom.

All she had to do was agree to become his consort in return.

No different than a high priestess. *Right?*

Medusa's eyes lingered on the god, wanting to say yes to his proposition. But she knew she needed to speak to her sisters first, to seek their blessing before making any decision. A lump formed in her throat as she mustered the courage to say, "I will talk to them tonight." Her words rang out confidently, yet her heart was pounding with anticipation and uncertainty.

She had no idea what Stheno and Euryale would say.

Medusa waited until nightfall to discuss Poseidon's proposal, carefully watching Stheno's reaction.

She was the one Medusa needed to worry about.

"Over my dead body," Stheno yelled, jumping off the bed, her plate of half-eaten bread and cheese crashing to the floor in a mess of crumbs and shattered pottery. "We are not having this discussion."

Medusa's eyes narrowed, her heart racing as she struggled to contain her growing frustration. Stheno wasn't even giving her a chance to explain, so she had no choice but to reveal the truth.

With a deep breath, she gathered her courage. "Athena has refused my prayers. I am no longer wanted." She squeezed her eyes shut, struggling to hold back the tears. "If we leave now, there will be enough time to choose my replacement before summer."

"How do you know?" Stheno whirled to face Medusa, her eyes flashing dangerously. "Did Athena tell you she wanted us gone?"

"No, but Poseidon said..." Medusa started.

Stheno's voice trembled with rage as she spat out, "Don't you dare utter that name right now." Her piercing green eyes glinted with a fiery mix of fury and loathing. "That god has done nothing but cause us problems. I knew he was trouble." She began pacing across the room, muttering insults under her breath.

Euryale shifted nervously in her seat, watching the heated argument unfold from a safe distance. "Please, Stheno," she murmured anxiously, "we don't know who's listening."

"You're worried about me?" Stheno laughed cruelly. "Your sister plans to start a war between Poseidon and Athena—just so she can run away from her responsibilities. And you're worried about what I'm saying?" She swung around, pointing her finger at Medusa. "A god, I remind you, that has more lovers than Zeus."

Medusa's voice pierced the air, a sharp and bitter tone laced with frustration as she fired back, "Who are we to judge the actions of the gods? You wouldn't complain if Athena ever decided to have a lover." Her fingers clenched tightly into fists, nails digging painfully into her palms.

"You're right!" Stheno yelled. "Unlike Poseidon, she's *not* married."

Her sister's words sliced through Medusa like a jagged blade, leaving deep wounds that throbbed with pain. She'd forgotten about Poseidon's wife, Amphitrite, and she never wanted to start a war between the two gods. Her shoulders slumped in defeat.

Stheno wasn't done. Her eyes held a knowing glint as she turned to Euryale, "Are you willing to stand by while Medusa robs us of our place in society? Our position within the temple? Our future?" she all but screamed the last word. Taking a deep breath, she fought to gain her composure. "Do you want to be remembered as the sisters of Poseidon's whore? Because that's what is going to happen." She walked over to the table and poured herself a glass of wine. "That's how history will remember us. As the monsters who started a war."

Medusa gasped, turning to Euryale for help. If anyone understood, it would be her.

Euryale saw the hope in her younger sister's eyes and felt a pang of sympathy. "Medusa, I understand you are unhappy, but please consider the consequences of your actions. Is it worth risking everything for a god who may or may not love you?"

"He does," Medusa whispered, trying to convince herself. Poseidon had never said as much. But she knew. Deep in her soul, she knew that he loved her. Why else would he risk Athena's wrath?

"Are you sure," Euryale prodded. "Sure enough to walk away from all of this?" she waved her hand about the room. "Sure enough to tell Athena herself?"

Medusa wrapped her arms around her body, suddenly feeling very cold and unsure of anything.

"We take it to a vote," Stheno said solemnly. "And I say no."

Euryale hesitated. Unable to bear any more heartbreak, she squeezed her eyes shut and whispered, "My vote is no."

Medusa nodded only once before leaving the room.

Two against one.

They would stay.

Chapter 18- Danaë

8th Century BCE, Argos, Greece

For three weeks, Zeus visited Danaë daily, and her happiness grew stronger each time. It had been a long time since she experienced pure contentment. He was more than just charming and light-hearted with his deep laughter. He was a breath of fresh air in the lonely tower. It didn't hurt that he was beautiful with chiseled features, a strong jawline, dark curls tumbling upon broad shoulders, and piercing blue eyes that held the secrets of the gods within them.

As their visits continued, Danaë developed a sixth sense about Zeus. She felt his presence before he entered the room, as if her soul was attuned to him. And when he did arrive, the air would be filled with the most delightful scents of ambrosia and honey, lulling her into a state of peaceful bliss. In those moments, Danaë knew they were fated to be together—two halves of a whole, brought together by the Fates.

The days slipped by effortlessly as they delved into the depths of conversation, trading thoughts on everything from politics to philosophy. Danaë couldn't believe how easily she kept up with his ideas, her mind soaking up his words like a sponge. But more than that, she was entranced by the sound of his voice - deep and husky yet soothing, like a warm blanket on a cold night.

But Danaë favorite moments were when Zeus would entertain her with fantastical tales of distant lands and exotic places she'd never even dreamed of. His kingdom extended beyond her wildest imaginations, and he shared stories of Phoenician traders who journeyed across seas to bring back riches from far-off lands like Mesopotamia and Egypt. He spoke passionately about the Celts, who inhabited Western Europe from Spain and Britain and shared their unique cultures, customs, and beliefs.

So different from hers, but the same somehow.

"But we all have different gods?" Danaë exclaimed as she surveyed the array of dishes on the table. Zeus had put a lot of effort into presenting platters of mouth-watering delicacies from every country he'd described to her.

"Not different gods. Same gods, just different names." Zeus leaned forward, pouring another glass of chilled fruit juice. The liquid sparkled in the sunlight, a deep golden hue enhanced by the spoonful of honey that swirled and dissolved into the mixture. "The ways of the gods are complex," he explained. "We take on the forms that are most relatable to our followers. We might look different but are the same "person," he air quoted.

"What do they see when they look at you?" Danaë reached for a pomegranate, and Zeus' eyes roamed over her figure. Embarrassed, she sat up straight, trying to ignore his approving gaze.

Zeus glanced away sheepishly, a small smile playing at the corners of his mouth. "I've never asked. I assume whatever they need to see to believe," he admitted.

Danaë paused to consider this. "So, what I'm looking at is not the real you?"

Zeus examined his arms, flexing them and admiring their muscular shape. "I see myself as I am," he stated confidently. "And I'd like to believe it's a pretty accurate representation because, let's face it, I'm quite handsome." He flashed a self-assured grin and playfully winked at her.

"Don't worry. You are stunning!" Danaë exclaimed before gasping and covering her mouth in surprise. Her cheeks flushed with embarrassment, a rosy glow spreading from her cheek to the tips of her ears. "I didn't mean to say anything out loud," she mumbled, flustered.

"Oh, but you did." Zeus's smile filled with mischief as his eyes skimmed over her body. "Mortals always give themselves away when they lie, and you, my dear Danaë, are no exception."

With a gentle push, he drew his chair close to hers, their knees almost touching. Danaë couldn't bring herself to meet his piercing gaze, instead choosing to fidget with her hands in her lap. The words that had just tumbled from her lips surprised her - she couldn't believe she'd spoken so boldly to the king of the gods.

"You can say whatever you want. If it's the truth." Zeus's voice was a warm caress, drawing closer as he gently cradled her hand between his. As their eyes met, she saw the sincerity in his gaze. "I believe you are the most stunning woman I have ever met," he continued, his admiration evident in every syllable. He pushed a strand of her hair behind her ear. "Strong. Confident. A warrior."

The weight of his words hung in the air, wrapping Danaë in a blanket of affirmation and affection, her heart fluttering in her chest. Was Zeus flirting with her? No one had ever dared to flirt with her in her sheltered existence. Being alone with a man, without any guards, servants, or the watchful gaze of her nursemaid Rhea, was an entirely new and thrilling encounter for her.

If anyone ever found out, her reputation would be ruined.

Danaë almost laughed out loud at her paranoid thoughts. No one could see or judge her. She sat trapped in a tower, imprisoned by her parents, for a reason she still didn't understand.

It was a sobering thought.

"Why did my parents do this to me? Danaë's voice quivered, a mix of anger and hurt evident. As tears welled in her eyes, she turned towards the small window, desperate for fresh air. The room suddenly felt suffocating and oppressive, the walls closing in on her. With trembling hands, she pushed herself up from the chair, needing to break free from the weight of it all.

"Sit down," Zeus growled, his voice soft and menacing. His grip tightened on her hand as he pulled her down. He grasped her chin firmly, commanding her attention. "Your parents will receive their rightful punishment in due time. Until then, you have only one thing that you need to worry about," he said, the words dripping with a dangerous edge as he leaned in closer, his breath hot against her skin.

"What's that?" Danaë's voice caught in her throat as she stared, unblinking, at the god before her. Her breath hitched as she took in the mesmerizing swirls of lightning within his eyes. She couldn't tear her gaze away from the dazzling display, transfixed by its power and beauty.

"Me. Us. Right now. Can you do that lil' warrior?"

He didn't need to ask. Of course, she could.

Because Danaë was falling in love with the king of the gods.

Chapter 19- Danaë

8th Century BCE, Argos, Greece

Danaë reclined on the bed, supported by a collection of soft pillows. Zeus relaxed at the foot, his legs stretched out and his arms folded behind his head. She idly twirled the fringe of one between her fingers, savoring the softness and texture against her skin. She imagined it was what Zeus' touch would feel: delicate, tempting, and sensual.

As if he knew what she was thinking, he extended his hand to caress her foot gently. The connection was electric, and her body reacted with a jolt of energy, her breath hitching. Her initial instinct was to pull away, but she couldn't resist the sensation of his warm hands on her skin.

To distract herself, Danaë mustered the courage to ask the question that had been weighing on her mind: "What happens if mortals forget about you?" With society shifting towards a more practical mindset, faith in the gods was dwindling, and she couldn't help but wonder about the gods' fate.

The dim lighting cast shadows on his face, revealing the tense lines etched into his features. He shifted to face her with a fleeting look of disappointment. "I have always known mortals would stop believing in us. When that day comes, we will be nothing but forgotten legends."

"Can't you do anything?" Danaë eyes widened in astonishment as she sat up, her words spilling out in alarm.

"I never said I couldn't do anything. All I said was it would happen." The words left Zeus with a calm, measured tone and a sorrowful smile on his face. "I will never take away mortals free will. Their decisions are something I have to accept."

"That's sad," Danaë mumbled, thinking about her parents and having to accept their judgment and sentencing with a say. Not having control over your life was a helpless feeling. "Unfortunately, not all mortals have good intentions," she said.

Zeus laughed. "I'm aware. But I have taken precautions in case they become too unruly."

"What?"

Zeus sat up, his muscular frame moving gracefully as he crossed his legs beneath him. His piercing gaze fixated on her. "When mortals were first forged, the gods had such hope for them. We molded them in our image, granting them free will to live as they pleased. To discover and create their own world. But as their numbers grew, so did their conflicts. The wars among mortals made the wars between gods seem like child's play. There needed to be a way to stop them if they got too out of hand."

"So you created a weapon?" Danaë interrupted.

"Weapon?" Zeus raised an eyebrow, considering the word. "I suppose you could refer to her as one," he thought out loud.

Danaë froze. "Her?"

Zeus reclined gracefully on his powerful arms, a small smile playing at the corner of his lips. "Yes, a woman," he confirmed, his voice reverberating with amusement. "Not quite a god, but not mortal either. We needed a unique perspective. Someone who understood and empathized with mortals and had the power and wisdom to decide when a reset was necessary." He shifted his weight, the muscles in his arms flexing as he ran his fingers up Danaë's smooth, toned calf. His movements were delicate yet purposeful, and she couldn't help but shiver at the sensation.

"Oh," Danaë breathed out, unable to form a coherent thought as he continued to massage behind her knee. She swallowed. "Where is she now?"

"On earth. I keep an eye out for her," Zeus said, his voice low and seductive as he watched Danaë's reaction to his touch with an unnerving intensity. He knew the effect he was having on her and reveled in it, savoring every moment.

Danaë shifted as his hands roamed higher, trying to ignore the god's advances. "And you gave all that power to a female?" she asked, her voice trembling slightly.

"How is that different from giving power to a male?" Zeus looked at her in confusion, his playful fingers pausing in their exploration. "Neither sex is greater nor lesser than the other," he declared, leaning in closer, his voice warm and seductive against her ear. "In this case, we chose to bestow the power to a strong, desirable female."

Danaë's breath hitched. Swallowing, she asked, "Is she happy?"

Zeus gently traced his finger down her neck, outlining the curve between her shoulder and arm. "I believe so," he murmured. "She found someone who matched her in every way, and together, they created a family." He kissed the sensitive spot just below her ear, eliciting a shiver from her.

"Does she know why you created her?" Danaë tried not to squirm as his kiss trailed lower.

"Yes," Zeus admitted, his powerful jaw tightening as he pulled back to look her in the eye. "She knows."

"What's her name?" Danaë pushed herself higher on the bed. She was uncomfortably warm and couldn't catch her breath. Zeus's touches were too much and not enough at the same time.

Zeus smiled, leaning back, giving Danaë the space she needed. "Pandora. But I think she calls herself Lilith now."

"That's a beautiful name."

"As beautiful as yours." Zeus rose reluctantly from the bed and knelt on the floor beside her. "I must go away for just a while," he said, his fingers tracing patterns down Danaë's arm as if trying to imprint her into his memory before he left.

"Where are you going?" she asked, her voice tinged with disappointment.

With a sheepish glance, Zeus rose and stretched to his full height. "I should make an appearance back home," he admitted. "If I'm gone too long, it might raise suspicion. Someone might come looking for me." His muscles tensed at the thought.

Danaë's heart lurched as she realized who Zeus was referring to - Hera, the queen of the gods. She had heard countless tales of the goddess's wrath and knew the dangers of making her angry.

Her delicate balance of surviving as a mortal in a world of gods was already precarious, and Danaë had no desire to add an enraged goddess into the mix. She clenched her fist, willing herself to remain calm and composed, but her mind raced with worst-case scenarios.

She could almost feel Hera's piercing gaze, ready to strike down the mortal her husband spent all his time with.

"Of course, you have to go," she said dismissively. "I have kept you too long from your duties. Thank you for everything." Danaë hoped her voice wasn't cracking as much as her heart was. She didn't want him to know how much his leaving affected her.

"I'm sorry, Danaë. But I promise to return for you." Zeus leaned in and lightly kissed her forehead, his eyes conveying a silent vow of something more between them.

"Of course. You know how to find me," Danaë answered with a half-smile, waving around the tower.

"Not for much longer, my stunning little mortal." Zeus leaned over and brushed his lips over her cheek once more. With a heavy sigh, he turned to the door, his footsteps echoing through the tower as he disappeared.

Even after he was gone, the warmth of his kiss stayed with her. Danaë forced herself to glance away from where he had stood and walk towards the painting she had been diligently working on. Each brush stroke reflected her heart and soul as she poured all her love into the piece. It was a gift for Zeus, a thank-you for everything he had done for her.

Danaë removed the covering cloth and examined her artwork critically. Her depiction of Mount Olympus was encircled by a sky filled with lighting, while a bustling city showcased all the gods she'd learned about. In the center sat Zeus, towering over them all, exuding power and authority.

At the bottom left corner, a mother and child stood waiting, looking up at him with love.

The symbol represented a hope and dream of Danaë's, but also a warning to herself for what her life would become if she chose to continue down the path she was on. With a heavy heart, Danaë abandoned the painting and moved to the window. She needed to figure out what to do.

Being in love with the king of the gods would only lead to heartbreak.

Chapter 20- Lilith

Modern Day- City of the Unspoken

Lilith strolled through the winding pathways of the Library of the Unread Gardens, enjoying the enchanting sight and scent of blooming flowers. Each turn revealed another carefully crafted arrangement, a colorful symphony of roses, lilies, and lavender. Sipping her coffee, she stopped to admire each flower's delicate petals and intricate patterns.

Nestled in the heart of the overbearing walls was her sacred sanctuary, a hidden oasis of peace amid the city's chaotic struggles. This secluded section, encased in ancient trees and flowing fountains, was a dark reminder of a time long ago.

A time when the Otherworld thrived, and magick flowed freely.

Lilith was on the hunt for one flower in particular. A relic of the past, it represented both the fragility and continuity of life. A constant reminder that beauty and death were forever intertwined.

It also served as a bold proclamation that the City of the Unspoken was ready to be revived and eagerly awaiting the one who would return it to its former glory.

Finding it blooming near the Fountain of Fates, she stopped.

And remembered.

Lilith stumbled upon the small village, her feet aching from endless days of travel.

Alone.

Her only guidance was to seek out the mortals and watch.

She couldn't understand why the gods were so invested in the mortals' daily activities. All they seemed to do was work and bicker, and their constant cycle of praying and sacrificing confused her.

Every day, some unfortunate creature met its end as a gift to appease the Original for a transgression they apparently committed. Today's victim was a goat. A large goat that could have fed the villagers for a week.

Instead, the creature's body lay motionless on a jagged rock, drenched in blood and crawling with a horde of flies. One of the men heaved it onto the raging fire, flames licking hungrily at the coarse fur and twisted limbs. The burning flesh and bone stench assaulted her senses, and Lilith wrinkled her nose in disgust.

These were the mortals that the gods designed in their likeness?

Were they the hope for the future of the world?

Lilith didn't understand how. But the gods were never forthcoming with their intentions, so she would have to make the best of the situation.

Over the last three days, she had quietly monitored the village, her sharp sense picking up concerning details about the two elders—a man and a woman. Unlike the rest of the villagers, their scent was off.

The elders smelled like mud and magick, while the others smelled like blood and fire.

And they were constantly on edge. Always glancing over their shoulders, worry etched into their faces, like someone was watching them, waiting for them to make a mistake.

With a grunt, Lilith adjusted the weight of her heavy pack on her shoulders, feeling the jar bouncing against her hip. Her fingers grazed its smooth surface, a silent prayer for protection for whichever deity was listening, and she headed down the mountain.

Lilith stayed with the villagers longer than planned, her days melting into months and years as she stood on the outskirts of their community. With each passing season, she better understood why the gods had chosen to place her here.

The mortals were carelessly walking down a path of destruction, unaware of the consequences that awaited them on their journey. She felt the weight of responsibility on her shoulders, knowing the fate of these careless beings rested in her hands.

Unfortunately, they didn't listen to her.

Lilith's efforts to gain the villagers' trust were in vain. She heard their whispers, convinced she was a test from god to see if they would stray from the righteous path. Their closed-minded convictions deemed her abilities witchcraft, condemned and forbidden by their society. Anyone caught fraternizing with her was immediately labeled as tainted and unworthy.

Through it all, Lilith stood tall and unapologetic, a vibrant dark rose among wilted weeds as they ignored her.

Except the children.

They loved her. And she found their innocence refreshing.

Lilith instantly connected with two young men, both sons of the elders. The pair were strikingly similar in appearance as if they were carved from the same stone. Their deep brown eyes sparkled with mischief, and their sun-kissed skin glowed in the warm sunlight.

The oldest, a sturdy and hardworking farmer, was lean, agile, and possessed contagious, carefree energy. The youngest, a sturdy and hardworking herder, exuded a sense of stability and reliability. Together, they made for quite a dynamic duo; she considered herself lucky to have them as friends.

Their rivalry started innocently, a playful game of trying to win their god's favor. Soon, a different kind of heat radiated between them. Sparks flew as they clashed in their pursuit, and simmering resentment grew hotter with each passing day. Both possessed a fierce desire to come out on top, and it was only a matter of time before their desire boiled over into a fiery contest of will.

Only after the damage was done did they understand the full extent of their actions and the ramifications that would follow.

One sin. One death. A lifetime of consequences.

Marked as a murderer, the oldest was banished and sent away to roam the world alone.

Lilith's tears flowed freely that day. Her heart broke with the realization that mortals were destined to bring about their own destruction. In their quest for power, they would ultimately destroy their future in brutal displays of dominance.

They blamed Lilith for their actions. Somehow, she'd become their scapegoat. But she refused to stand idly by and let it happen.

So she left, knowing that her story would be erased.

Lilith didn't mind. It was a relief. She didn't want to be tangled up in whatever happened next with them. She had her own path to forge and a story waiting to unfold.

The sun shined brightly the day she left. A symbol of infinite possibilities that lay ahead for her. As she crested the mountain, she found a solitary black flower embedded in the cracks of a large boulder.

Its velvety black petals stood out like an obsidian jewel in a sea of dirt and gravel.

Lilith smiled. It was a sign from the gods that beauty could still exist in death.

As she walked away, Lilith didn't notice the man who appeared next to the flower, watching her retreating form. With a grin, he bent down and plucked the flower before disappearing.

Chapter 21- Lilith

Modern Day- City of the Unspoken

Lilith trekked onwards, her feet dragging through the demanding terrain under the relentless heat of the scorching sun. Every step was a battle against exhaustion and pain. Her skin had turned from bright, blistering red to a deep, rich bronze. Her lips cracked and bleeding from the dry heat, but something deep within her urged her o n.

She had no idea where the trail would ultimately lead, but for now, she pressed on through the unforgiving landscape like a lone warrior.

Just as Lilith's determination was waning, she caught sight of a distant glimmer of light. She took it for what it was. A sign from the gods that she was on the right path. Her future was awaiting her. All she needed to do was keep going.

She scaled the peak of a rugged cliff, crawling on all fours as exhaustion took over, and gazed upon the breathtaking scene.

The body of water stretched out further than her eye could see, so vast and endless that it merged with the horizon. The ocean's colors danced and shifted from a deep, rich azure to a bright turquoise to a dark slate, mirroring the sea's ever-changing moods. The waves crashed against the jagged rocks, leaving behind a thin border of white foam that glimmered in the sunlight.

Lilith stood on the edge, the salty scent of the ocean filling her lungs and the gentle sound of wind whistling through the seagrass, driving away her disappointment in the mortals. Exhausted, she slumped alongside the massive boulder and waited.

She was about to give in to sleep when a spark of gold ignited in the sky, turning into a blazing trail of energy. With bated breath, she witnessed its descent towards the earth.

The impact of the falling star was so intense that it caused the ground to tremble and kicked up a cloud of sand. Lilith instinctively held her arm up to protect her face, struggling to get to her feet. Adrenaline pumping, she hurried down the cliff toward where it had landed.

As she reached the bottom, she could see a body lying motionless through the haze of destruction and chaos. The closer she got, the more she noticed the man's features - his battered face, his bruised and broken form. Lilith knelt beside him. Reaching out her hand, she felt the heat radiating from his skin and saw the shallow rise and fall of his chest with each labored breath.

He began to stir, his eyes slowly fluttering open as the mist of unconsciousness lifted. A mixture of annoyance and confusion was evident in his gaze as he strained to make sense of his surroundings. He turned his head towards Lilith, grimacing in agony.

And then their eyes met, two strangers connected by a single moment in time. An instant bond snapped into place, uniting them in a shared experience of pain and uncertainty.

"I've been looking for you." His hand trembled as he reached up to touch her face gently. "You're a hard person to find." He attempted to laugh, but his face twisted in discomfort at the movement.

Lilith's eyes widened. "Who are you?" she asked.

The man's parted into a sly smile as he replied, "Lucifer."

The name sent shivers down her spine, its weight heavy with implications. She couldn't tear her gaze away from the mysterious figure, unsure if she should be afraid or intrigued by his presence.

"Why are you looking for me?"

Lucifer's gaze lingered on her for a moment before he spoke. "Because we are going to change the world."

"Lilith? Are you out here?"

Lilith glanced back at the library door and saw Moll and Vivian in the doorway waving in her direction. She was grateful for the interruption; spending too much time with her thoughts made her miserable. They were a reminder of everything she'd lost.

"On my way." She tore her gaze away from the flower and began walking back to the Library of the Unread. Memories of happier days lingered in the back of her mind, but she pushed them aside, determined to focus on the present.

"Hurry. We have an issue," Vivian yelled.

Lilith's footsteps echoed through the grand hallway as she hurried to catch up, following them into the study. Moll glanced up as she entered, pouring a glass of whiskey for them both. The crystal decanter glinted in the soft light, its amber liquid swirling as Moll's trembling hands struggled to keep it steady.

"It must be serious," Lilith commented as she took her glass and sat before the fireplace, looking at the other two women suspiciously.

Vivian and Moll were rarely in the same room. Although they had agreed to work together, the uneasy truce did not mean they enjoyed each other's company. Both women had a protective mama bear attitude regarding who they thought the next Writer should be.

Vivian was adamant that Aelle should inherit the position, while Moll firmly believed that Chloe was the chosen one.

"It's Chloe." Vivian rolled her eyes. "She fell in."

Lilith's eyebrows shot up in surprise. "How did she manage that?"

"I don't know. All I can see is darkness. But she's alive," Moll confirmed, fixing a fierce look at Vivian.

"Well, that's good." Lilith sat back with a sigh of relief.

"Inconvenient if you ask me," Vivian said, gazing into her glass. "That girl is always getting herself into trouble."

"Do you think we should help them?" Moll asked, worry etched around her eyes.

Lilith raised her head slightly and shook it. "No," she said firmly.

"She might die!" Moll protested.

"She won't," Lilith countered as she rubbed a hand over her face. "No path leads to her death. Yet."

"Yet?"

Lilith shrugged noncommittally. "Death is inevitable, but worrying won't help us at the moment. We need to focus on other matters while we wait for them to arrive."

Vivian didn't make eye contact as she swirled her drink. "Like what?"

Lilith's stern gaze landed on her friend, "Like Aelle. How is she doing?"

Vivian glanced at the door as if she hoped to catch her daughter standing there, disappointment written on her face, before turning her attention back to Lilith and Moll. "She's managing. She only allows Max into her room and hasn't been out for days. I don't think she will forgive us anytime soon."

"Inconvenient if you ask me," Moll muttered, glancing at Vivian. "That girl is more trouble than she is worth."

Vivian leaned in to respond, and Lilith interjected to prevent another argument between them.

"We don't need her absolution." Lilith reminded the heartbroken mother. She empathized with Vivian's concerns, but this was not the time to dwell on past regrets. "Aelle will eventually come around. But the reality is that Aelle will do whatever we need her to do, regardless of whether she forgives you or not," she warned.

Vivian nodded, her curls bouncing against her shoulders as she straightened her posture and plastered on a stoic expression.

"Moll, is Esme back yet?" Lilith inquired, bringing their attention back to their objective.

Moll shook her head and sighed. "Not yet, but she will be soon."

Lilith nodded, relieved. Esme was renowned as the best tracker in both the mortal world and the Otherworld. Her impeccable sense of direction and knack for uncovering the truth had been an invaluable asset to Moll over the years.

And Lilith needed those skills now. The origin story of the Otherworld had mysteriously disappeared, and Moll was at a loss as to its whereabouts. So, Lilith gave Esme the task of finding it, knowing the risks involved in such a dangerous quest. But without it, all their hard work would be for naught.

Lilith had a sneaky suspicion of where it was.

With Taliesin. Somewhere on the island of Avalon.

"If she doesn't find the book?" Vivian asked, "What then?"

"We adjust." Lilith sighed, hoping that it didn't come to that.

Chapter 22- Chloe

Modern Day- Otherworld

The claws of the Sirens pulling me under the water was my last memory.

Then suddenly, I was standing on a cliff overlooking an ocean of breathtaking azure. Glancing down, I marveled at the sunlight dancing off the receding waters, revealing small pools teeming with sea creatures and patches of seaweed. The mist of the waves crashed against the coastline, dissipating into clouds in the gentle breeze.

Spinning on my heel, I darted my eyes across the land, searching for anything that might hint at where I had landed this time.

I was pretty sure that I wasn't in Scotland or the Otherworld.

Fed up with being jerked through history and not in the mood to play games, I sat down on a nearby boulder and decided to wait for whoever dragged me here. Picking up a rock, I threw it into the ocean, settling in for the long haul.

Hours later, I ran out of pebbles to throw. Which was quite a feat considering I was sitting on the edge of a cliff surrounded by rocks.

"Fine, you've convinced me. I'll explore," I mumbled as I grudgingly stood up and made my way towards the trees behind me. Not because I wanted to but because I was starving and had to pee.

When Moll first explained the role of a Writer, it sounded like the most fulfilling job in the world. I would be unearthing precious pieces of history and restoring the forgotten stories of mortals and myths. My pen would be my guide and my imagination my compass.

Now?

Now, I wanted to go home, get a decent cup of coffee, and curl up on my couch, putting this whole miserable experience behind me.

And take a shower. One that would burn off the top layer of my skin and the layers of dirt that coated me from head to toe.

Whoever said camping was fun lied.

I was dreaming about pumpkin spice lattes when a flickering light caught my eye through the trees. The aroma of fresh bread and roasting meats wafted through the air. I sniffed, my mouth watering, when I detected the familiar smell of something else drifting towards me.

I groaned. It was a scent I knew all too well: vanilla and raspberries.

Yup, I was in the right place.

Resigned to my fate, I skimmed the unfamiliar terrain. When I said I wanted to go on an adventure, I meant to go on a guided tour through the streets of Paris, not dive into a horror story come to life.

"I'm getting too old for this," I muttered as I tripped over a tree root. My nerves were on edge, but they were no match for the tantalizing aroma of dinner. My stomach growled in anticipation, and I took a deep breath and steeled myself to do what I needed.

Slowly inching through the trees, I swiped away at the cobwebs stuck to my face and dodged the low-hanging branches that snared my hair. Every rustle of leaves and scampering of squirrels had me stopping in my tracks.

"Whatever I'm supposed to find better be worth it," I grumbled as I stubbed my toe against a moss-covered rock.

Finally, I found my way out of the maze of doom and stepped into a small clearing. Before me stood a small cabin, its wooden walls built from intertwined twigs and branches, forming a sturdy protection barrier against the elements.

"Wasn't expecting this," I whispered as I wandered closer. The home was surrounded by terracotta planters packed with wildflowers. Near the entrance was a pile of hand-carved wooden toys and swords. A garden was situated between the house and the forest, filled with a vibrant array of vegetables and fragrant herbs.

Feeling confident that no one was home, I peered through the tiny opening that served as a window. A fire was burning in a makeshift fireplace built out of grey stones; on the mantel sat a single decorative jar, shimmering as the glow from the flames danced across it. Against the far wall stood a large wooden table with four stools surrounding it, already set with plates and mugs for dinner. A ladder led to a cove, and I could just barely make out a bed hidden in its dark corner.

A sudden movement caught my attention. I ran to the back of the home, peeking out from around the corner. Through the branches, I watched a man and woman emerge from the shadows, their figures illuminated by the rising moon. They turned down the path I had just come from, walking hand in hand toward the towering cliffs.

Unable to resist my curiosity, I followed, for no other reason than something told me they were the reason I was here.

"Please, no surprises," I whispered to the gods. "Let's try to make this a pleasant experience."

I wasn't exactly skilled at moving undetected, so I kept a safe distance behind them, being careful not to get snagged on any tree branches or trip over roots. When I finally caught up to them, they were already standing on the same cliffs I had just left.

Amazement filled the woman's voice as she gazed at the stars dotting the darkening sky. "They're incredible," she whispered to the man, her arms tightening around him.

He leaned in and kissed her forehead, whispering, "One day, we will be welcomed home and shine just as brightly as they do."

With a laugh, she kissed him on the cheek. "Hopefully in the far future." He smiled, brushed a strand of hair away from her face, and pulled her closer. Their fiery kiss made my cheeks flush, and I backed up slowly before I witnessed something highly inappropriate.

As it was, luck was not on my side, and I tripped. Falling to the ground, I tried to muffle my grunt of pain unsuccessfully.

The woman heard me. She shifted to glance in my direction.

Damn!

Her gaze darted to where I was holding my breath, and I was captivated by her striking appearance. Her long and curly hair flowed down to her waist in cascading waves. Her skin was flawless and smooth, like polished alabaster. But her eyes intrigued me the most, a piercing green contrasting with the darkness.

I stood frozen. *This is what magick looks like.*

The man pivoted, his alluringly dark and mysterious form contrasting the woman's radiant beauty. He was breathtakingly beautiful as if the hands of Michelangelo had carved him.

He towered over her, his athletic build a flawless silhouette against the darkening ocean, like an angel without wings. His penetrating eyes captured my attention, an intense silver dancing with glimmering black specks, almond-shaped and filled with intrigue and mystery.

I couldn't stop staring.

"She's here," he whispered, kissing the top of her head. He looked back in my direction, his eyes narrowing.

The woman's smile waned as she followed his gaze. "That means..." she started.

"Yes," he nodded, looking back down. "I will find you, Lilith. No matter how far apart we are, I will always find you."

"Until the end of time," she said as she wrapped her arms tighter around him.

"And beyond the farthest stars."

The world withered away as I brushed away my tears.

Chapter 23- Chloe

Modern Day- Otherworld

"What is she carrying? Bricks?" I held back a curse as Sydney lifted me over the boat's edge and dropped me unceremoniously onto the damp keel. He stumbled backward onto his seat, grimacing at the mud covering his jacket. "Well, that's just dandy," he said as he threw a piece of seaweed back into the river.

Try having it in your mouth. I gritted my teeth as a shard of wood prodded into my shoulder while water trickled down my face. Inhaling through my nose, I tried to wiggle my toes and fingers to regain blood flow, but the freezing water numbed my limbs like an ice bath.

I couldn't explain how I found myself in the River Styx once again or why the Sirens had let me go. But I was confident that the vision I had experienced was more than just a memory; it was a warning. No matter how hard I tried, I couldn't shake off the overwhelming sense of dread, knowing deep down it was somehow something I had done.

Or worse, I was about to do.

"I don't think she gets to pick and choose when it happens," Victor muttered as he pulled a chunk of algae out of my hair with a look of disgust.

"Is she alive?" Bree asked, leaning forward to press her ear against my chest.

"She's fine," Eidolon hissed as he pulled me into his arms, "just give her some breathing room."

Clean clothes and a hot cup of coffee were higher on my list of what I needed, but they weren't an option. So, instead, I murmured, "I need to work on my landing," as I shifted uncomfortably off a small piece of jagged wood.

Eidolon's face lit up with relief as he smiled and wrapped his arms tightly around me. "That would be great," he said, chuckling. "My pants are drenched."

Isabelle's delicate fingers gracefully moved through the air, coaxing the water from our clothes. The droplets lingered for a moment over me before evaporating.

I turned to stare; my eyebrows raised in surprise. "Nifty trick."

With a smile, she wiggled her fingers and said, "Whoever claimed magick was useless never had to rush to work with wet hair."

"Now that you're conscious, what did you find out?" Sydney asked. Bree nudged him with her elbow, and he turned to look at her, confused. "What? Eidolon said she's fine."

Bree let out a disdainful scoff and rolled her eyes. "At least her sit up before you start with your interrogation."

Sydney glanced back, a smirk on his face. "Why? She seems comfortable to me."

He was right. I was comfortable. Leaning against Eidolon's chest with his arms wrapped around me, I was the most comfortable I had been in weeks.

I could get used to this.

Eidolon let out a low laugh as he tightened his arms around me. I saw no point in trying to break free, so I let myself relax and leaned into him even more as I recounted the details.

"That sucks." Sydney ran a hand over his face.

"A prediction, not a memory," I clarified, directing my words to Bree. As I retold the story, her complexion turned pale, and her eyes shifted away. It was clear that she knew more than she was letting on. But before I could press for answers, Eidolon sat up straighter.

"We're almost there," he stated, eyes scanning the horizon.

Pushing myself off him, I peered over the boat's edge. The swirling mist of the coastline dissipated, and the City of the Unspoken came into view.

Imposing, frightening, and deadly were just a few words that could describe the monolithic barrier looming before us. Its walls, towering over two men's height, were adorned with intricate carvings and symbols that pulsated with an ancient and powerful magick, daring anyone to approach.

The air around it was thick and ominous as if a malevolent presence was preventing anyone from daring to explore deeper.

Which, of course, we were going to ignore.

"We're here!" I sang under my breath.

Charon navigated the boat towards the dock and gestured for us to disembark. He hadn't said a word the entire trip but called me over silently as I scrambled from my seat.

I glanced at Eidolon, and he nodded, his eyes never leaving Charon's. I squared my shoulders, pushed up my glasses, and slowly approached.

Charon extended his rigid and unyielding arm, offering me something from his clenched fist. My hand trembled as I reached out, wary of accepting anything from the ferryman of death. He placed the object into mine, the coolness of the metal sending shivers down my spine like an omen.

Give it to the one who cannot leave, he whispered without words, the sound carrying on the breeze as he pushed away from the shore and glided across the turbulent river. With each stroke of his arms, he blended in with the water, becoming one with its currents. I watched, rooted in place, as he floated away, his figure growing smaller and smaller until it finally vanished into the distant horizon.

Eidolon moved to stand next to me, casting a curious glance down. "What is it?"

I uncurled my fingers to reveal a small coin adorned with a coiled snake. The serpent was exquisitely crafted, its body intricately wrapped around the coin's circumference. Four legs extended from its form, each ending in sharp claws poised for attack. Flipping the coin over, we found the piercing gaze of an emerald eye. It felt like I held a piece of forgotten magick in my hand.

"That is a very unusual gift," Eidolon commented, reaching out to touch it before pulling his hand away as it burnt him.

"It's not for me," I whispered, my eyes wide as I glanced up at him.

"Who is it for?"

Uncertainty tinged my words as I glanced at the City of the Unspoken, "I don't know yet. But we are about to find out."

Chapter 24- Chloe

Modern Day- Otherworld

Shoving the coin safely into my pocket, Eidolon and I hurried to catch up with the rest of the group.

"Uh, it looks like we have a bit of an issue," Sydney announced as we walked up. "There is no way in."

"What?" Eidolon took a step closer, eyeing the barrier. "That can't be." He furrowed his brow and ran his fingers along the surface, searching for a concealed handle. With each unsuccessful attempt, his frown grew deeper.

"How long has it been since anyone's gone in?" I asked Isabelle as she moved to stand next to me.

"Better question is how long has it been since someone's left," she whispered out of the corner of her mouth.

"Have you tried knocking?" Eidolon asked, wiping the dirt on his jeans and glancing at Sydney.

"Why didn't I think of that?" Sydney grumbled, rolling his eyes. He pounded against the unyielding surface, the sound swallowed by the thick wall. No matter how much force he used, there was no response from the other side.

Eidolon and Watson joined in, their faces determined as the three hammered away at the barrier. Grunts and groans escaped their lips as they exerted all their strength, sweat glistening on their brows. After several more failed attempts, they stepped back and massaged their sore fists. Isabelle, Bree, and I watched in amusement as they huddled together, deep in discussion, before launching another assault on the formidable obstacle.

They failed again.

I raised an eyebrow and looked towards Eidolon, waiting for our fearless leader to reveal the details of Plan B.

But in the back of my mind, I was already drafting a new entry for the Book of the Veiled. I'd even created a title for it: "The Day the Door Won."

It *was* the City of the Unspoken. I didn't think someone would be waiting at the front door holding a welcome sign. The whole thing reminded me of when I couldn't get into the Raven Society on initiation night. It was Moll who showed me the way by reminding me that sometimes...

"We need to go back before we can move forward," I called out, adjusting my glasses. Six pairs of eyes fixed on me in confusion. Crossing my arms, I explained. "We need to find the backdoor."

"A backdoor? Seriously," Sydney retorted, glancing over his shoulder. "I don't think there is one. This place is a fortress."

"I bet you there is one," I said confidently, arching an eyebrow, "and that's how we get in."

"Maybe," Victor said, his brow furrowed in deep thought as he eyed the city. "There's likely a hidden tunnel or secret corridor." He sighed resignedly, his shoulders slumping like he couldn't believe what he was about to say. "We could split up and try to find it."

"Excellent idea!" Sydney exclaimed as he pivoted to face Bree. His eyes sparkled with enthusiasm as he stepped closer and wrapped an arm around her shoulders. "I pick Bree for my team."

Bree's face flushed, and she quickly moved out of his embrace. Sydney watched Bree walk to stand beside me; disappointment etched on his face.

"It's not a game of dodgeball," Victor chided, exasperated with the gentle giant.

"How do we let everyone know if we find anything?" I asked. The City of the Unspoken was massive, and none of us had cell phones.

"Can anyone imitate a raven's call?" Bree kicked a rock with her boot, avoiding eye contact with Sydney. "The Valkyrie used it as a form of communication. Two calls meant they found something, and four indicated they required backup."

"I can," Isabelle offered with a smile.

"Really?" Watson asked, eyeing her in surprise. "Since when?"

She shrugged. "When I was younger, my parents sent me to the Woodlands Camp every summer for two weeks. They taught us all kinds of animal calls in case we ever got lost and needed to ask the locals."

"The locals?" Eidolon asked.

"Yes, luv, the locals. The animals of the forest," Isabelle responded as if it were the most obvious answer. "Bird calls were my specialty," she boasted, tossing her braid over her shoulder.

"Beautiful and resourceful," Watson declared as he kissed her forehead. "It's decided. Bree, Sydney, and Victor, you go right. Isabelle, Eidolon, Chloe, and I will go to the left. Two raven calls if you spot a hidden entrance or ladder. If you run into trouble, four calls, and the rest of us will come running."

"Shouldn't we have weapons or something?" I asked. "Just in case?" The others burst into laughter, and I glanced around, unsure what they found funny. It didn't seem like an unreasonable suggestion to me.

Right?

Sydney adjusted the straps on his pack, ensuring his knives were secure and within easy reach. "There's no need to be nervous, Chloe. Trust me, we're well-equipped for whatever comes our way." He stretched his arms overhead, muscles flexing under his taut shirt. "We'll protect you," he winked at me.

My cheeks blazed with embarrassment. Talk about an ego blow.

Isabelle's expression twisted into one of disdain as she glanced at Sydney. "He didn't mean it like that. We all know you're capable of taking care of yourself. He's trying to say that we'll all watch out for each other," she clarified, giving Sydney a meaningful look and raising an eyebrow.

"Yeah, what she said," Sydney murmured. "I'm not saying you're incapable. I just don't think a book and a pen are useful in this situation."

"That's *so* much better, Sydney," Victor said, wrapping his arm around my shoulders. "I suggest you stop talking now before you dig yourself into a deeper hole."

My eyes narrowed as I glared at Sydney. I wasn't weak. I wasn't defenseless. But if this was what the group thought of me, I would have to prove myself.

"It doesn't matter," I waved away the sinking feeling in my stomach. "We need to find a way in, and no one else seems to have any ideas." Trying to sound cheerful, I forced a smile onto my face. "Unless you enjoy banging on the door, which has been incredibly unsuccessful thus far," I added with faux sweetness.

Watson laughed, and Sydney's cheeks flushed a deep crimson. Turning on my heels, I descended the path along the stone wall, silently praying we would come across a doorway. If not, I knew this humiliating moment would haunt me for years.

Chapter 25- Chloe

Modern Day- Otherworld

E idolon remained my constant shadow as we navigated around the City of the Unspoken.

Thankfully.

Considering my talent for stumbling over inconveniently placed rocks, I needed all the help I could get. Although Eidolon tried to hide it, I could hear him chuckling as I cursed and yelped every time I stubbed my toe or tripped over a tree branch. After two exhausting hours of a fruitless search, I was completely drained.

My mood had turned for the worse, matched only by the gloomy atmosphere and ominous storm clouds looming over me. On top of it all, the wind picked up, adding just another layer to my already challenging trek through the dense undergrowth of roots and shrubs full of sword-like thorns.

Despite its difficulty, I couldn't help but appreciate the ingenuity of the City of the Unspoken layout. The structure's purpose was clear: to keep out any uninvited guests. But it also made me question our ability to find a way inside.

"Steady there, hero," Eidolon chuckled as he grabbed my elbow. I rolled my eyes as I muttered a curse on all rocks.

A strong gust blew through my hair, the raven's caw barely audible over the howling wind.

Isabelle turned to me, pushing her braid out of her face. "Was that only two?"

"Shit! I think so," Eidolon whispered, straining to hear if another two followed.

None did.

Watson's eyes narrowed as he strained to see through the shadows. "I think it came from over there," he said as he pointed to the dark corner of the wall just ahead of us.

We took off running, dodging hidden roots and sidestepping tangled vines. Strands of my hair broke free from its bun and whipped around my face like wild snakes as I struggled to keep pace with the others. Rounding the bend, I stopped short. We were standing perilously close to the cliff's edge, and I eyed it cautiously. One misstep and it was nothing but an inevitable and painful fall onto the jagged rocks below.

"I don't see them," Watson called out as he danced across the edge, his sharp eyes scanning the shoreline for our friends.

"Are you sure this is the spot?" Eidolon yelled over the crashing waves from the River Styx.

"Yes," Watson yelled back, but the confusion in his eyes told me something was wrong. "Their scent is everywhere."

Hesitantly, I inched towards Isabelle; my hand pressed firmly against the rough stone to balance myself. Her hands glided over the surface, searching for something hidden. As she worked her magick, I fixed my gaze on the murky water, silently hoping we wouldn't find a body washed up on the shore.

"I'm going to look further down," Eidolon's voice pierced through the intense wind. Watson and I nodded, and he sprinted down the path.

"It's like the wall just...swallowed them." Isabelle peeked over her shoulder, her expression wrought with anxiety.

I headed to see what she was staring at, but the sound of heavy footsteps caught my attention. I turned around, ready to defend us. A wave of relief washed over me when I recognized the figure. But my reassurance was short-lived as Eidolon ran back, looking like he was running for his life.

"We have to go!" Eidolon cried, wrenching my arm as he dragged me down the path in the opposite direction. His face twisted in terror, and my throat tightened.

Watson rushed to Isabelle, who was still absorbed in examining the wall. "Let's go, darling," he urged, pulling at her arm.

"No!" Isabelle yelled, gesturing for him to back off as she frantically scanned the wall with her hands. "There's something else here I'm not seeing."

"You got to be shitting me." Eidolon pivoted, grabbing my pack to stop me from falling as I collided with his solid frame. "Isabelle, we need to go now. Whatever is out there is not a welcoming committee." He pointed into the darkness.

My mouth dropped. Shadows danced in the moonlight, casting eerie silhouettes of an exceptionally large animal.

Watson's eyes widened in terror, his grip on Isabelle's arm tightening as he pulled her away. From around the corner, two enormous wolves emerged, their sleek fur glistening. Their powerful muscles rippled under their skin as they stalked toward us with menacing grace.

The sight of the wolves alone would have been enough to send shivers down anyone's spine, but what made them truly terrifying was the fresh blood staining their sharp teeth and dripping from their jaws.

"Whose blood is that?" I asked, backing up.

"I'm not sure," Eidolon said as he grabbed my arms to bring me closer to him. "It didn't seem like the right time to ask."

The pungent scent of metallic blood and death permeated the air as the creatures edged nearer to us. They moved forward with measured steps, making no noise at all. Their scarlet eyes barreled straight into mine, never blinking, and I felt like I was in a bizarre staring competition where defeat meant becoming its next meal.

Is a wolf a dog? The thought caught me off guard, and I had to hold back a laugh before it escaped. In my defense, the question was fair, considering the situation. If I was about to meet my end, I wanted to know what kind of creature would have me for dinner.

"Isabelle, let's go!" Watson roared, tugging at his mate again, struggling against her unwillingness to move.

"I've found it!" Isabelle hollered, pushing her hand into a shallow indentation in the wall. The stone moved slowly, making a loud creaking noise as it rumbled along the rocky surface beneath us. A revolting scent of dead trees and wet moss filled the air. My stomach twisted in disgust.

The shifting door caught the wolves' attention, and their ears twitched. Their eyes glowed with hungry anticipation, and I nearly wept at the thought of being eaten alive.

The hidden entrance continued to move at a snail's pace, designed to give us a false sense of hope while providing the wolves with time to close the distance. Eidolon and Watson pulled at the small crack, trying to speed the process up.

"Just a little more," Watson grunted, sweat pouring down his face.

Isabelle moved beside me and grabbed my hand; her eyes never strayed from the wolves as they prowled forward.

"Did your summer camp also teach you how to talk to wolves?" I whispered as we inched closer to the opening.

"I think I missed that lesson," Isabelle replied, eyes darting towards me. "But I wonder if I can help lighten the mood." She glanced back at the wolves, who were no more than ten feet from us, and scrunched her eyes in concentration. The seconds felt like hours as I waited for her magick to work.

I peeked over to Eidolon and Watson, who had managed to open the door slightly wider, allowing a small beam of light to seep through. Sadly, it wasn't wide enough for us yet.

With a resigned sigh, all my happiest memories played like a silent movie, and a tear slipped down my cheek. I would miss so much, like my favorite coffee shop, Saturday afternoons at the bookstore, dinner with my family, food-truck tacos, and my dog.

Suddenly, a mammoth, dark figure streaked over the rugged terrain like a raging bull. A flash of silver trailed behind it, catching the glint of light from the entrance. The sound of a battle cry pierced through the air, sending shivers down our spines.

With a fierce lunge, two powerful horns belonging to an equally imposing ram launched a massive wolf through the air. The other wolf released a startled yelp as it fled in fear, barely evading its attacker's relentless flurry of sword strikes. Each movement was swift and calculated as if part of a brutal dance with one clear purpose: to kill.

I couldn't say anything as I fell to my knees in a sob and started shaking.

We were saved.

I would live to see another day.

I needed coffee.

Chapter 26- Medusa

13th Century BCE, Athens, Greece

As she stepped into the temple gardens, Medusa was met with a refreshing gust of cool air that hinted at an approaching storm. The scent of rain and earth mingled, creating an intoxicating mixture that made her smile. Winter was her favorite time of year—when the world slowed down, and people retreated to the comfort of their homes and families.

Something that Medusa was looking forward to because it meant fewer followers visiting the temple and demanding prayers, sacrifices, or help with petty disputes.

All she needed to do was get through the next two weeks.

After months of hard work and toil during the harvest, Athens's citizens eagerly anticipated the start of the Poseidonia festival. The city was abuzz with excitement and preparations for one of the year's most celebrated events. Merchants filled the markets with the last of their goods, and the aroma of fresh bread and roasted meats wafted through the streets. Decorations adorned every building, and a sense of exuberance hung like a sweet perfume.

The main event, without a doubt, was the Phallic Procession. A gathering for men to exhibit their physical strength and sexual potency. Each one competing to outdo the others with their size and thickness.

Medusa had never personally witnessed the time-honored event, but she overheard the servants gossiping about it. Men would coat their bodies in olive oil and strut down the streets for all to see. Rumor had it that those who were not deemed 'blessed' by the gods would be ridiculed and shunned. It was a show of wealth and prestige, praised for characteristics that set men apart from women, and they reveled in the opportunity to participate.

The women enjoyed it just as much.

Women would gather along the roads, jostling and vying for the best spot to view the parade. Medusa heard stories of how they would fight each other in a desperate bid to catch the eye of eligible men. Hair-pulling, fist-throwing, and name-calling were not uncommon among these women who, the day before, portrayed themselves as paragons of feminine grace and virtue.

As the day came to an end, lovers would slip away from the watchful gaze of their guardians and indulge in sinful and sexual bliss.

Under the pretense that Poseidon demanded it of them.

Medusa wouldn't know anything about it, of course.

She'd never caught the eye of a man daring enough to risk punishment for flirting with a high priestess. The closest she'd ever come to impropriety was when she tripped on the stairs, and a servant reached out to steady her, his hand grazing her chest. He was horrified by the contact, and even though Medusa told him there was nothing to worry about, he fled the city.

This time, it would be different. Medusa would take matters into her own hands. Today, she would have her first kiss.

And if she was lucky, from a god.

After completing her morning prayers, Medusa rushed back to her room to prepare for the opening ceremonies. To catch the attention of the sea god, she knew she had to look flawless. An hour later, she emerged from her room wearing a cloak the color of turbulent winter waters and a trident-shaped brooch, feeling confident and prepared.

Not telling her sisters, she headed towards the city square.

By the time she arrived, the festival had already begun, and the air was thick with the aroma of sizzling street food and the animated chatter of people. Street performers dazzled on-lookers with acrobatics while musicians serenaded the crowd with energetic tunes. Children ran about with glee, their colorful outfits adding to the vibrant atmosphere. Medusa couldn't help but grin from ear to ear as she took it all in.

It was everything she'd hoped for.

As she walked along the path, Medusa's attention drifted to the hypnotic movements of the Poseidon dancers around the elegant marble fountain. Their graceful movements and vibrant costumes captured her attention while the sounds of drums and flutes echoed off the nearby buildings, filling the air with infectious energy.

A large crowd formed around them, swaying and clapping in unison to the lively music. The warm winter sun shone on the dancers, casting a golden glow over their performance.

The lead dancer, a stunning young woman with cascading curls and a mischievous sparkle in her eyes, moved with effortless grace and fluidity. Her body was an extension of the pulsing rhythm as she twirled and swayed with the beat. It was as if she embodied the very spirit of the dance, enchanting all who witnessed her mesmerizing movements.

Hidden in plain sight, Medusa absorbed the animated conversations of those around her. The women were buzzing with anticipation, eagerly exchanging gossip about the arrival of Poseidon in disguise. Speculations were circulating that he would bestow a mysterious gift upon anyone who could uncover his true identity. The tantalizing possibility ignited daring and reckless energy among the crowd, and everyone was eager to unveil the sea god's secret.

Even Medusa couldn't help but feel a flicker of exhilaration at the prospect.

So far, no one had found him.

But Medusa was looking.

Her sisters forbade her from accepting Poseidon's offer to run off with him. But they never said anything about not enjoying his company. What did she have to lose?

Athena hadn't acknowledged her, and Medusa was convinced that her pleas to the goddess remained unheard.

If she wasn't listening, maybe she wasn't looking either.

Chapter 27- Medusa

13th Century BCE, Athens, Greece

As Medusa navigated the bustling crowds, she learned a valuable lesson: having fun alone wasn't easy. She'd even gone as far as participating in the festivities at the temple of Poseidon at Sounion, offering prayers and sacrifices. She even stayed for the parade, occasionally peeking out from under her cover eyes at the male displays of prowess.

As soon as the ceremony ended, she searched for the honored guest. Medusa was confident that if anyone could find him, it would be her.

She scanned the crowded streets for him, anxious and hopeful. But a vendor would grab her attention every few steps, begging her to sample their delicacies, sip their wine, or beg for a blessing. Medusa maintained a serene expression, as expected of a high priestess, but inside, she screamed in frustration.

Medusa had not come to play the role of high priestess.

She had come to enjoy the festivities.

As the day wore on, rumors circulated that she was in attendance. Citizens flocked to her with absurd petitions and demands, each more extravagant than the last. It was as if the intoxicating effects of the wine had clouded their judgment, and they had forgotten what was realistically possible.

In this lifetime or any other.

One man asked if Medusa would extend his mother's life. After losing his wife, he needed someone to manage his household and care for his children. His desperation seemed genuine, and she empathized with the agony of losing a loved one. Medusa wanted to help, but Poseidon ensured she knew that prolonging a mortal's life was a decisive 'no' for all the gods.

While the man pleaded his case, Medusa's gaze remained fixed on the fragile, elderly woman perched on a stool. The woman's feeble frame could hardly hold her up, and she emitted apparent signs of agony. It was clear that Charon would soon be escorting her to the afterlife.

From the way she watched Medusa, she was ready for his arrival.

"Your mother lived a long and fulfilling life," Medusa said, turning to the father with pity. "It's not my place to beg the gods for an exception. Death comes for us all. However…" she raised her hand as the man began to object, "there may be another option I can offer you. Have your mother come to the temple and find my sister. Euryale can help with her pain and assist you in finding someone to help with the children."

Medusa glanced at the elderly woman, noting the tears streaming down her face. With a trembling hand, the woman reached out and gently grasped her hand, kissing it in gratitude. Medusa's emotions welled, but she held back tears as she saw the profound relief in the old woman's eyes.

As Medusa turned the corner, another woman pulled her into a nearby booth. The anxious mother showered Medusa with gifts of olive oil, bread, and miniature cakes, pleading for her assistance in finding husbands for her daughters.

Medusa couldn't suppress the slight irritation as the woman continued chatting about her daughter's love life. She had no interest in participating in any matchmaking schemes, but she forced a smile and pretended to listen to the woman's pleas. Her eyes wandered to a man standing a few stalls away, watching her.

He was a towering figure, his height emphasized by broad shoulders and a well-defined physique. Medusa's heart raced as she met his gaze, desperately hoping he was Poseidon. When he flashed a dazzling smile, she averted her eyes in disappointment. He wasn't the sea god but a mortal with an uncanny resemblance.

Medusa took a deep breath and directed her attention back to the mother as she received another bag of food. "High priestess, if you know any suitable suitors, please send them our way. My daughters are getting older, and I worry about their chances of marriage." The woman leaned in, whispering, "I don't think my husband can take their incessant talking for much longer."

"I understand," Medusa comforted the woman. "Please have your daughters come by the temple on the next full moon, and we will pray together for Athena's assistance."

The mother readily agreed, and Medusa was only allowed to leave once she agreed to another donation of food. Sighing as she looked down at her heavy load, she scanned the area to find somewhere to put it all. Scanning the area, she spotted an unoccupied table and dumped the food. She knew that it would likely be gone as soon as she turned her back, but the temple already received enough donations.

Let it go to someone in need, she thought as she turned around and found a boy standing in front of her. His piercing golden eyes stared at her in wonder before he dipped his head. When he looked back up, he handed her a withered flower he'd been clutching.

Medusa's smile widened as she inspected the flower in front of her. "This is a wonderful offering," she remarked, kneeling to eye level. "What can I do to thank you for such a beautiful gift?"

The boy's voice hitched as he started to speak. "I have a request, high priestess," he said.

Medusa raised an eyebrow and motioned for him to proceed. It was uncommon for a child to seek her out, and she was curious to hear his tale.

The boy shared how his next-door neighbor, a greedy man with no regard for others, had been sneaking onto his land and stealing his father's prized cows. He wanted Athena, known for her swift justice and punishment, to strip the thief of his sight as retribution.

Medusa gasped in surprise. "That's quite the request," she started, choosing her words carefully. "Asking to take someone's eyesight is not to be taken lightly. His family will suffer alongside him. Is that what you want?" she asked kindly.

The boy's face fell, and he shook his head.

Medusa leaned in close, her eyes narrowing as she pondered. "I think I may have another solution for you," she whispered confidentially. "I have been looking for a new home for my cows. They tend to wander into the gardens and eat all the flowers. If you take them for me, I will know they are going to a good home." She leaned back with a smile. "And since they are branded with Athena's emblem, your neighbor can't claim they belong to him."

As Medusa explained her plan, the boy's face brightened with optimism, and his eyes lost their fear and anxiety, replaced by a spark of hope. "I have to go tell my father that Athena will help, just as I promised," he jumped up and down.

Medusa's smile widened as she watched him run off. Suddenly, he turned around and ran back to embrace her in a tight hug. "Thank you," he whispered in her ear before dashing off again.

As he disappeared into the crowd, Medusa fought back tears. She had never been hugged by a child before; it was a sensation she could hardly describe.

"It's nice to be appreciated," a rough voice sounded behind her.

Medusa spun around in surprise. Standing beside her was an elderly man, his face weathered and lined like the sea, lips chapped from years of salty winds, and his hair was wild and unkempt as if the ocean breeze had never left it alone.

"Yes, it is," she said as her eyes darted toward where the boy had run off.

"Are you willing to escort an old man around?" The old man extended his arm to her, revealing familiar tattoos on his forearms.

Medusa's lips curled into a smile as she nodded in agreement. To anyone else, the figure standing beside her would have appeared to be an ordinary mortal. But Medusa knew precisely who he was.

She'd finally found Poseidon.

Chapter 28- Medusa

13th Century BCE, Athens, Greece

"Lead the way," Medusa said with a sly smile. She linked arms with Poseidon, and they moved through the bustling crowd. To anyone passing by, they appeared as just another married couple, their bodies in perfect sync as they navigated through the crowds of vendors. Just two figures in a sea of faces, their forbidden relationship hidden under the guise of normalcy.

For the next few hours, they indulged in all the delights of the festivities. Mesmerizing performances filled the air with music while mouthwatering aromas from food stalls mingled and enticed them to enjoy freshly baked bread and local sweet wine. Poseidon was eager to explore every stall and admire the unique wares crafted by skilled artisans. His enthusiasm was infectious as he praised each artist for their talent.

Medusa couldn't deny he had charm and charisma when it came to connecting with the citizens of Athens. They adored him and treated them with the utmost respect, even as he paraded under the guise of an old man.

As they walked, Poseidon pointed out familiar faces he encountered on his journeys. They exchanged looks when they witnessed men attempting to impress and women unabashedly flirting while the elders gave disapproving stares. And when couples wandered off into the nearby fields, they shared a knowing smile.

For a moment, Medusa felt like an average person.

They were on their way to the racing field when an unexpected obstacle appeared- Stheno and Euryale. The air grew tense as the sisters glared at Medusa, their mouths tightly pressed together in fury.

"Where were you?" Stheno asked, glancing suspiciously at the old man. "We've been looking for you everywhere."

Medusa's heart raced as she anxiously glanced between her sisters and Poseidon, grateful neither recognized the god. She didn't want to risk them finding out who she was with. Her hand fidgeted with her cloak as she asked, "Has something happened?"

Tears welled up in Euryale's eyes. "Poseidon destroyed the gardens," she choked out, her voice quivering with emotion. "And now he's threatening to desecrate Athena's statue."

Stheno interjected, her eyes flashing with hatred. "He threatened to chop down the olive tree," she sneered, tugging Medusa's cloak and urging her towards the temple. "You have to convince him to stop before he ruins everything."

Medusa allowed herself to be dragged back to the temple, her thoughts spinning with bewilderment. She risked a look back at the god following closely behind. Poseidon didn't say anything, but the glint in his stormy eyes hinted at his amusement as they headed to the gardens.

The sea god was clearly enjoying himself.

Stheno and Euryale paid no mind to the intruder as they hurled venomous insults about the sea god, their voices laced with anger and frustration. Medusa's cheeks flushed with shame at each cutting remark, but Poseidon enjoyed the heated discussion.

"And to think you were planning on running away with him." The disbelief dripped from Stheno's voice as she hissed her contempt.

Medusa gasped in shock, feeling the weight of her sister's words like a physical blow. She glanced around, fear rising within her at the passersby, their curious gazes lingering on the tense exchange.

Medusa calmly nodded at a nearby vendor before focusing her attention on Stheno. "This is not the appropriate time or place to have this conversation," she whispered sharply, squaring her shoulders. Poseidon subtly moved closer to stand behind her, ready to intervene. Or to eavesdrop.

She held up a hand to stop him. She hadn't discussed her decision with him and did not want him to find out this way.

Stheno stood her ground, refusing to back down. "I know you don't want to discuss it, and you probably hoped we would change our minds. But the destruction he caused at the temple only serves as proof you chose the wrong god to fall in love with."

Waves of humiliation coursed through Medusa's body, and she desperately hoped Poseidon hadn't overheard. But a gentle cough from behind confirmed he had, his intense gaze fixed on the back of her head.

Medusa's shoulders slumped as she rubbed the bridge of her nose. Stheno had the uncanny ability to say the wrong things at the worst moments.

Poseidon gracefully sidestepped Medusa, a smirk on his lips and a honeyed tone in his voice as he spoke. "I've heard he is a most generous god," he said, casting a suggestive glance in Medusa's direction. "And I've also heard he takes care of his people." He leaned toward Stehno. "Rumor has it," he whispered, "that he is quite an attentive lover as well."

Euryale's inquisitive eyes scrutinized the god as she asked, "Who told you that?"

Poseidon waved a dismissive hand. "I can't recall," he said with a hint of indifference. "But I know he is the only god who has never ignored my prayers."

"You believe he truly cares for his followers?" Euryale asked, her eyes narrowing in consideration. She glanced at Medusa and back to him, a slight grin on her face.

Poseidon studied her for a moment before replying. "I know so. I've been to his kingdom." His chest puffed with pride.

"You?" Stheno scoffed, folding her arms across her body.

"Ah, yes," he exclaimed with a fond smile. "No other place in the world can match the breathtaking beauty of his palace. The architecture is a marvel, with gilded columns and floors of gleaming marble that seemed to stretch on for miles." He turned to Medusa. "Outside, as far as the eye can see, lush meadows lay like a patchwork quilt of wildflowers. The air was intoxicating with the sweet aroma of blooming blossoms and the gentle sound of cascading waterfalls. And hidden within the paradise are secret coves, accessible only by seashell paths that wind through the landscape." He paused, a wistful tone in his voice. "And once inside, you are completely concealed from the prying eyes."

Medusa held her breath, determined not to break their gaze, longing to accept everything he offered.

"It's not all water?" Euryale asked, shattering the moment they'd been sharing.

Poseidon reluctantly looked away first. "No," he chuckled, "it wouldn't be very convenient for those who can't breathe underwater if that were the case."

Stheno's expression grew more intense. "We'll see if you still feel the same way after witnessing what he's done to Athena's gardens," she hissed before storming off, everyone trailing behind her silently.

Medusa braced herself for what she was about to discover, hopeful Poseidon had nothing to do with it. But she couldn't dismiss the possibility entirely either.

Poseidon leaned close and whispered into her ear as they crested the hill. The warmth of his breath against her skin sent shivers down her spine. "I didn't," he said, his voice barely audible. His eyes searched hers when she glanced at him, wanting her to believe him.

"I had other things on my mind," he confided, his words laced with desire. Medusa's cheeks flushed, and she couldn't deny the crackling electricity between them.

"No," Stheno gasped and covered her mouth, shaking her head. Medusa glanced over to see what caused her reaction but couldn't hold back a smile when she saw the source of Stheno's distress.

The gardens were just as they had been when she last saw them. Clay pots sat along the outer wall, containing vibrant red saffron stigmas. Euryale's beloved ironwort, used for her famous teas, was meticulously arranged in precise rows, its leaves a deep shade of green. At the center, a gardener was caring for his prized Olympus Yarrow.

The air was alive with the sweet scents of blooming blossoms and the soft murmur of bees buzzing from one flower to another as they gathered the last of their honey before winter.

Poseidon's gaze glimmered with admiration as he took in the vibrant garden. "Impressive," he remarked, a smirk tugging at his lips. "I can see why Athena would be proud." He turned to Stheno. "But let's focus on the issue at hand. Where did you say the damaged section was? We need to assess the situation before we can make a plan." With a raised eyebrow, he awaited her response.

Stheno's hands fell to her side in defeat as she struggled to make sense of the situation. "I don't understand," she muttered, pivoting in disbelief. "Everything was destroyed...right?" She turned to Euryale, seeking reassurance that she wasn't losing her mind. "I could have sworn…"

Euryale nodded slowly, eyes scanning the gardens in wonder and relief.

"Maybe someone lied?" Poseidon asked, feigning innocence. "Or maybe an elaborate prank?"

With a sharp inhale, Stheno's gaze homed in on the god like a laser, her narrowed eyes locked onto his form. "And you are…?" she questioned, taking a slow, calculated step forward as if assessing her prey.

A warning flashed in Poseidon's eyes. "You never asked, and I never said." He extended his arm towards Medusa. "High priestess, I must return you to the contest. You promised to present the trophies to the champions. We wouldn't want you to miss the event because of your sibling's erroneous impression of the situation." He side-glanced the eldest sister with a frown. "Clearly, Poseidon hasn't done anything to Athena's temple."

With a slight nod, Medusa linked arms with him. But Poseidon wasn't done yet. He shot a hard look at Stheno and said, "I highly doubt the sea god has any desire to destroy his niece's gardens. More likely, he is off participating in the festival in his honor, not wasting his time on petty arguments."

Stheno's face reddened with anger, but she remained silent. Euryale walked over and grabbed her hand, giving it a reassuring squeeze.

With a triumphant smile, Poseidon led Medusa back to the city center, and she waited until they were far enough away before speaking.

"Don't be angry," she began. "They were only trying to defend the temple."

"Don't worry, I'm not angry," he reassured Medusa. "I find the idea of discovering the truth quite intriguing. And I have a hunch Athena may be involved somehow."

"You think she would do something like this?"

"Of course," he laughed. "It's nothing personal, just a bit of fun."

Medusa's mind raced with doubt as she looked at Poseidon. She couldn't shake the sensation that the incident wasn't a coincidence. Was Athena aware of her secret rendezvous with the sea god? Her eyes darted around, searching for any sign of the goddess.

"Come on," Poseidon urged Medusa out of her reverie. He leaned closer, "I have a surprise for you."

"What?" Medusa asked with excitement.

"A gilded tempest," he whispered alluringly as a sharp gust of wind whipped through the countryside, promising a night Medusa would never forget.

Chapter 29- Danaë

8th Century BCE, Argos, Greece

Unfortunately, Danaë's wish that some time apart from Zeus would diminish her affection for him proved futile. She could not push thoughts of him out of her mind.

Zeus was more than the king of gods. He had become a companion, someone she trusted and confided in. Danaë didn't want to admit it, but she longed for their relationship to evolve into something more.

She knew the idea was madness. What could she offer Zeus?

Was it worth the risk of incurring Hera's wrath? Sane people would say no, but Danaë had nothing to lose.

No one was coming to save her. Her tower, her prison, existed beyond reality.

Had anyone commented on her sudden absence? Did they even try to find her? Whenever she questioned Zeus, he would brush it off with vague promises that he would handle everything and ensure her safety. And that one day, she would be released.

But he never said when. So Danaë waited.

No one came.

The day Danaë's life changed ended with a gilded tempest. A breathtaking show of falling stars illuminated the night sky.

The heavens came alive as three comets blazed like a celestial bonfire through the darkness. Before long, the world transformed into a captivating gold canvas. The vast expanse roared with an ethereal choir of voices, singing a melody of hope, joy, and celebration.

Countless stars dotted the velvet sky, but one, larger and brighter than the rest, shot across it in a dazzling streak of light. Rhea's words echoed in Danaë thoughts, reminding her that falling stars were omens of things to come.

Whether it be good or bad.

Closing her eyes, Danaë took a deep breath and sent her fervent wish into the heavens, a flutter of longing growing within her. She knew nothing would change, but it didn't hurt to try.

She stood in the quiet darkness for hours, watching the stars descend from their rightful place in the sky. Each one was the soul of someone who had left this world to find their home in another. She wanted to beg them to stay. They had become her beacon. A reminder that one day, she would discover a real home.

But they faded into blackness, the memory of the person they once were lost to time.

Reluctantly, Danaë wiped the tears from her face and crawled to bed. It was only a matter of time before Charon came for her. And she was ready. Her entire life had been nothing but failures, defeat, and pain. With a deep breath, she shut her eyes and waited for what would come.

"Charon is a depressing old man," a voice chuckled from the shadows. "But I would be happy to summon him if you prefer his company to mine."

Danaë's heart fluttered as she caught a glimpse of the god striding towards her. Zeus's chiseled features were bathed in the soft glow of moonlight filtering through the window. The fold of his white robe clung to his sculpted muscles, highlighting every curve and angle of his divine form. She couldn't tear her eyes away, vulnerable and captivated by his presence.

Zeus had come for her.

"What did you think of the performance?" he asked.

"It was beautiful," Danaë whispered.

"Not as beautiful as you." Zeus stood before her, his intense gaze shining down on her. His golden hair curled over one eye, giving him a boyish appearance. He couldn't keep his eyes off Danaë as he subconsciously bit his lip, admiring her through the thin material of her gown.

Danaë's breath caught in her throat, her heart pounding wildly. She was dizzy with anticipation, her body aching with desire. Her hair tumbled in wild waves around her face, and she frantically smoothed it down, trying to regain some composure. The delicate fabric of her shift clung to her curves, emphasizing the rapid rise and fall of her chest.

She knew she looked a mess, but she didn't care. All that mattered was the person who stood before her, igniting every nerve in her body with his presence.

Zeus's fingertips traced the curve of her jawline, tucking a strand of her hair behind her ear before twirling another through his fingers. "Your hair is like a deep, endless void," he commented with a grin that revealed a dimple on his face. Danaë 's toes curl at the sight. "It's been ages since I've seen someone shed tears over the stars. They are my greatest creations, yet most people take them for granted. But you...you speak to them as if they are your dearest friends."

"They are my only friends," Danaë admitted, leaning into his touch.

"That's not true," Zeus chided. "All we need to do is remind the world of your existence."

"What if I don't want them to remember?" Danaë asked, biting her lower lip. If being remembered meant she couldn't be with Zeus, she'd rather be forgotten.

"Everyone wants to be remembered, even the gods." Zeus chuckled at her pouting, shaking his head. "Let's not dwell on such gloomy topics tonight," he whispered, tracing his finger along Danaë's chin. "I have other plans for how we can spend our time together."

"Oh," Danaë arched an eyebrow, feigning surprise. "What would those activities be?"

With a sly smile, he leaned close to her. "I'm going to make you a legend," he said, his voice husky and full of promise.

"Oh?" Danaë's stomach fluttered with excitement and nerves as Zeus pressed soft kisses against her skin. With his strong arms wrapped around her, she couldn't help but tremble.

"Do you trust me?" Zeus breathed in her ear.

Of course, she trusted him. Zeus was the only one who had never let her down, and he wouldn't abandon her. At least, that's what she told herself as she leaned in and lightly brushed his lips with hers. Pulling back, Danaë smiled and nodded confidently.

"Good." Zeus grabbed her, and suddenly, Danaë was in his arms as their mouths collided. The kiss was intense and urgent, igniting sparks within her body. She felt a heat spreading through her from the intensity of his touch, sending her into a frenzy.

"Beautiful," he murmured, tracing the curves of her breasts with his finger. "I would give you the world if you let me."

"I would go anywhere," Danae whispered, gazing into his eyes. "As long as I can stay with you."

Zeus' face lit up with a grin. "How could anyone say no to that?" He eagerly took his place on top of her, determined to fulfill Danaë's desires and satisfy her every need. With a careful and gentle touch, he took his time, giving her everything she wanted until she cried out his name loud enough for the entire heavens to hear.

Hera certainly did.

Chapter 30- Danaë

8th Century BCE, Argos, Greece

As the sun peeked through the window, Danaë gradually woke up to the delicate touch of fingertips trailing down her bare arm and the warmth of the body lying next to hers. With each gentle stroke, she was transported back to the previous night's passion, the intense heat and longing that consumed her.

The memories flooded back in a sensual rush, igniting a fire within her once again.

A rosy hue spread across her cheeks as she recalled everything they had done—everything she'd allowed him to do to her and everything he taught her to do for him. Her toes curled in anticipation of putting it all into practice again.

Zeus let out a soft laugh. "We should grab some food before we continue," he suggested, opening one eye and raising an eyebrow. "I can only imagine how hungry you must be."

Danaë's stomach rumbled. "I am," she admitted, biting her lip.

"Great, me too," Zeus replied, giving her a quick kiss on the cheek before jumping out of bed.

Danaë couldn't help but feel a twinge of disappointment as she watched him confidently stride across the room in all his naked glory. She didn't want to leave the warmth of the bed.

At least not yet.

Danaë shifted, propping herself on one arm to get a better view. She watched with a smile as he slid into his robe. The soft fabric cascaded over his broad shoulders and clung to his muscular frame.

She took in every detail, from how his hair fell across his brow to how his fingers delicately tied the sash around his waist. It was a simple act, putting on a robe, but to Danaë, it was a moment of pure beauty and intimacy between them.

She considered herself lucky that the god had shown her such kindness, allowing her to experience the joy and thrill of a physical and emotional connection. Danaë had been warned of the gods' unquenchable desire and how they would leave their lovers shattered and drained.

But with Zeus, she had felt protected, cherished, and loved. It never crossed Danaë's mind that he would ever hurt her.

No matter what transpired, she would always carry the memory of their night together. It was etched into her flesh and cemented in her thoughts. A story she would relive over and over again once he was gone.

A hunger she would never be able to satisfy.

Zeus glanced over his shoulder and smiled. Danaë blushed again, remembering he could hear her thoughts. "What are you in the mood for?" he asked seductively, walking back to the bed with a plate full of food.

With a sultry smile gracing her lips, Danaë pushed the smooth blanket down her body and arched her back. "For something only you can provide."

Zeus's eyes sparkled with desire as he set his plate aside on the nightstand and climbed back into bed.

"Your wish is my command."

Hours later, Danaë sat at the table, wrapped in Zeus's robe, as they finally ate.

"Are you alright?" Zeus questioned, taking small bites of the succulent ambrosia. Danaë inhaled deeply, savoring the fruit's alluring scent. The aroma was a blend of honey and roses, intoxicating and tempting.

Her mouth watered at the thought of experiencing its sweet flavor on her tongue. She wondered if Zeus would offer her a piece and quickly chided herself. No one dared to ask for permission to consume the nectar of the gods. One nibble of the forbidden fruit would grant her immortality, a gift exclusive to the divine.

But with it, she could be with Zeus forever.

A gift Zeus would never offer a mortal by his own decree.

Danaë pushed aside the thought and smiled sweetly, "Of course I am."

"Good. I was starting to worry," Zeus said, tossing the fruit away and picking out a fig. "I would hate to think that expression on your face was due to last night."

"I've never been better," Danaë responded with a smile that did not reach her eyes. Zeus must have been aware of her thoughts, but he ignored them. A wave of regret coursed through Danaë, but she refused to let it consume her. Instead, she grabbed a glass of wine and drank deeply, trying to wash away the bitter taste of disappointment.

"I would..." Zeus began but then hesitated and fell silent. His intense gaze shifted away from her and focused on something outside the window. He closed his eyes, and his facial expression tightened. When he opened them again, the room had a heavy atmosphere as he spoke with a mixture of sorrow and sadness. "I have to go," he stated, hanging his head down.

Danaë's gaze remained fixed on her glass as she brought it to her lips for a sip, a sense of foreboding settling over her when she realized he had been talking to someone else.

"Is everything alright?" she inquired, trying to mask the slight tremor in her voice.

Zeus tilted his head to the side, cringed, and cleared his throat. "Just family matters." He paused, frowning. "A battle is brewing between the gods. I need to step in before it escalates into a full-blown war."

"How long will you be gone this time?" Danaë dared to ask, playing with a fig.

Zeus rose from his seat and knelt in front of her. With a gentle hand, he brushed a strand of hair away from Danaë's face before placing a soft kiss on her cheek. His voice was low and serious as he stood before her. "I cannot say for certain," he began, "but I have left you something to remember me by in the meantime."

Zeus did not return, and a month later, Danaë discovered what the gift was.

She was pregnant.

Chapter 31- Chloe

Modern Day- City of the Unspoken

Wolves almost ate us.

That was all I could think as we sprinted through the gap and down a dimly lit tunnel. My heart was racing with adrenaline as I flew over the uneven dirt path, dodging rocks and leaping over puddles of water that seeped from the damp stone walls.

We were lucky that Sydney and Bree showed up when they did. I didn't want to imagine what would have happened.

Would we have survived?

I pushed the swirling thoughts aside, gasping for air when we reached a small clearing. My chest heaved with effort, and sweat trickled down my face, stinging my eyes and blurring my vision. I fumbled to clean off my glasses; their lens fogged from the heat and exertion. But my shaking hands made it difficult. Eidolon took them from me, wiping them off on his shirt.

I muttered 'thanks' in between gasps as I slid them back on my face. Eidolon nodded and glanced at Sydney and Bree, who looked pleased with themselves.

I'd never seen Sydney transform into his alternate form of a black ram, and obviously, he had been keeping some things from me.

Sydney was a behemoth of a creature, standing at least five feet tall, with impressive horns that curved gracefully upwards, adding to his intimidating presence. Despite being just being in a fierce battle against equally massive wolves, he moved with confidence and superiority as he strutted around the cave like a peacock displaying its feathers to attract a mate. Especially when his gaze landed on Bree, igniting a spark of desire and possessiveness within his eyes.

Bree was unfazed, ignoring Sydney, her determined watch fixed on the tunnel entrance before us. The strong-willed woman who just happened to tag along with us on this journey saved our lives without hesitation or a second thought. Bree wielded her sword elegantly and precisely as if it were an extension of her arm. Any doubts about her being a formidable Valkyrie vanished; she embodied the true spirit of a warrior in every way.

The two of them were beautiful and deadly.

"That was a close call," Watson exclaimed from the other side, arms wrapped around Isabelle. She leaned into him, not for her sake but his. She seemed unbothered by the recent events as if our narrow escape from death had not even made a blip on her radar.

Isabelle shrugged off Watson's grasp and strode deeper into the den. "The wolves weren't going to eat us," she said as she ran a hand over the walls. "They were trying to show us something."

"Sure. The blood trickling off their mouths and the fierce snarls were definitely signs of a peaceful discussion," remarked Eidolon. Watson let out a small chuckle as Isabelle gave him a disapproving glare.

"You'll see," Isabelle shrugged. Eidolon eyed her for a moment in confusion before looking at me.

Are you okay? He asked down the bond.

Sure, if being chased by wolves and almost becoming dinner is just another typical day, then I am good to go. Eidolon laughed, and I breathed deeply, enjoying the familiar scent of smoke and cedar surrounding him. Standing near him always brought a sense of calmness, and I let it wash over me, easing my nerves.

"Has anyone seen Victor?" I asked, mentally assessing everyone and realizing our group had shrunk to six.

"Right here," his voice called from the far dark corner of the room. I'll be with you in a minute. I'm just taking care of something." Sydney snickered, and I glanced at him in confusion when Bree elbowed him in the side.

"Victor got into a bit of a fight with one of the wolves." Bree's explanation caused Sydney to burst into laughter. She responded with another sharp jab from her elbow and a stern glare.

Sydney hung his head in embarrassment, but a small smile remained. "Get it? A bit?" he inquired, trying to keep his face neutral as he peeked at her through his lashes, amusement dancing in his eyes.

"Not funny," Victor retorted, his voice tinged with pain. I got up to walk over to him and was cut short. "Don't come any closer. I am not decent at the moment."

"Victor, what happened?" I demanded as Sydney laughed harder. "What the hell is wrong with you?"

Bree's voice was laced with pride as she announced, "Victor got hurt." Somehow, she seemed to think that an injury was something to be commended. "A minor scratch," she waved away my apprehensiveness.

"It's no big deal," Victor grunted. "A small casualty of the battle."

I narrowed my eyes, not understanding Victor's use of the term 'small casualty.' Sydney's face flushed red with amusement, and I knew he was itching to tell the story. But before he could speak, Bree interjected.

"Sydney and I were taking point while Victor was guarding our rear as we searched for the entrance." Sydney snickered, causing Bree to smack him on the back of his head. Victor let out an annoyed huff in response. Bree rolled her eyes and continued, " As we passed the door, the wolves crept up behind us, and before we could react, they latched onto Victor and pulled him back."

"In the ass!" Sydney offered with a wicked smile. My eyebrows shot up in surprise, and I stepped closer to Victor, but he stopped me again.

"A mere inconvenience, I promise you," he declared, still hidden from view. "Just a few more moments, and I will be healed."

"You said they dragged you back to this spot?" Isabelle asked, intrigued. Her thoughts were spinning as she tried to piece everything together.

"Yes, the damn things used my ass as a tither and brought me right back to where you found the door."

Isabelle smiled at Eidolon in delight. "When we encountered the wolves, they blocked us from passing by the door like they were pointing our way! I knew they weren't trying to eat us!"

I doubted they wouldn't have taken a bite from us if the opportunity had been presented, but she had a point. Naturally, I wished that there had been an arrow or label indicating the entrance. But beggars couldn't be choosers.

"But why?" I asked. "Why would the wolves want us to discover the door? A door, by the way, I said we would locate." I glared pointedly at Sydney, who was feigning interest in adjusting his weapons.

A deep, Norwegian voice echoed from the far end of the room. A sudden burst of light emanating from silver runes inscribed on the walls temporarily blinded us. "There is only one way in," the voice declared.

As my eyes adjusted to the glow, the chilly and somber cavern opened before us, revealing a serene haven of weeping willow trees—a winding trail carved through a collection of vibrant, unfamiliar blossoms. A waterfall crashed from a steep rock wall to my right, creating a pool of glistening, turquoise water below. The gentle breeze stirred the leaves, carrying a comforting, earthy scent mingled with the sweet fragrance of lilies.

It was a breathtaking panorama that was almost too perfect to be true.

Bree tiptoed around me, her movements as graceful and careful as a dancer's. She glided down the path, mindful of each step as if determined not to destroy even the tiniest grain of sand.

"Welcome back, Brynhildr," the voice called out. Bree stopped, her hand hovering above the hilt of her sword. It dawned on me why she had an expression of lethal intensity.

It wasn't what was in front of us that had her on edge.

It was who.

Chapter 32- Chloe

Modern Day- City of the Unspoken

Bree faced a towering man, his intense eyes cold and piercing like a frozen lake. His fiery red hair was untamed, adorned with long braids held together by black trinkets etched with enigmatic symbols. His physique was impressive, with a muscular chest and broad shoulders that hinted at years of warfare. His face bore the marks of countless battles, scars crisscrossing like a cascading waterfall below his chin. A patch covered his left eye, embroidered with intricate raven designs in silky black thread.

His outfit resembled the Valkyries: scuffed boots, brown leather pants that left little to the imagination, a crisp linen shirt draped over his muscular chest, and a black and red cloak fastened on his left shoulder with a shining silver raven symbol. His posture exuded grace and command, proving he was not just a fighter but a superior among fighters.

With caution, I edged closer, witnessing the tense standoff between them. But something about the man's expression captivated me: flashbacks of a man hanging from a tree, with birds and beasts encircling him as a weapon penetrated his flesh and crimson stains seeped into the earth below. His agony was evident, yet he did not fight against his destiny. A faint grin appeared on his face.

What are you doing? Eidolon hissed.

I waved him off. *I need to see something.*

Try not to get killed.

I couldn't help but roll my eyes in frustration. Death was not a priority on my to-do list for the day. But something about the enigmatic figure compelled me forward. Deep down, I knew he held all the answers I had been searching for.

Suddenly, he turned his focus from Bree to me. Surprised and self-conscious, I took a step back. My legs trembled as his one eye bore into me, almost as if he was reading my thoughts. We stared at each other for a moment before I gathered the courage to study the rest of his face.

My breath caught in my throat as I realized the markings on his face were not scarring but a complex arrangement of symbols and words etched into his skin. The design was intricate and almost mesmerizing, like a living work of art. His one good eye flashed hints of silver and blood red as he blinked.

I wanted to reach out and touch him, to read whatever story he immortalized on his body.

His deep, baritone voice greeted me with the warmth of a Norwegian ballad. "Hello, lil' Writer. I've been waiting for you." Bree snapped out of her daze and lowered herself to one knee, bowing her head respectfully.

"Honor in life," she said, her eyes lowered.

"Honor in death," he replied, his shrewd eye still fixed on me, analyzing my every move. A wave of unease washed over me. He then shifted his attention to the room, his expression turning sour when he spotted Eidolon before ultimately settling on Victor.

Victor emerged from the darkness and made his way towards Bree. As he drew closer, his eyes lit up with recognition, and he stood taller, his demeanor transforming from cautious to admiration.

The two figures stood staring at each other, a glimmer of familiarity evident in their gazes. As I took a second look, my eyes widened in shock. It was unmistakable that they were related; their stances and facial features mirrored each other.

"Odin..." Bree called out softly while still kneeling on the floor. I froze in shock, mouth agape, as I stared at the god before me. His one eye danced to me, and he gave a slight nod before looking down at the Valkryie.

"Bree, stand up. You've never lingered this long on your knees before; don't make a habit out of it now," Odin said in exasperation.

"As you wish," she murmured, her bold stare meeting his. She straightened up gradually, holding her head high and puffing out her chest, a challenging grin on her lips."

As I watched her, I couldn't help but silently cheer her on. It must have been incredibly challenging for her to face Odin again, especially after he banished her from the Valkyries and Valhalla. Watching him, I realized how brave she was for standing against his order to marry.

Odin ignored the slight jab and turned to face the rest of us. "Introductions are in order," he said.

"Obviously," Eidolon muttered, and Odins' one eye flashed in annoyance before pointedly ignoring him.

"I'm Odin, and this is the City of the Unspoken. I know you have questions now that you have arrived, but rest assured, they will all be addressed in time," he said, glancing at Eidolon as if anticipating his challenge.

Eidolon's voice trembled as he asked, "Where is my grandmother?" His fists clenched tightly at his sides, knuckles turning white from the force of his suppressed rage. Odin was unfazed by his threatening stance, but Eidolon's emotions were bubbling below the surface, ready to explode.

"As I said, all will be answered in due time. For now, I invite you to freshen up in the rooms prepared. Dinner will be served promptly at six."

"You were expecting us?" Watson asked, his eyebrows raised in surprise.

"Of course, we were. We've been waiting for your arrival for quite some time now. Now that you're finally here, we have a lot of tasks to accomplish," he said, wrinkling his nose. "However, I must insist you shower first; your unpleasant scent might disturb the residents. I smelled you from across the river."

I flushed in embarrassment, but Odin was right. We had been racing across the Otherworld so quickly that we hadn't had time to change out of our clothes.

My sweatshirt and jeans were smeared with dirt, and my boots had become unbearable to walk in due to the loud squeaking noise they made with every step. I ran my hand through the clumps of dirt in my hair, attempting to make myself somewhat presentable.

Which wasn't going to happen until I got a shower.

Even Isabelle, who always prided herself on her pristine appearance, now resembled a disheveled hunter returning from a disastrous trip. Her once perfectly tailored jeans were ripped and stained beyond repair, and her sweater was covered in filth. Even her signature long blond braid was tangled with twigs and leaves, starkly contrasting its usual sleek perfection.

Eidolon was the most worn-out of us all. His once bright and lively face now lacked confidence, his hair hung limply like dried straw, and his once-beautiful indigo eyes were now a dark black abyss. The words from the books within him scrambled to make sense of the chaos while his arms appeared as shapeless masses of ebony, twitching and swaying like a restless swarm of bees and shadows around him.

I reached out and took his hand; the chill of his touch startled me. His warmth had been replaced by ice, and a murky aura swirled more rapidly around him as he faced me.

What is wrong? I asked through our bond, not wanting to alarm the others as danger signs danced in my head. Something was seriously wrong with Eidolon.

Nothing, he replied dismissively. *I need to find Moll.*

We will. She is here. I can feel her, I assured him. The link between Moll and me was not as strong as between Eidolon and me, but a Writer always knew when another Writer was around. It tingled our skin and made us jittery- like two stories clashing. *Let's get you cleaned up and fed; then, we will figure this out.*

We'll see, he said as we followed Odin and the rest of the group out of the garden.

I was worried. Something was wrong. Eidolon was changing slowly in front of me. I couldn't pinpoint what was different- but something was off.

But Eidolon hadn't let go of my hand. And that was an encouraging sign.

Chapter 33- Chloe

Modern Day- City of the Unspoken

With each step, the weight of our feet echoed through the dark stone steps carved out of onyx and ivory as we followed Odin up. The flickering flames of small torches danced along the walls, casting an eerie shadow over us. Tiny windows lined the outside wall, offering glimpses of the murky waters of the Styx River beyond. I couldn't help but peer out with each step, searching for a glimpse of Charon's boat among the foggy mist that enveloped the river.

My legs ached, and my breath came in short, ragged gasps as we climbed the endless flights of stairs. Finally, we reached the entrance, and I collapsed against the wall. Unfazed by the climb, Odin opened the immense wooded door leading to the hallway. A knowing smirk played at the corners of his mouth as he glanced at me, his eyes sparking mischievously in the dim light.

"Welcome," he said as he pushed the door further open.

We took a few steps into the room and froze, awestruck by its magnificence. The doomed ceiling towered above us, casting a shadow over the stone floor. Candles flickered, highlighting the darkened windows. Tapestries depicting epic battles between ancient gods adorned the wall, with ornate paintings in golden frames scattered in between.

The room reminded me of the headquarters of the Raven Society.

Seven larger-than-life portraits adorned the richly painted walls, each commanding attention and respect. Each deity was depicted with intricate details and vibrant colors, emanating an energy that vibrated through the room.

The first frame captured a deity with sharp, curved horns that sliced through the air. Its piercing stare held an otherworldly intensity, sending chills down my spine. It appeared on the brink of breaking free from the confines of the frame, exuding a sense of raw power and authority. I felt the heat from its form washing over me, igniting a warmth within my body.

In the second painting, a goddess stood with a regal posture, her cascading locks of golden hair shimmering in the candlelight. Her eyes held a fierce intensity that penetrated my soul. She gipped a staff adorned with intricate carving and symbols in her outstretched hand, representing her divine power over the elements.

The third painting held a god unlike any other. Its lower half was a coiled serpent, intricately detailed and shimmering in vibrant hues. Its piercing eyes exuded a cold and calculating aura, hinting at ancient knowledge that would drive a mortal into madness.

The rustle of fabric and the shifting weight caught my attention, drawing my gaze to the center of the room. There, perched upon an opulent chair, was a woman of such stunning beauty that time halted in her presence.

Her long red hair cascaded around her like a beautiful silk robe, her complexion as smooth as alabaster, and her piercing emerald eyes seemed to hint at danger. Her lips were as soft as rose petals, and her figure was alluring, almost intimidating, making me feel inadequate in her presence.

Sydney blew a soft whistle, and Bree smacked him across the head. The mysterious woman gave him a sharp glare, her expression turning dark and menacing before settling into a neutral gaze.

The wolves we'd just escaped from were more welcoming than she was.

"I'm Freyja," she greeted us with a sultry voice. "I believe you've been looking for me." She stood with authority, an untamed warrior striding confidently toward us. Her steps were firm and measured, her movements deliberate, and her eyes watching us intently.

Every step she took across the room was like a magnet for the light. The candles flickered excitedly, their flames dancing in delight as she approached. She casually brushed away some stray strands of hair, revealing intricate tattoos on her neck that matched Odin's, spreading down her body.

"Brynhildr, it's wonderful to have you back. I trust that you had an uneventful journey," Freyja said, her gaze never leaving the young Valkyrie.

Bree nodded. "No issues at all, Freyja. Minus a slight incident with Geri and Freki, who got too excited about their role."

"They're known to be somewhat excitable." Freyja laughed. "Who did they attack this time?"

"What do you mean by 'this time'?" Victor walked around Sydney and stood up straight to his full height. "You call wild animals running rampant 'excitable'? I almost lost half my ass!"

Freyja gave him a once-over, her gaze focused on his lower half. A sly smile appeared as she remarked, "Looks like everything is in its proper place from where I'm standing."

"Because I grew it back!" Victor stepped closer, his eyes narrowing in contempt. "You think it's easy to grow back half an ass!"

"I would say no," Freyja replied dismissively before returning to Bree. "Aelle's in her room. She hasn't come out since she arrived. You might want to go see her after you clean up."

"Yes, Freyja." Bree turned to Sydney with a regretful look. "It's been an honor to fight beside you, and I would gladly do so again." She didn't glance back at the rest of us as she stalked towards a door tucked in the corner of the room.

Sydney watched her walk away, his confusion heartbreaking. Isabelle approached him and placed her hand on his back, trying to comfort him as he stared at Bree's retreating figure.

Freyja clapped her hands to get our attention and began speaking, "Now that that's over, we have a lot of ground to cover," she motioned towards the door. But first, Odin will show you to your rooms to freshen up before dinner." Watson opened his mouth to speak, but Freyja raised a hand to silence him. "Any questions or concerns can be addressed at that time."

"Where is Moll?" Eidolon asked through gritted teeth. He squeezed my hand, and I winced at the pressure.

"Be patient, Eidolon. It won't be much longer," Freyja said gently. "Now, go on. We'll reconvene for dinner." She turned and walked towards the door that Bree had just exited through.

"Unfortunately, due to the high number of visitors, there are only three vacant chambers. Will that be an issue for you?" Odin inquired, directing his gaze towards Eidolon and me. I quickly glanced at Eidolon. Luckily, he nodded in agreement, sparing me from a potentially awkward situation.

"Excellent. Let's go," Odin called over his shoulder as he opened a door across the room from where Freyja and Bree left.

After climbing four flights of stairs, my muscles were screaming at me. My treadmill workouts had not prepared me for this level of physical activity, and I struggled to keep up with the group. When I finally caught up, I gasped for air as Odin halted in front of a narrow hallway lined with three doors on the left side.

"Until tonight," Odin said, winking at me before turning and walking back the way we had come. My heart was still pounding from my second near-death experience, but I managed to muster a weak smile at him.

Chapter 34- Chloe

Modern Day- City of the Unspoken

"Sydney," Isabelle started after Odin left.

He raised a hand to stop her. "You don't need to say anything. I, for one, am delighted she's out of the picture," Sydney said with a tight sneer. "It'll be quieter without her."

From the look on his face, I didn't think Sydney meant it. But who was I to argue? Bree had obviously been keeping secrets from us. Why? I wasn't sure. At any point of the trip, she could have told us that she knew Freyja was at the City of the Unspoken. Or that the wolves weren't going to eat us.

But she hadn't. And I didn't understand why.

Isabelle's face scrunched up in a slight frown before she replied, "Sure thing, luv." We exchanged a knowing glance, silently promising to keep an eye on him. Forcing a light-hearted laugh, Isabelle smiled, "I don't know about you all, but I could really use a shower."

"Hear, hear." Watson gestured towards the door to their room, saying, "After you, my dear." Isabelle gave me a wink and walked inside, with Watson following close behind.

Victor and Sydney exchanged nods before walking down the hallway to the far room. I followed their retreating figures with my eyes until it was just Eidolon and me. Feeling a bit timid, I peeked up at him. "A shower does sound good," I said, trying to keep my composure.

Eidolon and I had plenty of time alone. We even spent the whole trip sleeping next to each other. However, sleeping in separate sleeping bags was way different from sharing a bedroom.

The bedroom was personal. Intimate. A sacred spot for couples.

"Ladies first." Eidolon pushed the door open and gestured for me to enter ahead of him.

Trying to hide my embarrassment, I quickly bowed my head and hurried in. Tossing my bag onto the luxurious, oversized bed, I took a slow, curious glance around the room.

It dwarfed my tiny apartment back home, with its high ceilings and lavish furnishings. The writing desk was a work of art, intricately carved with scenes of ravens taking flight, wolves howling at the moon, and stacks of books teetering on top of one another.

Shelves lined both sides of the massive window crammed with leather-bound tomes and weathered paperbacks. A warm fire crackled in the ornate fireplace, casting dancing shadows across the room. Two regal armchairs sat before it, beckoning me to sink into their cushioned embrace.

Perched delicately on a small table, a beautiful crystal pitcher filled to the brim with a rich, deep amber liquid caught my eye immediately. I wasted no time in pouring myself a glass. As the drink met my lips, the smoothness of the whiskey enveloped my tongue and spread a warm sensation throughout my body. It was exactly what I needed to calm my frayed nerves and steady my resolve.

"Want one?" I asked, pointing to the other glass.

Eidolon shook his head, the muscles in his jaw tight and tense. His piercing eyes remained fixed on me, unblinking and emotionless.

"Do you want to talk or just keep staring at me?" I asked, raising my eyebrows in question.

Eidolon blinked once before running a hand through his unkempt hair. "I need a shower." Without another word, he made his way to the adjoining bathroom.

"You can't keep avoiding me," I called out as he grabbed his bag. "Whatever is bothering you, we need to talk about it before dinner."

"Now is not the time, Chloe," Eidolon said, his hand hovering over the doorknob.

"Why?" I raised my hands and gestured around the room. "No one is here. What is going on? You've been up in arms since we got here." I scrunched my eyebrows. "Does it have something to do with Odin?"

"No," he glanced at me.

"Then what is it, Eidolon?" I asked, taking a step forward. "Moll's here. She's safe. What else is wrong?"

Eidolon's body tensed, his indigo eyes flashing. "They're hiding something from us. More riddles. I am exhausted from all these damn secrets." He stalked towards me, his movements calculated and predatory. "And I don't like the way Odin's looked at you." His voice was low and dangerous, filled with a protectiveness that made him seem more intimidating.

I laughed. "Jealous?"

"No, Chloe." Eidolon's sneer twisted his handsome features. "I'm not jealous. But I know when something's not right." He pointed towards the window. "Something happened in that river that you're not telling me. You came back different." Eidolon's sharp gaze scanned me from head to toe, assessing and searching for answers. "You smell different," he pointed out, his nostrils flaring.

"What does that mean," I huffed, wrapping my arms around me. "Of course, I smell different. I smell like muck, mud, and seaweed."

"No," he roared. "You smell like the City of the Unspoken. You smell like death."

My mouth hung open in disbelief. Of all the incredibly rude things Eidolon could say, that took the cake. "Thanks for the compliment," I muttered.

"You don't get it, do you?" Eidolon asked, staring down at me. "I know death. It's ingrained in me. I know when someone is about to die. And right now, you are marked." Eidolon tucked a piece of my hair behind my ear. "Odin knows. I could see it in the way he was looking at you. Freyja too. And then we find out that Bree is somehow involved? It's all a little too convenient."

A lump formed in my throat, and I swallowed hard. "I think you're reading too much into it," I whispered, my voice quivering slightly.

"Maybe," he shrugged. "But until I figure out what's going on, I don't trust anyone."

"You can trust me and everyone else," I argued. "And you have Moll."

Eidolon huffed, shaking his head. "No. Moll and I made a pledge—no secrets—and she broke that promise. She's somehow entangled in all this. I haven't figured out how or why yet, but I will," he promised. "Until then, you don't leave my sight."

I nodded.

"I will keep you safe." Eidolon's solid and protective arms wrapped around me. I leaned into his embrace, feeling the heat radiating from his body and savoring the warmth. The world melted, and I felt like I'd come home.

I just didn't know if it was him or the City of the Unspoken.

"I may smell like death," I teased, glancing up at him, wanting to steer the conversation in a different direction. "You, on the other hand, smell like a skunk's armpit."

Eidolon chuckled. "I'm not even going to ask how you know what that smells like." He glanced down at me and asked, "Do you want to shower first, or should I?"

"You first," I waved. Eidolon's words affected me more than I wanted to acknowledge, and I needed a moment.

The haunting song of the Sirens still echoed in my mind, their enchanting voices still calling out to me. Then, there was the vision, adding another layer of confusion. And everyone seemed so desperate for me to stay alive. But Eidolon said I smelled like death.

I sat before the fireplace, slowly sipping whiskey while he showered. As much as I didn't want to admit it, Eidolon was right. I was different. This whole experience changed me. There was a reason I was chosen as the Writer. Before, I thought it was because I was good at what I did: research, write, and listen.

But I was beginning to think it was something more than that. As I played with Charon's coin, I realized I was wrong. The coin wasn't for someone else.

Charon had given it to me because I was the one who couldn't leave.

Chapter 35- Lilith

Modern Day- City of the Unspoken

Lilith was lost in her thoughts when Odin came to find her, Geri and Freki flanking him on both sides.

"They're settled," he confirmed as he walked up, his one eye scanning the library for eavesdroppers. As always, Odin's natural wariness had him on guard, and he had some concerns he wanted to discuss with his long-time friend.

Lilith gestured to the chair beside her, signaling for him to sit down. As he settled in, she handed him a mug. "It's just us," she said.

Moll was secluded in her room, claiming exhaustion as an excuse. The children's interrogation and the incident with Chloe had stirred up emotions that Moll was still trying to process, and she wasn't quite ready to face Eidolon.

Neither was Lilith.

For years, she had meticulously crafted and strategized for this pivotal moment. And yet, now that it was unfolding before her, she couldn't shake the gnawing uncertainty in her gut. Was this truly the right path? Would her actions have unintended consequences? Deep down, she knew there was no other choice.

The fate of the supernatural rested on her shoulders, their stories and legacy at risk of fading into oblivion forever. The daunting responsibility weighed heavily on her as she recalled the pain from the last time she unleashed her powers upon the world.

Only this time, she wouldn't be using the jar.

No, the jar needed to stay safely hidden, far from the one person who would do anything to get their hands on it.

Taliesin.

From the moment Lilith met Taliesin, she knew he would eventually pose a threat. She couldn't have predicted the extent of his hatred, but she didn't blame him either. But she understood the desperation that drove him to act against the Fates.

The sight of his sister's lifeless body scattered among the battlefield debris struck Taliesin to his core. Morrigan had been callously discarded, left for scavengers to feast upon. Overwhelmed with sorrow and anger toward those responsible for her demise, Taliesin swore to exact revenge. He spent days tirelessly following the mortals' movements, determined to find the ones accountable. His relentless pursuit eventually led him to Lilith.

When he arrived, Lilith was mourning her own loss. The witch hunts had taken a toll on her family; despite her powers, she had been helpless to save them. Like him, she struggled with anger and a thirst for retribution.

"Open it," Taliesin demanded, his voice filled with rage. "Open it and unleash the wrath of the gods upon the vermin. Let them feel the same pain they have caused our kind." He continued to rant like a crazed man, vowing to find a way to bring back his sister and Lilith's children from the dead.

Together, they would seek vengeance for every supernatural life taken because of the Fates.

But Lilith said no. She promised the gods to protect the jar until there were no other options, and she wasn't going to break it—not for Taliesin, Morrigan, or even her children.

Lilith still had hope. They just needed to wait for someone to bridge the gap.

Taliesin hated her for that decision.

Now, they were all standing at the crossroads that could potentially lead to the destruction the gods hoped to avoid.

"What do you think? Are they up to the task?" Lilith asked, hoping Odin would see this was the right decision.

Odin mulled over her question. "Perhaps," he finally conceded, though his tone was hesitant. "But the challenges they will face are numerous and formidable."

"Life is full of challenges," Lilith shrugged. "They all bring something to the table that can't be underestimated."

Odin scoffed. "The girl couldn't catch a butterfly to save her life." He had been watching Chloe since her arrival in the Otherworld. While he would admit that she had a good head on her shoulders, he found her too easily swayed by emotion. She didn't have a strategic approach to battle; just willing to dive head-first into danger. She let her heart guide her instead of using her head.

And the decisions Chloe would have to make needed a clear mind.

"It's not a battle of the sword," Lilith said in a weary tone, understanding Odin's concern about Chloe. But he didn't know about the struggles Chloe had already faced and emerged victorious from. She had an uncanny knack for seeing three steps ahead when faced with adversity. "We need someone who can see through the lies and find a different path forward."

"And if she can't?" Lilith glared at him with a fierceness that Odin hadn't witnessed in years. It was the same intensity she had when Lucifer was ripped away from her, and she vowed to do whatever it took to bring him back.

"She will," she affirmed with conviction.

Odin took a deep breath and sipped his mead, the weight of worry on his shoulders as he knit his brows. The Book of the Veiled was more than just a collection of stories; it held power and knowledge of Lilith, Taliesin, and Morrigan's beginnings. If Taliesin were to obtain it, all the sacrifices made by Lilith and Morrigan to protect the supernatural and Otherworld would be for nothing. He would tear everything apart.

"Have you found out where they are hiding your book?" Odin asked, unable to contain his curiosity any longer. He was fascinated by Lilith's unexpected choice to hand over the books to the Fates for safekeeping. No matter how often he'd asked, she never revealed her reasoning.

"No. I had other things on my mind. But I am not worried. "

Odin leaned towards Lilith, his one piercing eye meeting hers with intensity. The wrinkles around his lips deepened as he spoke, his voice conveying authority. Like a king addressing his subject, demanding an answer. "What are you hiding, Lilith?"

With a nonchalant shrug of her shoulders, Lilith couldn't help but laugh. Odin may be intimidating to others, but to her, he would always be the young god who would find her after he lost a battle. Or some woman broke his heart. "Nothing," she said with a sly grin, knowing his curiosity often got the best of him. "I'm more concerned with protecting the jar. That's all."

Odin sat back in his chair, crossing his arms like a child. Geri and Freki whined at his feet. He leaned forward to pet them. "You make it seem so easy," he scoffed as Ferki licked his face. Laughing, he sat back and threw them a bone from his pouch.

"It hasn't been," Lilith admitted. "Resisting the temptation to open it for centuries has taken me to the brink of insanity." Lilith looked over and winked, "But it's safely stored and well-guarded. If all else fails, I doubt even Taliesin can break through my last line of defense." Odin's eyebrows shot up in surprise, and Lilith laughed. "Hell has no fury like a woman's scorn."

Chapter 36- Lilith

Modern Day- City of the Unspoken

Lilith sat in her favorite seat while everyone convened in the dining room for dinner. She ran her hand over the mahogany wood, so dark it reflected the light from the chandler. Looking closely, she could see intricate symbols engraved onto its surface, constantly shifting and changing as if the table were alive.

It was one of her favorite pieces. She and Lucifer designed it when they first decided to have a family.

Regrettably, they had never enjoyed it together, but she looked forward to the day when they could. Lucifer and she both deserved it. Assuming everything went according to plan, the day would be approaching soon, and she was determined not to let anything or anyone stand in her way.

Lilith's sharp eyes caught movement, and she looked up as Chloe and Eidolon entered. She took a deep breath, her nose twitching as she detected the mingling scents of the two, intertwined and inseparable. Seeing two individuals become one whole was a beautiful thing to witness.

At first, Lilith was wary when Moll revealed that they were destined soulmates, knowing all too well the cruel tricks the Fates could play on mortals. But as she watched them together, it seemed Moll had been right all along. Their bond was undeniable, their connection unbreakable.

They were fated just like she and Lucifer had been.

Lilith pushed the thoughts of her beloved out of her mind and turned her attention to the others in the group. Seeing them all appear well-rested after their arduous journey to the City of the Unspoken was a relief. It was strange for the River Styx to allow living beings to cross, but Charon had assured Lilith there wouldn't be any issues. Still, she couldn't help but worry after everything that happened to Chloe.

Not that she would tell Moll or Vivian.

The room fell quiet, every gaze fixed upon her in anticipation. "I'm sure you're all eager to find out why I've called you here," Lilith began.

"Where's Moll?" Eidolon asked, cutting her off.

Lilith glanced at him, her eyes flashing a warning. "She's currently occupied and requested I extend her apologies for her delayed arrival. But in the meantime, let's enjoy dinner and take this opportunity to get acquainted." Lilith's gaze shifted towards Isabelle, vibrating with excitement in her chair. "It seems like some of you have questions," Lilith stated with a knowing grin.

"That would be wonderful, luv," Isabelle chimed in. "I'm absolutely starving and would do anything for a homemade meal."

"And a stiff drink," Watson said with a wicked smirk. "Preferably a double."

"Already ordered, my dear Watson." Lilith clapped her hands, and the table burst to life with platters of succulent food, decanters of rich, velvety whiskey, and tall glasses of shimmering, golden liquid placed carefully in front of them. The aroma of roasted meats and herbs wafted through the air, mingling with the heady scent of aged wine.

Watson picked up the glass and inhaled deeply, filling his senses with the sweet notes of honey and vanilla before taking a swig and sighing. "What is this heavenly smell?" he asked, his golden eyes shifting to Lilith in pleasure.

Lilith gazed down at her glass, swishing it to watch how it glimmered in the light. "A weaker variety of Ambrosia," she commented, taking a cautious sip and smiling with delight.

Victor raised his glass and inspected the contents. "The nectar of the gods?"

"Some may call it that, but this version doesn't have the same strength." Lilith chuckled. "Everyone's mortal soul is safe."

"As my father used to say, 'When in Greece, do as the pretty lady commands,'" Sydney laughed and took a deep swig. "Any chance for a refill?" He held out his empty glass toward Lilith.

"Plenty to go around." Lilith waved her hand at the decanter before him.

Chloe's eyes flicked from her coffee mug to meet Lilith's, a questioning look on her face. "Why did you bring us here?" she asked. "Not that I'm complaining about the delicious spread," she gestured towards the dishes on the table, "but why now? Why didn't you tell us what we needed to know when we first met in Scotland?"

Lilith had been anticipating Chloe mentioning their initial meeting, and as expected, she wasted no time asking the hard questions. "I need your help."

The room fell into a hush, the only sound of Sydney's chewing breaking the silence. A satisfied smile spread across his face as he savored his first bite, moaning in pleasure.

"Help with what?" Chloe asked, stirring her coffee, frowning.

Lilith leaned back in her chair, folding her hands. "As you know, I have taken something from the Raven Society, and you are now tasked with recovering it. I want to help you find it."

Eidolon's eyes darkened with suspicion. "You're offering to help us find what you stole? You could've left them alone and not wasted our time."

Lilith met Eidolon's gaze head-on, allowing her godly power to radiate through her eyes. She watched as he recognized he'd crossed a line, and fear replaced his fury. He gestured for Lilith to continue.

"I believe one of those books belongs to me, young man. It's my story you have been keeping locked away in your secret library, hidden from its rightful owner," Lilith exclaimed, trying to keep her irritation in check. "Those books never belonged to you or the Raven Society. If I recall correctly, they were taken from me first."

"Where are the books now?" Isabelle's question cut through the lazy golden glow surrounding her.

Lilith couldn't help but find it amusing that Isabelle was attempting to control her emotions, but she didn't comment and instead breathed in the calming mist filling the room. After all, Isabelle was a direct descendant of Lilith herself, the granddaughter of an original witch.

"I'm not sure. After taking the books from the Raven Society, I immediately brought them to the Fates to handle as they saw fit." Lilith took a sip from her glass and braced herself for the barrage of questions she knew would follow.

"Why would you take the books to the Fates?" Victor asked, pausing mid-bite in surprise.

"I was guided by the Fates, Victor. Even I don't dare to question their commands."

"And you have no idea why?" Victor pressed, doubt filtering across his features.

"I do," Lilith nodded, setting her napkin on the table. "I was the one who warned them that someone was trying to steal them in the first place."

"And how did you know?" Eidolon asked.

"Intuition," Lilith replied, shrugging.

"What the hell does that mean?" Eidolon demanded.

Lilith sat back in her chair, crossed her arms, and looked at everyone. "For centuries, I have watched as one person destroy my children's story. And though I have engaged in enough battles with this individual to last five lifetimes, he was always able to find a way to work around my traps. It had finally reached a point where desperate times called for desperate measures. So, I turned to the Fates and explained the situation, and they decided to help me solve the problem."

"And who is the problem?" Eidolon asked hesitantly. Lilith watched as Chloe squeezed his arm lightly.

Ahhh, she knows. Lilith smiled, sure that Chloe had already solved this piece of the puzzle. She was everything Lilith had hoped for: listening when others were talking, watching when others were acting, and being willing to accept what was right in front of her—admirable traits that were not found in too many mortals anymore.

"Your father." Lilith finally said, looking at Eidolon. "And your mother."

Chapter 37- Medusa

13th Century BCE, Athens, Greece

The rest of the festival enveloped Medusa in sheer bliss. She and Poseidon indulged in a lavish feast, toasting each other with goblets overflowing with rich wine. As the melodies of lively music filled the air, they joined hands and danced with carefree abandon, their laughter echoing across the grounds.

Eventually, they slipped away from the revelry and made their way to their secluded spot on the edge of a rocky cliff overlooking Poseidon's magnificent kingdom.

As the warm sun dipped below the horizon, Poseidon let out a content sigh and stretched his muscular legs in front of him. With a flick of his wrist, he shed the illusion of an old man and returned to his true form. Turning to Medusa, his blue eyes twinkling, he asked, "Did you have a good day?"

"I did. Thank you." Medusa's finger traced the intricate details of a gold bracelet Poseidon bought her. The weight of it against her skin reminded her that she was no longer alone. She bent down and picked up a smooth stone, throwing it into the ocean and silently making a wish as it disappeared into the endless expanse of blue.

She didn't want the day to end. For a few hours, she felt like a normal person, free from the shackles of her position.

"If you keep tossing rocks into the ocean, I won't have anywhere to call home," Poseidon playfully scolded her. He plucked the other pebble from her and flung it over his shoulder before folding her hand in his.

A sudden, electric surge of energy swept through Medusa's body at the touch, a wave of warmth flushing over her. The sensation was intoxicating. "I wouldn't want to do that," she whispered, her voice trembling with longing.

"No?" Poseidon asked, eyebrows raised and a smile on his lips.

"No," Medusa shook her head, hoping the one simple word would convey the complexity of her emotions: need, passion, and regret.

She sighed. It was time. She had to tell Poseidon she couldn't go with him to his world, which broke her heart. Her sisters made their decision, and Medusa would honor it. But as she glanced at the god beside her, her determination wavered.

Gods, she wanted to go with him.

No, Medusa thought. She needed to tell him that she chose her family over her freedom. As she opened her mouth, Poseidon suddenly stood up and lifted her with one arm wrapped tightly around her waist. With his other arm pointing towards the dark sky, he held her close against him.

"It's beginning," he murmured, his warm breath sending shivers down her spine. "Watch."

Medusa stared in awe as the stars lit up the darkness with a stunning display of gold and silver. From above, they twinkled like cascading diamonds, swirling with breathtaking splendor before touching down and blending to create a kaleidoscope of vivid colors even more radiant than the sun.

"It's beautiful," she breathed.

Poseidon let out a low, hearty laugh. "Zeus and his grand gestures," he mused. "I wonder who this one is for."

Medusa shifted in his embrace to face him, her eyes meeting his. "What do you mean?"

Poseidon gazed back at her and gently tucked a strand of hair behind her ear, "It means Zeus is trying to impress someone."

Medusa arched an eyebrow in surprise. "All of this was for a woman?"

"What else?" Poseidon's eyes drifted back up to the stars. "She must be extraordinary if he's willing to make such a bold declaration."

Medusa held her breath in anticipation as she asked, "Is she a mortal?"

She wasn't sure which response she hoped for. On the one hand, she wanted Poseidon to say no because it would make saying goodbye less painful. However, some of her needed him to say yes because it meant mortals were worth fighting for, even if their time together was limited.

Medusa needed to know that it would be worth the sacrifice if she chose to turn her back on her family, duty, and home.

"It is but a small token compared to all I would do for you," he answered, gazing down at her with adoration. With gentle fingers, he traced the line of her jaw, reveling in the softness of her skin against his touch.

Poseidon's strong, calloused hands ran up her arm, sending shivers down Medusa's spine. His breath was shallow and quickening, mirroring her own as she allowed herself to be swept away by the moment. In a daring move, she gently slid her hands up his muscular chest. Medusa smiled as he let out a pleased growl at her touch, the sound vibrating through his body and into hers.

With a tentative balance on her toes, Medusa leaned in and pressed her lips against his. They were rough and salty, like the ocean breeze that swirled around them. The warmth of his body enveloped her, luring her in like a siren's song. It was a taste that both enticed and tempted her.

Poseidon grabbed her hips and effortlessly lifted her, wrapping her legs around his waist. A wave of desire washed over her entire body, from her toes to the crown of her head. Their tongues danced together like they were in a divine waltz. His lips were as fiery as the sun, but his touch was tender, loving, and passionate.

Medusa wanted to savor the moment forever, so she was surprised when he broke away from the kiss with a low groan. His expression softened as he lowered her back onto the ground and gazed at her with unbridled happiness.

He gently raised her hand to his lips, pressing a soft kiss against her fingers. His gaze never wavered as he spoke in a low, seductive tone. "I can see the hesitation in your eyes. But I swear, my dear, it will be worth it. I would give you the entire world if only you would grant me this one night to prove my love for you." His voice dripped with charm, lulling her into a trance.

Poseidon's vow echoed as the waves pounded against the shore. In the distance, she could hear the rhythmic chorus of the ocean and its creatures beckoning to her. Their voices were a symphony of magnificence and strength. Medusa shut her eyes and inhaled deeply, taking in the salty sea breeze and feeling the mist caress her skin. The ocean was calling out for her to come home.

She would say yes.

Before she could, a majestic white owl swooped over their heads, clutching a small branch from an olive tree. Its wings beat against the air with a concerto of sounds, echoing like swords clashing in battle. Medusa's heart raced as the bird approached; its swift and deliberate movements clearly showed its displeasure. The owl's piercing gaze, capable of seeing through the darkest night, locked onto Medusa before dropping the branch at her feet.

Wide-eyed, Medusa stared at it. Athena knew.

"I have to go back," she whispered. Medusa's destiny had been decided. She had Athena's full attention now. A whirlwind of emotions consumed her: sadness for what she was leaving behind and excitement at finally being recognized by Athena.

Poseidon reached down to pick up the branch, his fingers curling around it tightly. As he stared at it, a flicker of anger danced dangerously in his steely blue eyes. The muscles in his jaw clenched as he struggled to contain his emotions, but they continued to simmer just beneath the surface, ready to erupt.

"No," Poseidon responded, his voice low and rugged like the rumble of thunder on a stormy night.

Medusa was speechless. What did he mean? No?

Poseidon's voice was hoarse with emotion as he repeated the word and snapped the branch in half. "You are mine," he declared, eyes blazing with possessiveness. The broken pieces fell to the ground, a symbol of the shattered trust between him and Athena.

Medusa's confusion shifted to fear as she shook her head. "I have to go back," she pleaded. "I made a promise."

"What about your promise to me?" Poseidon growled.

Medusa stared. She'd never made him a promise. She'd considered his proposal but never said yes. Now that Athena knew, she had no choice. She had to return and beg for forgiveness and pray that Athena didn't cast her out.

"I swore no allegiance to you," Medusa declared, finding her voice. "I am Athena's high priestess. I will return."

"You think she cares about you?" Poseidon sneered. "She doesn't. To her, you are just a mortal willing to renounce her position, family, and city. Athena will see you as weak, unworthy, and unclean. You can't begin to imagine her punishment if you return now. Death would be a gift."

Medusa's face flushed with embarrassment and shame. She longed for love so much that she would have sacrificed everything for it—she almost had. "No," she whispered, taking a step away from him. "Athena will understand."

Poseidon's laughter rang out, but it didn't reach his eyes. "You underestimate Athena's standards. You will never be good enough for her. You are nothing more than a plaything that can easily be disposed of and replaced," he scoffed. "I am willing to overlook this small error on your part and forgive you, but you must make your decision now. Come with me, or face Athena on your own."

"Forgive me, Poseidon," Medusa whispered, hanging her head. Her heart was breaking, but she'd made a promise to her sisters. "I have to go back."

"Wrong answer," he roared.

The ground trembled under Medusa's feet as bolts of lightning danced across the night sky. Shaking from terror, she reached for the boulder to steady herself.

What had she gotten herself into?

The wind lashed around Medusa and tangled her hair into a chaotic mess. She desperately tried to brush it out of her eyes as she pleaded with Poseidon, her voice barely audible over the howling gusts. "Poseidon, please," she begged, "try to understand."

But Poseidon was not swayed by her words. With a fierce determination, he scooped her into his arms, holding her tightly against him. "You belong to me," he declared possessively, his grip unyielding as he jumped off the cliff and into the sea.

Chapter 38- Medusa

13th Century BCE, Athens, Greece

A searing pain coursed through Medusa as she lay on the cold marble floor. She cautiously peeled one eye open, only to be met with a sudden surge of agony that felt like a thousand needles piercing through her skull. Gasping for air, she painfully attempted to roll over, but her battered limbs refused to cooperate.

Gritting her teeth, Medusa took stock of her body, reaching down to touch the warm liquid slowly running down her legs. She brought her hand up and recoiled at the sight of blood. Letting out a small moan, Medusa tried to sit up. Every part of her was sore, bruised, and pulsating with pain. Carefully opening her other eye, she surveyed her surroundings; a gasp escaped her lips when she realized where she was.

Athena's temple.

How did she get back to the city?

The last thing she remembered was Poseidon telling her she was his—nothing more than a possession he could manipulate and control. And then, he left her at the base of the fierce goddess's statue to deal with Athena on her own.

It was a declaration of war. And Medusa was the bait.

Would Athena tolerate the mockery? Or would she seek revenge? Medusa wasn't sure. Tears flowed down her face as she slowly inched the inner flame, begging for the goddess's mercy and forgiveness.

Medusa's voice trembled with desperation as she pleaded, "Please come. I beg of you. Just listen to me this once and show me I am worthy."

Her words resonated through the empty chamber, echoing off the cold stone walls and filling the space with longing and sorrow. She clutched her hands together, her knuckles white with tension, and tears streamed down her pale cheeks as she waited for a response.

"No." The goddess's ethereal voice announced her arrival. Medusa froze in terror at the deafening sound of her refusal.

"Please, Athena," Medusa whispered, her voice hoarse from the pain around her throat.

"And why would I? You have no honor." Athena crouched low to face Medusa, startling her with the intensity of her beauty and strength. But Medusa saw only hatred and disgust in the warrior goddess's eyes. "You dared to become one of us."

"No," Medusa cried, lowering her eyes. "That was never my intention."

Athena lifted Medusa's chin, forcing her to meet her gaze. "Then why were you with Poseidon?" she asked probingly.

Medusa hesitated, realizing she would face the wrath of two gods no matter what she did next. With a resigned sigh, she decided to tell the truth.

"I believed he loved me. I thought I deserved at least one deity's love and approval." Medusa's words caught in her throat as she fought back tears. "I begged and prayed to you, but you never responded. I was abandoned and afraid, and I couldn't bear the thought of spending eternity alone."

As Medusa's confession sank in, Athena took a moment to consider them. For a second, Medusa thought maybe the goddess understood her pain. That Athena would embrace her and heal the shattered pieces of her heart that Poseidon had left behind. After all, as a female deity, surely she would have empathy for her high priestess.

Athena rose to her feet, brushing off her tunic. Her voice was measured as she spoke, "I understand now. It appears that I have erred in selecting you as my high priestess. You do not possess the qualities necessary to enter my temple."

Medusa let out a distressed cry, her spirit wrenching at Athena's dismissal. She wanted to protest, but the goddess silenced her with a wave.

"You pathetic excuse for a mortal," Athena sneered, her voice dripping with disdain. "How could you let Poseidon exploit the only thing that makes you remotely worthy?" She stepped away from Medusa as if being near her was repugnant.

"I didn't allow it, goddess," Medusa pleaded. "I still don't know what happened to me."

Athena drew her dagger and aimed it at Medusa's heart.

"I'll tell you what transpired. Poseidon manipulated you, deceived you with empty promises, and lured you into the embrace of another god." With each word, Athena pushed the dagger further against Medusa's skin until a trail of blood trickled down.

Despite the searing pain, Medusa struggled to rise to her knees. "It was never my intention."

"Not your intention," Athena laughed. "Did you not invite your sisters to accompany you to Poseidon's watery tomb? Did you not spend your entire day honoring the sea god, indulging in the antics of common mortals? And when he was in disguise, did you not pursue him and discover his true identity?"

"Yes, goddess," Medusa whispered, knowing there was nothing else she could say. Athena had seen it all.

Athena raised a skeptical eyebrow, her lips curling into a sneer. "So your motives are clear. You chased after the god of the seas, and now you seek my help because you believe he has wronged you."

"Yes, goddess," Medusa whispered, this time in defeat. "It is all true."

"You are nothing special," Athena mocked. "You were created as a plaything for the gods, a distraction from our daily lives, nothing more. Do you understand that now?"

Medusa's head bobbed up and down in agreement. "I acknowledge my wrongdoing, goddess. I will dedicate my life to making amends for failing you."

"Yes, you will," Athena agreed, a small smile tugging at her lips. "But not as you expected. You and your sisters are forbidden from re-entering my temple or Athens."

Medusa's eyes widened in terror. "Goddess, please, spare my family. They are innocent." She crawled towards Athena, begging for leniency. She was willing to accept any punishment as long as her sisters were untouched.

Athena's expression soured as she gazed at her statue. She took a few steps closer and brushed away a speck of dust with her finger. Frowning, she turned to face her high priestess. "Stheno and Euryale had every chance to stop your foolishness, yet they did nothing. Their lack of wisdom will cost them dearly. I have no use for such followers." Athena knelt before Medusa, gently lifting her face with her fingers.

"You, Medusa," she whispered, "will no longer be known as the most beautiful woman in Athens. Forevermore, your exterior will reflect the wickedness within. No longer able to deceive others with your outward appearance, all who lay eyes upon you will see the truth- you are nothing but a vile monster."

"Please, Athena," Medusa begged. Athena tightened her grip, and she fell silent as the goddess's nails dug into her cheeks.

"You will live the rest of your eternal days in solitude so that you can contemplate your decisions and their consequences. Your sisters will be granted immortality so they can think about their lack of discipline. But you will never see them again. They will only know that their punishment results from your choices."

The chamber filled with Medusa's piercing screams, bouncing off the walls and reverberating through the air. In an instant, a searing pain tore through her entire body. Her once smooth and tanned skin wrinkled and aged before her eyes. A wave of terror washed over her as she stumbled backward, a sharp and stabbing sensation penetrating her chest. As she fell to the ground, she could feel her heart hardening and shrinking as if it were turning to stone.

Her once luscious locks, a source of pride and joy, now writhed and hissed as serpentine creatures burst forth from her scalp. Each strand of hair elongated and twisted into a slithering snake, their scales glinting in the dim light. As the transformation overtook her body, Medusa let out a blood-curdling scream, gasping for air as her limbs contorted and warped in agony.

Athena glanced down at Medusa's form, lying in a heap on the floor, and laughed. "Let us see if your love saves you now. Or will he leave you to endure your punishment, as repulsed by what you have become as I am?"

Medusa opened her mouth to speak, but the words caught in her throat. Her eyes widened as she heard her sisters wailing and shouting for clemency. Stheno and Euryale had just discovered the consequences of Medusa's transgression and were on their way to the temple to find her. Medusa frantically turned to look at Athena, silently begging for mercy.

Athena stared at her. "What will you do?" she asked, her voice laced with ridicule. "Your sisters are almost here. Are you sure you want them to see you like this? I don't think they will survive the sight."

Medusa's entire being quaked with a mix of terror and fury as she struggled to stand, her legs trembling beneath her. Athena had robbed her of everything, but she would not let her sisters suffer the same fate.

"Do you honestly believe you can outsmart the gods?" Athena taunted, her voice echoing as Medusa frantically searched for a place to hide.

Her eyes landed on the west door, the entrance to the snake pit. What better location to seek refuge than with the same creatures that now tormented her? Medusa struggled to reach the entryway, each step causing pain to ripple through her body and a symphony of hisses to resonate from the tangle of snakes.

The screams of her sisters echoed in her ears as they were forcibly removed from the temple.

In an instant, her entire existence was erased—every memory, every connection, gone.

She was completely alone.

Forever.

Chapter 39- Danaë

8th Century BCE, Argos, Greece

Danaë held onto the hope that Zeus would return soon and that his absence was due to the ongoing conflict between Athena and Poseidon. However, a small part of her suspected that there might be another reason keeping him away.

His wife.

If she was in Hera's place, would she be willing to share her husband with a mere mortal? The answer was clear: Absolutely not.

Danaë also knew Hera would go to extraordinary lengths to keep Zeus away from any other women. She posed a potential threat to their marriage and, ultimately, to Hera's power and status.

But Danaë had been willing to wait.

In the beginning.

Nine months had passed since she last saw Zeus, and she had to accept the truth. He wasn't coming back.

Even though he was no longer with her, there were still regular deliveries of new books, canvas, and fabric for sewing baby clothes. At first, she saw it as a gesture from Zeus, a sign of his involvement in their child's life. But eventually, she realized it was just a form of compensation for his absence.

Zeus was willing to provide for her but didn't want to get involved.

He chose Hera and the gods over her and their child.

Although loneliness weighed heavily on her shoulders, Danaë refused to give up. Even in her despair, she clung to a spark of determination that grew stronger with each passing day. The tiny life growing inside her was a constant reminder to keep pushing forward, its gentle movements propelling her through the most challenging times.

At the end of each day, Danaë would curl up by the fireplace and let her mind wander to thoughts of her child's future. Would they inherit her features—dark black hair and deep brown eyes? Would their intellect match that of their father's? Would they possess unparalleled strength? Or perhaps they would have a passion for the arts, just like their mother.

The possibilities were overwhelming.

But they came with their set of challenges, too.

Tales of mixed beings, offspring of deities and mortals, sent shivers down her spine. Both worlds rejected these half-breeds; the gods saw them as lesser, while mortals feared their abilities. Danaë heard that being a demi-god came with constant challenges and dangers. The children lived a lonely life as they wandered the world, used as pawns in political games or for entertainment by the Fates.

Would her child suffer the same fate?

It was a harsh reality she had to face. The time Danaë and Zeus spent together was full of love, passion, and happiness - all genuine and tangible. However, now she was left to deal with the consequences alone, which broke her heart.

And it meant Danaë needed to take matters into her own hands.

The gods, the Fates, and her family conspired to put Danaë in this impossible situation. But she would no longer be a helpless pawn in their cruel game of destiny. She refused to be a victim any longer.

Her mind churned with thoughts and plans, preparing for the inevitable struggles ahead. She was determined to provide her child with everything she never had: the freedom to forge their own future and break free from the shackles of tradition and expectations.

She would escape.

As the night wore on, Danaë's mind buzzed with plans and preparations, but her body began to succumb to labor pains. She moved slowly around the tower, her hand pressed tightly against her swollen belly, trying to find some relief from the increasing agony. Each wave of contractions felt like a knife twisting in her abdomen, each painful throb reminding her of the strength and resilience within her.

She would face this challenge alone, embracing the pain as a symbol of the new life she was starting. Danaë's screams echoed through the empty tower as the moon rose higher in the sky, mixing with the sounds of distant howling wolves and raven calls.

Fortunately, it didn't take long for the baby to make its grand entrance into the world. The child's determination to arrive matched its mother's strength and endurance. As soon as the little one was safely in her arms, the new mother beamed with pride, tears of joy streaming down her face.

She swaddled in a soft blanket and held him close, whispering his name into his ear.

Perseus.

Destroyer.

Chapter 40- Danaë

8th Century BCE, Argos, Greece

As Danaë fell into the routine of motherhood and plotting their escape, her father was also on a mission.

Little did she know that the Oracle had already forewarned King Acrisius about his grandson's arrival and was rushing to the tower to witness it himself.

The Oracle delivered a dire warning to the king months ago: one day, his flesh and blood would overthrow him.

The prophecy tormented the king, and his mind became consumed with paranoia as days turned into weeks. He could find no peace and took to pacing the corridors of his palace. His erratic behavior sent chills down the spines of his servants as they watched their once-powerful ruler disintegrate before their eyes.

Ignoring the warnings of those who cared for him, including the queen, King Acrisius was resolute in his decision to visit the tower and confirm what the Oracle declared. His advisors all told him it would be a futile search; his daughter could not have survived, much less given birth. They reminded him that he'd spared no expense to create an impenetrable structure—a debt his kingdom was still paying for.

The king refused to listen. He had a hidden agenda that he didn't dare reveal to anyone.

The gods were exacting their revenge upon him. King Acrisius was all too aware of how he let down his daughter and disgraced his kingdom. Now, he was sure that the gods had cursed him. His once-fearsome armies fell in battle without a fight, his crops withered away, and his cattle perished from a strange illness. The entire realm was on the verge of destruction, his people losing faith in him while his enemies thirsted for his downfall. And it was all because of his own mistakes.

If his daughter had miraculously survived, he could plead with the gods for forgiveness and regain his lost honor.

However, his reign would be at risk if she were still alive *and* had a child.

That is why, while Danaë was planning, he was relentlessly racing to the tower.

Driven by gnawing fear and a fierce determination, King Acrisius urged his men and horses past their limits. The rapid beat of hooves against the ground echoed in his ear as they approached their destination. A sense of dread washed over him like a suffocating wave as he saw flickering lights through the single window of the looming structure ahead. A faint sound pierced through the air and stopped him in his tracks.

A child's soft, innocent cry.

"Open it," the king demanded, jumping off his horse and stalking to the doorway.

The guards labored non-stop, clearing away rubble and obstacles until the entrance was finally unobstructed. As they pushed open the door, a frigid gust of air hit them as if they were stepping into a tomb. A shiver ran down their backs as they cautiously entered the dark space. They exchanged worried glances, doubting that anyone could survive in such a desolate place.

The king imprisoning his daughter here had been madness. If she somehow prevailed, it had to be because the gods intervened on her behalf.

Despite their reluctance, King Acrisius urged them to proceed with their task, and they obeyed.

With torches in hand, they made their way to the spiral staircase, stretching endlessly upward, every creak and groan adding to their growing unease. Step by step, they ascended through each level of the tower, the air becoming musty and thick as they climbed higher. Finally, they reached a second door reinforced with bricks, clearly designed to keep anyone from entering and trap Danaë inside. The weight of their mission pressed down on them as they prepared to breach the final barrier.

Danaë heard them as they broke through, steeling herself for whatever was about to happen.

Breaking through, the guards stormed into the chamber, their armor rattling with each step. The king's daughter stood before them, her back straight and chin held high, a small child cradled in her arms.

Her eyes were fixed on her father, filled with defiance and disdain.

"How...?" The king stuttered in anger as he pushed his way through the guards, looking around in shock.

The room was no longer the heartless space he designed. Instead, it was a welcoming and comfortable home. A fireplace crackled in one corner. A large wooden table was overflowing with platters of food and bottles of wine. In another corner, a massive bed was tucked into an alcove adorned with vibrant blankets. The stone floor was covered in beautiful rugs, and tapestries depicting colorful scenes hung on the walls.

The king's gaze snapped to Danaë. "How are you still alive? And with a child?" He whirled around, his guards shrinking back in fear. "Who among you dared to disobey me?" he growled. "Which of you snuck in without my knowledge? Step forward and face the consequences of your treachery." The king's eyes scrutinized them, his face revealing the depth of his madness.

The guards backed up, shaking their heads in denial. None had known that Danaë was being held captive in the tower until now. The previous guards who brought her had mysteriously disappeared after delivering her to her prison. Rumors had been floating around that she had been sent to a faraway kingdom to be wed and would eventually return.

No one could have imagined she was a prisoner, abandoned to face death alone.

"Father," Danaë called out quietly, wrapping her arms tighter around Perseus, trying to comfort the crying child. "Are you here to take me home?" As she spoke, her tone was full of optimism. For a moment, she allowed herself to believe that her father returned to beg for her forgiveness. Together, they could return to the palace, where Perseus would gain the necessary skills and knowledge to become a great king - wiser and more effective than her father had been.

After all, he was not only the son of Zeus but also the future ruler of Argos.

But the king's expression made it clear that Danaë's homecoming would not be met with open arms. His eyes were filled with terror, panic, and anger as he scowled at his daughter and advanced toward her. "You were not meant to survive," he growled.

The guards stepped forward to protect the princess before the king whirled on them, and they shrunk back in fear.

"Clearly, I am alive and well." Danaë stood tall, her hand soothingly rubbing her child's back. She was determined to stay strong and not shed a single tear.

The king's eyes narrowed as he studied the small baby in Danaë's arms. Perseus timidly peeked at him before quickly burying his face against his mother's chest. "Whose child is this?" King Acrisius roared, his voice echoing through the tower.

"He is mine," Danaë answered, stepping back.

King Acrisius glowed with fury. "Who is the father?"

Danaë felt the burden of her choice weighing heavily on her shoulders. Would anyone believe her if she revealed the truth? And if they did, what would it mean for her?

Should she stay quiet?

As she watched the guards inching towards the entrance to the stairwell, she knew that remaining silent would only lead to her father turning on them. She lifted her head, squaring her shoulders. "Zeus."

King Acrisius's face reddened with shock as the gravity of his daughters' words sank in. If what she said was true, he could not act without angering the king of the gods. Anything he did would have catastrophic consequences for his kingdom.

He couldn't discount the possibility his daughter was lying.

Surely, the child belonged to someone else. But who else could have impregnated his daughter if not for Zeus? The tower was impenetrable, making it impossible for any mortal to enter. Only a god could have accomplished such a feat.

King Acrisius paced back and forth, lost in contemplation. He was facing a dilemma: If the child belonged to Zeus, he couldn't harm it, but he also couldn't let the child live long enough to one day challenge his rule.

What options did he have?

A sudden realization dawned on him. He could send them far away from his kingdom, where their identities would be unknown.

"My daughter," he said, turning to look at Danaë with a carefully crafted expression of paternal affection. "I have made a grave mistake." He stepped closer to her and placed a gentle hand on her cheek. "If Zeus blessed our family with an heir, who am I to go against his will?"

Danaë's breath caught in her throat as she asked her father, "Are you sure?" Despite everything, she clung to hope for a way back home. Once she made it there, she would figure out her next steps.

"Absolutely. Your son deserves all the privileges of being a child of Zeus." King Acrisius beamed. "We will begin his training immediately. This is a fantastic opportunity to strengthen our relationship with our neighboring kingdom to the north. When he is ready, he will return as a prince of two kingdoms and the ruler of one."

Danaë's narrowed her eyes, not trusting a word her father said. "He's just a child," she argued. "Who will take care of him?"

"You," the king announced. "You, my daughter, will accompany your child and ensure he is cared for."

Danaë gazed at her father, mulling over his proposal. She wouldn't return home, but the thought of being with her baby far away from the tower was enticing. They would finally have the freedom they deserved. With her son's body carrying divine blood, her father wouldn't dare harm them now.

"As you wish," Danaë declared, already thinking of the preparations required for their expedition. "I'll start packing."

The king waved his guard over, declaring there was no need for all the fuss. He promised to provide everything needed on the road. All she needed to do was grab what was necessary for the journey, and they would depart immediately.

"Are you prepared?" Danaë's father asked, breaking the silence. "If we want to reach the nearest town before nightfall, we must leave now."

Danaë took one last look at her prison. The tower taught her resilience and self-worth, turning into her refuge from the cruel world. With a deep inhale, she turned her back on it all.

Her life was in her father's hands again.

Chapter 41- Danaë

8th Century BCE, Argos, Greece

The group remained silent except for the occasional orders as they made their way to Temenium, a small town near the Gulf of Argolis. Danaë's father and the guards had little to say, but she was too preoccupied with her son and the sun's warmth on her skin to mind the quietness.

Freedom tasted like almond blossoms and honey.

As they traveled for hours, the seaside village slowly emerged on the horizon. Danaë's body was drained, and she could feel every ache as they pushed through the unforgiving midday sun. After spending so much time in the dark tower, her eyes were not used to the bright light or intense heat. She shielded her face with one hand while holding onto Perseus with the other, who squirmed and cooed with excitement.

The vast expanse of the ocean beckoned to her, its crystal blue waters shimmering like a sea of diamonds in the fading sunlight. As they grew closer, the rhythmic crash of waves against the shore filled her ears. Among the gods, Danaë had always harbored a soft spot for Poseidon. His spirit, loveable nature, and openness to mortals made him stand out.

Until she met Zeus.

Just thinking about the king of the gods still hurt. Danaë's heart hadn't yet healed from his rejection. During the day, she fought to push his memory to the side, but it was a different story at night. He continued to plague her dreams, leaving her to wake up and face the pain alone.

At least she had Perseus.

As if reading her mind, her son started howling in her arms. "Father," Danaë called out as the group stopped near the harbor. "Perseus needs his dinner."

"Of course," King Acrisius said with a dismissive wave as he dismounted from his steed. He instructed three guards to escort his daughter and grandson to the inn, claiming he needed to send a message to the queen to prepare for their arrival.

Grateful, Danaë handed her son into the waiting arms of a guard. As she slid off her horse, her legs trembled under the weight of exhaustion. She slowly worked out the strain in her back with a deep stretch, feeling each vertebra pop and release tension. The guard blew raspberries at Perseus, playfully bouncing him on his hip.

A small smile tugged at Danaë's lips. She was thankful for the moment of lightheartedness and human connection for her son, who had spent his young life isolated with only her for company. She reached up to take him, pausing when she saw the glimmer of tears in the guard's eyes. He glanced away before she could question him.

Danaë shrugged, deciding not to press the matter. The situation weighed heavily on everyone's shoulders, and emotions ran high. Despite everything, she couldn't shake the feeling of sorrow that washed over her for him and all the others who had to bear witness to her family's struggles.

"Thank you," Danaë said, following the guards up the winding road to the hostel. She glanced back at her father, hoping they might have dinner together, but he was already engaged in a heated conversation with the guard's captain. She decided to wait and let her father handle his business. They could talk in the morning.

Besides, she was spent, caked in a thin layer of dirt, and desperately needed a bath and a comfortable bed. Danaë sighed in relief when the owner led her to a tiny but immaculate room with a bed and a delicate hand-carved cradle.

In one corner, a small bowl of olive oil infused with the sweet scent of elderflower awaited her, along with a strigil used for scraping off the thick layer of dirt that clung to her skin.

Once Perseus was settled, she lay in bed, staring at the ceiling. She couldn't believe they had escaped from the tower alive. Her son was safe, and that was all that mattered. They would start a new life far away from her controlling parents. One day, when he was ready, Perseus would return and become ruler of the country, restoring it to its former greatness.

Smiling for the first time in months, Danaë was able to fall asleep and did not dream of the god she could never have.

Hours later, Danaë's eyes fluttered open, awoken by the faint sounds of men whispering outside her door. They were arguing about something, and she couldn't shake off the worry that it involved her. As their voices grew more heated, a chill ran down her spine.

"Do it yourself. It's bad enough that the king imprisoned her in the tower, but this? If that *is* Zeus's baby, whoever is involved will not walk away with their head still attached," a persistent voice whispered.

"We don't know if she is telling the truth," his companion said. "The baby could belong to anyone."

"You are dumber than you look if you think that child is anything but a demigod. Who else could enter the tower? It took us hours to break in. Did you see any signs that someone was there before us?"

The second man hesitated, his voice wavering. "I don't know," he answered. "But we can't disobey the king. Besides, we don't know if Zeus will even care. He hasn't intervened yet."

A heavy silence hung in the air as Danaë waited for their decision. She looked toward the window, calculating if it was worth the risk of trying to sneak out. But she knew she wouldn't have gotten far.

"You're right," the first man said with a sigh of resignation. "Let's go get her. May the gods protect her from what she is about to face."

Danaë's heart thudded against her ribcage as they burst into the room, calculating her chances of fighting back against the group of men surrounding her. But she was outnumbered, and resisting would be futile. They led her out of the hostel and escorted her down the winding streets and the empty docks.

Perseus

She pleaded with the guards to let her go, her voice raw with fear and desperation, but no one answered or even glanced in her direction. The cold ocean air danced on her skin as they pushed her towards a waiting ship, its dark sails billowing in the wind like a menacing storm cloud.

Tears streamed down her face, mingling with the salty sea air as she clutched the tiny bundle in her arms - her son, helpless and innocent, caught in the cruel hands of fate.

"Please, he's just a baby," Danaë cried, pivoting to face the guards.

Regret was etched on the captain's face as he delivered the devastating news. "I'm sorry, but it is a direct order from the king." A guard standing behind him passed over a thick wool cloak, a large bag of provisions, and a vessel of water. The captain gestured towards the boat. "Get in," he whispered.

Danaë's eyes widened as she stared at the boat and back at the captain, unsure what to do. "I don't know how to sail. What am I supposed to do? Where am I supposed to go? We will die out there."

"I am sorry," the captain said again. "We really are, but our hands are tied. If we disobey, our families will bear the consequences."

Danaë's eyes darted nervously around the group of men surrounding her. Their postures were tense and guarded, their hands resting on their weapons as they looked at her with a mix of pity and resignation. The captain's words rang true in their stances - they didn't want to harm her, but they had no choice.

Just like her.

With a soft touch, she patted the captain's face and gazed into his eyes, willing him to believe her. "I forgive you," she spoke softly. The gods will surely punish the one who ordered this heinous act, but my son and I hold no grudges for you and your guards."

The guards breathed a sigh of relief, their tension dissipating like smoke in the wind. With gentle hands, they assisted Danaë into the boat, careful not to jostle the sleeping baby. One handed her a bag filled with essential items they had secretly gathered for her behind her father's back.

With a quick nod to the guards, Danaë settled herself and Perseus, watching as they untied the vessel from the pier. She grasped the oars tightly, the rough wood biting into her hands. As she pushed away from the dock, the water lapped gently against the boat's sides, its rhythmic sound lulling her into a calm state. With each stroke of the oars, she was pulled further away from her home, carried by a gentle current.

The guards lined the wooden pier, their stoic faces watching her boat as it sailed away into the endless horizon.

In the tower, she had the protection of walls, a roof, and a stone fortress, but out here, she had nothing except for a small child and the unanswered prayers to the king of the gods.

Danaë lay down on the boat floor, cradling Perseus in her arms, and wept. Her life as she knew it was over. No one would ever know what happened to her. Her father, and by default, Zeus, had erased her existence.

She was now alone.

Chapter 42- Chloe

Modern Day- City of the Unspoken

I knew what Lilith had said wouldn't go over well with Eidolon. She just told him that his parents had something to do with the fall of the Otherworld and the lost souls.

And I wasn't wrong.

Without warning, Eidolon leaped to his feet, his chair crashing to the ground. His muscles pulsed with rage, and his tattoos writhed and twisted with his temper. I flinched at the sudden outburst.

Not good, Watson remarked.

I nodded, reaching up to grab Eidolon's arm, but he pulled away.

"My parents are not involved in this," Eidolon spat, his words dripping with venom. He glared at Lilith before storming off to the other side of the dining room.

"Take a seat, Eidolon." Lilith's order reverberated through the room. I watched in horror as Eidolon turned slowly, his gaze meeting hers. His lips pulled back into a sneer, a dark shadow drifting across his eyes as they bore into hers with malice.

The glint of steel caught the light as Odin's hand drifted towards the sheath at his hip. His fingers twitched with anticipation as they wrapped around the hilt of his weapon. "Final warning, ghost whisperer," he declared, fixing his sharp stare on Eidolon with an unspoken challenge.

I glanced over at him, weary, waiting for him to make his next move. Eidolon's face contorted, torn between seething anger and deep anguish as he struggled to decide. We could all see he was itching for a fight, but I prayed he would resist the urge and sit back down.

With an exasperated huff, Eidolon marched back to the chair and snatched it up in a rough grip. He slumped down heavily, his shoulders sagging with defeat. His fingers drummed anxiously on the armrest as he breathed a long, resigned sigh.

"That was intense," Sydney's voice echoed under the napkin as he wiped his mouth. I scowled at him as he scooped another serving of chicken and dumplings onto his plate. "No violence allowed during mealtime, as my mother always says," he joked as he reached for a piece of bread.

Victor swatted Sydney on the side of the head. He grimaced, rubbing the spot. "Seriously, why does everyone feel the need to hit me?" Sydney complained.

Victor retorted, "You have a talent for saying the wrong thing at the wrong time. We're hoping that you will take the hint." Sydney rolled his eyes in response and went back to eating his dinner.

I paid little attention to them, my focus solely on our hosts. Freyja's demeanor was stern and severe, while Odin appeared visibly annoyed as he gave Lilith a disapproving look. Clearly, they were assessing us, and we were falling short of their expectations. Without looking away from Eidolon, Odin reached for a bottle of whiskey and poured himself a glass, downing it in one swift motion.

The god was ready to fight. Eidolon returned his gaze, a confident grin spread across his face as if prepared to recreate a barroom brawl on the dining room table. Which would have been a shame, considering how lovely it was.

Lilith exhaled softly and took a small sip before gently setting her glass down. She was determined to stay calm and not say anything impulsive, but I could tell she was unhappy about the conversation's direction. She shifted in her seat, her regard flickering between me and Eidolon. I could see the turmoil in her eyes, a mix of regret and determination.

I placed my hand on Eidolon's arm, feeling the tension ripple through his muscles, and squeezed it quickly.

"I should start at the beginning," Lilith offered. We all nodded. Odin rubbed his eyes and sighed. "The story begins with Taliesin and Morrigan, the twins the gods created. Their powers were unique but interlaced, and they preserved harmony among the mortal and Otherworld realms. You never found one without the other close by.

"When they met Arthur, things changed." Lilith's eyes narrowed. "He was an impressive king with grand ambitions. At first, he believed in a united kingdom and freedom for all his subjects to worship who they wanted. Taliesin and Morrigan bought into the dream and offered their support to his cause.

"And despite the odds stacked against them, the trio managed to bring temporary stability to the land. Morrigan and Taliesin played a considerable role in the negotiations, using their extraordinary talents to sway opposing sides to agree on a treaty. However, the mortals remained distrustful and resentful of the supernatural and their religions. Taliesin grew apprehensive as time passed, becoming even more vigilant about protecting himself and his growing authority.

"Then, the period of peace ended abruptly and violently, as mortals and the supernatural engaged in a bloody battle. With Taliesin and Morrigan on Arthur's side, it was no surprise everyone assumed he would win."

"What happened?" Isabelle asked.

"Taliesin had a vision. He saw Arthur's death and the fall of the supernatural, their power fading, and their existence at risk. In a desperate move, he made a deal with the Fates." Lilith took a long drink. Looking over the glass at Eidolon, she said, "A life for a life."

"Morrigan's?" Victor asked, leaning on his forearms.

Lilith nodded, frowning. "Yes," she confirmed. "But Taliesin didn't know it at the time. He never specified whose life in exchange for Arthur's."

I raised an eyebrow. "What happened after Morrigan died?"

Lilith laughed, amusement dancing in her eyes. "Morrigan had her own arrangement with the Fates. She understood death was only a temporary inconvenience. She would lose her body, but not her soul."

Sydney's fork clattered onto his plate, forgotten as he leaned forward in rapt attention. "What did Morrigan get out of the deal?" he asked, engrossed in the story.

"Avalon," I whispered. "She asked for Avalon."

Lilith nodded, satisfied, and shot Odin a triumphant glance. "Yes. The last thing she did with her powers was help protect Avalon—a sanctuary designed for the supernatural who needed refuge. I've tried to go back there for years, but since Taliesin barricaded its borders, I can't break through the walls."

I shook my head, more confused than before. "Claire said Taliesin and Diana were protecting Avalon, and the barricade was to keep it hidden from you."

When Bree, Sydney, Victor, and I arrived on the shores of Avalon months ago, a misty fog cloaked the island like a shroud, obscuring its view from outsiders. Bree cautioned us about the fog's purpose as a protective barrier against trespassers. She claimed anyone lost within its labyrinthine depths would eventually succumb to madness.

Getting through pushed me to the edge of insanity, but when we got to the other side, we were in Avalon. I still remember how the city stole my breath away. Peaceful was the only word I could use to describe it.

But it was deserted. Caer Ibormeith, or Claire, as Bree instructed us to call her, warned us Lilith had been snooping around. As a precautionary measure, she moved everyone out of the city for safekeeping. Then she told us how to find the missing Book of the Veiled.

"Claire showed herself?" Freyja blurted out, clearly taken aback. "That's not like her—she usually stays in swan form when mortals are around." She cast a glance toward Lilith. "Something isn't right. That couldn't have been Clair."

Odin's intense gaze bore into me, his brow knitted and his massive frame leaning forward. "What else did this person tell you?" he pressed, his voice edged with suspicion.

Recalling the conversation, I repeated Claire's words: "Black symbolizes mystery and death and follows the path leading to the lost City of the Unspoken. Blue represents truth and sadness and leads across a vast body of water to a city built on top of another. Green, representing nature, wisdom, and envy, follows the path through a dark forest to reach a city that claims to hold the Gates of Secrets.

"Each road leads to a book, hidden in the shadows that will open with a key forged at the same time as it was written. Each one is a different possibility of what could be. Every road is obscured by darkness, threatening to overpower the magick of the books. Travel all three roads successfully, and you will reach where the Tree of Life and the Gates of the Otherworld are abandoned and dying. Then, with the blood of the last, you will be able to reopen the path for all."

Lilith's long, delicate fingers traced the rim of her crystal glass as she spoke. Her piercing gaze remained fixed on her drink, unblinking and intense. "Intriguing," she mused, her voice low and smooth like melted chocolate, "but it doesn't explain why Claire felt the need to protect the city from me."

Freyja's voice quivered with conviction as she spoke. "I tell you, it wasn't Claire," she repeated adamantly. "I don't know who or what it was, but it certainly wasn't her." Her eyes flashed with fierce determination, and her hands clenched into fists at her sides. "Claire would never reveal herself to mere mortals," she declared.

Victor furrowed his brow and stroked a hand along his chin, deep in thought. His eyes flickered with a mix of concern and curiosity as he spoke. "Claire also mentioned you took the Book of the Veiled to prevent the Otherworld from being fixed. She insinuated you were the mastermind behind their transformation into monsters."

My heart raced as I glanced at Eidolon, my words tumbling out under my breath. "Diana mentioned something similar to me," I began. "She spoke of a hidden agenda between you and Vivian and how Taliesin was trying to stop it." The tension in the room thickened as I spoke, the air heavy with secrets and unspoken truths. My skin prickled with unease as I waited for Eidolon's response to my declaration.

Odin and Freyja leaned back in their chairs and blew simultaneous whistles. Their eyes flickered nervously to Lilith, waiting for her reaction as if braced for a storm to break.

Fury painted Lilith's face red. "Why would I want my offspring to become monsters? Why would I deny them their paradise? What could I gain from destroying what I've helped build?" She scoffed at the idea.

My heart clenched with concern as I watched Lilith struggle to contain her seething anger. She balled her hands into tight fists, her knuckles turning white from the force, a hard line etched on her face. The tension in the room crackled with electricity, threatening to erupt at any moment.

I shuddered at the thought of what Lilith was capable of when pushed to her limits, and she was obviously on the edge.

Odin thought for a second before speaking. "It must have been Taliesin," he said. "Impersonating people is something he has done in the past. It's the only reasonable explanation." Freyja nodded.

Lilith shrugged her shoulders. "It doesn't matter who said what," she declared with conviction, "the result will remain the same. It's no surprise Taliesin still holds a grudge against me; he has a habit of making things difficult at crucial points." She looked directly at me with a cold and unwavering stare. "You know what you must do to acquire the Book of the Veiled, and that is all that matters."

"What's the deal with you and Taliesin?" Watson's eyes narrowed as he asked. "You two are always at each other's throats. Why?"

Odin let out a quiet breath and poured himself another glass of whiskey. "The bloodsucker just had to ask, didn't he?" Lilith scoffed while Freyja chuckled. "Might as well finish the story now that you've started, Lilith. No need to hold back."

Chapter 43- Chloe

Modern Day- City of the Unspoken

"I was at the Battle of Argerydd. I pleaded with the gods to let me participate, but they denied my request. Then Morrigan was killed. When she died, all her powers transferred to Taliesin." Lilith twirled her wedding ring as she spoke. "I felt it in my bones that something was wrong right away. He would go insane with that much magick inside him.

"After the battle was over and he found his sister's body, he sought me out. Taliesin was unstable and made a demand I could never fulfill. Rather than helping him, I left him to his own devices. That is why we are in this situation now," she concluded with a heavy heart.

"What does Taliesin want?" Victor asked.

"He wants vengeance for his sister's death. He holds the Fates responsible," Freyja scoffed.

"Did you have the power to do what he asked?" I inquired, pouring another cup of coffee and cradling it between my hands, relishing its warmth.

Lilith's head shook from side to side. "To a certain extent, I could have assisted in avenging his sister's death. Unfortunately, there was no way for me to bring her back," she replied. "Taliesin is convinced the only solution is to rewrite our stories - mine, Morrigan's, and his - to alter reality. He wants to change the trajectory of our narratives."

Watson draped his arm behind Isabelle's chair. His fingers moved rhythmically up and down her back. "What happens if he gets the books?" his deep voice rumbled with concern.

Odin's eyes blazed with determination as he revealed his grave announcement. "There will be a war between the Fates and the supernatural," he said, his lips twisting into an ominous grin. "Taliesin has been amassing an army for this very purpose. That is why he is tampering with history, manipulating Lilith's descendants into something so twisted even the gods fear them."

"A weapon," I murmured, my gaze shooting towards Lilith as realization dawned on me. Everything I experienced in my dreams and visions over the past few weeks suddenly made sense. "You have a weapon the Fates are afraid of. That's why Taliesin wants to rewrite your story. He needs it."

Lilith smiled at me. "I don't *have* the weapon. And no one will. I plan to keep it safe unless it must be used—a situation I am trying to avoid."

My mind reeled with the latest information. From far away, the deep chime of a grandfather clock rang out, marking a significant turning point in the story. As the chatter around me blended into background noise, I began to connect another piece of the puzzle.

Lilith had been telling us the truth from the beginning. She admitted to taking the books—not for revenge, as we had initially thought, but to keep them safe from Taliesin and his war against the Fates.

Watson and Isabelle entertained Lilith and Freyja with tales of their travels. Odin, Eidolon, and Victor delved into discussions about unsolved historical mysteries while Sydney helped himself to more food and occasionally added his input. Meanwhile, I remained lost in my thoughts, paying little attention to the conversations around me.

When the grandfather clock rang ten, Lilith stood up and announced we would reconvene for breakfast, along with Aelle, Moll, and Max. We all knew we should have requested to see them tonight, but everyone was too exhausted to protest.

In any case, I wanted to speak privately with Eidolon. The past three weeks had been hectic for him, and now, with Lilith claiming his parents had something to do with the missing Book of the Veiled, I was pretty sure he was overwhelmed.

In a daze, we made our way back to our room. No one said a word. As Isabelle and Watson reached their door, Isabelle turned to give me a small wave.

Good luck! She flashed me a sly grin and gave me an encouraging wink. My cheeks warmed at her implication; the anxiousness of what the night held in store started sinking in.

Eidolon gestured for me to enter, saying, "After you."

I quickly ducked my head and hurried past him. Eidolon followed closely behind, closing the door with a loud thud. He made a beeline for the minibar and poured himself a glass of whiskey.

"Eidolon?" I looked at him curiously as I poured myself a drink. Looking up, I noticed how his dark hair fell across his forehead, slightly covering his piercing eyes. With a surge of boldness, I reached out and pushed his hair back, revealing the intensity of his gaze.

"It's going to be okay," I reassured him. My hand lingered on his cheek for a moment before I pulled away. "We can get through this," I added.

Eidolon's voice was barely a whisper, tinged with vulnerability. His long eyelashes fluttered as he gazed down at me. "I know, Chloe," he said softly. "But it's like trying to swim in an ocean of emotions. It's overwhelming."

I took his hand and interlocked our fingers, feeling the warmth of our skin combine. His grip was tight, so I started to massage small circles on the back of his hand with my thumb.

"You don't have to face this on your own. We're in this together. What can I do to help?" I asked.

"I'll be okay," he reassured me, though his voice wavered. "Why don't you go freshen up? We can sneak down to the kitchen and grab some coffee," he suggested with a faint smile.

A slight nod passed between us, and I gathered my things before hurrying away to rinse off the lingering anxieties of the evening. I turned back to glance one last time. Eidolon was slumped in the armchair, his head reclined, eyes shut, and looking almost peaceful.

Smiling, I closed the bathroom door. There wasn't anything in the world that couldn't be solved over a cup of coffee.

Chapter 44- Chloe

Modern Day- City of the Unspoken

Thirty minutes later, I emerged from the bathroom, ready to head out. But Eidolon was nowhere to be seen. I was disappointed but reminded myself his absence shouldn't have been unexpected. If I were in his shoes, I would've needed time alone to sort through my thoughts and emotions.

It would have been nice if he'd said something or left a note telling me where he went.

I wandered around the bedroom, tracing a route on the plush carpet, at a loss for what to do. I wanted to ease Eidolon's pain, but I didn't want to pressure him into talking to me. Instead, I resorted to a tried-and-true method: pouring another drink and lounging on the massive bed, waiting for him to return.

And waited.

After waiting an hour, I grew frustrated that he hadn't come back. I went to refill my drink, but before returning to my seat, I decided to check the hallway for his whereabouts. Perhaps he had gone to visit Sydney and Victor or stopped by Isabelle and Watson's room for a drink.

As I peeked into the hallway, the happy couple was already there.

"Not who I was expecting," I muttered, disappointed, turning to walk back into the room. I crawled under the covers and glared at the intruders.

Watson's face lit up with a warm smile as he replied, "Well, hello to you too." He pulled two armchairs from in front of the crackling fireplace and placed them beside the bed. He motioned for Isabelle to sit. As she settled into the soft cushions, Watson walked over to the minibar and poured them a generous glass of whiskey each.

"How you doing, luv?" Isabelle asked as she reached for the glass Watson offered her. He settled in the other chair, propping his feet on the bed.

I frowned, arching an eyebrow at him. "I've definitely had better days."

"Better than this?" Watson dismissed the thought with a wave of his hand. "We're on an epic journey. The fate of the future rests in our capable but awkward hands. Fighting against evil for the greater good of humanity. This is the kind of stuff that inspires extraordinary novels."

I sipped my drink and muttered, "If this is what it takes to make the New York Best Seller list, then I'll settle for being a struggling author."

"No, you wouldn't," Isabelle scolded. "That's exactly why you are here, like the rest of us. We all feel destined for something beyond the ordinary."

I gave a noncommittal shrug and remained silent, curious about why they were in my room. But I was too tired and frustrated to ask.

Watson finally spoke up, breaking the tense silence between us. "Aren't you going to ask?"

I snuggled deeper into the bed and pulled the covers over my shoulders. "Ask you what?"

Watson raised an eyebrow at me. "You're not wondering why we're not in our room, enjoying a warm bed and pleasant conversation instead of being stuck with a grumpy woman who is giving us the evil eye?"

I couldn't help but roll my eyes at him. "Alright, Watson. I surrender. Why are you in my room instead of snuggling up with your mate?"

As he inspected his fingernails, Watson's voice was nonchalant, but his eyes were fixed on me from under his eyelashes. "He's searching for Lilith," he revealed, "and their last meeting was quite intense, if I recall correctly."

Watson watched me, anticipating a reaction. And he was about to receive one. My thoughts flashed back to our initial encounter with Lilith when she cast him under her spell, which I had mistakenly thought was some explicit movie.

A fear she didn't correct, and my anger reared its ugly head.

I wasn't typically jealous, but Lilith's beauty was undeniable. If I were a man, I probably wouldn't be able to resist her. Though Eidolon and I were still working through some issues in our relationship, he was still my 'better half.' I couldn't risk leaving them alone in the same room without supervision. It may have seemed possessive, but I couldn't help it. I glanced at Watson and Isabelle, who failed to conceal their amusement at my frustration.

Huffing, I threw off the covers and slipped on my shoes. "Fine. If you think we should save him, I can accompany you. But if he gets angry at us for intruding, know I'm blaming both of you." With that said, I hurried to the door.

Before they could get out of their chairs, I was out of the room and walking down the hall. I had no idea where Eidolon was, but I could feel the bond tugging me to the heart of the building. I followed its invisible pull, my mind filled with images of violently breaking through doors and obliterating anyone who dared stand in between us.

I typically relied on words to escape sticky situations rather than using my fists, but I felt today would be an exception for some reason. It may not have been the wisest decision to challenge the mother of all supernatural to a physical altercation. Still, considering all the strange events that had occurred lately, it didn't seem too far-fetched.

Let's do this, Lilith.

It only took a few minutes before I stood before the imposing wooden door. It loomed over me like a guard at a fortress, its sturdy frame and intricate carvings giving off an air of grandeur and mystery. My hand trembled as I reached for the ornate handle, curious and apprehensive about what awaited me on the other side.

Don't break down the door, please. It is older than Odin.

An expletive escaped my lips as I realized, too late, that Lilith could read my thoughts. The element of surprise was gone in an instant. Isabelle and Watson came to a halt beside me, their expressions mirroring the realization they, too, could hear Lilith.

With an exasperated tone, Lilith announced, "It's unlocked."

I hesitated, my hand lingering on the doorknob as I considered whether to enter the room. Taking a deep breath, I pulled open the door and braced myself for what might come next.

Chapter 45- Chloe

Modern Day- City of the Unspoken

My heart froze as we entered the room. It was like being back at the Raven Society. Six floors of mahogany bookshelves stretched further than the eye could see. A familiar spiral staircase adorned the outer walls, leading to hidden reading nooks on the upper levels. Natural light poured in through the dome above us, sparkling like diamonds.

The room was decorated with opulent forest-green velvet sofas and recliners scattered without any discernible pattern. Oversized decorative rugs and rich mahogany coffee tables accompanied them. Elegant writing desks lined the walls, tempting passersby to take a seat and begin crafting their masterpieces.

The aroma of coffee, paper, ink, and applewood mingled, filling the air and creating a scene that resembled a utopian library—a sanctuary for writers and readers alike to indulge in their love for literature.

Watson blew a low whistle. "This is luxury," he whispered, eyes scanning the room. "I could spend hours in here."

I nodded in response, momentarily forgetting about Eidolon as I imagined myself sitting at one of the desks with a steaming cup of coffee and an empty notebook.

My gaze was immediately drawn to a majestic painting above the fireplace. It depicted a breathtaking woman, her flowing hair and ethereal features surrounded by eight powerful gods. In her arms, she held a delicate jar cradled with care. As I took a hesitant step forward, my eyes still fixed on the artwork. A sudden movement caught my attention. Lilith emerged from the shadows with an air of intrigue and danger, her piercing eyes locked onto mine.

"Good evening," she greeted us with a welcoming smile, her emerald green eyes dancing with delight. "What brings you out so late at night?"

"We're searching for Eidolon." My eyes shifted between her and the picture on the wall behind her. It couldn't be. Or could it?

I delved into my limited understanding of Greek mythology and religion, trying to connect the dots. The woman in the painting was obviously Pandora. But the woman standing underneath it was Lilith.

And they looked eerily similar.

Was it possible that Lilith and Pandora were the same? Historically, there were some similarities between them. In the story of Prometheus giving fire to mortals and angering Zeus, Hephaestus was tasked with creating Pandora, the first woman. According to legend, she possessed beauty, curiosity, charm, and cleverness.

History and religious texts also whispered God created the first woman, Lilith. She was just as beautiful and cunning as Pandora, if not more so. However, her refusal to submit to Adam led to her being cast out of Eden, and her actions were deemed responsible for humanity's downfall.

Two women sent by the gods to be the destruction of mankind. But their tales had been twisted and rewritten so often that it was impossible to know who they truly were. My thoughts raced as I tried to process this revelation but couldn't find the words.

All I could do was stare at Lilith, my mind reeling with shock and confusion.

Lilith let out a soft sigh as her gaze flicked up to the painting, then back to me with a melancholy smile. "Eidolon is in the back, rummaging for something. I can call him for you if you want," she offered.

Watson took off in the direction indicated, calling over his shoulder, "No need. I'll find him."

Isabelle and I watched him saunter away, his strides purposeful and confident, before redirecting our focus to Lilith. With a graceful wave of her delicate hand, she beckoned us over to the crackling fireplace, its golden flames casting a warm glow across the room.

We settled into our seats, but I couldn't shake the suspicion that this had been Lilith's plan all along. Eidolon didn't come to the library to find her; she lured him here, knowing we would follow. My gaze narrowed as she poured us a drink.

"I've been hoping to have a moment alone with the two of you," Lilith said as she handed us each a glass. "As you can imagine, not many people visit the City of the Unspoken for a friendly visit."

I scanned the seemingly endless shelves filled to the brim with books and trinkets as I asked, "What is the City of the Unspoken? And how did it get here?"

Lilith's eyes swept over the space, a smile of pride appearing on her lips. "This was created as a sanctuary for lost souls. Within these walls lie the untold accounts and the hidden truths of our past."

My leg bounced in frustration as I let out a sigh. "What does that even mean?"

Lilith's elegant eyebrow arched, her gaze lingering on the bookshelf nearest us. The shelves were filled with ancient scrolls and dusty tomes untouched for years, their spines cracking and bindings frayed. "These are the lost stories," she murmured, her voice tinged with reverence. "Destinies that never had the chance to come to life. Lives destroyed by malice and greed."

"So, the books are orphans?" I asked, confused.

Lilith's features twisted in disapproval. "I detest the label 'orphans,'" she remarked with a firm tone. "Though, I suppose it's an apt depiction." She cocked her head to the side and furrowed her brow as she scrutinized me.

Isabelle's voice held a hint of sadness as she asked, "How did they end up here?"

Lilith met her gaze, shrugging. "They needed somewhere to call home. Just because the mortal world refused to acknowledge their existence doesn't mean they weren't real."

"And you guard them?" I asked, curiosity getting the better of me.

"Yes, with some help," Lilith nodded. "Not exactly the glamorous life I once had, but it keeps me busy."

My gaze widened as it fixated on the painting, and again, I was drawn into the scene. The colors were vivid and lively, giving life to the woman depicted. Her intense stare seemed directed at me, her golden tresses flowing in waves around her face. It was, without a doubt, Lilith. Each brush stroke captured her allure and strength, making it nearly impossible to avert my eyes.

Lilith's lips curled into a soft, amused smile as she saw what I was staring at. "Ah, a blast from the past," she remarked. "I like to think of it as a family photo."

"So, it is you," I said, my voice barely above a whisper. "You are Pandora? And Lilith?"

She took a small sip before gently placing it on the table. "The way others see me is subjective, based on their own outlooks and desires," she said, leaning back in her seat and clasping her hands together in her lap. "It's hard to explain."

"Try," I said dryly.

Lilith's lips curved in delight at the tone of my voice. "Consider the day a child is born," she began. "The mother's tale will focus solely on the moment they first saw their baby. They don't remember anything about the pains and struggles of labor.

"However, for a father, the memories are different. They recall the yelling, the helplessness of not knowing what to do, and the endless waiting. They remember the first glimpse of their child, but in a completely different perspective.

"Although the events are different, they both tell the same story. Just like how two people can have different experiences of the same event, the story of creation has multiple interpretations and perspectives. But the core message remains unchanged. One moment someone didn't exist, and then they did."

Isabelle and I sat in silence after Lilith's explanation. She was right. History constantly changed as new evidence was discovered. It was generally the same story, with different details added or altered over time.

"And your book has the original story? Is that why you are trying to protect it?" Isabelle asked, playing with her bracelets.

Lilith chuckled, her eyes sparkling with amusement. "Gods, yes," she replied. "Don't we all want to be remembered? The book contains my entire story, combining all the different versions. Each version is a vital part of the whole, and without one piece, I am incomplete. Erasing any part of me would change my entire identity."

I sat up, wringing my hands. "I had a vision." Lilith raised an eyebrow. "Two women. They didn't say anything to me, but they wanted to."

Lilith tilted her head to the side. "What did they look like?"

"I caught a quick glimpse, but I remember one of them had hair as black as raven wings, piercing dark brown eyes, and an infectious smile." I paused to organize my thoughts. "The other one had hair that moved on its own, almost like snakes. I believe it was Medusa, although I can't be certain."

I wanted to tell Lilith and Isabelle that the woman terrified me. That as she stared at me, I felt like I was turning into stone. And she was heartbreakingly sad—a kind of sadness that a person never recovered from.

Lilith ran a hand through her hair. "How intriguing. They never show themselves to anyone. I wonder why they decided to now." Her fingers drummed against the arm of her chair as she sat silent, lost in thought.

"Who were they?" I asked, holding my breath.

"Medusa and Danaë," Lilith finally stated, her voice heavy. "They protect something important for me and tend to stay hidden from outsiders."

"What are they guarding?" Isabelle asked, leaning forward.

The corners of Lilith's mouth turned into a deep frown as she focused her intense gaze on the painting. "A jar," she said, emphasizing each word. "A very important jar."

Chapter 46- Chloe

Modern Day- City of the Unspoken

Lilith's words hung in the air like a bolt of lightning, electrifying the stillness of the library. Before I could react, the heavy oak doors burst open with a loud crash. A whirlwind of chaos and energy swept into the room, carried by a lone woman at its center. Her piercing gaze scanned the area, searching for something or someone, until it landed on me with a fierce intensity, like a predator honing in on its prey.

Aelle!

The woman we left behind in Scotland was unrecognizable from the one standing before me. Aelle's usual poised and polished appearance was replaced with baggy clothing, dark circles under her eyes, and a gaunt face as if she hadn't eaten in days.

Her anger reverberated off the walls, filling the room with its intensity. The space seemed to magnify and reflect her emotions, sending them back toward us like a powerful wave crashing over our heads. I could feel it hitting me in the chest like a baseball as she shouted, "Where the HELL have you been?"

I winced, rubbing my chest. Isabelle and Lilith seemed utterly unaware of the situation, adding to my surprise. As Aelle's temper continued to rise, the room crackled with energy. The books on the shelf started to shift and twitch, reacting to her rage. The sound of rustling paper grew louder until it was a chaotic symphony of flipping and flapping pages as if the books were desperately trying to break free from their bindings.

What the...? I watched nervously, praying nothing came flying off the shelves.

"Luv, we just got here..." Isabelle started to say, but Aelle's glare silenced her.

"No," Aelle hissed. "I don't want to hear your excuses." She stalked forward, each word an arrow hitting its target. "I know you got here last night, and not one of you came to find me."

She whirled around, her anger directed solely towards me. "I was pulled out of my home, abducted by someone who shouldn't exist! No internet. No cell phone. No change of clothes. And to top it all off, I'll miss my academic article deadline! And here you are," she exclaimed, pointing at Lilith, "befriending the person who took me without a word about your whereabouts."

I turned to Lilith to gauge her reaction to Aelle's accusation. To my surprise, she smiled and tipped her glass in my direction, a subtle gesture of support. I fought the urge to roll my eyes and redirected my attention to the person yelling at me.

I crossed my arms and returned her glare. "Aelle, relax. We were planning on meeting you for breakfast. We would have found you sooner if we had known you were so angry. But," I raised an eyebrow, "we had our own issues to handle."

"As expected," Aelle scoffed, brushing her bangs away from her face. "I forgot everything always revolves around Chloe." She turned on her heels and headed towards the fireplace.

I wanted to retort, but the tears welling up in her eyes gave me pause. Aelle was the last person I would expect to cry about anything. Typically, she only had two expressions: anger and annoyance, which were always accompanied by her signature resting bitch face.

Her appearance was now utter misery, resembling a drenched and forlorn kitten. Despite my natural urge to feel sorry for her, I knew she would never accept pity from me or anyone else. Nevertheless, I couldn't shake off the feeling of responsibility for what had transpired, and I wanted to make things right.

"Aelle, we were going to rescue you," I said. "We would never leave you behind."

Isabelle nodded and moved closer, wrapping an arm around her shoulders. "Remember our talk about having each other's backs?" Aelle gave a slight nod. It means that no matter what happens, we will always come when someone needs us—even if one of us manages to get taken to the Otherworld."

Aelle's tremors ceased, and she brushed away her tears. "Well, you didn't have to take so long," she said with a scowl. "I haven't had a good cup of coffee in forever."

"Amen to that," I grumbled, pushing my glasses back up the bridge of my nose.

The tension between the three of us lingered but gradually faded away. I turned my focus back to the books behind us. The emotion emanating from them before seemed to have lessened, though remnants still lingered. Was it anger? Frustration?

Whatever it was, it stopped as soon as Aelle regained her composure. *Weird.*

"Well, the gang's all here," Watson's voice rang out from behind me, breaking the tense silence. He and Eidolon crept closer, their gaze on Aelle as they cautiously approached. By the expression on their faces, they overheard our heated argument.

"It's good to see you, Aelle." Eidolon reached out his hand, a hesitant smile playing on his lips. Aelle paused before accepting the gesture, her features briefly showing a hint of sadness before she masked it.

But not before I saw it. Aelle still harbored feelings for him, and I felt sorry for her again. There was nothing I could do about it. Eidolon and I were bonded. Not her. I could only hope she moved on sooner rather than later.

"Good gods, everybody is here," a familiar voice called from the doorway.

I smiled. Finally, a friendly face. "Max!" I exclaimed, rushing over to embrace him, relieved to see he was still in one piece.

Our friendship began when Max took us to the burial site of Taliesin in Scotland. We connected instantly, both sharing a passion for history and literature. That's when I discovered Max's interest in the Taliesin legend went beyond mere curiosity. His great-grandfather claimed to have worked alongside Taliesin, creating stories revolving around Merlin and the supernatural.

Initially, I doubted Max's claims, but he showed me passages from his grandfather's journal that backed up his story. As we delved deeper into our investigation, the clues we uncovered pointed towards the possibility that Taliesin and Merlin had been one person all along. Over the centuries, he seemed to have adapted by assuming different identities to suit his purposes.

I stepped away, noticing Max's gaze shifting past me. His features softened, and I followed his line of sight to see what caught his attention. It was Aelle, bathed in the dim light of the room. Her lips curved into a gentle smile, and her eyes shimmered as she looked at Max.

Well, I guess she's over Eidolon, I thought with relief before frowning. Max was the opposite of Aelle in every way - outgoing, kind, and full of affection. I couldn't help but worry about him getting his heart broken by someone as emotionally distant as Aelle. But as I observed her interacting with Max, my fears melted away. She seemed sincere, and for the first time, I felt genuine happiness for her.

"It's great to see you, Chloe. I was starting to get worried," Max said, squeezing my shoulders.

Shrugging, I apologized, "Sorry it took longer than expected. Google Maps doesn't have the Otherworld mapped out yet; it's quite disappointing."

"I don't doubt that," Max chuckled. "While you were busy, I had time to do my own digging. And let me tell you, I've discovered a wealth of information." His eyes sparkled with excitement as he ruffled his hair with one hand. Bending closer, he murmured, "You wouldn't believe the hidden gems lurking in this library."

I was about to inquire about his findings, eager to look through the library myself, when Eidolon suddenly materialized and wrapped his arm around my shoulders. His sudden touch startled me, and I jumped in surprise.

"Can we discuss this over breakfast?" Eidolon asked through clenched teeth as he pulled me closer. "It's late, and I need to get Chloe to bed."

My jaw fell open in shock. I couldn't figure out why Eidolon had taken an immediate dislike to Max, but the look on his face made it clear that the sentiment was mutual.

Max winked at me, ignoring Eidolon's thinly veiled warning. "I'll see you in the morning," he said with a playful tone. He looked over my shoulder at Aelle. "Are you ready?"

Aelle nodded and approached us, giving me a disdainful look from head to toe. "Do you need a formal invitation with directions? You seem to have trouble finding your way," she scoffed, and I couldn't help but roll my eyes in response.

Max groaned. "Aelle, we've already discussed this. You need to play nice with others."

"No problem, boss." Aelle's soft laughter caught me off guard, and I couldn't help but chuckle. But her stern look quickly ended any fun, her expression capable of curdling milk. With a huff, she walked out the door. Max mouthed 'sorry' in my direction before following her.

Eidolon whispered, "She really doesn't like you, does she?"

"Nope," I shrugged.

So much for girls sticking together.

Chapter 47- Chloe

Modern Day- City of the Unspoken

After the long night, we all stumbled to our rooms for a second time. All I wanted to do was crawl into bed and sleep for days. But my curiosity tugged at me even as I curled under the covers. "Did you find what you were looking for?"

A mischievous spark lit up Eidolons' eyes, and a playful grin stretched across his face, sending my toes curling. He reached into his bag and pulled out some clothes. "I'll tell you as soon as I shower," he promised.

"I'll be waiting," I gestured towards the bed. Eidolon's eyebrows rose in amusement, and my cheeks flushed with embarrassment. Did he think I was suggesting something more than just waiting for him? The thought made me cringe inwardly.

Oh gods, please let him not think that. Unless, of course, he wanted to. My face burned even brighter at the thought.

Before the awkwardness could settle in and make the moment unbearable, Eidolon made his way to the shower with a laugh. I rolled over, my face planted deep into the plush pillows, and let out a loud groan of embarrassment. Flipping on my back, I stared at the ceiling.

Eidolon was showering in the other room. So close I could almost touch him.

My mind danced with inappropriate thoughts. I snatched a throw pillow and squashed my face in it, muffling the screams threatening to escape.

Chloe?

I was startled when Eidolon reached out through our bond. I threw the pillow and scanned the room, half expecting to see him there. After a brief hesitation, I responded. *Yes?*

You realize I can hear you, right? Eidolon's amusement sent waves of humiliation crashing over me.

I snatched the pillow and pressed it against my face again, releasing a high-pitched scream of sexual frustration and exasperation. The urge to march in and pour a bucket of ice-cold water over Eidolon was strong, but I stifled it.

It isn't polite to listen in on people's private thoughts, I shot back.

I know, he replied. *But you didn't give me much of a choice. Your thoughts are loud.*

His enjoyment of my discomfort grated on my nerves. Of course, he would find the situation funny. He wasn't the one broadcasting inappropriate daydreams for everyone to hear.

Needing something to calm my irritation, I got up and poured myself a drink before settling against the bed's headboard. I was enjoying the warm amber liquid when Eidolon emerged from the bathroom, and I almost choked. He had swapped his clothes for comfortable sweatpants and a well-worn black t-shirt, his damp hair curling at the nape of his neck. I couldn't take my gaze off him as he walked towards me.

It was not right for someone to be that good-looking, especially when I knew how disheveled I looked. My sweatshirt was stained, my sweatpants had a small tear, and I hadn't had a good hair day since we arrived in the Otherworld.

"We need to work on your mental barriers. What runs through your mind is liable to give a man a heart attack," he grinned roguishly as he poured himself a drink and sat beside me.

I pulled the blanket closer, wrapping it tightly around my body as his words sent a shiver down my spine. Eidolon had a way of making me flustered and exhilarated all at once. I tried to ignore my heart racing as he sipped his whiskey, his eyes never leaving mine.

"Whatever," I muttered. "I thought we were going to grab a cup of coffee," I reminded him.

"You know, Chloe, your love for coffee borders on an unhealthy obsession." Eidolon's deep and contagious laugh caught me off guard. It had been a while since I heard him laugh, not since I returned from Avalon. A grin spread across my face as our connection solidified once again.

My eyes lingered on him, admiring his toned muscles and taut abdomen. I couldn't help but feel an overwhelming desire to touch and explore every inch of his sculpted physique. "So?" I asked, trying to push the thoughts away.

Eidolon lifted an eyebrow, a sly grin creeping onto his face.

Great! I just got caught thinking inappropriate thoughts. Again!

"So, are you going to tell me why you were in the library?" I asked, trying to change the subject. "When I got out of the shower, you disappeared. I was worried you were angry with me."

"I've already told you. I'm not mad," Eidolon clarified softly, his eyes never leaving mine.

"Really?" I raised my eyebrows in surprise. "Just like that?"

"Just like that," he snapped his fingers. My warm cocoon of blankets was suddenly disrupted as he tucked it around his legs. "I was intrigued by something Lilith said, so I went to the library to investigate."

I swallowed hard, trying to focus on anything else besides Eidolon's leg pressed against mine. "What did she say?"

"When we asked her about Avalon, she responded with a question of her own: why would she want to destroy something that she helped bring into existence? However, she conveniently omitted mentioning who or what she created." Eidolon paused. "Or with whom."

My mouth dropped. Eidolon was right. If Lilith was considered the mother of all supernatural, then it was logical to assume there must also be a father. My mind raced with questions as I recalled my vision: a couple holding each other tightly, children's toys scattered across a lawn, and a sense of warmth and belonging.

I flung the blanket off me. "Lilith is married...or was married. That's who I saw in my vision—Lilith and her husband!" I stared at Eidolon in excitement, pushing my glasses up. "He was breathtaking—like an angel." I sighed, my heart racing as his image flashed in my mind.

"Well, tell me how you really feel. Don't worry about hurting my feelings," Eidolon muttered, and I playfully tossed a pillow at him.

As if he wasn't as good-looking as the man in my vision.

"Not like that. I mean, he didn't look like a mortal. I can't explain it, but I know they loved each other."

Eidolon arched an eyebrow, "I hope so. Because I think you're right. It had to be her husband. There is no other explanation."

"Why do you say that?"

"Because I stumbled upon his book in the library, tucked away on a forgotten shelf. All the other books were coated in a thick layer of dust, untouched for years, but not this one. It was well-loved and well-worn. But that wasn't even the strangest thing," he hinted with a mischievous glint in his eye.

"What?"

"I found it sitting beside a case with only one item inside. A white feather." Eidolon paused, running a hand through his hair. "I think her husband is Lucifer, the original fallen angel."

Well, now. That's a plot twist.

Chapter 48- Medusa

13th Century BCE, Athens, Greece

For hours, Medusa leaned against the door to the Chamber of Serpents, waiting until nightfall before she made her move. Her last memories of her sisters would haunt her forever.

Athena's verdict had been swift and severe, banishing them to an unimaginable fate—immortality on a desolate island. Medusa's sisters were forced to endure the one thing she desired, but they had never asked for. Their pleas for Medusa's return fell on deaf ears, unable to sway Athena's ruling.

The goddess hadn't even told them what she had done to Medusa. She let them believe she had run away with Poseidon and turned her back on her family.

That was the worst punishment of them all. Medusa would never be able to tell them the truth.

As the sun peaked in the afternoon, the chamber became unbearably hot. Medusa fought to stay conscious, enduring the pain surging through her body. She took advantage of the time to reflect on the past few days' events.

She thought of Poseidon, the god she loved, and his actions that shattered her heart and left her broken. The memory of his betrayal seared like acid in her veins, poisoning every thought as she replayed the moments of deceit and manipulation. The thoughts left a bitter taste in her mouth and fueled the burning fire of vengeance, consuming her.

A wave of numbing sorrow washed over Medusa as her body gave out, and she crumbled to the ground. She was mindful not to disturb the twisting serpents who coiled and slithered around her shoulders, their scales glimmering in the dim light. The weight of their presence, both physical and symbolic, added to her exhaustion.

She had dedicated herself to the temple, only for it all to come crashing down in a single blow. Her relationship with her sisters and her place in society was destroyed, all because she fell in love with a god.

But it wasn't just Poseidon who betrayed her; the goddess who should have protected her held the most blame. Medusa's anger towards the sea god faded as she fixated on seeking revenge against Athena.

Poseidon stole her innocence and left her with the repercussions of his actions.

But Athena took her self-respect and belief in humanity.

And left her with a head full of serpents, their sleek bodies coiling and uncoiling around her skull. The added weight made her neck pulse and her body shudder. Every time she shifted, the smell of moist earth, decaying leaves, and foul decay wafted toward her, invading her senses and making her stomach churn with disgust.

But despite their intrusive nature, they weren't dangerous. Not for Medusa. She was encircled by their cold forms, forming a shield as they attempted to comfort her.

A sudden movement caught her attention as she was about to drift off. From the depths of the chamber emerged serpents lured by her scent. Their smooth, obsidian scales glistened as they slithered closer. Medusa frantically scanned the chamber for a place to hide and gradually made her way up the wall, inching closer to the right. The snakes eagerly pursued her, emitting hisses of anticipation.

She swallowed a scream. But then the unexpected happened.

Her withering locks hissed their own warning, and they lurched forward, growing longer and larger.

The serpents stopped, and Medusa held her breath. For a second, no one moved until, finally, the intruders turned back to where they came from.

It was time to go. She pressed her ear to the door and listened for the sounds of movement. Satisfied that it was clear, Medusa pushed against the weighty stone door, grimacing at its scraping noise as it opened.

Her serpentine hair coiled and hissed in anticipation as they moved down the dimly lit hallways. Medusa held her breath, her eyes darting back and forth like a viper's as she maneuvered past the looming statue of Athena. Her heart raced as she continued, navigating the treacherous maze of corridors until, finally, she was out of the temple.

She hurried through the deserted streets of Athens, the biting cold gnawing at every inch of her body. She shivered and pulled her cloak tighter, trying to shield herself from the frost. The dark alleyways and abandoned buildings around her seemed to hold secrets and dangers beyond her imagination—a brutal reality for someone who had once lived a sheltered life in the temple.

Now, she was running for her life.

Her first priority was finding something to wear. Her torn and tattered clothes offered no defense against the piercing elements, so she grabbed a thick black cape that was left out to dry. As she moved on to the next house, she spotted and snatched an overlooked bag. Scouring through the alleys, she collected food and other useful items, including a small cup adorned with a beautifully etched snake that sparkled in the moonlight.

Fitting for her new life.

Navigating the empty city streets was unsettling. Usually bustling with people and vendors, the lanes were deserted. The frigid wind raged, hurling snowflakes against her face. She'd only seen snowfall a few times before, which had always brightened her spirits. But tonight, it felt like a cruel punishment from Athena.

A chilling gust of air swept in from the north, and Medusa's cloak flapped around her body. She held onto it tightly, trying to protect herself. The salty air from the nearby sea carried echoes of Poseidon's tales of deserted islands, sparking an idea.

She changed course and made a beeline toward the dock. She glanced over her shoulders and saw a figure trailing behind her. Adrenaline surged as she quickened her pace, hoping whoever it was just stumbling home after a night of drinking.

The sound of footsteps drew closer. Whoever was tracking her was now only a few strides away. Medusa turned, her eyes blazing with rage, ready to defend herself. Her serpentine locks rose defensively, their warning hisses and strikes echoing through the street. But before they could attack, a figure emerged from the shadows.

Poseidon!

As Medusa watched him casually approaching her, her anger boiled over. Just seeing him made everything worse; he was the reason she was in this predicament in the first place. But as he drew near, her determination to make him pay wavered. Despite all the harm and suffering he caused, she still loved him. She would have sacrificed everything for the god.

Well, until the end, Medusa admitted to herself. And then she told him no. With her head held high, Medusa was determined not to hide the changes forced on her.

Poseidon stopped, his gaze swept over her form, taking note of her transformed hair and aging features as if he were searching for a glimpse of her former beauty. When one of the snakes lunged toward him, his eyebrows shot up in surprise, and he instinctively stepped back.

"Medusa?" Poseidon's voice was barely above a whisper as he uttered her name, filled with shock and dismay.

"Don't you dare say another word," Medusa's voice hissed like the serpents wrapped around her. "Unless you can give me back the life you and Athena stole from me."

Poseidon shook his head, his eyes fixed on her hair. "I can't. Only Zeus has that power."

"Then talk to your brother," Medusa spat. "Surely, if you explain to him what happened, he will understand."

The sound of Poseidon's laughter echoed through the air. "Do you really believe Zeus would undo this?" He shook his head incredulously. "It goes against everything he stands for. Punishment is his ultimate pleasure, especially if it lasts forever. He calls it justice."

"But he may find pity. If not for me, at least for my sisters," Medusa protested. "I didn't do anything wrong." She paused, lowering her eyes. "At least not intentionally."

Poseidon stared at his feet, kicking off the snow clinging to his boots. He lifted his head, meeting Medusa's gaze through his long eyelashes. A frown creased his face as he confessed, "I've already asked him. And he refused. Instead, Zeus imposed a truce between Athena and me. She is forbidden from entering my territory," he paused, wincing at the memory. "And I am not allowed to intrude with her decisions."

Medusa's eyes widened in surprise. Even her serpents stilled. Poseidon petitioned Zeus on her behalf. She couldn't believe it. "Then why have you come?" she asked in a hushed tone.

Poseidon hesitated before taking a step forward. "I swore not to interfere with your punishment, but I said nothing about helping you escape."

Medusa's heart sank. Escape. That was her only option. She struggled to collect her scattered thoughts as she paced back and forth. If Poseidon couldn't help her, then there was no hope left. The absurdity of it all weighed heavily on her, like a stormy sea crashing against the shore.

"Let me help you," Poseidon pleaded, watching her with a weary look.

"So, now you want to help me?" Medusa laughed as she locked her gaze on the god and moved closer, her eyes narrowing in suspicion. "After leaving me abused, broken, and alone on Athena's doorstep? After stealing my innocence and then discarding me like trash? Don't try to play the noble god now."

Poseidon moved closer to Medusa, his expression filled with rage and sparks of fury igniting in his eyes. "I have not taken anything from you. Before making any accusations, remember who truly robbed you of everything." He pointed a finger at her. "And I advise you to seriously consider accepting my offer of protection before rejecting it."

Medusa opened her mouth to argue, but Poseidon held up his hand to stop her. "I can take you somewhere safe. Far from Athena and the mortals who will likely spend their days hunting you down. You don't have much time to decide. Time is no longer your friend."

"What do you mean?" Medusa asked, bracing herself.

Poseidon let out a tired sigh as he rubbed his face. "By sunrise, her retribution will be fulfilled. And to ensure I cannot intervene, she imposed another curse. Anyone, mortal or divine, who lays their eyes on you will meet their demise," he paused before adding, "or the eyes of your serpents."

Stepping back, Medusa could feel the weight of Athena's banishment. Cursed with serpents for hair and a decaying body, she was already doomed. But to also be denied any chance of companionship was an unbearable blow. "Athena wouldn't..."

Poseidon nodded, his expression grave. "I swear to you, she inflicted the final punishment not on you but me. I begged for your life and offered to take you back to my kingdom. But this only enraged her further, and Zeus sided with her demands."

Medusa stared at him in horror.

Poseidon's voice was filled with regret as he gently turned her chin to face him. "I am sorry," he whispered. "I never intended for any of this to happen. I only wanted you and foolishly thought Athena would reject you, allowing me to bring you home. But never in my wildest dreams did I imagine things would turn out this way. Please, let me take you somewhere safe before the sun rises. I will do my best to help from a distance, but this is all I can offer."

Medusa gave a solemn nod and followed Poseidon to a waiting boat. He assisted her as she stepped into the small vessel, and she sat towards the front. Sitting upright confidently, she allowed the sea breeze to dry her tears as the sea god took her to her new home.

She never turned around, refusing to gaze upon the city that once meant so much to her.

That life was over.

Chapter 49- Medusa

13th Century BCE, Sarpedon Island

As the first rays of sunlight began to peek over the horizon, Poseidon expertly guided the boat through the choppy waters towards a distant beach. Medusa's eyes never left the island looming closer and closer, her heart heavy with anticipation and fear. Beneath the surface, a school of shimmering fish darted in and out of view, their movements like a graceful dance beneath the waves.

Medusa looked down to watch, brushing back the tears as they swam away, wishing she could go with them.

When they landed, Poseidon gracefully hopped out. The waves danced around his legs as he extended a hand to help Medusa onto the soft, sandy shore. She took hold and felt a jolt of electricity shoot through her body at his touch.

Poseidon's sea-blue eyes met Medusa's, and they exchanged a wordless glance before turning away from each other, their unspoken emotions hanging heavy in the air.

There was nothing left to say.

Medusa tempted a god, and now she must face her punishment. Alone.

The island that he brought her to was far from welcoming. She struggled against the overwhelming stench of seawater, rotting seafood, and a slight whiff of decaying wood. Medusa pushed forward towards the center of the island, her gaze fixed on the bleached and shattered bones and skulls scattered at her feet.

But what made her most apprehensive was the eerie silence enveloping the island. As she walked further up the beach, she couldn't help but notice the absence of any sound besides the gentle rustle of air and the distant lapping of waves. Time had frozen on the desolate land, leaving an unsettling stillness that sent shivers down her spine.

It was Death's Island, and she was its master.

Poseidon stood behind her, watching as she took in her new surroundings. He knew the curse could have already taken effect, but it didn't matter. Medusa had no desire to see him, to look into his loving eyes, feel the warmth of his touch, or remember how his smile made dimples appear on his cheeks.

The sea god felt the tension between them and knew his presence only made things worse. He wasn't sure what to do—part of him wanted to leave and give Medusa space to come to terms with her new reality, but he didn't want to go just yet.

He frowned as his heart experienced an unfamiliar emotion that mortals often called guilt, which was surprisingly intense for him.

Medusa was also struggling. Although she was thankful for Poseidon's help, she would never forget how he betrayed her. And she didn't want him to see her as she was now. If he was going to remember her, she wanted it to be as she once was, not what she'd become.

"Medusa, I have to go," Poseidon said as the sun danced along the horizon. He played with his ring. "I regret..."

"There's no changing the past with regret," Medusa interjected. We both made mistakes and now I must face the consequences." She held back tears as she fiddled with the bracelet Poseidon had bought her—the one item she'd brought with her to remember happier times.

Poseidon stepped closer, his words promising, "I will find a way to fix this. I won't give up until the curse is lifted." When Medusa said nothing, he asked, "Do you believe me?"

"Yes," she answered, knowing it was nothing more than an empty word. Mortals were of little concern to the gods; her happiness and well-being were unimportant in the grand scheme. As Athena explained, humans were mere playthings for the gods, a source of amusement during their eternal existence.

He would forget about her soon enough, but Medusa vowed to take revenge on the goddess. She was practically immortal, a creature of such immense power that she could kill even the king of the gods.

Athena unintentionally gave her the power, and she would use it to carry out her vengeance.

And it would only take one look to do it.

Poseidon's heart weighed heavily in his chest as he turned away from Medusa, her back stoically facing him. The salty sea air stung his eyes as he gathered her belongings and carefully laid them on a large boulder. His stomach churned with sorrow, a deep ache that radiated throughout his entire being.

He cast one last glance at the woman he loved, not knowing how long it would be before he could see her again.

Poseidon had never planned for this to occur, but it had—now all that remained was for him and Medusa to come to terms with their destiny. He looked at the sun rising in the sky and squinted at its blinding light. He needed to leave now, or he would become Medusa's first victim.

Silently, he cursed his brother and his niece. Athena may have won this battle, but he would win the war.

Medusa's heart sank as she listened to Poseidon leaving without a word. She turned her head, hoping for one last glimpse. All she saw was the water lapping at the shore. Poseidon had vanished into the depths.

She was alone.

The sky above her darkened as thick clouds full of rain loomed over her. Medusa's survival skills took over, and she quickly gathered her things and bundled up in her cloak. With determined steps, she headed towards the dense forest. In the distance, a small hill rose against the horizon, its silhouette suggesting the presence of a cave. She would need to find shelter if she wanted to survive the incoming storm.

Chapter 50- Danaë

8th Century BCE, Seriphos Island

Danaë leisurely wandered through the bustling public square, her senses inundated with the lively sights and sounds surrounding her. Food stalls overflowed with an array of savory delicacies, while taverns beckoned passersby with cheerful laughter and clinking mugs.

The pungent scent of freshly pressed olive oil wafted through the air, intermingling with the briny aroma of the fishermen's catch displayed proudly on their stands. Their animated voices filled the square as they regaled each other with tales of their morning fishing expeditions.

Everywhere she looked, a sense of life and energy pulsed through the square, making her feel alive and invigorated.

The passage of time had been both a blessing and a burden for Danaë as she and Perseus settled into their new life on Seriphos Island. It had been years since she was imprisoned in the tower and cast away on a small boat at the mercy of the treacherous Aegean Sea.

But with each passing day, Danaë found strength and resilience within herself, slowly recovering from the traumas that threatened to overwhelm her. She had faced her worst fears and emerged victorious, basking in the warm embrace of her newfound freedom on the island.

All thanks to her husband, Dictys.

It had been eighteen years since he found Danaë and Perseus on the shores and brought them into his home. At first, their relationship was purely platonic. Danaë took care of the household while raising Zeus's son, and Dictys would spend his days fishing and trading in the nearby city center. As time passed, they grew closer and eventually got married. Danaë found comfort and security in the man who rescued her, leaving her old life behind without regrets.

It took some time, but eventually, Danaë disclosed every horrendous aspect of her time in the tower to her husband. She revealed details about her relationship with Zeus, her father's betrayal, and her son's true lineage.

The couple kept Danaë's origins a secret to safeguard themselves from her father. By keeping this part of their lives private, they could ensure her safety and freedom in marriage and motherhood. However, there was one thing they couldn't hide forever: Perseus' growing powers.

From an early age, he displayed exceptional agility and intelligence that set him apart from other children. He was never afraid to question the beliefs and practices of those in authority, much to his mother's dismay. In fact, he seemed to have a fearless nature bordering on recklessness, always seeking out danger no matter the potential consequences.

For years, Perseus accepted his mother's half-truths that the gods blessed him. But this lie had consequences.

The local kids taunted and provoked him, constantly pushing him to get into fights and arguments. The village elders frequently reprimanded him, and his teachers scolded him. One day, after a particularly tough day at school, Perseus confronted his parents, demanding an explanation for why he felt like an outcast among the other children.

Danaë hesitated to reveal the truth about his bloodline, not wanting to burden her son. However, Dictys believed Perseus deserved to know his biological father's identity.

She relented and told Perseus the truth in all its gory details over dinner.

Perseus kept his emotions tightly guarded. With a steely resolve, he replied curtly, 'If Zeus didn't want to acknowledge their relationship, then neither did he.'

Danaë, on the other hand, couldn't hide her mixed feelings. While she was relieved to share their past, it still stung that Zeus had abandoned her and their son. She knew that even if she were ever to come face to face with her former lover, she would struggle to contain her emotions and keep from lashing out. It was best to keep her distance and let Perseus handle this new knowledge about his lineage.

Thankfully, Perseus held no ill will towards his mother despite her secrets and lies. The family banded together and continued living as if nothing had happened, agreeing to keep their identity a secret.

And today marked the nineteenth anniversary of their arrival. Danaë had planned a special meal and wanted to find the perfect gift for her husband to show how much she appreciated him and all he did for her and Perseus.

As she walked through the busy streets, her gaze was drawn to a man standing at the corner of the square. He stood out amongst the crowd with his tall, slim build and sharp blue eyes that tracked her every step. Despite his simple clothing of a tunic and pants, he emitted an air of danger and confidence. He took a swig from his flask as she grew closer and slyly winked at her.

Danaë's spine tingled with unease as his piercing gaze traveled up and down her body. She tried to divert her attention to the colorful wares at the marketplace stalls but couldn't help glancing back at him. Her fear intensified when their eyes met again, sending a warning chill down her spine.

Frantically, she turned down a bustling alleyway, hoping to blend into the pulsing crowd and lose her pursuer. The feeling of being watched gnawed at her, making her skin prickle with unease. Despite her best efforts, she could hear swift, determined footsteps following behind. She risked a glance over her shoulder and saw the shadowy figure looming just a few feet away.

Her voice trembled as she turned to face him, asking, "Who are you?"

A slow, menacing smirk spread across his face. "Just a passerby," he uttered, his gaze lingering on Danaë. "But I couldn't help noticing you in the market. You don't look like you're from this island."

Danaë's heart dropped as a wave of mortification washed over her. She had always felt out of place among the fair-haired and porcelain-skinned people of the island. Her dark, olive skin tone seemed to stand out like a bruise against their flawless complexions. But never had anyone pointed it out so bluntly, leaving Danaë feeling exposed and vulnerable.

And worried.

Before she could devise a way out of the situation, he closed the gap between them, standing so close that she could feel his warmth radiating toward her. A bead of sweat rolled down her face as she realized she had been tricked into his trap. He arched an eyebrow, his knowing eyes drilling into hers. "You're not from around here, are you?"

The intensity of the man's gaze sent nervousness coursing through Danaë. He was commanding, and she worried he was somehow connected to her father. She needed to find Perseus and Dictys fast. They would have to leave the island if he was one of her father's guards.

"My apologies, sir," Danaë said in an even tone, trying to move around him. "I'm looking for a present for my husband. He and my son are waiting for me at home, and I have taken too long already."

"Your husband?" he asked in amusement. "I wasn't aware you were married."

"Yes, I am. My husband is Dictys, and he is waiting for me." Danaë tried to step the other way, but the man blocked her way again.

"Dictys? The fisherman?" the man asked, his lips curling up in a knowing smirk. She nodded in confirmation. "You don't seem like the typical fisherman's wife. To me, it looks like you have royal blood."

Danaë glanced up at him in surprise. How did he know?

The man chuckled, "Ah, yes. You do, don't you? I can see it now. You have a queen's face."

"You are mistaken. The sun is playing tricks on your eyes. Now, please excuse me; I must head home."

The man's eyes remained on Danaë as if he were trying to solve a puzzle. He slowly backed up, allowing her to escape. Keeping her composure and poise, she walked away without another word.

However, her steps faltered when she heard him shout, "I will see you soon, Danaë. We have much to discuss."

Danaë ran all the way home.

Chapter 51- Danaë

8th Century BCE, Seriphos Island

Panic flared in Danaë's eyes as she frantically threw her clothing into a chest. Her voice rose as she called out to her husband, "We must leave now!"

Dictys perched on a rickety wooden stool, his azure eyes reflecting deep concern as he watched his wife with furrowed brows. "Danaë," he asked, "is it possible you're jumping to conclusions? Are you sure he knew who you are?"

Danaë nodded, her long dark tresses bouncing against her flushed cheeks as she tossed Dictys' fishing gear into a nearby basket. "He said my name," she cried.

Dictys stood up and wrapped his arms around her waist, brushing back the stray strands of hair falling over her eyes. "Love, everyone knows who you are," he reminded her.

Danaë's sobs muffled her words as she pressed her face into her husband's tunic. "He knows where we are now," she sobbed, "and he'll find me. My father will take us back. I'll be trapped in the tower again."

"Don't worry, Mom. We won't let anything happen to you," Perseus called out, his voice unwavering as he stood in the doorway, his tunic damp from sweat. He had raced home from the temple, sensing something was wrong and needing to ensure his family was unharmed.

Danaë's eyes narrowed, her hands clenching tighter around her husband's arm. "You don't know my father. He'll stop at nothing," she scoffed. "Believe me. I have been on the receiving end of his madness."

Perseus stood up taller. "I'm sure we won't have a problem," he declared, his gray eyes sparkling with excitement. "After all, I am Zeus's son..." Mid-sentence, a gloved hand covered his mouth as he was pulled backward into an iron-tight hold. Perseus fought to break free, but the man's grip was too firm.

"Knock it off, kid," a voice growled in his ear. "You're only making it worse for yourself." Perseus' eyes watered from the stench of the man's breath, a combination of alcohol and decaying teeth, but he stopped struggling.

"Just the woman and child." Danaë tensed as she heard a familiar voice call out from outside the house. "They are to be unharmed," the voice added as an afterthought. Two more men rushed into the home, and her heart sank as she realized it was the royal guard.

"Stop!" Dictys yelled, a desperate plea as a guard shoved him against the wall. Pain exploded through his body, the cracking of bones echoing in his ears. He grimaced as a foot connected with the back of his knee, and he fell to the ground.

Another guard grabbed his wife, effortlessly overpowering her smaller frame. She struggled and writhed in his grasp, trying to bite him. The man's hand tightened around her fragile neck, cutting off her air supply as she desperately fought for survival.

"I will kill you myself," Dictys spat, his words laced with fear and determination as his face collided with the unforgiving plaster. The impact echoed through the room, leaving a sickening crack in its wake, and blood began to trickle down from a gash on his forehead. His vision blurred for a moment before he shook off the dizziness.

The guard let out a low, amused chuckle as Danaë broke free from his grip and ran for her husband. With surprising speed, he snatched her back up in a tight embrace. "Careful now, Dictys," he warned with a smirk. "That's not what the king wants to hear." His eyes flickered with both amusement and underlying menace. "Thanks to his divine grace, you still have your life. But this woman and child will come with us."

Danaë let out a piercing screech, her body thrashing as she kicked the guard dragging her towards the door. "You can't do this!" she yelled, fighting against his hold.

The man waiting outside strolled into the room, eyes scanning the area with disgust before landing on Danaë. "I assure you," he declared confidently, "I have the right. According to law, someone of royal status cannot marry an individual of lower standing." His gaze flickered to where Dictys was being held captive. "That's why I'm here," he announced, "to rescue you."

Danaë's breath hitched in her throat. The man had traded his casual city clothes for an extravagant tunic, a midnight blue cloak, and a delicate crown made of gold and albite. His face offered nothing as he gazed at her, anticipating her response.

"King Polydectes!" Dictys exclaimed in disbelief as the guard freed him to bow before the ruler.

The king offered Danaë a warm smile as if he expected her to be relieved and overjoyed at his rescue. His sharp gaze narrowed in annoyance as Danaë remained silent.

He blinked once. "Imagine my surprise when a tiny bird fluttered into my court with news of King Acrisius' daughter hiding on my island. I couldn't resist the opportunity to see for myself if the rumor were true." The king's voice dripped with sarcasm as he shook his head in disbelief. "And lo and behold, here you are." His expression was cold and calculated, carrying a threat that lingered in the air like a thick fog.

Danaë's disdainful glare surprised him as he fought back his rising anger. "You have a choice," he said through gritted teeth. "Either make this easy for us both or make it difficult. A life for a life - what will it be, princess?"

Danaë could barely stand on her own, relying on the guard's grip to keep her from collapsing. But her words came out measured and dripping with warning. "Release my husband. He knows nothing."

King Polydectes grabbed her chin, tilting her face upwards to meet his gaze. "It's against the law to lie to the king." He let out a frustrated sigh, shaking his head. "I have no desire to punish your husband for your transgressions. Come with me, and he lives."

Perseus' howl of fury echoed through the room, startling everyone. Danaë's mouth gaped in awe as she watched an ethereal aura swirl and envelope her son. In a dazzling burst of energy, Perseus unleashed a powerful blast that sent guards flying across the room like ragdolls. The king dropped to his knees, shielding his head with his arms.

Time stood still as Perseus stared at his hands in disbelief, then turned to his mother with a bewildered expression.

The room fell into a hushed silence as King Polydectes slowly drew himself up to his feet. He straightened his cloak, brushing off the dirt with a self-satisfied smile playing on his lips. "Ah, the child of Zeus. Your reputation precedes you," he chuckled, eyes gleaming with amusement. "You may attempt to attack me, but I assure you, your so-called father will lie lifeless on the ground before you lay a hand on me. The choice is yours." He pointed to the guard, a knife poised to slit his father's throat.

Perseus's body tensed with rage as he stared at Dictys, still on his knees. He prepared himself to retaliate, but his mother's eyes begged him to hold back, her head shaking from side to side.

With slow, calculated steps, the king approached Zeus's son. His words dripped with disdain, a venomous tone that oozed from his mouth like poison. "I always get what I want," he spat with a sneer. "Demigod or not, you will not stand in my way." King Polydectes leaned in closer, his warm breath grazing Perseus' cheek. "Your mother is now mine."

Perseus clenched his hands into fists as he glared at the man before him. "My mother belongs to no one," he shot back, his voice dripping with defiance. The muscles in his jaw flexed as he fought against the anger bubbling inside of him. "You will not get away with this."

The king's voice sounded rich and regal as he spoke, "Of course, I will," he replied, his words dripping with arrogance. But then, a wicked smile crossed his face as he asked, "Unless you are willing to make a deal."

"What?" Perseus asked, his eyes narrowing as he studied the man before him.

"Retrieve a weapon for me," the king said, a hungry gleam in his eye.

Perseus scowled at the king, considering his unusual request. All he wanted was a weapon in exchange for his parents? It sounded too easy. "Why haven't you sent one of your guards to get it?" He motioned to the man holding his mother captive. Perseus arched an eyebrow, leaning in and whispering, "Or are they not competent enough to find it?" His lips curved into a smirk, provoking the guard, who growled in response to the insult.

King Polydectes raised a hand to stop his man, admitting, "I have dispatched many, but none have returned." He paused, considering the boy in front of him. "But perhaps you, son of Zeus, are better suited for the task."

"If I bring you this weapon, will you let my parents go? Unharmed?"

The king shrugged. "Yes. Fetch me the weapon, and you will be free to return to your insignificant life without further repercussions."

Perseus turned a deaf ear to his mother's desperate plea. The weight of his family's lives hung in the balance, and he needed to do whatever it took to save them.

Perseus schooled his face into a bored look. "What do you need me to find?"

"It is not an *it*," King Polydectes replied. "A lone woman residing on a deserted island—a simple task if you think about it."

Perseus was taken aback. "You want me to bring back a woman for you?" he asked, ensuring he heard the king correctly.

The king took a moment to think, tilting his head thoughtfully. "She is not just any woman," he clarified. "She is a beast who defied the gods and suffered their retribution. If you deliver her head to me, I will release your parents from captivity."

Perseus gazed at the king, his expression filled with shock. "You want me to retrieve a head for you?" he questioned.

The king nodded.

Perseus paused to consider the proposal, glancing at his mother for approval.

Danaë met her son's eyes before looking up as if seeking the god's guidance. A sorrowful expression he had never witnessed before cloaked her face. She turned back to him, straightened her back, and gave her consent with a simple nod.

Perseus pivoted to King Polydectes. "I will do it," he declared. "I will defeat the monster and return with its head."

The king clapped with satisfaction. "Excellent," he exclaimed. "Your parents will be taken care of while you retrieve their ransom." He stepped forward, lowering his voice so that only Perseus could hear. "But let me make this clear, son of Zeus: my patience has its limits. If you are not back within three full moons, your father will meet his end, and your mother will become my bride."

Perseus nodded once, and the king motioned for the guards to leave. As tears streamed down Danaë's face, she glanced once more at her son, whispering a prayer for his safety.

Dictys followed. Before he left, he glanced back at the young man he raised since infancy. "Be safe, my son."

"I will see you soon, Father," Perseus promised. "One way or another."

Chapter 52- Lilith

8th Century BCE, City of the Unspoken

L ilith wanted nothing more than for the woman beside her to stop crying. The incessant sound was like nails on a chalkboard, testing her patience. She'd been trying desperately to connect with her for hours, but despite her best efforts, they were making no progress.

"For the love of the gods, we are wasting time." Lilith grabbed Danaë's hands and pulled them away from her eyes. "Just listen. I'm offering you a chance to make amends."

Danaë's eyelids fluttered as she struggled to compose herself, using her sleeve to wipe away the tears streaming down her face. "I... I killed her," she whispered in agony, her voice cracking with emotion as she grappled with the weight of her actions.

Lilith tilted her head from side to side, attempting to loosen the tightness in her neck. "You did," she replied, exasperation clear in her tone. "It's unfortunate, but we can't change what's already been done. Now you must right the wrong," Lilith retorted in frustration, standing with her hands on her hips.

Danaë fell to her knees, grasping Lilith's cloak with trembling hands. She buried her face into the fabric, soaking it with tears and muffled sobs. "They took everything away from me," she cried out, her voice choked with grief and anger. "I didn't deserve any of this."

Lilith released a long, defeated breath. "I know," she acknowledged, feeling the weight and urgency of her mission pressing on her. She couldn't waste time comforting Danaë's broken heart; they were running out of time.

"The gods have abandoned me!" Another piercing cry echoed through the air, and Lilith's last thread of self-restraint snapped. She reached down, forcing Danaë's eyes to meet hers.

"That's quite enough," Lilith commanded, exuding her power like threads of shimmering silver that tightened around the woman, rendering her motionless. If she wouldn't cooperate willingly, Lilith would make her. "Yes, all those things have happened. You made a decision: a life for a life." The woman's eyes opened in horror, but Lilith pressed on.

"Neither choice was ideal, I admit. But you must live with the consequences and decide what to do now. Are you going to spend your days crying over the past or do something with your life?"

Danaë's eyes narrowed. "I never wanted this. I never asked to live forever. And I certainly never wanted to be responsible for taking a life." She stared at her hands as if she could see the blood that stained them.

Lilith couldn't help but feel pity for the woman. She knew all too well the torment that haunted Danaë every night and would continue to do so for the rest of her long life. A small token from Hera, a reminder of the horrible deed Danaë committed.

The unthinkable sin.

Danaë fell in love with a god and had a son with him.

Danaë bore the burden of that decision despite the fact that Zeus initiated their relationship, and she was simply an innocent victim. When Hera found out about Perseus, her wrath knew no bounds. It was then that she and Athena presented Danaë with a supposed 'choice,' even though it wasn't truly a choice in the end.

Spend an eternity living with the guilt of her sins or watching her son die at Medusa's hands.

Danaë ultimately chose the path Lilith anticipated. While it may not have been ideal, it was Danaë's only way forward. In the end, her son became a unifying force for a divided kingdom and ushered in an exciting era for his country.

But she would also be the reason an innocent died.

After Perseus returned from his mission for King Polydectes and brought back Medusa's severed head, Danaë and Dictys fled Seriphos Island. They followed their son, but when Dictys died, it was time to fulfill her end of the agreement.

Fortunately, luck was on her side. Poseidon intervened and helped her escape Hera's revenge, bringing her to the City of the Unspoken along with the one mortal he dared to love. A gesture of mercy for the woman his deeds had condemned to an eternal existence of isolation and death.

Medusa.

Lilith's lips curled up into a small smile as she thought back to Medusa's arrival. Despite being beheaded, immortality was an inescapable destiny.

Despite losing her head, Medusa remained surprisingly calm and dismissed it as a minor setback. With Poseidon's help, Arawn reversed Athena's punishment within the limits of the Otherworld. Her form was restored to its original state, allowing her to reunite with her sisters again.

In a strange and unexpected turn of events, Medusa decided to keep her hair as a writhing mass of serpents.

The wriggling creatures were her salvation, providing comfort, protection, and strength to become the confident and resilient woman she was today.

They also taught her a valuable lesson: never give in to fear.

"Being immortal is not a curse if you use it wisely," Lilith explained, returning her attention to Danaë. "That's what I'm offering you: an opportunity to become something greater. I offer you forgiveness and the chance to leave a legacy."

"What do you want me to do?" Danaë asked cautiously.

Lilith understood her hesitation. Danaë had every reason to be cautious of the gods, having witnessed their cruelty firsthand and narrowly escaping with her life.

"Protect something of mine. Something that mortals and gods are looking for. Something so powerful, it could change history," Lilith explained.

"And in return?"

"I will give you a life worth living." Lilith's hand gently cupped the woman's cheek as she made her promise. She showed Danaë glimpses of her past, plans, and goals. As Danaë absorbed these images, she nodded in agreement, understanding what Lilith was proposing.

"I accept," Danaë said, and Lilith breathed a sigh of relief.

She hadn't revealed everything. She couldn't bear to burden the woman with the crushing weight of what lay ahead, a fate too cruel and overwhelming for anyone to handle. But Lilith reveled in her bold defiance of the Fates, knowing the consequences would be dire.

Chapter 53- Lilith

Modern Day- City of the Unspoken

Moll's voice echoed through the long, dim hallway, punctuated by her cane tapping against the stone floor. "Lilith? Are you in there?" she called out, her words bouncing off the walls and disappearing into the shadows.

A smile tugged at Lilith's lips as she got up from her favorite chair by the roaring fire, stretching to relieve the stiffness in her neck. It had been a long night already. Moll's restless thoughts had awakened her hours ago, and she'd been anticipating her arrival.

Not that she needed to eavesdrop. The Library of the Unread had been stirring with life since Moll arrived. Books shuffled and whispered, pages rustled and turned as if eager to be remembered. Lilith didn't understand how or why, but the library knew when a Writer was near—as if it understood the one person who could breathe new life into its forgotten tales was within reach.

And now there were three.

With Moll, Chloe, and Aelle within the walls of the City of the Unspoken, the books were more energetic than usual. Just last night, Lilith had to sprint after a particularly mischievous book that had escaped from its shelf and was making its way up the stairs towards Aelle's room. It took all her strength to wrangle it back into place and secure it with a heavy leather strap. Even then, she could feel it vibrating with rebellious energy beneath her touch.

"In here," Lilith called out, heading to the coffee cart. "I made a fresh pot," she offered, holding up a mug. Moll nodded, leaning heavily on her cane for support, and Lilith eyed it with interest.

The cane was a weathered extension of its owner, crafted from dark wood and adorned with intricate carvings that told her life story. Lilith had never seen her without it, serving as a walking aid and a symbol of Moll's strength and resilience. But every now and again, a new carving would appear, etched into the surface with delicate precision. Each carving held its own meaning, a tribute to a moment or person in Moll's past she wanted to keep close in memory.

Moll caught her stare and slid her hand over the new addition with a frown.

"Did you sleep well?" Lilith asked, opting not to question her about it. She poured a generous amount of whiskey into Moll's mug and handed it to her. Moll lifted an eyebrow. Lilith chuckled as she added a little more.

"I was working," Moll replied, taking a sip. She let out a self-satisfying sigh before glancing over at the grandfather clock. "Time is not on our side."

"Did you find it?" Lilith asked, interested. Moll hoped to figure out what Book of the Veiled the Fates hid in the Library of the Unread. One of them had to be nearby. They just didn't know which one or where. One thing was for sure: the Fates did an exceptional job concealing it from them.

Moll rubbed her tired eyes, her shoulders sinking in defeat. "No," she said with a heavy sigh. "Nothing useful, at least. But I'm fairly certain it isn't yours."

Lilith shrugged, trying to hide her disappointment. "It's not a big deal," she said. "My book is out there somewhere. Lucifer and I have waited this long. What are a few more weeks?" She moved back to her chair, and Moll settled next to her.

They both fell silent, lost in their thoughts. The grandfather clock chimed in the background, the constant ticking a reminder of how time was slipping away. Everyone would gather in just a few hours, and the next chapter in their lives would begin.

Lilith's finger traced a slow, steady path around the rim of her mug as she asked, "Is that what's bothering you? Not finding my book?"

"No." Moll's slender fingers grazed the cool metal of the key tucked away in her pocket, tracing the familiar ridges and indentations along its worn corners. She pulled it out slowly, staring at it as she said, "My book only has three blank pages."

Lilith's eyes opened in surprise as her friend's words sank in. "I never knew Writers could see the end of their books," she exclaimed, her voice tinged with awe and curiosity.

Moll shook her head, realizing the rarity of the situation. She had never heard of it happening before; the Fates wouldn't allow it. But now, with only three pages left, Moll knew her story was approaching its inevitable conclusion.

"I think my story ends with you, Taliesin, and Morrigan," she admitted.

Lilith rose, her movement hesitant as she kneeled in front of Moll. She took her friend's hand into hers. "I'm so sorry," she murmured, her voice laced with genuine remorse and sadness.

Moll chuckled and wiped away Lilith's tears. "My dear, I never desired to live forever. Trust me, I've already seen more than my fair share of the past, present, and future. Now it's time for a younger person to take on the responsibility."

Lilith's heart ached as she asked, "What about your daughter? Will you get to see her again?" Lilith knew Moll had never stopped looking for Diana and was willing to bet that death could not stop her from continuing the search.

"If the Fates allow." The love and determination in Moll's eyes were a testament to the unbreakable bond between a mother and child.

Lilith leaned back, her weight shifting onto her heels. "Will you tell the others?"

"No," Moll frowned. "And neither will you."

Chapter 54- Chloe

Modern Day- City of the Unspoken

Eidolon and I stayed up until the early morning hours discussing Lilith, Lucifer, and the imprisoned souls in the Otherworld. By dawn, I barely mustered enough energy to stumble into the shower.

Steam rose in delicate wisps as hot water poured over my body, soothing my aching muscles. Standing there, I couldn't help but reflect on how much my life had changed in such a short period.

As someone who usually despised change, I was surprised to find that instead of feeling overwhelmed or anxious, excitement rose within me. It was a sensation that had been absent for far too long—the thrill of something unfamiliar and unpredictable, the potential for endless opportunities. Each droplet of water hitting my skin felt like shedding my old self and emerging as a renewed version of who I wanted to be.

I was shaking off the shackles of growing old before my time.

Everything was possible now.

Like falling in love.

My history of making sound decisions about love was not exactly stellar. Embarrassingly, I once fell for a man who claimed to be separated from his wife, but later, I found out they were still married. Looking back, I should have seen the red flags. But instead, I got caught up in the fantasy of a perfect happily ever after and paid for it in the end. The asshole drove off into the horizon with a brand-new set of tires, and I got left with the bill.

Or the best friend turned boyfriend who preferred playing video games and leaving dirty laundry strewn around. I put up with him for a year before realizing all he wanted was for me to cook his meals and stay quiet while he finished 'just one more round.'

During my twenties, I was infatuated with a man I believed was my soulmate. Ignoring the fact that he only wanted to be 'friends,' I convinced myself that he would eventually realize that I was the one for him. He found his perfect match—it just wasn't me. Six months later, my dream guy married his dream girl, adopted two dogs, and had two beautiful children.

I got an upgraded coffee pot.

What I wanted was the type of love Isabelle and Watson shared—one that could last 700 years and still feel like it wasn't enough. I wanted someone to look at me with the same adoration as the man in my vision looked at Lilith. Someone who would make me feel like I was the center of their universe. Somebody who knew my favorite coffee and would take me to a bookstore on a date.

A sigh escaped my lips. The idea was lovely, but I couldn't pursue it. Eidolon and I may have been meant to be 'soul mates,' but the thought had to take a backseat for now.

Our priority was finding the Book of the Veiled. If I was being honest with myself, it was a task that excited me more than the idea of falling in love.

Three floors beneath me was the most magnificent library, hidden from the world's knowledge. It held a compilation of tales spanning thousands of years, containing all humanity's forgotten moments. Within its walls lay the truths behind the inconsistencies in history and every story missing from the ancient archives.

If I wanted to, I could spend eternity walking up and down the aisles of bookshelves without ever reading the same title twice. But it would also mean staying in the City of the Unspoken. Sacrificing myself for knowledge, just as Odin did.

Something Eidolon couldn't do. I couldn't explain how I knew, but I just did. He didn't belong here anymore than I belonged in the Otherworld as a mortal.

As I turned, the water cascading over my head and down my back, a frown deepened on my brow. The decision before me was heavy, its magnitude pressing down like a physical force. To gain full access to the Library of the Unread, I would have to make an impossible choice. I would have to walk away from everything I knew and loved, leaving behind any possibility of a future with Eidolon.

Not that drastic decisions hadn't been made before for knowledge.

Odin gave up his eye, plunging it into Mimir's well, and impaled himself on his spear, Gungnir, in a symbolic act of sacrifice. Then he hung himself from Yggdrasil, the tree of life, for nine days and nights, seeking the wisdom of other realms and understanding of the runes.

In a moment of temptation, Adam and Eve chose knowledge over blind obedience, which resulted in their expulsion from paradise as punishment for their wrongdoing.

Knowledge was dangerous according to all the myths and legends.

'But so was hope.' My eyes darted around the bathroom, searching for the source of the unfamiliar voice. It wasn't Eidolon. It was a woman. Soft and delicate, like a breeze from a fairy's wing, the ethereal tone danced between reality and imagination, creating an eerie atmosphere in the small space.

"Hello?" I whispered, praying for no response.

'Hi!'

My eyes widened in shock as I leaped out of the shower. Grabbing a soft towel, I raced to get dressed, convinced I was losing my mind.

'You are not going crazy,' the voice reassured me with a chuckle.

My body tensed as I frantically scanned the room for the source of the mysterious voice. "I beg to differ," I retorted. "Hearing voices is the textbook definition of crazy."

The voice sighed. *'We have been waiting for you, daughter of Morrigan. Have you returned to finish what she started?'*

"Depends," I murmured, leaning towards the mirror. "Who is she, and what did she start?"

'She promised to find us a home,' the woman said sadly. *'But she never came back.'*

"A home for who?" I questioned, baffled.

'The ones whose stories never got written.'

I leaned heavily against the cool, porcelain sink, my fingers gripping the edges. Was I talking to the books Lilith told me about? The orphans of the Library of the Unread?

"I think you've mistaken me for someone else. You should talk to Eidolon. This kind of stuff falls into his realm of expertise," I explained, staring at myself in the mirror and feeling foolish.

'No, daughter of Morrigan. You are what we need. Eidolon can only see what has lived. Not what hasn't.'

"What exactly does that mean?" I asked, my eyes narrowing. "Are you saying you're not human yet? If you're not human and not figments of my imagination, what are you?"

'We are the library,' the voice responded.

I froze. The library was alive, just as I suspected. My thoughts raced with the implications of what my new imaginary friend was saying. If the library was alive, it could help me find the Book of the Veiled.

"Chloe? Who are you talking to?" Eidolon's voice called from the other side of the door.

I jumped back from the sink, bumping my head against the metal towel rack. My head throbbed in pain as I reached up to rub the injured spot, grimacing at the sting.

"Nobody," I called out with a shaky voice. "Just singing to myself."

"Didn't sound like singing. Sounds like you are talking to someone."

"Do I criticize you when you hum while eating? No. So, no comments from the peanut gallery about my singing," I snapped back, annoyed.

"Okay," he laughed. "Once your so-called serenade is finished, we need to head to breakfast. We're going to be late," he warned. "And I don't hum when I eat," he muttered, striding away from the doorway.

"Hello?" I whispered, not wanting Eidolon to hear me. "Are you still here?"

The bathroom was quiet, and I felt a twinge of disappointment. Trying to brush the strange conversation off as my overactive imagination playing tricks on me, I finished getting ready. Taking a deep breath before mustering a smile, I entered the bedroom. Eidolon's dark, piercing eyes followed my every move as I purposely avoided eye contact.

"Ready?" I asked, pulling my damp hair into a haphazard bun and throwing on a somewhat clean sweater and boots.

When I turned to face Eidolon, my stomach plummeted. He looked amazing, dressed casually in jeans, a hoodie, and a backward baseball cap. I blinked twice, my glasses sliding down my nose. I readjusted them, embarrassment washing over me as Eidolon watched in amusement.

"Ready," he winked. "Let's go save the Otherworld."

Chapter 55- Chloe

Modern Day- City of the Unspoken

As we entered the dining room, Moll sat at the head of the table, her face a mask of forced politeness. My fingers instinctively tightened around Eidolon's hand. He squeezed back, his gaze fixed on his grandmother. A tumultuous mix of emotions was visible in his eyes—relief mingled with barely contained anger.

Eidolon took a deep breath, calming himself. "Moll," he greeted as she struggled to rise from her chair. She leaned heavily on her cane for support and slowly closed the distance. Every step was a battle against discomfort and weakness, but determination sparkled in her eyes as she finally stood before him.

"Eidolon," she whispered, her voice trembling as her eyes locked on his. "I'm sorry..."

"You lied to me, Moll," Eidolon interrupted. His voice was heavy with accusation, and his grip on my hand tightened to the point of pain. "The one thing we promised we would never do."

"I can explain..."

"I don't think you can." Eidolon's voice carried a weight of emotion as my focus flickered to the strange noises coming from the library. "You knew where my parents were and who my father was," he accused.

Moll's shoulders slumped, and tears gathered in her eyes as the ground began to tremble. Wide-eyed, I watched the chandelier sway, its crystal prisms casting shimmering patterns across the walls. A low, ominous rustling sound echoed through the room—a warning of something dark and dangerous approaching.

The library was reacting to the intense emotion again, and I couldn't shake the sinking feeling that whatever was about to happen would not be pleasant. My breath caught in my throat as I tapped Eidolon's shoulder to get his attention. He ignored me.

"Eidolon, please try to understand," Moll said, her voice strained as she looked past him.

I followed her gaze to the dining room table. My mouth dropped. The table's carvings shimmered with a dazzling silver light, their movement resembling the dancing lights of a moonless night on the ocean.

"What the hell?" My whispered question hung in the air, swallowed up by the chaotic rattling of paintings in their frames and the clattering of objects on the buffet. It was as if the entire room had come alive, trembling with an unknown force.

Aelle burst through the doorway, her eyes wide and filled with fear. Her breath came in quick gasps as she took in the scene before her. "What the hell is going on? The whole damn house is shaking."

Our eyes locked. "You feel it, too?" I asked.

Aelle's sharp, assessing gaze swept over the room, settling on the billowing curtains. Despite the closed window, they danced and twisted with energy, intensifying the unsettling atmosphere. She nodded once, frowning.

"It was me," Moll confessed, her voice thick with emotion. Her brows furrowed as her eyes darted nervously around the room, unable to meet anyone's gaze. "I got carried away," she continued, her tone filled with regret, "and the library responded."

"What do you mean, 'responded'?" I ask slowly, struggling to understand.

Moll motioned for us to take a seat. I hesitated, eyeing the silverware. I wasn't in the mood to get stabbed by a finicky butter knife. Eidolon noticed my uncertainty and pulled out a chair for me.

"You good?" he whispered into my ear as he drew his seat closer to mine.

I nodded, shifting my gaze towards Max, casually leaning against the doorframe with his eyes glued to Aelle. She remained fixated on the pictures, her brow furrowed as they righted themselves.

He sighed, running his fingers through his unkept hair before walking over and touching her on the elbow. She darted a glance at him, her expression tight. As he leaned in and whispered something in her ear, his hand moved down to rest on the small of her back. A smile formed on her lips, and they both took their seats.

Lilith materialized from the inky shadows as if summoned by some unseen force, her unnatural eyes shining like two orbs of molten gold and green. Moll greeted her with a reassuring smile. She nodded in acknowledgment before settling into her seat and pouring herself a drink as Moll sat beside her.

"It's not just me. It's the three of us," Moll clarified, glancing sheepishly at me and Aelle. She ran her fingers over her cane, tracing the lines of a half-carved face. "As Writers, we have a unique bond with the library, which responds to our heightened emotions. I've never experienced it before, but my predecessor warned me it was possible."

"See, I told you I wasn't insane," Aelle declared in triumph, looking at Max with an annoyed expression. "He thought I was losing my mind when I refused to enter the library. He accused me of being over-dramatic." Max blushed at being called out but didn't try to deny it. "Things got even stranger when Chloe appeared," Aelle continued, shooting me an irritated glare. "Especially at night."

Lilith's eyebrow arched in surprise. "That's why you wouldn't come out of your room?"

"Why else?" Aelle scoffed and rolled her eyes. "I wouldn't have avoided the library if I hadn't sensed something was wrong. Every time I entered, I felt an odd vibration and heard murmurs. But no one else was in the room. The sensation would fade once I left," she shrugged. "So I stayed away until somebody could clarify what was happening."

"I had the same experience," I offered. "I heard bizarre noises in the library last night. Then someone or something decided to make an appearance while I was taking a shower." Eidolon glanced at me questioningly. "I didn't want you to think I was losing my mind," I admitted, embarrassed.

Lilith's curious eyes sparkled with intrigue as she leaned in, resting on her elbows. "What did it say?" she asked.

I paused, unsure of how to explain the strange conversation. "It asked if I was here to finish what she started."

Lilith's mischievous eyes darted a sly glance at Moll, her lips curling into a small triumphant smile. She turned her attention to Aelle. "What did they say to you?

Aelle's stormy gaze narrowed, her jaw muscles tensing. Max reached out and placed a comforting hand on her arm. She briefly looked at his touch before meeting his eyes. He nodded in support.

"They told me I had work to do," Aelle said with a tinge of exasperation. Her attention flickered to Moll. "And then the library literally threw books at me."

"Books?" Eidolon asked. Aelle nodded.

Lilith's eyes danced as she asked, "Where are they now? The books?"

Aelle shrugged. "Probably still strewn about on the floor. When one nearly hit me, I ran."

Moll and Lilith exchanged a knowing glance, their unspoken communication almost undetectable.

"Do you two know what books she is referring to?" I questioned.

Moll's lips curled into a secretive grin. "We might have an idea. We'll investigate after breakfast." The anticipation in her voice was palpable and piqued my curiosity even more.

"Did someone say breakfast? Great! I'm starving," exclaimed Sydney as he walked in, his stomach growling in agreement. Victor, Isabelle, and Watson followed close behind.

"What's going on?" Watson asked, his eyes scanning the room and resting on each of us in turn. He pulled out a chair for Isabelle. "You look like you've seen a ghost."

Aelle gave a wry smirk as she poured herself a cup of coffee and reached for a flaky pastry. "Depends on how you define ghosts," she replied cryptically.

Chapter 56- Chloe

Modern Day- City of the Unspoken

"So, what was everyone up to last night?" Sydney asked as he piled bacon on his plate. "There were some rumblings in the castle, but I was too tired to get up and investigate."

Moll, Aelle, and I exchanged surprised glances. "You felt it, too?" Moll asked, sounding taken aback.

"Of course, I could," Sydney said with a mischievous smile, buttering a piece of toast and slathering it with raspberry jam. "Being a shifter has its perks," he claimed, taking a bite. "When there is a disturbance in the force, we know."

"That will be helpful," Odin declared as he swept into the dining room, his deep voice resonating through the space. His midnight black cloak billowed behind him, giving the impression of a powerful storm brewing. Geri and Freki padded silently by his side, their sharp eyes scanning the room.

As soon as they spotted Victor, they headed towards him with calculated steps. A faint smirk tugged at my lips as I monitored Victor's uneasy expression, his gaze darting nervously between the wolves and their master.

"Don't worry, they already ate," Odin commented as he took a seat.

Victor frowned. "Reassuring," he muttered.

Freyja stepped into the room, her linen shirt splattered with blood. Her leather pants were in a less-than-ideal state, with stains, dirt, and an unknown black substance covering them. A beautifully crafted dagger was strapped to her thigh, adorned with a slender rawhide grip and a glimmering blade that caught the light from the chandelier.

She sat in her customary chair to the left of Lilith, reaching over to pour herself a cup of coffee. "We once had a group of shifters working with us. In terms of hunting skills, they were unmatched. I would give anything to have another pack," she commented, looking up at Sydney appreciatively. "Bree told me your fighting abilities match your instincts."

Sydney's posture straightened at the mention of Bree's name, and his expression contorted into a scowl. He only uttered a disinterested "hmmm" before resuming his breakfast. Freyja raised her hands in surrender, chuckling at his reaction.

"She leaves in the morning," Lilith mentioned, glancing at the shifter. "I know she would appreciate some company."

"She's probably got more important things on her plate. Secrets to keep, other men to aggravate," Sydney scoffed as he took another bite. "Wouldn't want to get in her way."

"I believe you may have underestimated young Bree. Don't be too hasty in saying no. Listen to what she has to say first, and then decide. She's currently in the training arena," Odin said as he sipped his whiskey, observing Sydney above his glass. "Then again, this is a judgment-free zone if you're too scared."

Odin's suggestion took aback Freyja, but she kept her thoughts to herself. Instead, she turned to Sydney and gave him a wicked smile. "Leave the young shifter alone, Odin. We Valkyries are a formidable bunch. Not everyone can handle us."

Sydney's jaw tensed, the muscles in his defined jawline rippling as he placed his fork on the table. With a scowl, he glared at Freyja. "There is nothing I can't manage," his voice dropped to a dangerous level. "Not even a Valkyrie." Freyja merely shrugged and speared a piece of fruit from the bowl in front of her. He shifted his attention to Eidolon, "What do you think?"

Eidolon leaned back in his chair, rubbing his chin. "I think it's your decision. But if it were me, I would go."

Sydney sat on the edge of his seat, deep in thought. After a moment, a small smile curled at the corners of his lips as he faced Victor. "Think you can run things while I'm gone?" he asked, trying to sound severe but failing as a hint of amusement danced in his eyes.

"I'll do my best," Victor replied in his usual dry wit. I had to suppress the urge to laugh.

"It's decided then," Sydney declared as he stood up and stretched. "I'll go. We can't risk Bree wandering off alone; she might get lost."

"I am sure she will be relieved to hear that," Freyja agreed, and I caught her rolling her eyes. If there was anyone who didn't need saving or help- it was Bree.

Sydney's head bobbed with the assuredness of a seasoned fighter as he surveyed the faces around the table. "Are you guys sure you'll be okay without me?" he asked, his eyes betraying a hint of uncertainty. They landed on me, and I knew that I was the one he was most worried about. He had promised to protect me and leaving me behind was going against his instincts.

"Go, Sydney," I said. "It's your opportunity for the next great adventure. And don't worry about Eidolon," I motioned towards him with my head. I'll make sure to keep him safe. God knows he needs all the help he can get." As predicted, Eidolon's expression twisted into a scowl while Isabelle erupted into laughter.

Sydney laughed lightly before walking over to me and embracing me warmly. He bent down, his voice soft as he whispered in my ear. "You're tougher than you think, lil' Writer. Remember to take care of yourself." As he stood up, he playfully ruffled my hair with his giant hand and flashed a bright smile. "And whatever you do, don't die," he joked as he left the room, whistling.

I watched Sydney's tall figure as he walked out of the room, gradually disappearing from my line of sight. Despite his attempts to lighten the mood, I couldn't shake off the growing unease and concern. We had been friends since the beginning, and I would miss his jokes and fun-loving personality.

All I could hope for was that wherever he and Bree were headed, they would stay safe.

"Will he be alright?" Isabelle's question dripped with anxiety as she looked back and forth between Odin and Freyja. The two of them exchanged a knowing grin before nodding reassuringly.

"You should be more worried about Bree. She's met her match, and I'm not sure how she will react when she realizes it," Freyja said with a mischievous smirk.

"I heard you could heal yourself, boy," Odin pointed at Victor, changing the subject. "When did you discover that unique talent?"

Victor puffed out his chest in pride. "Car accident a couple of years back. Should have died, but I didn't." He winced at the memory. "Damn painful process."

Odin's laughter echoed through the air. "I've thought the same thing once or twice," he admitted, a playful grin spreading across his face. "After breakfast, we'll set off on our own adventure. It's about time someone showed you your true potential." Victor eagerly nodded in agreement.

I couldn't help but feel a pang of jealousy that I couldn't join them. I almost invited myself along on their journey, but then Lilith cleared her throat, giving Odin a pointed look. "Let us not forget why we are here. Max, why don't you tell everyone what you've learned."

Max sat up straighter and fixed his glasses. Aelle retrieved her small red notepad and a pen from her back pocket. I silently groaned, knowing that once she started taking notes, the story would drag on with an excessive amount of unnecessary details.

"Of course," Max started with his story. "After you all left for the Otherworld, Aelle and I stumbled upon an old black journal hidden in my grandfather's closet. It was something I had never encountered before. But when I read it, its significance became clear as to why he kept it concealed."

"What did it say?" Eidolon asked, intrigued.

Max glanced down at the notebook page Aelle was pointing to. "According to one entry, the Tree of Life would be destroyed. Taliesin believed that something so evil had arrived that even Arawn feared it. He went on for pages about a fallen angel who vanished without a trace and a weapon capable of eradicating everything."

"Lucifer?" Eidolon asked carefully.

Max shrugged, "I don't know. Maybe. He never mentions a name."

Watson's brow furrowed in confusion. "Why wouldn't he mention his name?" he asked. "Everyone knows about Lucifer. It's not like it's a secret." His eyes darted to Lilith. "Right?"

Lilith frowned. "At that time, the term 'Lucifer' wasn't commonly used. It was coined during King James's translation of the Bible. The scholars working on the conversion had limited knowledge of Hebrew and Greek, so they made assumptions when they couldn't find direct translations. They attempted to translate 'luciferum,' which means 'constellations' or 'crowns.' But it ended up being linked to the phrase 'morning star,' and eventually became Lucifer."

"So, Lucifer isn't a person? He's a star?" Isabelle asked, even more confused.

Lilith couldn't resist smirking as she took another sip of her coffee. "No, Lucifer exists. But not like how he's depicted in the Divine Comedy. He doesn't have three faces or blow icy winds through hell with his wings." She paused. "Well, he did have wings, but they weren't quite like how Dante imagined them."

"Was he an angel?" I asked.

"He was for me." Lilith's eyes drifted towards the window as she spoke. Tears glistened in her eyes, and it was clear that the conversation was painful for her.

Isabelle gently patted her hand, asking, "What happened luv?"

Lilith inhaled deeply and composed herself before facing us again, her expression calm. "Angel means messenger, and that is what Lucifer was. Initially sent by the gods to oversee humanity, he eventually became a protector of the supernatural. He refused to let mortals harm those with abilities and worked to create a haven for us."

"The Otherworld?" Victor asked.

"Yes and no. Arawn and Lucifer devised a plan to divide the space between the dead and Lucifer's descendants. Each had their own territory to rule, governed by strict laws and regulations that ensured separation between the two factions."

"Avalon?" I guessed. Lilith nodded.

"That is why historians got confused. They both were located in the Otherworld," Watson reasoned, taken aback by the revelation. Odin nodded in confirmation. "But why did the supernatural return to the mortal world? Why not stay in Avalon?"

"Free will…" Lilith mumbled, almost to herself. "Some supernatural wanted to see if things would become better over time. They wanted to help create what the gods had originally envisioned. A world of both."

"But why did Taliesin alter Arawn's and Lucifer's stories? Why combine them into one person?" Eidolon asked.

Lilith's eyes hardened at the question. "One of Lucifer's roles was guarding the Tree of Life. When Taliesin asked him to restore his sister, Lucifer refused."

"So, Taliesin was rejected by both you and Lucifer," Eidolon remarked. "It's no wonder he's furious with you two. But I still don't understand why he would take such drastic measures. Why rewrite the entire history of the supernatural and leave them with nothing?"

Lilith's eyes hardened. "That is not my story to share. I don't know what Taliesin's final breaking point was, but it *was* extreme."

Odin reached over and put his arm around her, giving her a slight squeeze. Frejya shifted in her seat, uncomfortable.

"But if you won't tell us…" Victor started.

"She won't because it's my story to tell," a voice emerged from the door frame. The woman I had seen in my first vision stood in the shadows, still and silent.

The woman who brought Lilith back to life.

Aelle's mother.

Vivian.

Vivian glided into the room, a smile forming on her lips as she caught sight of her daughter. But instead of a greeting, Aelle sneered at her. Vivian's steps faltered before she shifted her gaze to Lilith. "Do you mind if I share?"

Lilith's hand gracefully motioned to the unoccupied chair next to Victor, inviting her to sit. "By all means, please do."

Vivian took a seat and reached for the bottle of whiskey, pouring herself a shot that she downed in one swift motion. "The story was like a painting, stained with heartache and infused with magick and a mother's unrelenting love."

"Just like most epic and tragic tales," Watson said as he moved his seat closer to the table.

"It all started the day I decided to kill Taliesin," she said as she poured herself a cup of coffee, avoiding our eyes.

Chapter 57- Chloe

Modern Day- Avalon

Vivian stood atop a small, grassy hill on an island in the middle of Loch Bél Dracon, her heart pounding with anticipation for Taliesin's return. The mist from the lake below rose and swirled around her like a cloak, adding to the mystical atmosphere surrounding her.

She had been his steadfast companion for years, using her powers to aid him in his magick and help him create a new world for the supernatural. After everything she sacrificed, the Fates finally blessed her with the one thing she desired most: a baby.

Vivian lovingly caressed her stomach, feeling the gentle curve of a small bump beneath her hand. She marveled at the miraculous growth inside her body, cradling the precious life developing into a strong and independent woman. Every kick and flutter reminded Vivian of the hope and promise that lay ahead for her child.

Aelle.

The title was usually reserved for kings, but Vivian firmly believed her daughter would surpass any ruler in strength, integrity, and grace. She carefully selected the name to reflect her unwavering faith. She knew the child would bring healing to Taliesin after his devastating loss.

For the last year, Taliesin traveled through vast landscapes, scaling mountains and crossing valleys in a relentless pursuit of a single oak tree.

Its location was shrouded in mystery. But he was convinced it held the power to unite the realms of life and death and bring his sister back from the dead.

Vivian stood by him but had reservations. Everyone knew a soul couldn't return from the Otherworld without a physical vessel to inhabit, and Morrigan's body had vanished without a trace.

Morrigan was lost, and Vivian desperately wished Taliesin would accept it and let it go.

For a moment, Vivian thought he had.

Months ago, they stumbled upon an old tavern for the night. The dilapidated building stood stoically amid a sea of overgrown grass and weeds. Inside, dust motes danced in the dim light, filtering through grimy, oilcloth-covered windows. The smell of stale beer and musty wood assaulted them as they squeezed through the crowded tables and chairs. Unsavory types with weathered faces and rough hands laughed loudly, their voices slurred by alcohol. As they drank, they regaled each other with wild stories of days gone by, adding more and more embellishments with each retelling.

Despite Vivian's pleading, Taliesin refused to leave when he overheard a man spinning a tale about an old god, Arawn, and his key to the Otherworld. The man's voice was laden with ancient mystery, and shadows danced across his wind-swept face as he spoke. Taliesin was entranced by the story, and so, much to Vivian's dismay, they remained.

Taliesin pushed past the jostling men and chairs, his eyes dancing darkly. "Tell us, where can we locate this Arawn?" he demanded, his voice laced with a hint of danger and urgency.

The man's eyebrows raised in surprise as Taliesin sat on a stool beside him at the table. The man gave a disapproving look, clearly offended by the unexpected company. In an attempt to smooth things over, Taliesin motioned for the barmaid to come over and waited for her to pour a glass of amber liquid into the man's mug.

"Now, where do we find Arawn?" Taliesin asked again as the man took a sip.

The stranger's hand slowly released his drink, setting the glass down on the wooden table with a soft thud. He leaned back in his chair, his sharp regard fixed on Taliesin as he spoke in a low, calculating voice. "Legend has it that the entrance to the Otherworld lies within an ancient oak tree, standing tall amidst a shadowy forest. They say its presence is unmistakable; its branches aglow with an ethereal blue light."

"And it's nearby?"

"By the River Tweed." The man's curious gaze swept over Vivian, and she suppressed a shiver. He seemed oddly observant and almost otherworldly for someone sitting in a rundown pub, nursing a pint of subpar ale. His sharp stare made her uneasy.

"You will take me to this tree!" Taliesin's piercing stare locked onto the outsider, daring him to defy his command. With a raised eyebrow, he waited for the man to agree.

The man chuckled. "No, I will not be taking you there. The forest doesn't allow fools to enter it. If that were the case, anyone could access the tree." He took another drink, eyeing Taliesin over the rim. "Even with your black magick, you couldn't gain entry."

"His powers do not stem from dark magick. They were granted to him by the gods," Vivian defended her lover, offended by the stranger's tone.

The man's eyes flickered with silver light as they darted back towards her. She leaned back in her seat, feeling his powerful aura surpassing even Taliesin's.

"Believe what you want, girl, but any individual who derives their abilities from another's blood is involved in dark magick," he pointed to Taliesin, "and your companion's hands are tainted with her blood." His scowl shifted back to Taliesin, his mug pointing accusingly at him. "She is dead. Abandon your foolish plan and accept responsibility. You can't change what you have done."

Taliesin's anger boiled, his fist slamming down onto the tabletop with a resounding thunder. His resolve was unwavering, his determination fierce. "I will not rest until I bring her home," he declared through gritted teeth.

The man chuckled deeply, the sound rich and aged. "A soul for a soul," he spoke knowingly, leaning closer to Taliesin. "That was your deal with the Fates, and it cannot be undone." His voice held a hint of warning, "If you continue down this path, death will surely find you." The gravity of his words hung heavily in the air, like an ominous storm cloud looming over them.

Taliesin sneered, confident he had outsmarted the man before him. "I cannot die," he stated with amusement. "I am the embodiment of eternity in a mortal body."

The stranger shook his head. "You may not die, but you will be doomed to a fate worse than that. Your legacy and identity will vanish, your name lost and distorted until it becomes unrecognizable."

"I have the power to change the story in my favor. Words written will live forever, just like the gods." He lifted Vivian from her stool, eyeing the man with anger. "Last time I ask, friend. Decide now which side of history you want to be on. Will you help me?"

"No, Taliesin, I will not," the man said with finality. Vivian's breath caught in her throat. They never disclosed their names. He continued before she could ask. "But listen closely. Understand there will be someone who can stand up to you—someone with the determination and wit to unravel your intricate web of deception."

Taliesin leaned in, his eyes glinting with genuine curiosity as he asked, "Who?"

"Your child," the stranger said with a mischievous grin. He took another drink and waited.

"You lie," Taliesin whispered with a quiver in his voice. "I will not let it happen."

The man arched his eyebrows and grinned. "That's what the ancient gods claimed as well. But history shows us how it ended for them." He stroked his chin thoughtfully. "I'm pretty sure it was their offspring who overthrew them. I'm sure you remember. I believe they called themselves the Titans."

Taliesin's face drained of color as he grabbed Vivian's arm and pulled her out of the pub. They ran through the darkness, with only the moon to guide them, the wind whipping against their faces and clothes. Reaching the shoreline, Taliesin quickly loaded Vivian and their belongings onto a nearby boat and raced across the bay. As they approached their island, Vivian's heart raced with fear. Without saying a word, Taliesin dropped her off on shore and disappeared into the night darkness.

For weeks, Vivian mulled over every word the man said, pacing back and forth in her home like a caged animal. The wooden floors groaned under her restless footsteps, and the flickering candlelight cast eerie shadows on the walls. She had to choose what was best for herself and her unborn child.

On the one hand, she was devoted to Taliesin and loved him above all else. But on the other, she couldn't ignore the prophecy that weighed heavily on her mind. If she stayed, Taliesin might harm the child.

As time passed, Vivian's anxiety lessened. She convinced herself that Taliesin would be thrilled to hear that he would have an heir to carry on his family line. A child was all he needed to move past the grief of losing his sister. Together, they could build a new legacy.

Taliesin eventually returned home after weeks away. Vivian couldn't contain her excitement, dancing around the house, ensuring everything was pristine before making her announcement.

Her heart pounded as she sat beside Taliesin, watching him eat the stew she'd prepared. Finally, summoning all her courage, she spoke softly, "Taliesin, we are to have a child!" She searched his face for any emotion, but it remained expressionless. "Taliesin? Did you hear me?" Her words hung in the air like a fragile thread, awaiting his response.

He didn't look up from his bowl. "No."

"Did you mean 'no' to my statement or 'no' to the child?" she chuckled. "Because, at this point, there's no turning back. The baby is on her way."

"No." Taliesin's voice boomed through the room, a deep, guttural sound that shook Vivian to her core. She jumped up in fear, her heart racing as she took in the intensity of his words. "There will be no child," he declared. His voice was soft and dangerous. The finality of his statement hung heavy in the air, filling her with dread and sadness.

Tears filled her eyes as he moved closer, his pupils shining silver and blue electricity crackling around them.

"We will not have a child," he sneered. "You will die before I let it happen."

"Taliesin, please. You don't know what you are saying." Vivian's voice trembled as she pleaded with Taliesin, desperation evident in her tone. She stumbled backward until her back pressed against the cool stone wall behind her, her hands grasping the rough surface for support.

"You heard the man; I will not let a child stop me from completing my mission!"

"Your sister is gone, dead, and not returning. Don't waste your life trying to bring her back. Don't you dare throw away mine." The words exploded from Vivian's mouth in a fiery rage, the anger at his stubborn refusal to listen drowning out any trace of fear.

"I will do whatever is necessary." His words dripped with venom, each syllable laced with warning.

"Then so will I," Vivian vowed, her voice barely above a whisper as she stared at the man before her with cold determination in her eyes. She would move mountains, swim through oceans of fire, and do whatever it took to ensure her child's safety. And anyone foolish enough to stand in her way would meet a swift and brutal end at her hands.

Even the man she loved.

"Whoa!" Watson exclaimed, leaning back in his chair with a whistle. He glanced over at Aelle. "That's insane. You've got some deep-seated daddy issues, my friend."

Aelle slowly shifted to face him and gave a subtle nod of agreement. She turned her unwavering gaze to her mother and asked, "How old am I?"

"1,424 years old. Give or take a few years," Vivian said with a small smile and a glimmer of hope in her eyes.

"I look really good for my age," Aelle remarked, looking down at her hands.

Vivian's eyes filled with tears, and she nodded. "Not a day over 39."

Isabelle offered Vivian a slight nod of approval as she asked, "Did you kill Taliesin because he was going to harm Aelle?"

"No," Vivian replied with a shake of her head. "I intended to end Taliesin's life, but I couldn't bring myself to do it. Instead, I set a trap for him and imprisoned him. It was an ingenious technique he taught me long ago."

"How did he escape?" Watson asked.

"We don't know," Lilith offered. "We weren't aware he could until he came for me and Lucifer."

As the voices around me blended into a jumbled mess, my mind became enveloped in a thick fog of confusion. The conversation, once clear and distinct, faded away. The sweet scent of vanilla and raspberries filled the room.

Please, oh please, not now, I silently pleaded. Something about this vision was wrong. My senses were in overdrive. I could feel each hair on my body, the slightest gust of air against my skin, and the faintest sound echoing in my head, like an orchestra off-key.

I struggled against the visions, faint shadows flickering around me.

The darkness won, engulfing me until I disappeared into its depths.

Chapter 58- Chloe

Modern Day- Avalon

My body stirred, slowly awakening as I sat up, surrounded by a mountain of pillows. A patchwork quilt enveloped me, the comforting scent of vanilla and raspberries filling the air. I squinted against the sunlight beaming from the enormous stained-glass window. Rubbing my eyes, I opened them to find a breathtaking valley stretching out into the distance. Houses dotted the landscape, their colorful facades blending into the natural scenery.

Wrapping a throw around my shoulders, I looked around the room, trying to get my bearings. A massive stone fireplace at the back provided some light, but it wasn't enough to warm up the chill that had seeped into my bones. In the center of the room, a small dining table was set with an assortment of dishes and a large pot of coffee. The smell of sizzling bacon, eggs, buttered toast, and fluffy pecan pancakes wafted through the air, and my stomach growled in anticipation.

A woman's voice greeted me as she entered the room. "You're finally awake! I was afraid you would spend the entire day sleeping," she exclaimed with relief.

I groaned in response, rubbing my temples.

Diana.

One eye cracked open as I watched her glide gracefully further in. Diana's resemblance to Eidolon was unmistakable, from her intense gaze to the deep indigo shade of her eyes to the sharpness of her jawline and the fullness of her lips. Her jet-black hair flowed down her shoulders in a smooth cascade, accenting the elegant forest green dress adorned with delicate golden ravens on the cuffs. A pair of brown leather boots completed the look, along with a gleaming silver belt at her waist, holding a raven-shaped pendant.

She was as beautiful as the first time I met her, and it was difficult to believe she was trapped in a prison.

"There's got to be a better way to get my attention." The words tumbled out of my mouth in a grumble as I reluctantly left the warmth of the bed and shuffled to the table. My muscles protested, and I stretched to work out the kinks in my back. With a frustrated sigh, I pulled out a chair and plopped heavily, turning my back on her. "Something a little less painful."

"It was a necessary evil, I am afraid," she said as she sat across from me. "I had to take some precautions before bringing you here."

Rolling my eyes, I filled my plate with food. "What do you want, Diana?" I asked between bites of pancakes and sighed in pleasure. They were divine - light and airy with just the right amount of crunch from the pecans and slathered in an unhealthy dose of butter that oozed down the sides.

"We needed a private conversation." Diana fidgeted with her pendant, her fingers tracing the intricate design as she avoided meeting my gaze.

My eyes widen in surprise, darting about the room. "Taliesin doesn't know I am here, does he?" I guessed, popping a bacon strip into my mouth.

Diana glanced around anxiously and shook her head. "No, this is between you and me. I wanted to warn you about what you're about to face."

"What do you mean by 'warn'?" I asked, stabbing at my eggs. "Is there something I should be worried about?"

"It's a long story," she started, but I cut her off.

"Why don't you give me the cliff notes? Because as soon as I finish my breakfast and have another cup of coffee, I'm heading back."

Diana's eyes narrowed with annoyance as she locked her gaze with mine, a faint frown creasing her brow. I met her glare with a nonchalant shrug, arching an eyebrow. I wasn't in the mood to deal with her half-stories and lies. I wanted to get back to Eidolon and the others. We had things to do.

"Your life is in danger," she finally said when I refused to back down.

I laughed. "You're not exactly telling me something I don't already know." Pouring a cup of coffee, I waited.

"Taliesin figured out how to open the portal to the Tree of Life." She paused, her fingers tapping on the table nervously. "But there is a key element he is missing." I raised my eyebrows, curious to hear more. "Your blood," she added with urgency.

A flicker of concern crossed my mind as I processed her statement. "Alright, I'm listening," I said, placing my cup back on the saucer and clasping my hands together.

"The only way to bring Morrigan back is through her blood," Diana said, her voice tinged with sadness.

"And when you say blood, what does that mean exactly?" I questioned, leaning back in my chair.

"It means a soul for a soul. Morrigan can only return if you switch places with her. Your body, her soul."

"And Taliesin just figured this out?" I asked, anxiety clawing in my gut.

"He made the connection when we last saw you. He could hear his sister's blood calling out to him. Taliesin spent weeks trying to figure out how. He would have never solved the puzzle if it wasn't for the damn cat," she clarified with a sneer.

Cat? What cat? I racked my brain, trying to remember if I had encountered a cat before. Then, it hit me—the first time I met Taliesin. The feline was sitting on a book on the spiral staircase leading up to the second-floor library. It watched me like a predator assessing its target.

"What did the cat do?" I asked.

"It was protecting a book," Diana looked up at me, visibly upset. "When Taliesin wrestled it away, he disappeared. When he returned, all he said was that he needed to find you before you reached the Library of the Unread."

I slowly processed what she said, trying to make sense of it. "Let me get this straight—you brought me here to warn me not to come here?"

"I had no choice; I can't leave, remember?" Diana said, waving her hand around the room. "I needed to warn you somehow."

I shook my head, pushing my food around the plate with my fork. "I'm confused. You said I needed to stop Eidolon from coming to the Otherworld. But now you're saying Taliesin needs my blood to bring back Morrigan. So, who am I really protecting, Diana?" I raised my eyebrows. "Me or your son?"

She sighed. "Both. Lilith needs Eidolon to help her regain her identity, and Taliesin needs you to bring back his sister. Both need the Tree of Life restored." She paused, running a finger along the edge of her cup. She looked up, eyeing me. "It's a race to see who achieves their goal first."

My mind raced with a thousand thoughts, each competing for my attention as I got up and paced the room. Diana's weary eyes followed me, her concern evident in her gaze. The flickering flames of the fireplace cast a warm, orange glow on the antique hourglass that sat atop its mantle. My eyes were drawn to the fine grains of sand slowly trickling down, each one marking the passing moments of my time with Eidolon's mother.

It was like watching my life slip away, grain by grain, as I struggled to come to terms with the weight of the information she had just given me.

"Why are you telling me all this?" I demanded, pivoting to face her.

"Taliesin is working with the Fates." Diana's eyes followed me as I started pacing again. "I think he made another deal."

I stopped, turning to face her. "So?"

"The last time he made a deal, his sister died," she reminded me. "Whatever he is planning now will be worse than that."

My breath hitched, and I ran a hand through my hair. What was worse than having your sister killed? "What do you want me to do?"

"Stop him," she said simply.

With a sigh, I stalked back to my chair and plopped down, crossing my arms in frustration. Leaning in towards her, I lowered my voice to a whisper. "I'm not sure if you remember, but I'm just a mortal. A witch with no witchy powers, remember?"

Diana leaned closer, a dangerous glint flashing in her eyes. "You don't have to kill him. You need to find his book and rewrite the chapters after he becomes Taliesin."

A sharp intake of breath escaped my lips, the disbelief in my voice ringing out. "You want me to erase your husband? The father of your child? How does that work?" My mind raced, trying to comprehend the consequences of such a choice. Suddenly, understanding dawned on me. "How would Eidolon exist?"

Diana's words were barely audible, a whisper carried by the gentle breeze. "Eidolon would survive. But as an unspoken story," she said, her voice trembling with emotion. "There is no other option. Taliesin will destroy everything we worked so hard to build. We have no other choice."

I jumped up from my seat, knocking over my chair and spilling coffee across the table. My plate of pancakes tumbled to the ground with a loud thud, but I didn't care. All my attention was focused on the woman before me. "There is always another choice. This is insane."

"Are you willing to risk it all for Eidolon?" Diana questioned gently. "His soul is immortal; it can never truly die. But the rest of the Otherworld will if Taliesin lives. It's as simple as that. One soul for a chance to save millions. The decision is yours, Chloe."

I followed her gaze toward the hourglass and noticed her worried expression as footsteps echoed down the hallway, growing louder with each passing second.

"You need to leave now," she whispered, and with a flick of her wrist, my world crumbled around me.

Chapter 59- Chloe

Modern Day- City of the Unspoken

"**S**he's coming around." Eidolon's voice was a gentle murmur in my ear as I regained consciousness. I was sprawled out on the floor, my head cradled in his lap. As the fog cleared my mind, I could see the concern in his dark eyes as he eyed me. Lilith, Odin, and Freyja stood behind him, looking at me like they had just seen a ghost.

"Odin, if you keep huffing and puffing, you'll have a heart attack," Lilith scolded, giving the god beside her a sideways glance. "You remember what happened last time?"

Odin glared at her momentarily and then shrugged, his visible eye dancing with amusement. "Not my fault. I told the mortal that it'd been a while." Lilith rolled her eyes.

"Why is everyone making such a big deal over Chloe fainting?" Freyja asked, her brow furrowed in disapproval. "I've gone without food and water for three weeks while hunting, and no one helped me when I passed out."

"Probably because you're immortal," Odin joked with a sly grin, nudging her with his elbow. "Why bother fixing you when we all know you would have stood right back up, sword in hand, and yelled about us invading your 'personal space'?" he chuckled.

"It would've been nice to know someone cared," Freyja said, hands on her hips.

"We care, Freyja. We just care about keeping our body parts attached more. Do you know how long it takes to grow back a hand or a leg?" Odin laughed as he poured himself another drink.

"Unless you start treating me better, I can make something else disappear," Freyja suggested with an evil smile. Odin straightened, shielding his vulnerable area with his hands while his complexion paled.

"She must have traveled," Lilith commented, not paying her friends any mind. She had never seen anyone travel before. In all her years, she could never catch the moment a Writer disappeared into the past or the future. They usually did so in secret. But this was different.

And Lilith wanted to know why.

"Where do you think she went?" Odin leaned in, whispering. "Do you think it concerns the Book of the Veiled?"

"Of course, it has something to do with the books. But what did Chloe see?" Freyja commented dryly.

Wouldn't you like to know? I had been listening to their conversation, taking the opportunity to regain control of my limbs. As soon as I remembered Diana's warning, I sat up abruptly. Eidolon's eyes followed me, puzzled, but there was no time for me to reassure him I was okay.

I fixed Lilith with a stern gaze. "We need to talk. Now." She nodded in agreement and silently trailed behind me as I marched toward the library.

Freyja's voice was a whisper as she leaned in towards Odin, her eyes flickering with curiosity. "Should we follow them?"

"Lil' Writer seemed awfully mad. We should stay close just in case," Odin replied, following us. Eidolon and Freyja were close on his heels. The rest of the group shared a glance and followed suit.

Nobody wanted to miss this conversation.

As I stepped through the library's threshold, my heart pounded like a relentless drum. The deafening ticks of the grandfather clock served as a cruel reminder of time slipping away, each second bringing me closer to my and Eidolon's inevitable fate.

A musty stench hung in the air, permeating my nostrils and making me dizzy as I navigated through rows of ancient books and scrolls that whispered secrets and warnings as they rustled on their shelves.

"Where's Taliesin's book?" I demanded, whirling on my heels to face Lilith.

Her steps faltered slightly, her brow furrowed in concern and determination. With a deep breath, she composed herself and gestured for me to join her in the sitting area by the fireplace.

"I don't know," Lilith said as she smoothed out her skirt wrinkles. "That's why you're here, isn't it? To find the books?" Her gaze flickered up to me, her green eyes sparking with touches of gold—a subtle warning to me not to push her too far.

A warning that I ignored. "Fine," I huffed. "Then you can at least tell me why Taliesin wants yours. What's the end game, Lilith?"

My questions shot out like a machine gun on rapid fire as Eidolon joined me, placing a steadying hand on my shoulder. I shook it off, glaring at him. "No. I'm done playing games." I turned my attention back to Lilith. "No more half-truths. No more lies. What the hell is going on?"

"What do you want to know, Chloe?" she asked kindly, and I almost screamed in frustration.

"Do you still have it?" I asked, annoyed she was playing games with me.

Lilith's gaze lingered on me, weighing her words before responding. "That's not an easy question to answer."

"Sure it is. Do you or do you not have Pandora's box?" I said each word slowly, hoping she understood how serious I was about this conversation. Eidolon stepped forward, surprise flickering across his face before composing himself. Dark shadows danced around his body as his tattoos shifted.

Odin stepped behind Lilith, eyeing Eidolon, his hand on his dagger's hilt. "Technically, it's not a box," he offered, his voice low and smooth like distant thunder rumble.

"Then what is it?" Max's voice rang out. I peeked at the doorway and saw the remainder of the group sneaking in, trying to be inconspicuous.

My eyes flickered back to Lilith, anticipation building as I waited for her answer. I already knew the jar belonged to her, but what was inside remained a mystery. And it was time to find out.

"I have Pandora's jar," Lilith said, her voice tense. "But it is well guarded by two people I trust with my life. Rest assured, nothing and no one will ever discover its whereabouts."

Watson and Isabelle settled into the chair next to Lilith. "Sounds like a fascinating story," Watson remarked, perching himself on the armrest and extending his legs in front of him. "Who are they? And what's in the jar?"

Lilith's eyes flicked towards Odin, and they exchanged a wordless exchange. He responded with a nod of encouragement, urging her to carry on. She drew in a deep breath as Freyja moved to stand by the fireplace. She positioned herself casually against the mantel but standing at the ready.

"They were the star-crossed lovers of two ancient gods," Lilith confessed, her gaze falling to her hands. "But their love came with a heavy cost. They were cursed with immortality and forced to endure the consequences of their choices for eternity."

"Consequence? As in, they are being forced to guard Pandora's jar?" Victor asked, standing on the other side of Eidolon.

Lilith's gaze snapped up, ablaze with intense anger. "No one has been forced into anything against their wishes," she declared through gritted teeth. "I simply made them an offer, and they agreed to it willingly. In return, I ensure their safety." The atmosphere around her vibrated with tension as she balled her hands in fists. Odin leaned over and whispered something into her ear, and Lilith's fury slowly dissipated.

"Why do they need protecting?" I asked when she gained her composure.

Lilith arched an eyebrow. "Just because you're hiding doesn't mean you can't be found," she stated firmly, looking at me. "You, above all others, would understand that, wouldn't you?"

My mouth dropped. "I don't know what you're talking about," I sputtered.

Lilith's piercing regard bore into me, her head tilting to the side as she leaned forward. Her dark eyes held the universe's secrets, daring me to reveal mine. "Really?" she asked. "You don't?"

Eidolon's questioning gaze flicked towards me as he asked, "What is she talking about, Chloe?"

I pushed my glasses up the bridge of my nose and drew in a deep breath. "It's not a big deal," I said, my voice wavering. "It has come to my attention that Taliesin is looking for me. I might have something he needs."

Eidolon's face was etched with rage as he closed in, his tattoos writhing in sync with his pulsing fury. "What is he looking for?" he demanded.

"Apparently, my blood is one of a kind," I chuckled, trying to find humor in the situation's absurdity. "Who knew?" Eidolon and I stared at each other as he tried to control his emotions.

Without warning, his strong arms pulled me out of my seat and wrapped around me. "My father will not touch you," he vowed, his voice menacing. "I will kill anyone who tries." I pulled back to look at him. Eidolon was struggling with his darkness. I could see it in his eyes.

Forcing a smile, I brushed a piece of his hair off his face. "I didn't expect any less." I tilted my head. "But let's try to get through this without bloodshed. It would put a damper on our parade." Eidolon nodded once, still fighting to control himself.

Isabelle sat up in her chair, leaning forward. "Why does he want your blood, luv?"

I turned, pulling out of Eidolon's arms but linking our hands and giving him a quick squeeze.

"Because of her bloodline." Victor speculated, glancing at Lilith for validation. She nodded in agreement. "Chloe comes from Morrigan's line, which means her blood carries the same power."

"Why Chloe? Out of her bloodline, what sets her apart from the others?" Freyja's voice was filled with genuine confusion and suspicion as she scanned me from head to toe.

"Chloe has an unusual ability," Moll replied, appearing out of nowhere. I hadn't even seen her come in with the group.

I raised an eyebrow, intrigued. "And that would be what?"

Moll paused. "You don't fear death," she stated plainly. "In fact, you welcome it. While most people run away from it, you steer towards it."

Eidolon's arm wrapped around my waist, drawing me closer to him. "Chloe isn't going to die," he assured Moll through clenched teeth. "What do we need to do?"

Moll's expression turned grave as she regarded Aelle and Max. Aelle was taken aback and raised one eyebrow but remained silent. "We must locate the book. It is the only solution."

"Wonderful! We have a plan," Watson exclaimed, jumping up from his seat. He ran a hand over his jacket, smoothing out the wrinkles. "What does it look like?"

"We don't know," Odin confessed sheepishly.

Watson frowned. "That's fine. Which one are we looking for then?"

Odin's piercing gaze shifted to Freyja, who shrugged her shoulders in response. "To be honest, we don't even know ourselves."

Watson's face twisted into disbelief and shock; his eyebrows furrowed as he processed the information. "Just to clarify," he began, his voice tinged with frustration, "we are searching for a book, but we have absolutely no idea who or what it looks like."

Max stood up and ran a hand through his hair. "I think I know," he said, pausing.

"Are you intending to share?" Eidolon's voice was on the brink of breaking, his frustration barely contained as he clenched his jaw. I squeezed his hand again, trying to calm him down. His intense gaze locked onto mine. A fire burned behind his dark eyes, hinting at the depths of emotion he struggled to control.

"Take a deep breath," I whispered. "It's going to be okay." He nodded, his body still tense as he turned his gaze back to Max.

Max reached up and rubbed the back of his neck, a habit he had when deep in thought. "It must be Taliesin's. There's no other possibility."

Odin arched an eyebrow, his one good eye narrowing. "Why do you think that?"

"Some may debate Lilith's existence, but there is no doubt she was real. Morrigan's passing in 537 A.D. is documented, solidifying her reality. However, the same cannot be said for Taliesin. Unlike his counterparts, he remains shrouded in mystery." Max pointed to the bookshelves. "Like these books."

"Wouldn't somebody have found by now?" Eidolon asked doubtfully.

"I initially thought the same. But the more I considered it, the less convinced I was that someone would have stumbled on it." Max spun to face Lilith. "I think it's linked to Lucifer somehow."

Lilith's eyes widened with shock and dread as she slowly turned to face Odin and Freyja. They stared back, wide-eyed in horror, their usually confident expression marred by fear. Moll gasped and reached for Lilith's hand, intertwining their fingers tightly.

"What?" Eidolon asked. "What's wrong?"

Lilith's face paled. "I know where the book is," she said, looking at me.

Chapter 60- Lilith

December 1589- Nether Keith, Scotland

Lilith lay enveloped in darkness. The dying sunlight from the open door and the glowing embers in the fireplace were the only light sources in the room. Despite being bundled up under multiple layers of blankets, she couldn't shake off the biting cold that penetrated her bones.

She wondered if she would ever feel warm again.

Lilith remained in bed for days, staring at the thatched ceiling above. She exhausted her mind, trying to remember what had transpired. But all she could muster was a vague memory of rushing water and birds scattering in panic.

She needed to remember.

Why couldn't she remember?

A faint rustling sound snapped her out of her thoughts. She scanned the room, but nothing was out of the ordinary. Still, she couldn't shake off the sensation that someone was watching her from the shadows. It felt like a familiar presence. Someone she should remember but couldn't.

Lilith's eyes darted to the ceiling, searching for answers as tears gathered in the corners. Flashes of memories came back to her in bits and pieces: an explosion, colliding with an object, then falling into a pile of soft lichen. A glimpse of a magnificent tree glowing in the darkness, cruel laughter ringing in her ears, the faint sound of a man's groan. And then everything turned black.

The one memory she could remember was being held in the arms of a small woman with golden hair that shimmered in the sunlight and bright green-yellow eyes that radiated kindness. The woman carried Lilith for miles as if she weighed nothing. Throughout the journey, Lilith's mind was consumed by the thought of returning. She felt like she had left something or someone crucial behind.

Her rescuer walked through the door, and Lilith turned to look at her. "Did you bring it, girl?" she asked, her voice hoarse and rough.

"You know I did," Vivian replied sharply as she turned to face her. "Unless you can get your broken and half-dead body out of bed, you can be quiet and let me finish in peace!"

Lilith suppressed a sharp retort and forced herself to roll over on the lumpy, threadbare mattress. A violent cough wracked her body, wringing out the last of her strength. Every movement sent a piercing pain through her chest as she tried to find a position that offered even a fraction of comfort.

She shut her eyes and inhaled deeply. She couldn't let her feelings control her; she needed to stay composed for her own sake. Her very existence relied on the other woman's generosity and kindness, and she appreciated everything Vivian did for her.

But she hated feeling trapped.

Lilith listened as the woman pulled and chopped bundles of ingredients, accompanied by calming words that infused the room with peace. The air was thick with the scent of rich earth, salty sea breeze, sweet raspberries, and warm vanilla. As Lilith inhaled deeply, her mind was transported back in time, the shadows of memory dancing around her once more.

What had she left behind?

The flames crackled and danced in the hearth, casting a warm glow over Vivian as she stirred the contents of a bubbling pot. Her voice was firm yet tinged with doubt as she asked, "You will uphold your end of the bargain?"

Lilith struggled to hold back another violent bout of coughing, her hand pressed tightly against her chest. She gasped out a weak 'yes,' determined to reassure the woman of her commitment despite the agony coursing through her veins.

Vivian's hopeful gaze met Lilith's, her voice trembling with anticipation as she poured the liquid into a mug. "You promise all my dreams will come true?"

Lilith felt a twinge of annoyance at the constant questioning, but she forced a smile and nodded reassuringly, "Yes. All your dreams will come true. Now give me the drink!" Lilith demanded, harsher than she meant it.

With a flick of her hand, she beckoned Vivian over, mustering a weak grin. Her lips parted as the warm liquid touched them, and she couldn't help but sigh contentedly as the drink flowed down her throat. In an instant, a wave of healing energy washed over her, its soothing touch spreading through her body. It seeped deep into her bones, reawakening forgotten memories locked away.

She remembered standing atop a grassy hill, the salty ocean breeze whipping through her hair as she gazed up at the vast, star-studded sky. By her side stood a man, their bodies entwined in a loving embrace. With one arm wrapped around her shoulders and the other hand gently resting on her waist, he held her close as they took in the beauty of the night together. She leaned into his warmth, finding solace in his protective hold as they watched shooting stars streak across the midnight canvas above them.

One day, they will welcome us into their home, and we will shine as luminously as the rest of them. Lilith registered his words, but when she looked up, the man's face was hidden in shadow - only his intense gaze with flickers of silver could be seen.

Hopefully, in the far future. Lilith spoke the words, although she couldn't recall saying them. It was her body, but it felt unfamiliar to her. She still had her memories, yet not a single one was recognizable.

Who was he? They had an undeniable connection, as if their bodies shared the same soul. Every beat of her heart synchronized with his own, and their magick intertwined in a mesmerizing rhythm that felt like coming home. Even though she couldn't remember him, something deep within her knew he belonged to her.

A few moments passed before he spoke, kissing Lilith's forehead and embracing her. *She's arrived.*

Lilith looked around, but no one else was there. She went to tell him he was mistaken, but he disappeared into the shadows, leaving her standing alone.

You need to find the girl. She will have the key to reuniting us with our family. The man's voice called out from afar, and Lilith's heart ached for him. Yet, she stood alone in the silent woods, with only the sounds of a cawing raven and an echoing owl. She searched the treetops for the curious birds but instead locked eyes with a woman watching her.

A middle-aged woman with matte reddish-brown hair, stained clothes, and clunky wet boots. She was disheveled as if she had been dragged through a river and taken away by the current.

Lilith studied her closely, committing her face and body language to memory. Was this the woman the man spoke of? Could this be the person who held the key to bringing her family back together?

As quickly as she faded into the memory, she evaporated back into the smokey, dark room that was her unwelcome sanctuary.

"I returned to the site today after collecting the items I needed," Vivian said as she cleaned up her work area. "The area is still destroyed, but I discovered something interesting."

"What?" Lilith said, still staring up at the ceiling and wondering why it would matter if Vivian found something. She couldn't remember anything.

"A single white feather."

Lilith turned her head to face Vivian, her eyes narrowing in annoyance. She let out an exasperated sigh and raised an eyebrow. "What does a bird's feather have to do with what happened to me?"

"This is no ordinary feather. It stretched the length of my arm and weighed as much as a turkey's leg. I haven't seen any birds around here that could leave a feather this size behind."

"Where is it?" Lilith asked, her curiosity piqued. Vivian reached into her basket and retrieved it, placing it in Lilith's hands. The feather was massive, larger than Lilith's arm, and as pure white as freshly fallen snow. Specks of light danced across its surface, giving it a shimmering appearance.

The weight surprised Lilith. *How could something fly with wings made of something so heavy?*

A distant memory emerged from the depths of her mind—a figure with the face of an angel descending from the heavens and landing upon the shoreline.

"Does it look familiar?" Vivian asked.

Lilith's brow furrowed in deep thought as she admitted, "I think so. But I'm not entirely certain. It feels like a name, but nothing more than that."

"Who's?"

"Lucifer," Lilith replied, looking up at Vivian with confusion etched into her features. "Does that name hold any significance for you?"

Vivian's face fell as she shook her head. However, her mood quickly changed as she brightened up and suggested, "But that doesn't mean we can't figure it out. We'll get you fixed up and search for a Lucifer. The Fates will know. We can ask them."

Lilith slowly nodded, her head heavy with exhaustion as she rested it on the pile of rough fabric that served as her makeshift pillow. Her eyes were set intently on the feather cradled in her hands, her fingers tracing its delicate edges. She may not have fully comprehended the concept of a 'Lucifer,' but something inside her told her that following this path was the right choice for her.

Chapter 61- Lilith

Modern Day- City of the Unspoken

"What do you mean he is looking for Lucifer?" Eidolon's footsteps echoed in front of the roaring fireplace as he paced back and forth, his agitation tangible in the air. His eyes burned with anger as he fixed them upon Lilith, who stood defiantly before him.

Lilith stood tall, her golden green eyes unflinching as they met his calculating silver gaze. She coolly replied, "He's searching for Lucifer's feather."

"Why would he be looking for Lucifer's feather? Victor asked at the same time Eidolon demanded, "Do you know where it is?"

The atmosphere in the room shifted as Odin's features hardened into a scowl, his jaw clenched and eyes blazing with anger. He closed the distance between him and Eidolon with measured steps, his lips curling into a sneer.

"Watch your tone, boy," Odin growled.

Eidolon's frown turned into a menacing snarl, his muscles coiling like a predator ready to strike.

Before the situation escalated further, Freyja placed herself between the two, her hand instinctively reaching for her dagger to protect Eidolon from harm.

"He is just asking Odin," Freyja cautioned, placing a hand on Odin's forearm. "There is no need for blood," she said, returning her attention to Eidolon and Victor. "Of course, we know where it is. It's safe."

"I am confused. What does Lucifer's feather have to do with Taliesin's book?" Watson's gaze was fixed on Odin as he positioned himself protectively in front of Isabelle. The atmosphere in the room had become increasingly tense, and I knew it was only a matter of time before a fight broke out.

"Lucifer's feather has nothing to do with Taliesin's book. We need to concentrate on one thing at a time," Odin said, nonchalantly shrugging his shoulders and watching Eidolon like an owl about to swoop down and snatch a field mouse.

"Odin," Lilith called out. Odin's good eye glanced over. "You're wrong. Lucifer's feather has everything to do with Taliesin. It's the one piece of my husband that I have left. If Taliesin gets his hands on it, all hope of bringing him back is lost." The thought brought tears to her eyes, and she struggled to speak through a choked sob. "He will use Lucifer to destroy everything we've worked for."

"Lilith is right," Isabelle said from her seat, a soothing aura radiating around her as she tried to quell the heated atmosphere. "We must find Taliesin's book and Lucifer's feather." She stood and moved over to Aelle, resting a hand on her shoulder. "And you are the only one who can find it."

"Why me?" Aelle asked, stunned, eyeing Isabelle's hand wearily and stepping to the side.

"Because the library likes you. Why don't you try asking for its help? And be polite about it," Isabelle added with a wink.

Max nodded. "Aelle, she's got a point. Maybe the voices were trying to tell you that you had something to do with locating the book."

"I don't think so." Aelle moved further away from Isabelle, still eyeing her wearily. "It's not just one voice in that library. There are thousands of them, all demanding attention. I refuse to enter until someone performs an exorcism or something."

Moll spun to face the exit, declaring, "We don't require an exorcism; we need someone to listen while Aelle is off looking for answers. Come on, Chloe. It's time for your next lesson on what it means to be a Writer."

Chapter 62- Chloe

Modern Day- City of the Unspoken

Moll claimed everyone needed to leave the City of the Unspoken for us to work.

Not something I wanted to hear.

Odin invited Victor and Max to Valhalla, and after a heated discussion with Lilith, the invitation was extended to Eidolon as well.

Eidolon was uneasy about leaving me behind, but I encouraged him to go. Maybe he and Odin could work out their issues and be done with them.

And it would be easier for me to find the answers to how to save him without him asking questions about what I was doing.

Freyja asked Watson and Isabelle to accompany her to the Fólkvangr plains, where Isabelle could focus on honing her abilities in a safe environment. She insisted that Isabelle's control over her magick would be essential to our mission's success, and I had to agree.

It seemed like the team was splitting up again, and I wasn't sure how I felt about it. But I was also extremely curious about the next lesson Moll hinted at. I had no idea what it was, but I was excited we were finally doing something.

I held back tears when Eidolon walked over, engulfed me in a huge hug, and kissed my forehead. *Try not to die. It would be inconvenient,* he said to me through our bond. *I still owe you a cup of coffee.*

I won't, I replied with a slight frown, tired of everyone telling me not to die. I wasn't intentionally trying to. It was actually the other way around; everything was trying to kill me. Before I could argue, he kissed me firmly, and I melted in his embrace.

When I return, we will explore some of those delicious thoughts you had about me in the shower.

My toes curled, and my face reddened at the mention of my inappropriate thoughts, and he laughed.

I'll see you soon. I kissed Eidolon again before turning him around and steering him towards Odin. Watching them leave, a wave of sadness hit me as a small part of my heart broke. Would I find a way to stop everything? Could I save Eidolon and the Otherworld souls?

Or was Diana right? One person for the millions?

I pulled on the bond connecting me to Eidolon and felt his presence firmly anchored to mine. As long as the connection remained intact, we would be safe.

Isabelle and Watson walked up after he left. I composed my expression to hide the tears that were threatening to spill.

"Looks like 700 plus 700 to me," Watson said with a wink and quickly hugged me. I couldn't help but smile.

"Stay safe, Chloe," Isabelle said, hugging me next. "We have some major shopping to do when we go home." I laughed, enjoying her embrace before she let go, and they followed Freyja out of the room.

Then there were just three.

I glanced wearily at Moll and Aelle, an unspoken tension between us. I took a deep breath and smiled at them, hoping I was putting off an air of self-assurance rather than a scared middle-aged woman walking into a tomb of death.

What could go wrong?

Silently, we all turned and headed further into the Library of the Unread, mentally trying to prepare ourselves for our next task. As we approached the corner of the library labeled *Ancient History*, Aelle tensed up.

With a quiet tone, I turned to Aelle and asked, "What do you hear?" She was watching Moll intently as a single bead of sweat trickled down her forehead. She didn't respond to my question, but her eyes danced nervously around. She stepped closer to me, and our shoulders brushed against each other.

Knowing Aelle was just as frightened as I was made me feel better. Not much. But a little.

As we ventured further in, the voices returned, becoming louder and more urgent as we pressed forward.

Have you found us a home?

Can you tell me my story?

Where are my parents?

Can I go home now?

Have you seen my husband?

Where are my children?

The questions echoed around me, the overwhelmingly different cries blending into one enormous roar. The keys around my neck vibrated with frustration and pain. All the stories had a distinctive identity, yet I couldn't understand them. Their anonymity felt so desperately painful.

How many souls were forgotten because no one told their stories? How many lives had disappeared into the City of the Unspoken because there was nowhere else to turn?

This was so much worse than the supernatural forced to live in the City on the Mountain. At least they had some sense of life. They were remembered. Maybe not in their true forms, but their legends were still documented in one way or another.

But these books? These lives? They never existed except in the world of engraved leather and gold lettering.

I was so lost in my own world that I didn't realize Moll had stopped until I crashed into her. When I looked up, my mouth hung open.

Books upon books overflowed from shelves, walls, and even the floors, stretching as far into the shadows. Some were so old that a layer of grime and disintegration fluttered into the air when I blew lightly over them. The selection was never-ending: leather, animal hide, papyrus with golden edges, and embedded gems, stone, or wood .

What struck me as bizarre was the sudden absence of voices, as if time erased their ability to speak. They had fallen as silent as the dead.

Aelle's voice was barely a whisper as she asked, "Can you see anything?" I followed her gaze to the aisle and saw nothing but books. Yet, I could feel their desperation, their silent cries for help.

I shook my head, and Moll fixed her gaze in the same direction.

Hopefully, we didn't need to go down there.

"This is where we need to focus first." Moll nodded confidently.

But do we really? I inwardly groaned.

Aelle disappeared down the aisle, leaving me no time to object. She ran her hand along the bookshelves, gently grazing the spines of each book. "They are crying," she whispered and turned to look at Moll. "Why are they crying?"

"Because they have no story left to tell. If we opened these books, we would find the ink has faded away into nothingness. All that remains is the knowledge that they are lost to time."

"Can we help them?" I asked, stroking my fingers across an exquisite blood-red cover that smelled of olive oil, mold, and honey.

Moll turned to look at me and nodded. "Yes, but it will come at a cost," she said solemnly. "To recreate a story as it once was, you must breathe new life into it."

I turned back to the book. "Seems simple enough."

"It's not," Moll warned. "The life you give to these books will take a piece of yours."

Aelle and I paused, speechless at the gravity of Moll's words. I stepped away from the book.

"What do you mean by 'taking a piece of ours,' Moll?" Aelle asked, her eyes still fixed on the bookshelves.

"Each story you bring to life will take a part of you. It may be something as simple as a memory or as precious as a dream. But know, you can never get it back once you give it away."

A shiver traced its way down my spine, the icy tendrils of fear and excitement intertwining. Was this what it truly meant to be a Writer? To pour pieces of your soul onto the page, sacrificing parts of yourself for the sake of art?

Looking back, every tale I crafted had taken a toll on me. A fragment of my heart resided within the pages, forever lost. And no matter how satisfied I felt upon completing a new novel or short story, a lingering weariness clung to me, mingled with sorrow. The words I spilled onto the paper were like blood from my veins, leaving me drained yet fulfilled simultaneously.

It was a bittersweet existence as a Writer, but one I wouldn't trade for anything in the world.

But how much would it cost me to tell these stories?

Aelle appeared unperturbed by the potential dangers. "I'm willing to take the chance," she declared. "These books need to have their stories heard."

I hesitated, torn between wanting to run away and wanting to stay. But as I spotted shelves of forgotten books, their covers covered with dust and cobwebs, I realized I couldn't leave.

"So, you think Taliesin's book is somewhere in Ancient Greek history because..." Aelle asked.

"I can't say for sure, but he's searching for Lilith's weapon. The women protecting it lived in this era, and though their truths have been lost to time, their names still echo. My intuition tells me that if we uncover their stories and learn about their lives, they will lead us to Taliesin."

"What do we need to do?" I inquired, readying myself for the challenge. I wondered how much of myself I'd have to surrender to remember their stories. Hopefully, not too much, but something told me it would be more than I expected.

"Aelle, you must find the books while Chloe prepares to venture into their realities to find the truth."

"And what will you do?" Aelle asked, her eyes narrowing at the older woman with suspicion.

"I will be the one to rewrite them," she responded calmly.

My eyes narrowed. "But you said each time we recreate a missing story, it takes a piece of us. No offense, Moll, you don't have much to offer right now. You look like a breeze could blow you down."

"True," Moll agreed. "But neither of you has tried before, so it must be me. You will need to watch, learn, and remember."

"So, I just need to look for the two books?" Aelle asked, turning to head down the aisle. "Seems simple enough. There is nothing better than an Easter egg hunt in the middle of an emotional storm of tears and agony. Easy peasy." Her voice faded as she moved away from us.

"So, what do we do while she searches?" I focused on the books again, wondering whose story I was looking at.

"I have something to give you," Moll said as she pulled a small, leather-bound book from her dress pocket.

I turned to look at it and stepped back. "What is it?" I pointed to the book, my fingers tingling with the need to touch it. To protect it.

"It's the blueprint for the Otherworld."

Chapter 63- Chloe

Modern Day- City of the Unspoken

"Arawn's book? Emma found it. Where?" I asked, surprised Emma had returned and we hadn't seen her. I filed the information away to think about later.

"It doesn't matter where, only that we have it. Our top priority now is to keep it safe," Moll said pointedly, daring me to object. The keys I was carrying started singing as if they were greeting an old friend, and I put my hand up to silence them.

"No offense, Moll, but I've got a lot to handle. Can we find someone else to take charge of the construction manual?"

In truth, I couldn't manage Arawn's book and everything else I was worried about. With the keys and my copy of the Book of the Veiled, I was hanging on by a thin string. The manuscript tugged at me, filling me with unease. Part of me was drawn to it, but another part feared I would be trapped in the Otherworld forever if I took it

.

"I am not giving it to you," she countered. "It belongs to Arawn and whoever decides to stay and help rebuild."

An anxious flutter tightened in my chest as I glanced at the book in Moll's hands. "Does it have a lock on it?" I asked, my fingers unconsciously tightening around the key hanging from my neck. The

335

cool metal warmed against my skin, and I couldn't shake the feeling that the two were somehow linked.

Moll's eyes widened in surprise, her gaze flickering from me to the key. "You think they are connected?" she asked, her tone filled with amazement.

I handed it to her. "I thought the key was symbolic. Like a 'Welcome to the club' kind of gift." Moll's fingers brushed the metal, tracing its edges and curves. Her lips tightened into a slight frown as she turned it over in her palm. I adjusted my glasses nervously and asked, "Did you know?" The weight of the question hung heavy between us as I waited for her answer.

"I had wondered," Moll whispered. She looked up at me. "May I?"

With a grimace, I nodded. I didn't have a choice, it seemed.

The key slid effortlessly into the intricate lock that bound Arawn's book together. With a twist, the click of the lock echoed through me, sending a shiver of unease down my spine. She opened it to the first page, staring at it in confusion. Her eyes met mine.

"I can't read it."

I took the book from her with shaky hands. The first page was worn and yellowed, and the ink faded from years of age. It was covered in unfamiliar symbols and glyphs—the language of the gods. As I traced my fingers over it, I could feel a strange power emanating from within, as if the words were alive and pulsing with power.

I turned the page, and the symbols shifted, rearranging into a different language filled with spells and incantations, each more powerful than the last. As I read them, a wave of emotion washed over me—a mix of awe and sadness. The words carried a cold, frightening energy that cascaded down upon me. Even though I understood them, I couldn't bring them to life.

A witch with no witchy powers.

"We have a problem," Aelle's voice floated from the end of the room.

I breathed a sigh of relief and closed the book. Arawn's book would have to wait. Closing the manual, I slipped the key back around my neck.

"We will deal with it later," I declared, eyeing Moll. She'd aged in the last few minutes, and it scared me. "Moll, are you alright?" I asked, placing a hand on her shoulder.

"Fine," Moll said dismissively, shaking me off her. "Let's find Aelle."

I followed behind her, the sound of her cane reverberating against the stone floor. I couldn't shake the suspicion that she was keeping something from me—something ominous and unsettling. But I knew better than to pry. I would let her keep her secrets, just as I kept mine.

Aelle stood in front of a small, dark bookshelf adorned with intricate rosette carvings. The richness of the wood was complimented by the soft glow of lamplight casting shadows across its surface. Next to it sat a pedestal holding a leather-bound book. Behind it, a glass display box caught the light, revealing delicate etchings of stars accented by shimmering gold hinges and an ornate lock.

Inside sat a single white feather.

"I can't get to it," Aelle said as we stood in awe. "Is there such a thing as an invisible wall?"

"If that is what I think it is, Lilith said Lucifer's feather was protected. That might be why we can't get near it." I reminded her.

Aelle turned and narrowed her eyes. "But by what? And is that Taliesin's book?"

I shrugged because I had no idea and glanced at Moll, hoping she had some answers.

"I think so," Moll whispered. "But it's so quiet."

I paused to listen and realized she was right. The silence was deafening. A chill ran down my spine, and I whirled around.

"Someone else is here," I whispered, my voice barely audible in the thick quietness.

Aelle's head snapped up as she scanned the area with wide eyes. "You're right," she agreed. "But whatever it is, it's not alive."

"Listen," Moll whispered, her eyes brimming with tears. "And tell me what you hear."

Aelle rolled her eyes before closing them, and I did the same. We stood silently for a moment, unsure of what to do next. But then, I heard a faint melody from behind Taliesin's book.□

O ROWAN tree, O rowan tree! thou'lt aye be dear to me!
Intwined thou art wi' mony ties o' hame and infancy.
Thy leaves were aye the first o' spring, thy flowers the simmer's pride;
There wasna sic a bonnie tree in a' the country side.
O rowan tree!
How fair wert thou in simmer time, wi' a' thy clusters white,
How rich and gay thy autumn dress, wi' berries red and bright!
On thy fair stem were mony names which now nae mair I see,
But they're engraven on my heart—forgot they ne'er can be!
O rowan tree!

The sound of the woman's voice was an exquisite blend of pleasure and sorrow, and I let myself be swayed by the song. Her tune filled the air with a beautiful melody that drew me deeper and deeper. I was pulled away from reality and into a lush meadow. In the middle stood a towering rowan tree, its bark covered in shimmering letters beckoning me closer until I stood under the large branches. As the last note faded away, words formed together until they created a message.

Names!

The bark was inscribed with thousands of names, and my finger grazed the etched symbols. I saw flashes of faces that would have kept me in a trance had a sharp pain not shot across the back of my head, jerking me out of my vision.

"Chloe!" Aelle shook me with more force than was necessary.

Rude!

"What?" I asked, rubbing the sore spot and giving her a dirty look.

"What did you see?" Moll asked, looking at me strangely.

"A tree with names written on it," I told them. "I think they belong to the books."

"Excellent! We are where we need to be," Moll said excitedly, tapping her cane against the floor. "Aelle can start researching. If all works out, the stories will reveal what guards Taliesin's book and tell us how to get around it."

Chapter 64- Chloe

Modern Day- City of the Unspoken

We spent the next few hours crowded around a desk with a straight line of sight to Taliesin's book and Lucifer's feather. Moll and Aelle were whispering to each other, but I couldn't stay focused.

Now that I was standing face to face with Taliesin's book, I worried more about what Diana said.

He must stay in the Otherworld—one life to save the thousand souls trapped.

Had I gotten it wrong? Was Charon warning me about Eidolon? Was he the one who couldn't leave the Otherworld?

The idea was heart-wrenching, but it seemed to fit. Eidolon was the Librarian, holding onto the Book of the Veiled, and gifted with the ability to talk to the dead. He was also the one person who could open the veil between the Otherworld and the mortal world.

He was the link.

The rest of us weren't immortal. Even Victor, with his incredible self-healing powers, was still subject to mortality. But Eidolon? He was an intercessor between life and death, a ferryman of souls controlling the gateway to the realm of the living and the afterlife.

He belonged to the Otherworld.

"What do you think, Chloe?" Moll asked, and I turned to see her looking at me expectantly.

I pushed up my glasses. "Sorry. What were you saying?"

Moll sighed and leaned back in her chair, crossing her arms over her chest. "We were just talking about the next step," she explained. "Aelle has some ideas, but we wanted your input too."

"Off in dreamland again," Aelle muttered, not glancing up from the red notebook she was writing in. She was encircled by books and scrolls of various shapes and sizes, sticky notes surrounding her, and a yellow legal pad with a weird timeline sketched on it. The small desk light cast an eerie shadow across her face, highlighting the deep stress lines around her lips. "It's not like we are right in the middle of something."

"Are you alright?" Moll asked. "You seem distracted."

Of course, I am distracted. Eidolon's life is in danger, I wanted to yell. Instead, I shook my head and glared at Aelle, hoping her pen leaked and stained her hands with permanent ink. "I'm good. Just thinking."

"If you're sure..." Moll said slowly, looking back down at the book in her lap. "Aelle thinks she found something."

I took a seat and crossed my arms, waiting for Aelle to reveal her latest discovery. *Of course, she would find the next clue,* I thought bitterly.

Aelle's silence spoke volumes. She furrowed her brow and stared intently at her notes. I braced myself for whatever unpleasant news came out of her mouth.

"Without Max's help, this is a long shot. But after going over my notes and comparing them to the names Chloe found on the tree, I think we are looking for Medusa and Danaë."

I leaned forward excitedly; this was fantastic news. I had been wondering how the two were connected to our mission, and now we were about to find out. But my excitement soon faded as Aelle continued.

"And I think I know what's in the jar," Aelle glanced up at me, a hint of concern in her eyes. "Hope."

"Hope?" I questioned. "Like the feeling?"

She nodded. "Take hope away, and the world crumbles like a sandcastle in the rain."

"So, it makes sense that Medusa and Danaë would guard the jar," Moll continued. "From what Lilith told us, all they had left after the gods' punishments was hope."

"Okay," I nodded in agreement. "But how does Lucifer play a part in all of this?"

"I was thinking the same thing, and I believe I have found the answer. First, Lilith is Pandora." She held up a finger to keep track of her points. "Secondly, Medusa and Danaë are guarding her jar. Thirdly, Taliesin needs not only the jar but also Chloe's blood, the Book of the Veiled, and the Tree of Life to bring back his sister. Fourthly, Lucifer protected the Tree of Life. Finally, Taliesin's book was discovered next to Lucifer's feathers. I think Taliesin needed to get rid of Lucifer somehow but couldn't because Lilith is protecting a piece of him," she concluded, lowering her hand.

I narrowed my eyes, thinking out loud, "So, this feather is keeping Lucifer alive? The Fates must have known and hidden Taliesin's book with it. Talk about a plot twist." I joked half-heartedly.

"It would seem the most likely conclusion," Moll agreed, getting up to walk to the window. "But it doesn't help us figure out how to get through whatever is blocking us from Taliesin's book or how to help Lucifer."

"I think Medusa and Danaë have the answer," Aelle suggested, looking at me. "We need to find them."

"Awesome! And how do we do that?" I asked with a frown.

"I think Charon is waiting for you," she said, her finger outstretched towards the dark, swirling depths of the River Styx.

Aelle and I exchanged nervous glances before joining her. Charon's face was shrouded in shadows, but his piercing eyes were fixed on us from beneath his hooded cloak.

It's time, I heard him say, and the cold grip of death shivered down my spine.

"Did you hear that?" Aelle whispered. I nodded. "Well, our chariot awaits," she said, shrugging and turning to Moll. "Are you ready?"

Moll shook her head, begging us to understand. "I am not invited to this part of the journey."

"I don't understand," Aelle said, looking confused. "Of course, you have to go. We have no idea what the hell we are doing."

"I was never meant to see this part of the story," she said sadly, gripping her cane tightly.

I glanced back down at Charon and saw him still staring at us. "We have to let the rest of the team know. How long will it take to get them back here?"

"No," Moll said firmly, turning to look at us both.

"What?" Aelle and I cried at the same time.

"No," she repeated. "They can't come with you."

My jaw dropped as I looked at Moll. Sure, we had split up before, but this was different.

Wasn't it?

"I don't understand. Why can't they?" Aelle asked.

"Because Medusa and Danaë don't want people wandering around, asking questions, and making a nuisance of themselves. Those women have been through enough, and we will respect their privacy."

Moll was right. There was nothing the rest of the group could do; this was a job for the Writers. I tried to reach out to Eidolon through the bond to let him know, but he was too far away. I could still feel our connection humming, making me feel better.

"Then I guess it will be the two of us," I said with a forced smile to Aelle and winced at her frown. Any hopes that this would be a bonding experience vanished like a birthday candle blown out by a five-year-old.

"Fine," Aelle muttered, returning to the desk and picking up her notebook and three pens. "Anything to get out of this place."

I understood why she was anxious to leave. Since we started researching the Rowan tree names, the voices in the library began to get louder again. From the look on Aelle's face, she was having a hard time dealing with it.

We started heading for the door when Moll called out to us. "Try not to get yourselves killed."

Chapter 65- Chloe

Modern Day- Otherworld

A elle and I cautiously descended the slick, marble-gray steps toward the murky waters of the River Styx. Halfway down, a light rain began to fall, making each step treacherous on the slippery surface. My fingers dug into the stone ledge, my knuckles turning white as I clung on for dear life. A sense of foreboding filled me as I peered over the edge, my heart sinking at the sight.

The choppy waves crashed against the rocky shore, their relentless force churning the dark waters. And in the distance, a thick fog crept in from across the river, shrouding everything in an eerie mist.

That is not at all an ominous sign, I thought bitterly.

The rain intensified into a heavy downpour, drenching my hair and penetrating my skin. The wind howled around us, and each drop hit the ground with a deafening clap. I started to tremble and regretted not bringing a jacket. The darkness thickened so we could barely see a few feet ahead of us, and I feared we would never reach the bottom of the stairs.

Minutes later, our feet hit solid ground, and I almost dropped to my knees and kissed it. Aelle gestured towards a faint yellow light ahead of us, and we trudged towards it. The biting cold rendered my fingers almost numb, and I could hear Aelle's teeth chattering over the crashing waves.

I silently prayed that Charon had a cover for his rickety boat, but I doubted he cared much about the cold. The thought of encountering him again filled me with dread. Our previous interaction left a bitter taste in my mouth, and I hoped our paths would never cross again.

As we approached the dock, the atmosphere grew eerily quiet, like standing in the center of a storm. I halted at the river's edge, peering out at the murky waters shrouded in a thick fog that made it impossible to see more than a few inches ahead. My heart skipped a beat as memories of my previous journey across the treacherous waters came flooding back, accompanied by a wave of fear. Aelle's hand intertwined with mine, and I felt her fingers grip tightly.

"Are you ready for this?" she asked, her voice barely a whisper.

I nodded, swallowing hard as I gazed at the swirling currents. This was it—the next step in our quest to find the Book of the Veiled. We had been searching for months, and now, we were one step closer.

Who would have thought it would be just Aelle and me on the mission?

"Hi, Charon," I said, trying to sound like I was looking forward to the boat ride. "I heard you were taking us somewhere."

Charon stepped forward and pointed to the boat, directing us to get in. His eyes were an abyss, like Fyodor Dostoevsky's mind reaching into humanity's darkest spaces.

"Sure thing, friend," I commented as we stumbled onto the rocking boat. "Do you happen to have a raincoat? It's freezing out here, and we mortals aren't immune to frostbite or runny noses. I'd hate to show up to meet Medusa and Danaë half-frozen and looking like drowned rats."

Charon didn't say a word as he retrieved the long oar from the bottom of the boat and pushed us into the current.

The boat glided through the River Styx as Charon expertly navigated its course. The air was thick with the stench of death and decay. The only sounds were the creaking of the boat and the occasional mournful wail of a lost soul. I watched the Otherworld pass me in a blur of twisted trees and shadowy figures. The cold mist stung my face, chilling me to the bone. Aelle and I clung together to preserve our warmth. Charon's face remained stoic, his eyes fixed on the horizon as if immune to the eerie atmosphere.

We journeyed in silence for hours, our teeth chattering from the bitter cold. Every so often, the distant hoot of an owl broke through the stillness. I couldn't believe I allowed myself to be dragged into this. The contrast between wherever we were and the Otherworld was jarring.

The Otherworld may have deteriorated, but it had some semblance of life at least.

This place, though? It was designed to keep people out.

Through the fading light, I spotted a distant glow flickering. Wherever Charon was taking us, we had arrived.

We approached the shore, and a large bonfire came into view. I leaned forward anxiously, my eyes fixed on the flames that promised warmth and maybe even a cup of coffee. When we pulled up, I saw two figures standing next to the dock, waiting for us. The flames from the fire cast long shadows on them, and I couldn't make out their faces. But one of them had hair that waved at us in greeting.

We had finally found Medusa and Danaë.

Chapter 66- Chloe

Modern Day- Tartarus

A kind and inviting voice rang out, beckoning us forward. "Welcome. We've been expecting you. I'm Danaë," the woman called. Her accent was gentle and soothing, like a soft breeze on a summer day. I instantly felt a sense of comfort and security wash over me.

Maybe this wasn't going to be so bad.

But as I looked at the woman beside her, my optimism waned. Her cold glare pierced through me like a sharp knife, and her head of writhing snakes seemed to mirror her agitation. They slithered and coiled around each other, their hoods flattening as they hissed in my direction.

"Thank you, Charon," Danaë called out. "We will take it from here."

Charon nodded in acknowledgment and pushed his boat back into the murky waters, the oars slicing through the strong current as he drifted away.

Wait! Where was he going? He was our ride back.

I avoided looking directly at Medusa, directing my attention to Danaë. "I'm Chloe," I introduced myself, unsure if it was appropriate to shake their hands. Meeting characters from Greek mythology was not something I had prepared for, but I wanted to make a good first impression. "And this is Aelle." I gestured to her, noticing she was staring at Medusa.

Please, please, please be on your best behavior, I thought. Aelle was never great at first impressions, and we needed their help.

"Does it hurt?" Aelle asked

Medusa looked at her in surprise, and a small smile tugged at her lips. "Only when they are hungry."

"Makes sense." Aelle shrugged. "What do they eat?"

Seriously? That's what you want our first question to be. The feeding habits of her hair?

"The souls of annoying people who show up at dinner time unannounced," Medusa answered, her face indifferent.

"Understandable. It's one of my pet peeves, too," Aelle agreed, and Medusa almost smiled again.

"What my friend was trying to say was that we made dinner," Danaë cut in, casting a sharp glance at Medusa, and I choked back a laugh.

They were the Greek doppelgängers of Aelle and myself: one oozed sarcasm while the other exuded kindness. I had a feeling we would hit it off right away.

"Sounds great!" I said, walking up the beach. Aelle followed, looking around the island wearily. "We are starving. Do you have any coffee?"

Danaë nodded, and they both turned and walked towards the tree line. We followed a well-trodden path through the forest, and as the rain stopped, the physical activity warmed me up. When we arrived at a small clearing, I halted in my steps. Before me stood the same house that had appeared in my vision, complete with pots of flowers on the front porch and a smoke shack behind in the back.

"This is where you live?" I asked in awe.

"Yes. Lilith brought it here for us. She said some of her happiest memories were in this home, and she wanted to start us off on the right foot." Danaë said happily. "I think it's wonderful."

"I think it could use some more insulation," Medusa mumbled.

"Don't mind her. She's not used to having company," Danaë said over her shoulder as she walked through the front door.

We followed, but I was careful to keep a safe distance between Medusa's hair and me. As we stepped inside, the warmth from a crackling fire in the hearth greeted us, and the tantalizing scent of stew and freshly ground beans filled the air. My stomach growled at the thought of finally satisfying my hunger and enjoying a cup of coffee.

The room was cozy, with two armchairs, a wall-length bookshelf, and a small kitchen area. Two intricately carved doors adorned the back wall; one featured a tall tower against a starry backdrop, while the other showcased a vibrant ocean scene filled with leaping dolphins. I assumed these led to their bedrooms. In the center of the main room stood a round oak table covered in a blue tablecloth, with plates, silverware, coffee mugs, and wine glasses already laid out.

They had been expecting us.

"Please, sit down and make yourself comfortable," Danaë called, waving to the table and heading to the kitchen. She poured bowls of stew and carried them over on a tray with bread and a pitcher of golden liquid that looked a lot like what Lilith told us was a watered-down version of ambrosia.

Aelle remained near the entrance, her gaze interested in every detail of the house. She strolled to the bookcase and traced her fingers along the titles' spines. Medusa joined her, and Aelle glanced at her notorious hair before focusing on the books. "These books are in the Library of the Unread," she said. "But they were blank."

"I would assume they would be. Those stories belong to a time that has been forgotten."

"Are they blank too?" Aelle asked, her eyes sad.

"No," Medusa answered. Aelle looked at her in astonishment. "These are the stories we remember—stories of our families and people we have met over the years. We have been saving them."

"For what?"

"For you," Medusa said. I glanced over in surprise. Oddly, Aelle didn't seem affected by the statement and only nodded.

"Time to eat, you two," Danaë's voice echoed through the room as she set a bowl of stew in front of me and poured a steaming cup of coffee. I eagerly took a sip, savoring the rich flavor with a touch of cinnamon. It was truly a treat. Aelle and Medusa joined me at the table. Danaë poured Aelle a cup of tea and Medusa a glass of ambrosia.

"Lilith tells us that you need our assistance," Danaë said as she buttered a piece of warm bread and handed it to me.

I took a bite of the stew, savoring the delicious combination of meat and vegetables in a thick gravy. Sitting in my seat, I couldn't help but dance with delight. Finishing my bite, I looked up. "We were hoping you could help us retrieve Taliesin's book," I said. "Maybe you could give us some pointers on how to get around the barrier."

"You can't," Medusa said, looking at me sharply. I stopped mid-bite and stared at her.

"What Medusa is trying to say is that you can't," Danaë said, staring at Medusa pointedly. "The protection around Taliesin's book is strong, and a mortal can't go through it."

"I don't understand," I stumbled, setting down my spoon and focusing on her. "We need that book to fix the Otherworld," I said, trying to hide my desperation.

"You're not listening, Chloe," Medusa replied slowly as if I were a child. "She said a mortal couldn't pass it. She never said it couldn't be done."

"I don't understand," Aelle said, drawing Medusa's attention to her. "Why can't mortals pass through the barrier? The Fates hid the books specifically so Chloe could get them. And if she can't get to Taliesin's book, this was all for nothing."

"First, the Fates assigned Chloe to find the Book of the Veiled. Not necessarily to retrieve them. Second, Chloe knows the answer," Medusa said, looking back at me. "How does someone find something that can't be found?"

What in the hell was she talking about? I hadn't a clue how to locate something that couldn't be found. It didn't even make sense. But what did was my anger, and it was beginning to boil. I didn't have time for more games. I needed to get back to the City of the Unspoken and find a way to save Eidolon from being written out of existence.

Not sit here and be toyed with.

Medusa continued to stare at me, her snakes dancing happily around her, taunting me with their mischievous snake smiles and incessant hissing. "Come on, Chloe, think about it. What do you do when you can't find something that doesn't want to be found?"

"I don't know, Medusa," I replied angrily. "I don't know what you are asking. Why don't you tell me and save us all the trouble?"

"No, Chloe. You need to figure this out for yourself. You're the Writer. You're supposed to know what to do," she taunted me.

"Medusa, that's enough," Danaë warned. "You're making it worse."

"No," Medusa yelled, hitting the table with her fist and sending my coffee flying. "The Fates have tasked her with this. She needs to stop playing around and answer the question." Her eyes flew to me again, anger dancing through them. "What do you do when looking for something that can't be found?"

Aelle and Danaë's eyes were wide, glancing between us. But I didn't notice. I was staring at the woman I was ready to throttle. How dare this woman, this myth, yell at me like I was a small child.

But a touch of suspicion also crossed my mind. Medusa was right. I was the Writer and was supposed to know what to do. I could travel through memories and find missing pieces of history, but I didn't understand how to control them. I didn't know how to find things that were misplaced. Hell, half the time, I lost my keys in my purse. And I was constantly retracing my steps to find out where I had left a book or my phone.

"We have to go back to the beginning," I whispered.

Medusa looked at Danaë triumphantly and then back at me. "Yes. And what started all this? Where does Taliesin's story begin?"

"With his sister's death," I replied, another puzzle piece falling into place. "Taliesin became who he is now when his sister died." I looked in horror at Aelle. "When he exchanged a soul for a soul."

Chapter 67- Chloe

Modern Day- Tartarus

Aelle's brow knitted into a deep furrow as she turned to me. "What on earth are you prattling on about?" Her fingers drummed an impatient rhythm against the table, her gaze sweeping over the three of us with annoyance. "What beginning?"

"The prophecy," I said, my eyes fixed on my discarded bowl of stew. "Taliesin's child would be the one to bring an end to him, just as Zeus had done with his father, Kronos." I glanced up to see Danaë staring at me with a somber expression. "That's why the Fates led us here. Because you know how Zeus did it."

Aelle's fingers froze mid-motion, her eyes widening in shock and disbelief. She turned to face Medusa, her features contorted in anger and accusation. "And you're sure?"

"Yes," Medusa replied, her eyebrow arched. "Don't you dare tell me you didn't put two and two together before you arrived." Medusa looked at her pointedly. "You're better than that."

Aelle paused, and the two locked eyes before a resigned smile formed on Aelle's face. "I had a suspicion."

My mouth dropped in surprise. "You knew?" I pushed my glasses up. "How?"

"A soul for a soul," Aelle's words were simple and to the point. "It clicked when you told us that Taliesin needed your blood to bring back Morrigan. A part of me hoped that the prophecy was referring to Eidolon because he was already connected to the Otherworld. But as it turned out, I was chosen for sacrifice."

"Aelle…" Her name escaped my lips as I got up to hug her.

"Don't even think about it," she warned, her voice laced with tension and emotion. I could see the inner turmoil in her eyes as she fought back tears. I sat back down. Taking a deep breath, she turned her attention to Danaë. "And you know what I need to do?"

Danaë nodded.

"What?"

"Only the one linked to Lilith, Morrigan, and Taliesin can walk through the barrier," Medusa explained. "And you have the key."

Aelle's hand trembled as it reached for the small key entrusted to her during her initiation into the Raven Society. It hung delicately on a silver chain around her neck, glinting in the room's dim light. The weight of its importance seemed to bear down on her as she fumbled to grasp it between her fingertips.

With her gaze fixed on it, Aelle whispered, "I have responsibilities back home. I'm a guest lecturer at the university and have an article deadline in two weeks. I can't stay in the Otherworld."

Medusa leaned back in her chair, sipping her ambrosia. "The choice is yours," she shrugged.

Aelle's eyes flew to the woman, sneering. "You mean save me or save the Otherworld? What the hell kind of choice is that? Both options suck."

Medusa chuckled. "I admit, neither option is perfect," she said with a sly smile. "But then again, when does life ever go as planned? We all have to make difficult choices." She narrowed her gaze, staring intently at Aelle. "The real question is, what will you choose to do now?" She raised an eyebrow and added, "You are not obligated to say yes. We can simply send you back to the mortal world and pretend none of this ever occurred."

"And the other?" Aelle asked.

"You take over as caretaker for the Library of the Unread. Watch over the books until they can find their voices again."

"But I have to give up my soul?"

Danaë reached out and grasped her hand firmly. "Your soul will always be yours," she said, glancing at Medusa. "That is something the gods can never strip away from us." Her expression turned sorrowful as she shifted her gaze back. "But in exchange for Taliesin's book, you will sacrifice your body."

My mind spun with confusion as I listened to the conversation unfold. Moll's words echoed in my ears, her ominous decree that a sacrifice must be made to save the books. But I could never have imagined she meant our lives. It all seemed so extreme, so drastic.

Aelle would be the one who had to stay in the Otherworld. Not me. Not Eidolon.

My heart raced with panic, and protest rose within me, but before I could speak, Medusa's piercing gaze snapped in my direction. Her serpent hair writhed and hissed, warning me against any rebelliousness. I lowered my eyes and waited for Aelle's decision.

"I will do it," Aelle declared, squaring her shoulders. "At least I won't have to worry about lesson plans now," she joked half-heartedly.

A smile played on Medusa's lips as her snakes wriggled in excitement. "Excellent. Now, let's discuss the next steps."

For the next three hours, the four of us devised a plan for how Aelle would retrieve Taliesin's book. It was pretty simple. Moll had told me that keys were a way to protect the things that we held dear or hide something that we didn't want to be found. In this case, Aelle would cross the barrier between us and Taliesin's book and secure it by locking the door behind her—figuratively.

"You just need to make sure that you give his book to Eidolon before the door closes," Danaë warned.

"Why Eidolon?" I gasped. "Why can't Aelle just hold on to it?"

"Because Aelle is walking into a plane of Taliesin's existence," Danaë explained. "She is locking the door to who he was when he learned about the prophecy."

"And because he's the librarian," Medusa huffed. "Did you think that the Book of the Veiled were real books?"

I stared at her because I had. I thought they were tangible books, like my copy of the Book of the Veiled. That I could carry around in my rucksack as we went to find the others.

She sighed. "No, Chloe. Their stories are part of the bigger picture. One juncture in time changed the course of the world. That is what you are searching for—a single moment."

"It's okay, Chloe," Aelle said. My eyes flew to her. She shook her head. "Eidolon will be fine. He can handle it."

I snapped my mouth close. Here, I was arguing that it was unfair that Eidolon had to do his job when Aelle was about to make the biggest sacrifice of her life. "Aelle, I'm sorry." I hung my head in shame. "I didn't mean it like that."

"I know," she reassured me. "I understand. You're just worried about him." She shrugged. "I would be too. But he's going to be okay; he's a big boy." I nodded. She turned her attention back to Medusa. "I think that's everything."

"Okay then. Let's get you back." Medusa stood up, clapping her hands.

Chapter 68- Chloe

Modern Day- City of the Unspoken

In the blink of an eye, we were transported back to the Library of the Unread. Moll stood at the window, her figure silhouetted against the dark sky, gazing down at the murky waters of the River Styx, lost in thought. I took a moment to soak in the familiar scents of old books and musty paper.

I wasn't ready for this next part. But I had no choice. I needed to respect Aelle's decision. Squaring my shoulders and taking a deep breath, I called out, "Hey, Moll. Look who we found."

Moll spun on her heel, coming to an abrupt halt as Medusa and Danaë appeared at my side. Her complexion drained of color, her expression frozen in shock like she was looking at a ghost.

"It's good to see you again, Moll," Medusa greeted, her snakes waving at Moll like they knew each other.

"You too, Medusa. It's been a long time," Moll said, leaning heavily on her cane and walking towards us. "I assume everything went alright?"

"Yes," Danaë said with a smile that didn't meet her eyes. She reached into her satchel and pulled out a lock. "We brought you something."

Moll hesitated before accepting the gift, her expression betraying disappointment despite her attempt to hide it.

"Why do you need a lock?" I asked, stepping forward to examine it, but she quickly slipped it into her pocket.

"Never you mind about that." She shooed me away. "Did you figure out what we need to do?"

Aelle moved closer, positioning herself next to Medusa and giving a slight nod. "I've decided to stay," she said.

"Are you sure," Lilith's voice called from down the aisle, and I turned to see her and Vivian striding toward us. "This is not a decision to take lightly."

"I'm sure," Aelle nodded. "It feels right—a little scary, but right."

"Don't be scared. We will be right here," Vivian said, walking up to her and putting her hands on either side of her face. For once, Aelle didn't shy away from the contact but looked at her mother with a glimmer of love in her eyes. "You were destined for this. From the moment you were conceived, I knew you would be more powerful than me or your father."

"You're not disappointed I'm not going to be the next Writer?" Aelle asked.

"No, child," she tsked. "You were never meant to be a Writer. I see that now. You are meant to be the Caretaker. You will be the one to give the unspoken stories a home. I am so proud of you."

Aelle nodded. "What happens now?"

"It's time to use your key to unlock your destiny," Moll said as a tear ran down her face. "I don't know what happens after that. A Writer is not allowed to know the ins and outs of a Caretaker's job."

"Does this mean I will disappear?" Aelle questioned.

"No, not disappear," Lilith shook her head. "A soul never disappears if their name is remembered."

"So, this is the sacrifice you were talking about?" She glanced around at the library sadly. "I suppose it's worth it."

Aelle turned and narrowed her eyes at me, and I took a step back before she started laughing. "I guess we won't be in competition anymore, lil' Writer," she joked. "But just so you know, Eidolon can still talk to me even if I am dead. So, I will keep my eye on you," she said with a wink.

"I wouldn't expect any less," I said dryly. And before I could say anything else, Aelle hugged me.

"Try not to die," she whispered in my ear, and we both laughed as she pulled away.

"Enough of this sentimental stuff. I'm ready," Aelle said, squaring her shoulders and eyeing Taliesin's book. "And you're sure the book will transfer to Eidolon as soon as I get my hands on it."

"Yes," Moll reassured her.

Aelle's jaw clenched as she stared at the book she was about to lose her life for. "And Lucifer's feather? What will happen to it?"

"I don't know," Lilith said sadly. "It may be linked to Taliesin, or it may be still bound to the Tree of Life. We will have to wait and find out. But Aelle, if you see him..."

Aelle turned her head and looked at Lilith. "I will tell him you are waiting for him," she promised.

"Thank you."

Aelle nodded once, her head tilting to the side as she strained to listen to something beyond the reach of our ears. "I can hear them," she whispered, her voice barely audible. The air around her vibrated, and she started shimmering. Words formed in her eyes as they darkened to a black abyss. She looked at her mother. "Thank you."

Vivian's breath hitched, and she ran forward to hug her daughter. "Whatever happens, I will find you."

"I know you will." Aelle pulled out of her mother's embrace.

She took a step forward and was gone.

"What just happened?"

When I heard Eidolon's voice echoing through the library, I immediately raced to where he was. The others were already gathered in the foyer, their expressions filled with confusion. My eyes quickly found my soulmate in the group, and I hurried toward him. As we embraced, I couldn't help but feel grateful he wasn't chosen to stay behind, but also saddened by the sacrifices our friend made for all of us.

"That's not the welcome home I was expecting," Eidolon laughed as I gave him a firm kiss. "Not that I am complaining."

"How do you feel?" I asked, sliding out of his arms and looking him over. He didn't look any different, but I wasn't sure how someone looked after another book was added to a body.

"Heavy," he admitted. "Like something punched me in the chest and landed in my stomach. What the hell happened?"

"Where's Aelle?" Max asked before I could explain, looking around the room. "I found something I think she will find interesting." He looked over at me, a question in his eyes. I glanced away, not sure how to describe what happened.

"Aelle is gone," Lilith said simply as she strolled into the room and headed for the bar.

"What do you mean gone? Like she went back home? Without me?"

"No," Vivian answered, tears in her eyes as she took the drink Lilith handed to her.

"She was the one, wasn't she?" Max asked. "She was the soul for a soul." He sounded so defeated that I started tearing up and walked over to put my hand around his shoulders.

"I'm so sorry, Max," I began, but he waved me off.

"It's okay. A part of me knew." I looked at him in surprise. How did he know?

"The library called to her," he shrugged. "And while she acted like she didn't want to be anywhere near it, I caught her standing at the doorway more times than I could count. She was just afraid of what would happen if she went in."

"She seemed to be at peace with her decision," I told him.

"I'm sure she was. It's everything she ever wanted," Max said, eyeing the books with a small smile. "I'll see her again. Our story isn't over yet."

I wasn't sure what he meant, but from the determined gleam in his eye, I was sure he meant it.

Max had an interesting background. His great-grandfather had been able to see the supernatural, and maybe he inherited the gift, too. But I did know whatever happened next, Max wasn't going to leave the City of the Unspoken anytime soon, at least not without Aelle.

"Where are Medusa and Danaë? I wanted them to meet everyone," I asked, noticing they weren't in the room and wanting to change the subject before I started crying.

"They went back," Lilith answered. "They don't like crowds, but they told me to tell you they were finally glad to meet you."

"Oh," I looked down at my feet, disappointed I hadn't gotten to tell them goodbye. I had so many questions I wanted to ask them, and I wasn't going to get the chance now.

"I wouldn't worry about them, Chloe," Lilith said, taking a seat and leaning her head back in her chair. "They got to tell their side of the story, and that's all they wanted—for history to know their truths. And you gave them the opportunity."

"So...what now?" Watson asked, walking over to the bar and pouring himself a drink.

"We find the next book," I said, reaching out to take Eidolon's hand. "One down, two to go."

Afterword

The charm of myths and folklore is that you can spot similarities in all of them. What is true in Scottish mythology has echoes of the same themes existing in Welsh, Roman, Greek, Indian, Chinese, and so many more. All these tales offer insight into the unknown and give us explanations for what we can't understand.

Most of the characters of the Raven Society are rooted in a narrative that has been passed down through many generations, adapted, and reinvented along the way. These tales are the ones that hold us together, whether we're living through our highest highs or lowest lows. And when they come together, these stories can help reveal who we truly are deep down inside.

As you read The Myth and the Monster, I hope you recognize something in its characters - a piece of yourself or your beliefs. Myths and folklore are mysterious yet complex stories that can show readers the extent of human experiences, the good and the bad. Every story deserves to be told, and I hope this book convinces you that not all monsters are created equal.

Eidolon- Librarian: Inspired by an E.A. Poe poem, 'Dream-Land,' the term Eidolon represents something real or imagined. In Greek, it translates to 'spirit' or 'image.' The poem follows a traveler as they explore an alternate universe filled with ghosts and other supernatural beings found in the underworld. But it was also in the underworld that the reader could find comfort and peace in death. And that in itself is beautiful.

Moll: The life of Moll Pitcher, a renowned clairvoyant from early America, serves as the basis for this story, which I found by chance one rainy afternoon. She was born to Lydia and Aholiab Diamond in 1736 in Marblehead, Massachusetts, and married Robert Pitcher in 1760.

Moll's childhood in The Writer and the Librarian is interwoven with references to Wizard Diamond, her grandfather. He was an expert at guiding ships through stormy seas into port. Moll also had an intimate knowledge of the sea, and while Wizard could navigate boats safely to shore, Moll could tell if the voyage would be doomed before they even left the harbor. It's said that sailors would refuse to set sail if she'd predicted a treacherous journey.

Moll was also a seer specializing in tasseography—divination through tea leaves. For over fifty years, she read for the famous and influential. She was so well known for her accuracy that even Henry David Thoreau mentioned her in his personal journals. George Washington called upon her to predict who would ultimately win the Revolutionary War and was relieved when she told him he was on the winning side.

Moll's predictions of the future can be considered nothing short of amazing. She accurately predicted inventions such as the radio, car, submarine, and humans venturing into space.

Taliesin- Merlin: Historical documents suggest that Taliesin was indeed a man. His tale is recounted in various medieval Welsh texts, such as *The Tale of Cullhwch, Olwen Historia Brittonum,* and *Y Gododdin,* thus practically elevating him to the level of a mythological figure. His name in Welsh translates to 'radiant brow' - an apt title for Taliesin due to his legendary beauty. It's said that the white witch endowed him with both beauty and the power of Awen.

He was a handsome man with a special gift: the ability to see what was yet to come. Consequently, he became well-known as an adviser to kings. Several of the most renowned kingdoms—Briton, Saxon, and Roman—invited him to serve them as seer and strategist. He accepted the invitation of three British monarchs, including King Arthur's court.

And how do we know that there was a form of Merlin? It's hard to say for sure, but he's first mentioned as a fictional character in Geoffrey of Monmouth's book *Historia Regum Britanniae*, composed in the 12th century.

Whether he was Taliesin or Merlin, or sometimes referred to as Myrddin Wyllt, there was a man behind the myths, and I wanted him to be remembered.

Lilith: Lilith's history is found in many religious and cultural texts, from Mesopotamian accounts to stories of Christianity and Judaism, as well as Greek and Roman mythology. Her most remembered role is that of Adam's first wife or the Queen of Demons.

In the 2000 years since her first appearance in Mesopotamia, straddling the Tigris and Euphrates rivers, what's now known as Iraq, Iran, and Southern Turkey, Lilith has been depicted in various ways. From a servant of Inanna to a succubus to a terrifying harpy, her references from this era paint a varied picture. One thing is still true: even if each tale casts her in a different light, Lilith was referenced enough to be considered an essential part of the culture then.

In Greek mythology, Lilith is represented through Lamia, the Queen of Libya. Born to Poseidon and Lybie, she was one of Zeus' favorites. However, when Hera found out about the relationship between her husband and Lamia, she murdered all of Lamia's children in a jealous rage. In response, Zeus granted her the ability to look into the future with her prophetic sight and gave her the power to detach her own eyes. To take revenge on Hera for the tragedy she caused, Lamia would kill other children.

In Roman mythology, Lilith is equated to Libitina- the goddess of death, funerals, and corpses. Much like the Grim Reaper of today, she was depicted as wearing a black hooded cloak and having great dark wings. Temples were built in her honor, including one at the Colosseum to remember the fallen gladiators' spirits.

Lilith is mentioned in many Jewish contexts, including legends and stories in the Talmud and Kabbalah. The Jewish Zohar names her one of the four angels of promiscuity. There is no confirmation that Lilith was a real person, though it's obvious enough from the tales passed down through time that someone must have been the author of her story.

Medusa: Medusa is a well-known mythological creature renowned for her ability to turn men into stone with her gaze and for wielding snakes as weapons. Hesiod and Pindar first mentioned her in poems and stories during the eighth and fifth centuries B.C.E. In these tales, Medusa has two sisters, Stheno and Euryale, who together make up the trio of Gorgons.

Medusa has been featured in many ancient art forms, each with a unique interpretation of her physical features. Though the details have changed significantly over time, the full-frontal pose is always recognizable. While most figures are depicted sideways in Greek artwork, Medusa stares directly at the audience no matter the style or material used to create her image.

Writers, artists, and lore keepers from the ancient world to today's popular culture have long been inspired by the story of Medusa. They capture her image and tale through literature, legend, and art. She symbolizes female power and strength and is an iconic representation in modern entertainment, such as films and Netflix series.

The symbolism of Medusa has been significant when discussing the history of sexual assault and the blame placed on its victims. She has been both protected and vilified as a monster by society. I wanted to tell Medusa's story from her side, and while I may not have gotten all the details right, I hope that I have been able to do justice in recreating what her reality may have been. It didn't sit right with me that we had never heard her side of the story.

Danaë: The story of Danaë, while not as widely known as some other tales in Greek mythology, still has far-reaching implications, affecting the stories of Perseus and Medusa, Hercules, and even the founding of Ardea near Rome.

The earliest depictions of the myth of Danaë can be found in Greek Attic red-figure vases dating back to the fifth century B.C.E. The Louvre houses a krater that depicts Danaë lying on a bed in her tower while gracefully receiving the amorous attentions of Zeus.

In Greek literature, Danaë is celebrated as a powerful gift of the gods, while Roman poets interpreted her story as a tale of avarice and immorality. Centuries later, during the fourteenth century, she was transformed into a symbol of modesty and decorum. Her tower then became representative of pureness and innocence.

Several artists, including Titian, Rembrandt, and Gustav Klimt, have captured the story of Danaë in their paintings: Titian's Danaë (1554), Rembrandt's Danaë (1636), and Klimt's Danaë (1907). She is nearly always pictured the moment Zeus visits her in the form of a shower of gold.

Arawn: In Celtic/Welsh mythology, Arawn is the ruler of Annwn (the Otherworld) and is responsible for honoring promises, defending his realm, and upholding justice and tradition. He is associated with honor, duty, war, vengeance, death, terror, and hunting. His mythical kingdom was an idyllic place of rest for the dead.

Arawn was known by many names— 'the Virtuous,' 'the Provider, and 'the Guardian of The Lost Souls'—as he reigned over the heavenly kingdom of Annwn. Despite its peaceful reputation, Arawn was seen as intimidating due to his close ties with death.

As Christianity was accepted in the British Isles, Arawn's reputation as death's servant caused him to be seen as a demon. Annwn, the Welsh Otherworld, became a place for doomed souls, and its ruler, Arawn, was viewed as their lord. In addition, his hounds were linked with hellhounds pursuing the spirits of evil. This contrasting theory of what 'hell' is or is not made me want to write Arawn into this series. I wanted to share that what we now consider 'hell' was not always the case.

Charon: Charon plays a crucial part in the ancient Greek's understanding of death and the afterlife. As the ferryman of Hades, it is Charon's job to transport souls seeking judgment by Hades. Depending on their sentence, they may continue to Elysium, similar to the Christian concept of heaven, or Tartarus, a miserable abyss comparable to hell. But first, all souls must meet him.

Charon guides souls across the river so that they can continue their travels. But nothing is free in this life, even after death! In return for his help, he requires payment in the form of a single coin. Typically, it's either an Obolus or Danake coin; both have little value.

In the past, a coin was placed in the mouth of the deceased to represent proper funeral rites. It was believed that without it, the dead would not be able to pay the boatman and cross the Styx. Consequently, they were said to remain stuck as ghosts on the banks of Acheron for hundreds of years—similar to purgatory.

Charon is a prominent figure in Ancient Greek art, often portrayed as an intimidating character. He's typically depicted as unsightly in paintings and sculptures, like an aged man with facial hair frowning in indignation. Many of the earliest works featured him as a gloomy and grizzled elderly person.

In later versions of art, Charon was depicted in a much more frightful manner. Some interpretations portrayed him with wings, hellish eyes, and a visage of terror.

Odin: The name 'Odin,' written in Old Norse as Óðinn, was derived from two parts: óðr, meaning "fury, rage, passion, ecstasy, or inspiration," and the masculine definite article suffix -inn. Depending on the translation, it could mean 'the Fury,' 'the Furious,' 'the Passionate,' 'the Inspired,' and more accurately, 'the Inspiring.' Odin was thought to bring forth feelings of fury, passion, and ecstasy even as he personified these characteristics himself.

Odin, known as the 'all-father' and bore many other titles, was often depicted in art with one eye and a long beard. His familiars—the wolves Geri and Freki and the ravens Huminn and Muninn—would usually accompany him, as would his eight-legged horse, Sleipnir.

Befitting his royal stature, Odin was renowned as an invulnerable warrior on the battlefield. It was said that he had never been defeated in any of his battles, and some even believed that he couldn't be beaten.

Though Odin was a great warrior, he often ignored the conventions commonly associated with warrior-kings. He kept his court in Valhalla, found in Asgard, one of the Nine Realms of Norse mythology. However, he preferred to wander around as a traveler.

He was devoted to gathering knowledge—of his enemies and of the future—and sought it from mystics, fortune tellers, and spirit-sighting wizards. His words danced in verse and riddles, and he could control animals, even occasionally taking on their shapes.

Freyja: The Norse goddess Freyja is connected to love, sex, lust, beauty, sorcery, fertility, gold, war, and death. Her name translates to 'lady' in old Norse and was used as a sign of honor among women. Freyja has had many aliases over the years, with names like Freja, Freyia, Freyja, Fröja, Frøya, Frøjya, and Frua being some of the more popular ones. This diversity in language gave rise to the theory that Freyja was synonymous with Odin's wife Frigg and may have been Gullveig - the völva narrator who predicted the fate of the gods during Ragnarök in Völuspá.

Freyja was a deity of both battle and demise. According to Norse mythology, Freyja gathered one-half of the spirits of warriors who passed away during battle to reside in her Folkvangr home. Odin collected the other fifty percent to live in Asgard's majestic Valhalla Hall. Here, until Ragnarök, the twilight of the world, the souls would stay until they were summoned back to fight.

Bree: Brunhild, the beautiful, proud, and willful heroine in the stories of Teutonic mythology, had a tumultuous love life. Also known as Norse mythology, these tales date back to around 400 A.D. and revolve around the Valkyries—goddess-maidens sent by Odin, the leader of the gods—of whom Brunhild was the most graceful.

In the heat of battle, Brunhild strikes down Hjalmgunnar, a king who had been promised victory by Odin. Angered at her disobedience, Odin orders her to marry as punishment. But Brunhild refuses; she swears that she will only marry a man who can defeat her in combat—a nearly impossible feat. Odin, frustrated, puts her under a magic sleep and circles her with fire. Eventually, Sigurd (known as Siegfried in German legends) bravely rides into the flames and rescues her.

Brunhild and Sigurd fall in love, yet it ends in tragedy. Sigurd marries Gudrun, a Teutonic princess, and helps her brother Gunnar win Brunhild for his bride. Disguised as Gunnar, Sigurd defeats the unsuspecting Brunhild in combat, and she agrees to become Gunnar's wife. Years later, when Brunhild discovers Sigurd's deceitful trickery, she is overcome with rage and orders one of her servants to kill him. Fulminating with guilt over what she has done, Brunhild throws herself onto Sigurd's funeral pyre to join him in death.

The tales of Brunhild the Valkyrie did not appear in writing until they were included in works created in Iceland and southern Germany in the 1100s. The oldest references to her stories are found in *Poetic Edda* and *Volsunga Saga*, which both originated in Iceland. However, German writers added their own twist to the character by changing the spelling of her name to Brynhild or Brünhild in the *Nibelungenlied*, a German epic poem composed around 1200. While multiple sources tell different versions of Brunhild's story, these tales inspired Richard Wagner when he wrote his famous opera cycle, *The Ring of the Nibelung,* in 1876.

Acknowledgements

To my best friend and husband. We have been through more than any normal couple should have, but we have somehow managed not to walk away from each other. We have suffered through the blazing Afghanistan sun, Alaska's bone-chilling winters, and a rough patch of living partially off-grid. We have both bought and sold houses. We have raised snakes and built libraries. You taught me how to ride a motorcycle and criticized how I drove my truck. We created a life that most people would never understand, but it works for us. And somehow, we survived it all. And most of the time we still like each other at the end of the day. Who could ask for more?

Thank you for supporting my dreams and standing by my side when the voices in my head got too loud.

To my sister. I thought about you when I wrote this story. You have never been content to follow the norm, and it amazes me how strong you are. Your joy for life is infectious, and I am truly grateful that we finally live in the same state. Thank you for helping me learn how to laugh again and showing me where all the good breweries are.

To my father and backstage manager, you were always there when I needed you, flying across the country to celebrate my big moments—promotions, deployments, and births. It has never occurred to me to wonder if you would support me or drop everything if I asked for help—I have always known you would. Thanks for letting me 'borrow' your lawnmower. One day, I will return it to you. And I NEVER took your Irish flat hat. That's all on JoDee. I swear.

To my children, it doesn't matter where you are or what you are doing; I will always be here with a light on. I am so proud of the men you are becoming, and you all amaze me more and more each day. Keep living your best life because it gives me plenty to brag about to all my friends.

To my mother, you understand. You heard the story before it was written. You remind me of the women in this story—strong, passionate, creative, and able to face life's challenges with quiet dignity. I hope I become half the woman you are!

And finally, to the one thing that helped me keep my sanity during this whole process- coffee. You have been a faithful friend and confidant and have never complained when I cry into you. I couldn't have done this without you.

About the Author

R.L. Geer-Robbins is a Reader, Writer, Veteran, and Coffee Connoisseur. On warm days, you can find her riding her Harley with her husband or watching the History Channel. On rainy days, you can find her plotting out her next story by researching the myths and fables that have created our reality.

Social Media Links:
Website: **https://rlgeerrobbins.com/**
Twitter: **https://twitter.com/RLGeerRobbins**
Facebook:**https://www.facebook.com/RoseLGeerRobbins**
Newsletter: **https://rlgeerrobbins.com/newsletter/**

Also By R.L. Geer-Robbins

Does a person truly exist if no one remembers their name?
Long ago, when someone died, their fate was sealed. Their stories would become a memory that faded with every generation until nothing was left but whispers in the wind before they were forgotten forever Unless you could find the one who had the ability to move between life and death.

****

The Raven Society has uncovered the first missing Book of the Veiled, but it came at a great cost. Now, they must regroup as they navigate the turbulent history of fanatic religious leaders, mad Kings, and crypt prophecies.

Time is not on their side as they uncover the dark secrets that lurked during a long-forgotten era when displaying even the slightest hint of magic could send a person to death.

Two women, one prophecy.

History doomed to repeat itself.